THE INEVITABLE FALL OF TOMMY MUELLER

The INEVITABLE FALL
of TOMMY MUELLER
a novel

by

R. Tim Morris

EMPIRE STAMP

Empire Stamp trade paperback edition: April 2019
ISBN 978-1-7750598-5-1 [eBook]
ISBN 978-1-7750598-9-9 [Paperback]
ISBN 978-1-7750598-4-4 [Hardcover]

PART I

~~~

THE LETTER
~~~

CHAPTER ONE
Tom's Restaurant – Morningside Heights

2004.

I've known Thomas Mueller long enough to know most everything about him, except perhaps the most important thing of all. I watched Tommy that morning as he took a bite out of the big apple. Of course, the metaphor was ridiculously obvious, but that had always been his way. The man was palpably metaphoric. It was clear just how much Tommy loved the city: New York City. The CKY Grocery on Amsterdam had giant, bright red, Spartan apples every day of the year, even if it wasn't the right season. He loved that grocery, and the old, shaky Persian man who owned it. Tommy emphatically, yet erroneously, believed the CKY Grocery was the genuine heart of the great city. All five boroughs embodied distinct feelings for him, but there was only one he'd ever truly romanticized. To him, Manhattan was the entire world.

He loved everything between the East River and the Hudson; from the Financial District up to Harlem; from Avenue A to Zabar's. He loved the four seasons, although autumn was easily the most anticipated. To Tommy, Central Park's bright, almost copper hues in the fall were the epitome of orange. He loved the unique perfume of deli meats and subway steam. He loved the rain with such verve that every time it so much as drizzled, he would turn to the sky so he could feel the drops sprinkle onto his teeth. Because every raindrop that hit him had already experienced the much-envied journey from the tips of the skyscrapers all the way down to the cracked and foot-stamped sidewalks. He believed every inch of the city had its own predetermined genre of music that suited it to a tee. The modal jazz of Miles Davis and Wayne

Shorter was absolutely meant for the Upper East Side, north of 61st Street. Precisely between Gershwin and gospel. He loved the view from his apartment, even if it was just the leaves of the tree outside in July or the thin shadows of its bare branches crawling along the plain brick wall in January. Tommy loved his career. He loved his friends. And he loved that first big bite of apple I watched him take each and every morning.

Everything was perfect in the city, and as long as things remained the way he wanted them to, Tommy Mueller would continue to love the city forever.

Which is exactly why his jaw dropped when he opened the letter he found in his mailbox that morning. The first bite of still un-chewed apple fell out of his mouth and firmly planted itself within the crack of that 113th Street sidewalk.

<div style="text-align:center">~~~</div>

"You guys are *not* going to believe this," Tommy said as he removed his coat and scarf. He sat down next to Kate and across from Jesse, placing the still-not-quite-yet-brown apple core onto Kate's empty plate. She hated that about him, how he'd walk into the coffee shop every day as though he owned the place.

"Not now, Tommy," Kate interrupted. "Jess was just about to spill the details of his date last night."

Jesse struggled, but managed his best ear-to-ear smile. Still, Jesse's fake smiles were far more beautiful than most of the city's genuine ones.

Tommy was impressed. "Our man Jesse finally scored himself that elusive second date, huh? My, oh my! If this day were any other, I'd say that kind of conversation wins out." He reached into his coat pocket, and waved the envelope around in an attempt to gather up their attention. "But not today, my friends. Not. To. Day."

"Whatever," Kate spat out, not the least bit interested in whatever news

Tommy had brought along with him that morning. She anxiously slapped her palm on the table, allowing the salt and pepper shakers a tiny jump. "Come on, Jess. Out with it."

Jesse finished his last drop of coffee and immediately signaled the waitress for a refill. "It's not such a big deal," he said. "We ate dinner and saw a show. End of story."

Tommy knew for sure it wasn't really the end of the story, and he was fine with that. But although Jesse's highly unimaginative yarn was adequate enough for him, Tommy knew Kate wouldn't be as easily satisfied.

And she wasn't. "Dinner?" she asked, with one of her infamous one-word questions. Kate didn't like to waste words, unless of course it was to tell someone how disappointed she was in them.

The waitress returned with the refill. She knew well enough to leave sufficient room for Jesse's preferred amount of cream. Jesse concentrated on the steady stream of shining coffee pouring into his cup. "The Wing King's on 87th Street," was his answer for Kate.

"Show?" There it was again: the one-word question.

"Some off-Broadway play. Honestly, I don't even remember the name."

Tommy laid the envelope onto the table, only to see it continue to go ignored. He positioned it so it sat precisely in the middle of all three of them; he calculated the measurements in his head. And he was careful to make sure the letter sat outside the shadows of the ketchup bottle and napkin dispenser.

"You have got to be kidding me!" Kate grumbled. "You squeeze out a second date and the best you can do is take the girl out for *chicken wings*? There's got to be a *bazillion* better restaurants in this city you could have picked."

"At *least* a bazillion," Tommy mimicked under his breath. He slowly circled the envelope with his index finger, hoping for some interest. Like a shark around a boat, eager for just one curious bite.

"Actually, it was *her* choice." Jesse sprinkled two packets of sugar into his steaming drink. He focused on the granules as they plopped in one by one. It was almost as though he was attempting to count each single, glittering speck. The tiniest droplet of coffee arced from the cup to the letter on the tabletop. Observant as ever, Tommy was the only one who noticed. He rubbed the globule off with the back of his hand.

"Cab?" Kate asked again, unrelentingly.

"I hailed her a taxi and gave the driver a twenty," Jesse answered. "I thanked her for the night and walked home by myself. That was all."

"What? Seriously? No kiss? No discussion of date number three?"

Jesse hesitated to answer any further. He looked at Tommy, for what might have been the first time since he sat down, hoping maybe his friend could help put an end to Kate's meddlesome barrage of questions. But Tommy refused to interfere.

"And really, Jess," she continued. "A twenty-dollar cab ride wouldn't have gotten the poor girl farther than *three blocks* in this city." Truthfully, twenty dollars equaled about twenty blocks — "a buck a block," they say — but Kate's sarcasm was on the right track.

"All right, all right," Tommy finally complied. "Jess, we all know it was you who picked the restaurant. The last time I checked, you were the one with the freezer full of chicken wings, right? And are we really expected to believe you didn't take her to go see Wicked, and not some way-the-fuck-off-Broadway shit show?"

"Haven't you seen Wicked like a *kajillion* times already?" Kate added.

"At *least* a kajillion," Jesse conceded. "Okay, fine. We did see Wicked. But it was *her* suggestion. Really!" Without thinking, he dumped another pack of sugar into his coffee cup. "How could I possibly refuse though?"

"You couldn't," Tommy said with conviction. "And Kate should really know you better by now, don't you think?"

Tommy, Kate, and Jesse had been best friends for nearly fifteen years; having known one another since high school. The three of them had shared so many ups and downs over the years their bond was virtually unbreakable. They met at that exact booth every morning. Sometimes it was only two of them. Rarely was it just one. And it was unusual for the fourth seat to ever be filled, but it had happened on occasion.

The shadow from a crowd of people outside spread across the tabletop. "Hey!" Tommy banged on the window to get their attention. "Fuck off, already!" He cursed seemingly at random, but there was nothing arbitrary or illogical about it to Tommy. He did it all the time. The only reason the group started coming to that particular coffee shop on a regular basis was because it had Tommy's name on the sign: "Tom's Restaurant." Besides, as it turned out, that coffee shop made the best soft-boiled eggs too. It was also immortalized in the "Seinfeld" sitcom, the stand-in for what was known as Monk's Coffee Shop, so it was not unusual for its windows to be crowded with fascinated tourists; taking pictures of one another outside; posing as though they were the first to ever do so. On the other side of that glass were a million faces Tommy did not want watching him slurping coffee and stuffing breakfast sausages into his mouth. He banged his fist on the window again. The crowd scuttled away like startled spiders, but his friends didn't flinch at all. They never did. The framed poster of Cosmo Kramer watched them from the back of the restaurant. Again, Tommy carefully repositioned the envelope between them on the table.

And finally, Kate gave in. "Okay, fine. So, what's in the envelope, Tommy?"

"And he thought you'd never ask!" Jesse joked, tapping out the last of the sugar from the packet with his fingertip.

"The two of you can laugh all you want, but I've got some serious news this morning." He motioned as if he was going to open the envelope, but then leaned back in the booth, content to continue on with his proclamation.

Tommy savored any moment in which he could hold everyone else's attention. "Actually though, this is *beyond* serious. This is *more* than trivial. It's bigger than Jesse scoring two consecutive dates with someone in his own age bracket!"

Jesse balled up the tiny sugar package and flicked it across the table into Tommy's face, right between his eyes. His aim was uncanny, and if Jesse didn't hate sports so much, he would have been very good at them. Tommy ignored it completely though; his exuberance carried him on, and he emphasized every word with an extended index finger. "The contents of this envelope just might have the potential to significantly change *everything* we know."

Kate's attention had already been diverted; she took her purse and dug deep inside for some money. Typically, she was the first to lose interest in anything Tommy wanted to carry on about.

"Hey," Tommy said. "I'm not done yet. What are you doing?"

"Paying for breakfast. You know how long it takes to get change back in this place." She found a ten and flagged down the waitress. "And I've got to get to work. Some of us still have *real* jobs, you know."

"Wow," Tommy proclaimed. "Bitter much?"

The waitress was quick to take the money and she whirred back around robotically to find some change. "You know what I mean, Tommy. Jesse and I have to get up every morning and you don't." Kate slipped out of the booth and turned her eyes away from the two men, hoping they wouldn't notice her deliberately avoiding eye contact.

"Hey, I get up in the morning. Of course, it's usually just to come here for breakfast and talk to the two of you."

"Why don't you tell Jess all about your life-changing letter and he can fill me in later?"

"Trust me. This is something *both* of you will want to hear."

"Tommy," Kate began, but her words were abruptly hampered by emotion.

For a moment, the envelope in front of them was forgotten. There was now another force distracting the trio. They each had something different weighing on their minds that morning, each had their own personal black cloud hanging above them, but at that moment, Kate's bad attitude seemed to be the prevalent issue. Whatever it was, it seemed to infect that one, single table within that particular Morningside Heights coffee shop at that precise moment.

Quietly, Kate removed her coat from the rack. Tommy was the first to say something. "Kate?" he asked. "What's going on? Are you all right?"

"You want to hear something funny?" she spoke, still purposefully looking off somewhere else. One of the waitresses was placing a fresh strawberry-rhubarb pie behind the glass pastry display. The cashier was having trouble closing the register, and slammed the drawer shut over and over and over. Kramer seemed to disapprove of everything within his sight lines.

"Why do I get the feeling this isn't really going to be something funny?" Tommy said.

"I don't think I'm in love with Gene anymore," Kate answered. Tommy was right: it definitely was not funny. But it wasn't a total surprise either. The marriage of Kate Prince and Gene Schneider had been one of the strangest couplings of all time. Intuitively, both Jesse and Tommy reached their hands over and placed them on the tips of Kate's fingers, which were still anchored to the tabletop. "I'd like to believe I *was* in love at some point. But to be honest, I'm really not so sure now." Her eyes darted back and forth between her two best friends. "I think I might have made a mistake." Breaking her hand away from theirs, Kate slipped on her coat and wiped her eyes with one sleeve, just to make sure nothing incriminating had leaked out. It might have been the first time in her life Kate had ever admitted to making a mistake.

"Jeez. Now I feel bad for telling you about my date last night," Jesse confessed.

"I just feel bad Kate's been stuck with a dude named Gene for three years," Tommy said to Jesse, managing half a smile with the corner of his mouth.

Friends like these never need to say the all-too-obvious "I'm sorry's" and in some ways, their own empathic conventions were actually better anyhow. Their normal reactions were much easier for them to take than any overflowing sympathy.

"Have you talked to him?" Jesse asked, hoping the answer would be a yes.

Kate took the change from the approaching waitress. "No. Not yet. I just realized it all this morning, before coming here. But of course, I should tell the two of you first, right? Isn't that how we do things around here?"

"It's how we've *always* done things." Tommy's words were comforting. In a microsecond, their entire friendship weaved its way through all three of them. This wasn't the first time they had run into a difficult obstacle together, and it certainly wouldn't be the last.

"Come on, Kate," Jesse said, taking one last gulp of coffee and rising from his seat too. "I'll walk you to the subway."

Tommy took note of the fact that the details of the letter on the table were not questioned again. "Call me if you need anything," he said, watching them exit the restaurant.

The waitress collected their dirty plates and asked Tommy if he wanted his usual for breakfast. He replied with a look that seemed to ask, Why wouldn't I?

The plate with the apple core disappeared into the kitchen where it would be dumped into a bag amongst various items which were only ever destined to be forgotten. Tommy clutched the letter in his hands for a few minutes before sliding the envelope back into his coat pocket, worrying about whatever change the future might hold. He knew well enough Manhattan would always send signals, if only its residents could stop and feel them.

The city itself breathes in with every tragedy: every obituary in the New York Times; every jackhammer upon its streets; every time a girl leaves a boy; every slight transgression that takes place within its invisible walls. And every time New Yorkers breathe a collective sigh of relief — every time they find peace in themselves, every time they find each other again, every time they bring new life into the world, or enjoy a good book, or put a fresh coat of paint on an old, cracked wall — Manhattan exhales.

The city breathes in. The city breathes out.

Breathe in. Breathe out.

I knew precisely when Tommy could feel it, but he still had no way of knowing just what was waiting for him around the corner. He banged on the window beside him once more as another body blocked his view of Broadway.

Breathe in.

CHAPTER TWO
Midtown Comics

I watched Jesse Classen enter the coffee shop that morning, but when he exited its doors not even forty-five minutes later, the burgeoning changes within him were already evident. Jesse and Kate walked to the 110th Street Station. He rode with her to Times Square before saying goodbye and transferring onto the 7-Train to Grand Central. For a Tuesday morning, things seemed particularly quiet. Grand Central Station was the nucleus of commotion in the world's busiest city, but Jesse couldn't place the sudden wave of serenity. He didn't know what to make of Kate's news that morning, but he knew the man she married had never been quite right for her. He was just as unclear about the contents of Tommy's letter. Whatever the unremarkable envelope contained, it certainly had seemed important to him. But Tommy always had a way of blowing things out of proportion. It was something Jesse and Kate had grown accustomed to. Was this simply another one of those moments or was it indicative of something much greater? Jesse stopped for a moment to process it all.

Of the three of them, Jesse had always been the one to dwell on mistakes made. He was the first one to regret poor decisions but he was also the likeliest to make such poor decisions in the first place, which is why Jesse was far more comfortable being a follower rather than a leader. He knew next to nothing about New York when he and his friends moved there after high school, yet he followed Tommy blindly. He knew Tommy's choices could always be trusted, no matter how preposterous or random they might have seemed. There were very few other things Jesse Classen was completely sure of:

seafood chowder, Will Eisner, and that one Savage Garden hit from the 1990s which he still swore was great. He believed in the American justice system, but like the majority of Americans, he clung to the hope he would never have to be selected for jury duty. He also believed in Bigfoot, even though he knew there had never once been a shred of concrete evidence to support the creature's actual existence.

Jesse was small in both presence and stature. He had a block-shaped head with a messy haircut and muttonchops he refused to let go of. He had the slight crater-like remnants of a bad acne outbreak in high school. At times, he would display paranoid tendencies, afraid somebody was trying to sneak up behind him. Nevertheless, he insisted on wearing the same square-framed prescription glasses with the wide arms which blocked his peripheral vision enough to make him misjudge his turns, and he would often find himself bumping into the hard corners of brick buildings.

Jesse had narrowed down his life's greatest moment to the time he climbed up and balanced himself on the very tip of the Alamo, the black rotating cube which lured tourists onto its curious concrete island at Astor Place and Fourth. He, Tommy, and Kate found the Alamo while wandering drunkenly around the city one night. Kate snapped a picture of him. In it, he appeared to be in the midst of a deft Karate Kid stance, but in actuality, he'd slipped and was making a failing attempt to regain his balance. He chipped his tooth when he hit the sidewalk and his nose had been wrapped in bandages for three weeks. But Jesse remembered the look in Tommy's eyes as it happened: it was clear Tommy had never been more proud of him. The photo had been taped to Jesse's fridge ever since, reminding him of a time when he had been guided strictly by impulse.

Behind that photo sat a freezer full of chicken wings, just one of his culinary vices. At restaurants he could always be counted on to create new condiments with whatever ingredients were immediately available, be it "chocolate milkshake & Tabasco sauce mustard" or "coffee creamer, egg yolk & three-cheese ranch salad dressing." His favorite candy was black licorice. His preferred literature was "The Amazing Spider-Man" (circa 1974). He was a stickler for organization, as his rather sizable collection of comic books attested. He liked to play poker, although he was not one for the particulars of the game's intricate strategies. It annoyed his friends to no end whenever he referred to spades as "shovels" or clubs as "curlies."

And whenever Jesse second-guessed himself, or when he was caught in moments of personal uncertainty, the world around him had always seemed to slow down a little, almost to a near-perfect silence. Which was exactly what was happening at that moment. But the hushed clamor of Grand Central he had found himself in the midst of, was seemingly much more than that. His intuition had never been recognized as being anything close to exceptional, but Jesse had to brace himself on a railing for a moment longer in order to help narrow down these feelings. His palms were cold and wet, yet his grip was simply mediocre.

<div align="center">~~~</div>

Only the glistening mosquito-like tip of the Chrysler Building could be seen from the second-story window of Midtown Comics, but it was just enough to remind Jesse of how much the city could love him one minute, only to prick him the next.

For five years, Jesse had been the assistant manager of Midtown Comics, Manhattan's preeminent comic book store. It was a career decision borne somewhere between childhood dreams and grown-up regrets. He had always been inspired to create art, yet he'd consistently been limited not only by his bank account, but also by his on and off again lack of self-confidence. Jesse dreamed of taking comic art and bringing it to life on a grand scale. Not in the ways Roy Lichtenstein, Richard Donner, or the Thanksgiving Day Parade had done before him, but to an entirely new level. Something different he could never seem to put his finger on. Eventually though, Jesse was forced into accepting the simple life of retail in order to make ends meet. And his dreams had paid the price too; they were now reduced to something unlikely to add up to any more than a half-page addendum to his life story.

Jesse still owned the very first comic book he was ever given, a rolled-up treasure found in his stocking one Christmas morning. Beneath its ratty, tattered cover there still existed the dozens of spectacularly patterned four-color images that had laid the foundation for his desire to experience New York City firsthand. But it wasn't the drawings of Greenwich Village or Forest Hills or even the George Washington Bridge that stood out to Jesse. No, from the very first time he'd read his very first comic, it was the simplest of details that caught his attention: the bold silhouettes of rooftop water towers, the colorful billboards with their cracked and peeling artwork, the kicked-in steel garbage cans, and those portentous, ever-steaming manhole covers. This was the essence of what New York had been to him when he was a boy, and they were the very same details he was ever so quick to take note of the first day he emerged from Grand Central Station.

For more than eighty percent of his life, comic books had been the escape hatch from Jesse's reality to the comfortable recesses of his inexhaustible imagination. The mysterious origins, the fantastic powers, and the incredible weaknesses. His secret headquarters was actually the hollow tree in the woods behind his childhood home. It wasn't Jesse who failed the tenth grade and had to repeat it the following year but rather his luckless secret identity.

Yet amid the dreams and desires and heroics that continued to linger inside Jesse, evil continued to play its part. And his name was John Galloway.

~~~

It was four years earlier when John Galloway first ascended the stairs of
~~~

Midtown Comics. I recall how he stood out of place so perversely amongst the store's usual rabble of consumers. This man of fastidiously cultured tastes, wearing a pin-striped suit and fedora rather than brightly-colored, oversized shirts and countless, varied facial piercings barely visible beneath greasy mops of hair. Like the one stark white seagull amidst a sky full of ravens. Though it was far from uncommon for suits like his to make an appearance around such shops — even men of his remarkable age had been known to peruse the newest issues week after week — it was the feeling of the man himself that made those around him take notice. A business tycoon since he was twenty-five, it had been nearly fifty years since John Galloway had made his first million on Wall Street. And the smell of the U.S. dollar seemed to emanate from the crags in his finely weathered skin.

When Jesse had first taken note of the man, he realized the entire store had gone silent. The bustling street traffic outside faded away completely. He didn't know what else to do but ask the man if he needed help looking for something. It turned out John Galloway *did* need help: he wanted to speak with someone who would be interested in buying his collection of old comic books. He wasn't really all that different from anyone else in the store after all; he just came with a few extra million dollars in his bank account. Jesse quickly came to realize he would never be able to afford any of the books in John Galloway's possession, but when he explained he might know of some buyers who could possibly afford such a rare and sizable collection, Jesse was offered a business card nonetheless. And yet still, when taking the card in hand, Jesse was instructed to come to John Galloway's home and take a look at the books himself. It was an offer he couldn't refuse. And in retrospect, it's easy to say he probably should have.

And so, I followed Jesse to Gramercy Park six days later. The modest townhouse was indicative of the money John Galloway had made, but it certainly did not stand out from its own tiny neighborhood of genteel 19th century mansions. Jesse knocked on the door, only to be met with silence. It was the same way the world often slowed down to an empty, hollow hush and tried to warn him of something he could never ascertain. There was a doorbell, but for some reason Jesse thought he should avoid it. He knocked again and fidgeted uncomfortably in the continued silence. He shifted his footing from his left to right and back again. I could feel the front steps wince beneath his uneasy balance. Instead of walking away at that moment, Jesse allowed himself the time to wait. He waited for the door to open, and by then, just as destiny is known to work, it was far too late to go anywhere.

Edith Galloway opened the door. She was a little suspicious of the drearily-clothed and shaggy young man in her doorway; the uneasy kid standing on her finely woven doormat which proudly read: "The Galloways." Edith was comfortably into her forties. She was a woman who had an obvious familiarity with the elite tastes of Manhattan's upper class, a lifestyle she had settled into through her marriage to John. But within that slender frame was a woman who desired something more. Many claimed there was a feeling about her; a feeling palpable enough to know Edith Galloway could never be fully satisfied.

Jesse produced John's business card, and with stumbling words, he explained his reasons for being on the Galloways' doorstep. He was graciously welcomed inside — Edith's arm coiled around his shoulders like an all-too-playful python — and within ten minutes, Jesse was on the Galloways' fine European sofa sipping herbal lemon tea from an heirloom cup. Another fifteen minutes would pass before he found himself underneath Edith Galloway, as she made her own intentions uncomfortably clear.

Jesse had not acquired any comic books on that visit, nor was he lucky enough to catch even a glimpse of the immense collection. What *had* come out of that visit was the triumph of Edith Galloway's aching infidelity. Her marriage was not where it had once been, and Jesse was unfortunate enough to arrive on her doorstep the very morning Edith had awoken from such unsatisfactory dreams and made her decision: *This would be the day.*

Breathe in.

Jesse had learned many secrets about John Galloway that morning, most of which were certainly not the kinds of tidbits one stranger would ever want to know about another. Information such as how often John would clip his yellowed toenails, or how much more often he did not. He learned the man hadn't had an erection since the Reagan administration and that also no amount of medication he'd ever taken had yet to help the dreadfully degenerative skin condition on his backside.

To all of which Jesse could only reply: "I just came to look at the comic books."

And so began Jesse's affair with the intoxicating Edith Galloway. It didn't take him long to go from calling her "Mrs. Galloway" to "Edith," and it took even less time for him to finally settle on "Edie." Neither of them was sure about whether or not the other was proud of the situation, but it continued nonetheless. Jesse had shared every detail of the torrid relationship with Tommy and Kate, and even though they sometimes joked about his predicament, neither dared to make mention of "Harold and Maude" or "The Graduate." It was one of the hardest things Tommy ever managed, watching his tongue when there was a perfect joke to be made.

From the clandestine rendezvous outside Gracie Mansion while John hobnobbed inside at mayoral functions, to hiding in the guest room closet for three hours the one time John had come home unexpectedly, Jesse had quietly found himself woven into the tapestry of the Galloways' upper class Manhattan lifestyle. For three years, Jesse was almost upper class himself, living vicariously through Edie's personal bank account. Lunches, shopping, and even weekend getaways were all part and parcel of their surreptitious situation. Jesse remained in the same studio apartment on West 116th Street he'd lived in since they first met, but thanks to Edie, he now had all of the most modern amenities imaginable. Prior to their relationship, there was no way he could have afforded his wardrobe, his computer, or even his own dishwasher. Before Edie, Jesse's apartment was mostly just a single bed and weathered boxes full of comic books. Even his Silver Surfer underwear had been traded in for Calvin Kleins.

Edith had also been responsive to Jesse's artistic dreams. Through her financial backing, Jesse had spent a full year preparing for his first significant art show. He imagined people traveling to the city just to see it. The only unfortunate part being the city in question was Jersey and not New York. Jesse's art would eventually be presented in a massive warehouse in New Jersey, in a space large enough to accompany the size and the magnificence of his work.

But of course, it was inevitable John Galloway would one day discover his wife's secret. It seems these things are always inevitable. John had entered Midtown Comics and handed Jesse his business card, but it was through that card, he had also unintentionally handed the young man private access to his own life. And it was that night in which the furtive relationship was ultimately revealed. Jesse had sometimes wondered if maybe it wasn't revealed intentionally.

Edith was never one to show much consideration for entertaining her husband's concerns regarding her whereabouts, but there was a small shift within the tiniest of details on that inexplicably snowy October night. It only took a few hours for everything to change. As Jesse and Edith prepared to leave for the show's opening, Edith had left a note behind for John. There was nothing suspicious written on the note. She was known to attend many art galas and other such festivities around town, but perhaps it was merely the existence of the paper itself that had aroused suspicion. In any event, John Galloway returned home early that evening to find the note, and he had made the critically uncharacteristic decision to drive to New Jersey and meet his wife at the show.

From what I've been told, Jesse's artwork was met with ambivalent reviews, leaning heavily toward the negative variety. But it was both the entrance and the exit made by John Galloway that night that would prove to be the most memorable for those in attendance. It had been nearly three years since John had handed his business card to the clerk at Midtown Comics, but he recognized Jesse immediately. Edith tried to stop him, but it was no use; his rage could not be arrested. And it was on that one snowy night when John Galloway would firmly cement his place amongst our hero's rather insubstantial and mediocre gallery of villains.

~~~

The phone in Midtown Comics rang just like the old 1960s Batman theme song, and it distracted Jesse's attention from the glimmering tip of the Chrysler Building. "Midtown Comics. This is Jesse." He was so terribly sick of that theme song.

It was Kate. "Hey, Jess. Busy?"

"It's Tuesday, Kate." Jesse's voice echoed in the empty store. "New books come in on Wednesdays, so Tuesdays at one-thirty are like a second-week showing of a Kate Hudson movie. There's nobody here."

"Pond Scum?" Kate asked. There were five staff members at Midtown Comics, one of which was a bulbous man-child named Pond, whom Jesse believed to have quite possibly the all-time most ridiculous name ever for a man. Another shining example of hippie love. Fortunately, Pond was also a good enough guy that he didn't mind it when everyone would continually refer to him as Pond Scum. Probably because in his lifetime he'd heard much worse anyway.

"Pond's on his lunch break. I guarantee you can spot him on Number Sixteen at this exact moment." Manhattan had a number of online real-time
~~~

cameras situated around the city. One of these was Camera #16, located at the intersection of Lexington and 42nd, where there sat a perogi stand which was visited by Pond every single day. Kate was fascinated by these cameras, and had many of them running on her computer screen at work all day.

"Hold on—" Kate's mouse clicked on the other end of the phone. "Oh yeah, there he is. Wow. Didn't I see him wearing the same Elvira shirt last week?"

"That's not Elvira, Kate. That's Vampirella."

"Whatever. It's still inexcusable."

Jesse's neck was beginning to cramp from holding the receiver between his ear and his shoulder. He always held the phone that way, even though he could often be heard complaining of neck pains. Part of the reason why Jesse still didn't own a cell phone was because he couldn't find one big enough to hold with his clavicle. Why did cell phones have to keep getting smaller and smaller?

The clicking on the other end of the phone ended abruptly. "Listen, Jess," Kate said. "I'm sorry about mentioning my problems to you and Tommy this morning. I don't know what happened there. It just kind of poured out of me."

"It's fine, Kate," Jesse assured her. The traffic outside seemed to slow to silence once more. "I don't think I've ever heard you complain about Gene before now. I think maybe you were overdue." Jesse moved toward the giant cardboard Incredible Hulk blocking the window. He peeled back the Hulk's corrugated kneecap in order to take a peek outside, to make sure life on Lexington Avenue had not come to a complete halt. But the city was still breathing.

"Jess. What I meant was, when I left you this morning, I realized maybe a failing marriage wasn't something you'd want to hear. You know, with Edie and everything."

Without a response, he looked west up 45th Street.

"I just wanted to apologize, okay? Whether I needed to or not."

Jesse didn't have anything else to say on the matter. Life persisted outside Midtown Comics, and that was good enough for him.

"When's the last time you saw John, anyway?" Kate asked.

"Not since that night. But I'm sure he's still wandering around the city. Like the lonely little eye within the hurricane of delivery trucks and foot traffic. Like my arch-enemy, just waiting for the right time to strike."

"Don't you ever wonder if he's okay?" Kate asked.

"Nope."

"Not even a little?"

"Nope."

"Can't you just admit you're still angry, Jess?"

"*Of course* I'm still angry. I didn't think it was something I actually had to admit to. It's been a year, Kate. One year! But it's still not easy."

"I know," was all Kate could muster for a response. She began clicking her mouse again on the other end of the phone. "Listen, Jess. I'm sorry again about this morning, okay? I just wonder if I should have seen any of this coming."

Yes, thought Jesse. A most definite *YES*.

"I'm wondering what I should tell him."

Jesse wanted to say: *You tell Gene it's over. And you tell him the two of you should never have gotten married in the first place.* In his head, Jesse had the utmost confidence to answer any question.

"And I wonder what I should do next," Kate continued.

He wanted to tell her: *Move on. Go treat yourself to a fine meal at The Wing King's. All by yourself. Go see Wicked again. Alone. And you lie to your best friends about being on a second date rather than spilling the entire embarrassing truth of it all to them.* But that isn't what Jesse told Kate. "Tough to say," is what he told her instead. "But we all have messes to sort through. And if you're anything like me, you'll just want to start forgetting.

You know, instead of bottling it up."

"You can't forget everything, Jess." Kate didn't mean to point her answer so directly at Jesse, but her words applied to his memories nonetheless. "And you shouldn't."

No? Just watch me, he thought. "Have you spoken with Tommy?" he asked, not really intending to change the subject, but happy he had.

"I tried calling him already, but he didn't answer his phone."

"Tommy never answers his phone. Did you leave a message?"

"Tommy doesn't check his messages. You know that. But he always checks the caller I.D. and calls right back."

"So, did he call you back?"

"Nope. You don't think he's ignoring me, do you?"

"You know how Tommy is. He's probably just mad we didn't ask him about that letter this morning."

Kate stopped. "What letter?"

"You don't remember? It was practically glued to his hand."

"I remember he kept trying to interrupt us with something. But I had other things on my mind."

"We all get other things on our minds sometimes. How about I meet you at the coffee shop tonight at seven?"

"Christ. I think Pond just shoved four perogies into his mouth at once."

"And I think you really need to find a new website."

"I can't. This city is just too damn interesting. I'll never get enough of it."

Until it's had enough of you, Jesse thought. Sometimes Jesse wondered if he would have been better off having never emerged from Grand Central Station with his friends so many years ago.

"Yeah, I'll you see you later then," Kate finally agreed. "Thanks, Jess."

"Love you," Jesse concluded. But the words that came out his mouth were already exhausted from being set free.

CHAPTER THREE
Pendulum Publishing – Midtown

"Love you too," Kate said, ending her conversation with Jesse. She elongated her neck until she could view the labyrinth of cubicles surrounding her own. Heads of hair bobbed up and down and back and forth, as the bodies they were attached to read and typed and processed miles upon miles of aimlessly insipid and seemingly never-ending manuscripts which never had a prayer of being published. Midtown Manhattan's afternoon light poured through the windows and created a fuzzy glow above the thin layer of dust covering every horizontal surface higher than five feet from the floor. Thousands of discarded, yellow sticky notes sat crumpled out of sight, whatever reminders written on them had fallen to the wayside; and yet no one seemed to have ever noticed their absence. Only rubber bands and clumps of hair had now found themselves attached to the notes, and they blew gently from the freezing breeze of the office's amped-up air conditioners.

There was a note stuck to the top of Kate's partition; she reached out and unfolded it. All it said was: "LUNCH WITH GENE," in her own chaotic, right-handed printing. She had invented the art of writing notes in the office with her right hand, while reserving her natural left-handedness for the real world outside. What would happen if a co-worker should one day discover some sort of incriminating information? Kate's jumbled, right-handed printing could never be traced directly back to her, could it? Maybe it was paranoia, but Kate figured just a sprinkling of paranoia was a lot better than the alternative: that someone in the office might know when she had to pick up her vaginal antifungal cream, or when she was reminding herself to record reruns of "The

Osbournes" she had already seen. Kate stared at the wrinkled note in her hand — the yellow paper not even yellow anymore — and she couldn't recall if she'd ever made it to that once-promised lunch date with her husband. She crushed it even tighter in her fist before tossing it into a nearby wastepaper basket.

From one of the bobbing heads came the words, "*Swish!* Oh yeah! Kate's got game!"

"Fuck off," Kate mumbled in the direction of her unseen fan.

Katherine Prince was a strong person, but her natural self-doubts, jealousies, and competitiveness continued to pull her in weak directions. She was an inappropriate dresser, always selecting the wrong wardrobe for any occasion. She would wear business suits for greasy coffee shop lunch dates with Tommy and Jesse, but then choose worn, tattered, bohemian skirts and Jamaican knit hats for meetings with authors and literary agents. Still, she braggingly described her own fashion sense as being, "Somewhere between a Park Avenue spinster on a bad day and a Meat-Packing District hobo on a good day." She had an embarrassingly vast collection of printed tights, the argyle or checker-pattern being the most popular of late. But there was always the chance of the once-favored purple cow pattern still showing up for an early morning meeting.

Her face was impossibly oval. Her hair, rich with beautiful curls, was always wrapped behind ears too small for her head. Once or twice a year, she considered cutting her hair short, but would always reassess when Tommy reminded her of the flack Felicity took after butchering her hair in Season Two. She had the delicate wrists of a high-end mannequin and legs that were made to show off, although she'd cover them up as often as possible. At times, her generosity was unheralded: she was never opposed to paying for a friend's meal, and she could always be counted on to remember a birthday or anniversary. Her kitchen calendar was the most thoroughly complicated chart anyone had ever seen. She considered herself to be a polite pedestrian, navigating her way through the city's crowded sidewalks using a variety of courteous tricks she'd garnered over the years. She would plan her moves seconds in advance, finding empty pockets to slip through, and she would always shoulder check before swerving from side to side. She claimed to have names for many of her more popular moves, but would never divulge them. In her dreams, Kate was the city's greatest bike courier, but in reality, she was a below-average book editor.

Kate's favorite food was anything hot from a street vendor: kebabs; chestnuts; pupusas. Her favorite cereal had always been Frankenberry, which she thought was discontinued until she discovered the Sunny Mart, a dusty Filipino market on 128th Street, was the only place in Manhattan that still stocked it. Her favorite gum was Nicorette, not because she was trying to quit smoking — she'd never smoked more than one-and-a-half cigarettes since I'd known her — but because to her there was nothing quite as satisfying as the combined flavor of mint and nicotine. Her favorite color wasn't even a color, it was really just a complicated explanation. Her favorite place in the city to sit was the artsy, tiled benches near Grant's Tomb in Riverside Park: on summer evenings, she enjoyed watching the lightning bugs dance across their colorful surfaces.

She always seemed to have so much in her hands when unlocking doors, that there was the inevitable need to be holding something between her teeth. Every year she hoped for a technical malfunction during the city's New Year's Eve celebration so she could say: "They really dropped the ball on this." It was a joke she never told anyone else so she might receive the best possible reaction, should the opportunity ever present itself. She was still paying for a gym membership she hadn't used for six years. She loathed anyone who clapped at the end of movies. She never wanted to have kids but she still had baby names picked out in case there was ever an accident: Creston for a boy and Liberty for a girl. And Kate always wanted to write a book, however her inability to think of something worth saying was what continued to obstruct her progress.

Kate worked at Pendulum Publishing in Midtown. Pendulum was intended to be no more than a stopgap between school and the life she'd once imagined for herself. But as it stood, Kate had been an assistant editor now for much longer than she'd planned. After seven years of self-inflicted promises, Kate was still fine-tuning her first novel. The book's titular journey began once upon a time as "Paper Fences," but eventually turned into "Hold for Applause," followed by "The Breakfast Special Comes with Toast," which soon after became known as "Am Not, You Are." It was labeled "The Things We Forgot" for what must have only been a day or two before it had once again embraced its original and ambiguously titled roots as "Paper Fences." But this was still just considered a temporary title until Kate finished her latest rewrite. Essentially, the story hadn't changed much: it had always been about a wallflower of a girl who'd grown up to become a woman living a life of regret. It was about bad decisions and poor choices and the character's desperate fight to win back her lost childhood. There was a reason the book had been turned down so many times, and it was never because of the title. Tommy knew it, and he'd tried on numerous occasions to convince Kate she'd be well-served in detaching herself altogether from the whole unworkable mess, to start fresh with a blank piece of electronic paper. Internally, Kate agreed she probably should, but her competitiveness toward Tommy prevented her from ever doing so.

The real difference between Kate and Tommy was she was quicker to make excuses for not writing. The barking dog from somewhere in her neighborhood was the latest in a series of prime examples. Tommy never once made an excuse for himself. His first novel, "Blanc," was published three months to the day after his very first draft was finished. It was an instant success — even having its own movie adaptation — and Tommy followed it up with four more books in the critically acclaimed series starring the erudite Detective Buster Broome. While Kate couldn't help being jealous, it was the strength of their friendship that kept her real feelings quietly simmering just below the surface. She didn't even realize it, but those feelings were all blatantly confessed within one paragraph of "Paper Fences." It was directly in the center of page two-hundred-and-forty-nine.

Kate's brain was still trying to piece itself back together after one of the most inane staff meetings the Pendulum office had organized that year. The last three publications had utterly tanked, and the higher-ups whose voices were actually heard decided it would be best to find fault with how their employees were working rather than why certain employees were even there in the first place. The consensus put forward was thus: editors and copywriters were no longer allowed to listen to their iPods while working. Apparently, the prognosis was if an editor was listening to a song they liked, they were more likely to give the final approval on something, no matter how bad it was. And, as Troy "The Shark" Dunlop of "Consumer/Media Relations & Employee Motivations" (the sign on his office door said just that, in those exact words) so eloquently put it: "Especially if it sucked really, really hard." Conversely, if said employee were listening to music they didn't enjoy, works of genius were quite possibly being tossed into the slush pile, never to be seen by human eyes or touched by human hands again until its next life as recycled toilet paper. The only reason Kate had raised a hand during the morning meeting was to ask: "Why would anyone have music they hated on their iPods in the first place?" A valid point, but once it was established Kate didn't even own an iPod, her case was quickly dismissed and everyone was sent back to their cubicles where they could hear the muzak version of "Livin' La Vida Loca" softly playing over the constant static of the office intercom speakers.

The meetings were constantly unnecessary, her co-workers were fundamentally unreliable, and the work was tedious, but it was also a paycheck. Kate had even started to mold the slow, pinheaded older brother who worked part-time at the failing party supplies store in "Paper Fences" after Troy Dunlop, so Pendulum had also been a good source for creative inspiration.

Kate fumbled through a mess of notes on one of the books she was currently editing, but they were nearly illegible to her. She found herself staring at one page for nearly a full minute before realizing it was upside down.

From beyond her cubicle, Kate could hear the squeaky wheels of an office supply cart approaching. Suddenly, a head popped up from behind Kate's partition. The head belonged to Dwayne Reamer, one of Pendulum's temporary workers. Although "temporary" didn't really seem to apply to Dwayne anymore, since he'd been there for well over two years now, and he didn't appear to have any dreams of leaving. "Hey, Kate! You get my email?"

"Nice going, Dwayne," Kate said as she reached over and added another notch to her open notepad. In her notebook, in a series of marks of five, Kate recorded every time she heard the phrase "Did you get my email?" around the office, or some variation thereof.

"Oh, shit! That one was completely unintentional too." He argued his case, but it was already too late.

"Dwayne, you know there's pretty much only one thing I hate more than people wearing their backpacks on the subway and idiots who repeatedly hit the crosswalk button: when someone in the office asks someone else if they got their email."

"I know, I know—"

"I mean, if they're going to come sauntering over looking for some sort of self-gratifying confirmation on whatever meaningless drivel they just spent twenty minutes typing up without their supervisor knowing, they may as well have just come on over and asked what they wanted to ask and not have sent the fucking email in the first place. At least that way they'd be getting some exercise too. Do you know what I mean?"

"Kate, I'm pretty sure I've heard the 'did-you-get-my-email' rant from you before."

"Oh, I'm positive you have."

"Maybe even a couple of times last week."

"I wouldn't doubt it."

"Should I say 'I'm sorry' again?"

"It couldn't hurt."

"Okay then. Kate, I'm sorry for whoever pooped on your muffet this morning, because they're sure to get it later."

"Hold on. Pooped on your muffet? Isn't the saying, 'Who *pissed* in your *Corn Flakes?*'"

"Nah. Muffets are better for you than Corn Flakes. And they've got twenty percent of your daily fiber." Dwayne Reamer's claim to fame was his constant attempts at revamping old catchphrases. Or better yet, starting new ones of his own in the hope they would one day catch on. "Times are changing, Kate. You gotta keep up." Dwayne's only dream was to one day overhear a catchphrase of his own creation uttered on the subway by strangers.

The one he was most proud of was a little saying known as: "You're on, Huron." Definition: *It's a deal, buddy; I'm totally in agreement with you, pal.* Kate could only assume the Huron in question was some sort of reference/homage to Lake Huron, but she wasn't entirely convinced. And she had never cared enough to ask Dwayne either, even though he could be heard saying it around the office a few times a day.

"Listen, Dwayne—"

"That's what I'm doing," he butted-in.

"I appreciate your continuous attempts to try and keep me just as chipper as can be, but I'm really not in the mood today. No offense."

Dwayne swiveled his ear a little closer to Kate.

"And I know I say that every day, but today I *really* mean it."

"You're on, Huron!"

Kate turned back to the mound of paperwork on her desk. She rarely found herself intimidated by her workload, but she hadn't been in the right frame of mind all morning. Her realization that Gene wasn't, and probably never had been, the right choice for her had made Kate question the relevance of basically everything else in her tiny world. "Listen—" she began again.

"I'm still here." He didn't mean to be, but Dwayne Reamer could really be quite irritating.

Kate slid the pile of paperwork in closer and thought for a moment about laying her head down and simply waiting for an end to come. "I've got submissions from design artists to sort through. I've got facts that need checking. And I've got a whole other manuscript to rewrite. My copy editor called in sick, so I've got to finish *her* work too in order to get this fucking thing out by five o'clock."

"So, you're extremely busy. Is that what you're trying to tell me?"

"Dwayne, please."

"You've sure been saying *Fuck* a lot lately. Do you realize that?"

Kate wondered for a moment if she had possibly muttered the word at the morning meeting. *Fuck*, she thought. *There was probably a pretty fucking good chance.*

"It seems to me, Kate, there must be something else on your mind, because you've had these kinds of deadlines before and you've always hit them. And — might I add — you've also never complained about it. Before now, that is. Unless, of course, I interpreted your complaining as some sort of semi-jovial nitpickery."

Kate was hoping the pile of work before her might disguise what was really on her mind, but no mountain of paperwork could ever be distracting enough for Dwayne Reamer. "Nice work, detective." Dwayne rolled his forearm in front of him, and bowed as though he'd just sawed Kate in half and there was a cheering crowd surrounding his stage. In truth, Kate felt like she really had been opened right up. "There is something," she started slowly. "And I don't know why I'm even telling you this, but—"

Dwayne crooked his neck forward, his interest officially piqued. "Spill it, Vesuvius."

"But I'm having some, marital...*dubieties* at the moment."

His shoulders slumped. "Shit, Kate. I'm sorry."

"I didn't even realize it until this morning. I knew something was wrong, I just couldn't put my finger on it. But now I know what it was."

Dwayne twisted his head back a little, as if to ask: *So, what is it?*

"I hate my husband."

Dwayne continued to lean over the partition of Kate's cubicle. "Well, shit." He wanted to extend a little more sympathy, but some unknown factor was holding him back. "I don't know how you could miss something like that, Kate."

Kate leaned back in her ergonomic office chair, and looked up at the ceiling panels with murky brown eyes. "I was up before him this morning. Gene's usually gone by the time my alarm goes off, but today he said he wanted to sleep in a little. So, I brushed my teeth, had a glass of orange juice, and I—"

"Wait, you drank orange juice *after* you brushed your teeth?"

"That's right. I actually prefer it that way."

"Weird."

"Anyway, Dwayne. I got dressed in the bathroom and when I went back to say goodbye to him, I realized he was already asleep again." Kate stopped for a moment, but her silence went uninterrupted. She assumed this would have been a difficult conversation, and the thoughts in her head would be wearing away at her, weakening her, word by word. But they weren't. It was actually easy for Kate to acknowledge the fact her life was on the cusp of being torn apart. "You know those picture frames people have? The ones that don't have any pictures in them, and they're just hung from the ceiling, suspended in the air like some inane, ineffective room divider?"

"I hate those things."

"Me too, Dwayne. Me too. But we have them in our bedroom, right beside the bed. Like they're windows on some kind of invisible wall."

"Wait. Why on earth would you need windows if your walls were invisible?"

"It doesn't matter, Dwayne. So, when I came back into the room, instead of waking Gene to say goodbye, I just looked at him through that picture frame. I don't know what it was — whether I felt like I was watching him from another room, from across the street, or from another world. Or maybe it was like a television."

"Or a picture frame?"

"Exactly! But there was only *one* single thought that occurred to me at that moment: Why am I here? I hate this man. We have nothing in common."

"I'll ignore the fact there were three thoughts right there, and not one. So, why'd you marry the guy then?"

"Let's just say I've made some embarrassingly bad relationship decisions in my life and leave it at that."

"Hasn't everyone? Shit, I could write the book on bad relationships, if you wouldn't mind editing it for me."

"I doubt you could compete, Dwayne. In fact, you probably wouldn't even qualify."

"Hey, I've got stories."

"Have you ever had anonymous phone sex on your lunch break?"

"Uhh—"

"Ever licked the neck of a cab driver?"

"Eww."

"How about a threesome in the back of a deli?"

"Um, well no, but—"

"Have you ever given a hand-job to a co-worker in the supply closet?"

"Which closet?"

"Take your pick."

Dwayne groaned as his imagination began to run wild. Compared to Kate, his book of bad relationship decisions instantly became more like a brochure, or a playbill at best. "I did it with a Furry one time."

"Please, Dwayne. Who hasn't? Honestly though, I think I might have been hiding these feelings for so long because I'm afraid my marriage is headed in the exact same hopeless direction as my novel."

"Ah yes. 'The Things We Forgot.' How's that coming anyway?"

"Actually, it's back to 'Paper Fences' again."

Dwayne thought to himself for a moment before responding, "Hey, can I use that?"

"Use what?"

"That line: *Back to paper fences.* You know, like if you've found yourself right where you started. Or when it's a Monday morning and you're trudging back to work."

"Sure, Dwayne. Do whatever you want with it. Fill your boots."

"You're the best!" Dwayne paused for a moment before Kate's story fully cycled through his mind. "Jeez, Kate. I would never have pegged you for someone who would have those hanging picture frames."

"Everyone's entitled to a few secrets. Just don't tell anyone else, you hear?"

"Your secret's safe with me." Dwayne grabbed the few pieces of mail from Kate's outbox and filed them into his cart. "You know, Theo told me he's changed the name of his book too."

"Theo? From Finance?"

"No. Theo from Sales."

"I didn't know Theo from Sales was writing a book. Is it a novel?"

"*Everyone* here is writing a novel. And the majority of them are being typed up right now on company time."

"Really? How is it you know that and I don't?"

"I'm the mail room temp, Kate. I pick up and deliver all their mail every day. You think you're the only one I talk to around here? Some of the staff I don't even know, I only know them by their book titles." Dwayne looked to the ceiling, trying to list off a few from memory. "There's 'Frozen Lake' in Editing. 'Soul Blood' is in Accounting. And I work with a guy named 'Piddle Paddle' in the mail room."

"*Soul Blood?* Fuck."

"Yeah, and Theo's just changed his title to 'Running Through Gravity.'" Dwayne put a finger in his mouth, hoping to gag himself in reaction to the author's choice. "So 'Paper Fences' is not so bad, really."

"It's been a pleasure as always, Dwayne." Kate assumed that would signal the end to the conversation, and Dwayne's arms would begin sliding slug-like from her cubicle wall until he'd melted from sight completely, but the Temp's visit was not so temporary. He continued to hang in front of her. "What did your email say, anyway?" she asked.

"Oh yeah," he said, recalling the reason he came by in the first place. "I think I found out who's been stealing my yogurts from the fridge."

"You're doing a bang-up job around here, Dwayne Reamer. And if I'm actually interested in the details, I might even read it later."

"Awesome sauce! Well, it's back to paper fences for me." With that, Dwayne finally disappeared from sight. The squeaky wheels of his supply cart could be heard for a moment, but then stopped suddenly. Just as Kate had thought about opening the marked manuscript, Dwayne's head popped right back into place. "And, Kate—?"

"Hmm?"

"I just wanted to say I'm sorry again. Even if there's really no requirement for me to be."

Kate gave him a nod of appreciation and then immediately turned back to her work.

~~~

Thirty minutes later when Kate thought to check her email, she noticed the message from Dwayne (with the subject line: YOGURT THIEF!), and was amused to find Dwayne accusing Cliff Barnes from marketing of stealing his precious fruity yogurts from the nineteenth-floor refrigerator. Kate smirked to herself knowing Dwayne would never suspect it had actually been her all along. There was also one email from Teresa (sent out to the entire office, letting everyone know her cat's hip surgery was a success), one from reception (a reminder that this month's employee prize was a new iPod) and one from Troy "The Shark" Dunlop (he of 'Consumer/Media Relations & Employee Motivations') — sent precisely thirty-one seconds after reception's email — again stating the office's new iPod policies. In it, he even had the audacity to use the phrase, "bass ackwards." Jesus.

And just when Kate decided she would call Tommy again, to let him know she and Jesse planned on meeting at the coffee shop later, a second email from Dwayne the Temp's account suddenly popped up:

SUBJECT: "RE: YOGURT THIEF!"
Hey Kate,
Just wondering if you'd like to have dinner with me tomorrow night.
Actually, I'm free pretty much any day.
-DR-
~~~

For the first time ever, Kate felt guilty for stealing the Temp's yogurt. She deleted the email and went right back to work.

CHAPTER FOUR
Airport Runway – Seattle

He boarded the plane on Pacific Time, but he would be landing on Eastern. Most of the passengers were already setting their watches accordingly. He didn't wear a watch anymore.

The overhead compartment was completely full, but he didn't feel the need to blame others for what was only a minor inconvenience. Instead, he asked the large, Southern woman seated behind him if she would mind terribly if his bag was stored with hers. With an abundance of politeness, she told him there was still plenty of room, and she could even just hold onto her purse should he require more space. He said that wouldn't be necessary, and thanked her for her courtesy.

He thought of his friends. How long had it been since he'd seen them, he wondered? It had to be at least ten years now. Time passes so slowly when you're not paying careful attention to it, slow enough you might not notice when something is gone from your life completely. He wondered just how much they must have changed. It's possible they may have moved on as well and left the city behind for better opportunities elsewhere. Except for Tommy. There was no way Tommy would ever leave New York; he knew that much, at least. But would he be accepted back into their world? It had felt like such a permanent world so long ago, but now it seemed like a world he'd only ever temporarily known.

The lid of his water bottle had been screwed on so tight, his fingers burned trying to open it. He soon realized he'd already finished the last drop. Rubbing his dry throat with an open hand, he closed his eyes in an effort to settle his nerves. He hated flying. The plane would be taking off shortly, so he secured his seatbelt, and made sure he was sitting in a full, upright position. He made a note of where the emergency exits were situated, just in case the flight attendant forgot to mention it. He caught himself as he checked his wrist for the time and tried to recall when he'd last worn a watch. He couldn't remember.

It took him a few moments before he realized the plane was already moving along the tarmac and it was deep into the sky before he knew it.

He was anxious. Nervous. Optimistic. Terrified. Was the plane supposed to be making such noises? At once, it reminded him of the chaotic echo of a New York subway, a zipper being pulled tight, a barking dog behind a fence, and the remote control being dropped on the glass coffee table in middle of a scary movie. His sweaty hands clenched the shared armrest.

The woman behind him placed her perfectly still hand on his shoulder in order to let him know things would be fine. "Let fate do the rest," were the words he heard in his head. But he was unclear where the words had emanated from. He also realized then that accepting fate was the one thing he'd never really been comfortable with.

He turned in his seat just enough to get a look at the time on the woman's watch, hoping it might comfort him. But he couldn't make out the digits due to the shaking airplane.

CHAPTER FIVE

Tommy's Apartment – Morningside Heights

The first thing Rachel noticed when she entered Tommy's apartment was the opened letter. It was on the couch, crumpled into a ball, as though tossed across the room in a moment of emotional recklessness. It was an immediate distraction since the apartment had always been so incredibly bare. Tommy didn't like clutter; he boasted often about his extreme, minimalist attitude. And yet, his apartment still seemed to be begging for knickknacks: dusty picture frames filled with family from generations removed; cracked lamps with their cords winding through shag carpeting like snakes through grass; maybe some ornithological chotchkies lined up along the kitchen windowsill. Wooden owls. Glass seagulls. Plastic penguins. Rubber ducks. There was never much in his refrigerator aside from a few days' worth of fruit from the CKY Grocery, a carton of chocolate milk which remained perpetually half-full, and two-dozen bottles of iced coffee. His walls had an assortment of framed movie posters: "Manhattan", "The Apartment", and a limited-edition print of "The Royal Tenenbaums" signed by Wes Anderson which Tommy had purchased on eBay a number of years ago and had always questioned the signature's validity. All of these seemed explicably linked by their common locale, the object of Tommy's inescapable obsession. New York City coursed through his veins as Atlantic waves lapped the shore of Brighton Beach. Growing up in Seattle, he had never yearned to visit Manhattan; he only ever wished to live there. To Tommy, there was a very significant difference between the two, although no one else could ever seem to appreciate the dissimilarity.

Tommy lived in Morningside Heights, on the sixth floor of the same apartment on West 113th Street he'd been in since he first moved to New York eleven years ago. Over that time, he graduated from sharing a first-floor tar hut with an ever-changing collection of college roommates to living on his own in his sixth-floor penthouse. The door buzzer only ever worked intermittently, and Tommy was quick to hand out copies of his keys to anyone who meant anything to him; sometimes to individuals he only mildly cared for; sometimes even to those he met on the street and simply had a great conversation with. Tommy had a whole drawer full of the things. The Engine Company 47 firehouse was right next door, but the blaring sirens never bothered him. In fact, he convinced himself the racket was actually helpful whenever he would sit down to write. His desk by the window had nothing but an old banker's lamp and a laptop on it: no other instruments of any kind. At the moment, there was a copy of his first novel, "Blanc," on the desk as well as a hand-written manuscript for his latest book, "The Manhattanite." There were never any lights on in the apartment and the television was rarely used, but Rachel could hear its muffled static coming from the bedroom.

When Rachel reached for the letter on the couch, I couldn't help but stop and question her reasons for doing so. Rachel Ponzini was not a complicated girl but she had a certain muted quality about her that teased others into stopping dumbfounded at the most unexpected of times.

She was the kind of beautiful that made the average looks of those around her seem all the more lacking. She had a smile that often made men fool themselves into thinking they loved her, but it was simply her disposition that carried such propensities behind her like a balloon on a string. She was smart enough to know things like when to walk out of a bad movie and she was always right when guessing the reasons for subway delays. Rachel was not inherently nosy — nor was she overly obtrusive — but still, she could not resist taking the letter into her hand.

Carefully peeling it open like a suspect piece of fruit, she found both the diligently typed one-page letter and the envelope crushed within one another. The envelope was addressed to Tommy, but to his old address: the apartment on the first floor where he hadn't lived for as long as she'd known him. The current resident of Apartment 104, the Middle Eastern man with the wooden leg, must have redirected the letter for Tommy. It read:

Tom,

I'm sorry to contact you in such a way, but you were the only one I was certain I could reach. I've got to say, I do sometimes miss your shameless predictability.

I know we've lost touch over the years, and I realize I have to be accountable for my actions, but I've got some news for you. And I'm not entirely sure how you'll take it, but here it is: I'm moving back to Manhattan.

To be honest, things in Seattle are not so good right now. In retrospect, it's easy to say I never should have left New York. But by that logic, perhaps I never should have left Seattle in the first place either, right? Who knows though. Maybe I'll regret this decision too. I'm not certain how much news might have gotten around. I'm not sure if friends and family talk the way they used to. But suffice it to say, I was once again in need of a change and one has finally and most opportunistically presented itself.

I hope we might have the chance to sit down again. You, me, Katie, and Jesse. Just like old times.

Anyway, I'll keep things short for now, and save the rest of it for when I arrive in NY. I hope I'll see you when I get there.

Miss you guys,
Patrick

Rachel was unsure what to make of it. She didn't know who Patrick was or what kind of connection he had with Tommy and his friends. She was certain Tommy had never mentioned him before, and there was something very cold and clinical about the words which had been written. But whoever Patrick was, he seemed to be somebody both close and distant, and the letter left the impression that there was some kind of friction, or possibly even bad blood, between them all.

Rachel left the letter unfolded on the couch, and she stepped cautiously toward the bedroom, where she could clearly make out the unmistakable echo of the Six O'clock News. She peered around the corner into the dark room as though she didn't belong there; as though she was an intruder in her own boyfriend's apartment. She was expecting to see him lying on the bed like he always did. But instead, Tommy was standing in front of the television, his back turned to her. She couldn't help herself from quietly taking him in with her eyes before making her presence known.

Thomas Mueller was tall; tall enough he would make rooms seem smaller than they were, and his boisterous personality had a way of making him seem even bigger. He could tolerate getting his hair cut no more than twice a year, and would cringe on that 116th Street barbershop chair like a lamb sheared before the abattoir. Tommy's skin was unusually dark, making his coffee-stained teeth appear whiter than they actually were. His clothes were always clean and pressed, and generally brand new. A few times a year he would change his entire wardrobe and give his old clothes to Goodwill, prompting Jesse to joke about Manhattan's homeless numbers seeming much lower than the city claimed them to be, since the majority were walking unnoticed in Tommy's old clothes. As often as his look changed, Tommy could always be counted on to wear one item in particular: an old New York Rangers hockey sweater, which, despite his generous frame, was still somehow a size or two too big for him. He didn't care that the first and last letters had come unstitched and fallen off the front. Now all the jersey said was "ANGER," and Kate was always quick to suggest he start wearing a different emotion.

The city's midnight din invigorated Tommy, and he would slide his window wide open and use that time to write exclusively, never sleeping for more than a few hours. He absorbed the sound of the traffic, the wind-carried yelps of both pleasure and violence, and the buzzing of the streetlights, transplanting those feelings into words. Tommy knew the power of words, and he could say the most wonderful things at times; he once told Rachel he always thought his grandmother's smile was the most beautiful sight he'd ever known. But he also said many juvenile things, and still found the word "dick" to be tremendously funny. The first time he ever met Rachel's father ("Pleased to meet you Tommy. I'm Dick Ponzini."), Tommy couldn't help but snort rudely to himself. There was nothing funnier than that word.

His favorite tune was "Auld Lang Syne" and he could often be heard humming it, not caring at all when others informed him the song was only ever sung during New Year's celebrations. When drunk, he would often quote obscure lines from movies and he would not relent until someone guessed the correct film. Tommy had a keen sense of direction, and never felt discombobulated. Even inside an office tower, he would always point the right way when speaking of a specific location. He never felt inferior around anyone, but there was a devilishly handsome man in the apartment who never failed to make Tommy feel uncomfortably mediocre. That man intimidated Tommy beyond imagining, especially when he wore his newborn infant in that front-loaded baby carrier, or whenever he would chivalrously hold the lobby or elevator door for him.

Tommy had habits that could always be counted on. He was not a germaphobe, but when Tommy used a public washroom he would lift the toilet seat with the toe of his shoe. When he rode the subway, he would sit in the last car, claiming it made the ride last longer. He refused to eat meals with three-pronged forks. He insisted upon sprinkling capers onto nearly everything he ate. And when he watched the Six O'clock News he would always lie with his stomach on the bed. It was exactly how he and his brother would lie on the living room floor when they were kids, watching the nightly broadcast with their parents.

But Rachel observed him as he stood there, wearing his favorite ANGER sweater and holding the remote control to his neck as though it was a razor blade. The top story was a report about a plane crash somewhere in the Midwest.

"Look at this," Tommy directed her, not surprised at all by her sudden appearance.

"How did you know I was here?"

"Come on, Rachel. You're about as stealthy as a garbage bag full of broken glass."

"What are you watching?"

"Plane crash. It left Seattle this afternoon and crashed somewhere in the Midwest. Kansas, I think. Destroyed six farms."

"Was anyone hurt?"

Tommy set the television to mute, and tossed the remote onto the bed where he sat down. "Everyone on the plane was killed," he said, his palms pressed together under his chin, as though praying. "And *six farms* were destroyed," he reiterated.

"It sounds to me like you're more concerned for the farms." Rachel sat down beside him on the bed. "Your sympathy seems a little misguided, Tommy."

He didn't have more of a reaction to her words than shrugged shoulders. They silently watched the flickering flames on the television for a minute or so longer. The words, "ALL 212 PASSENGERS AND CREW KILLED" continued to scroll across the bottom of the screen. The letter on the living room couch aside, Tommy's past was not a complete mystery to Rachel. She knew Tommy once had a twin brother. His name was Leyland, and he died in a plane crash years before somewhere over the Pacific Ocean. That, along with the memories of September Eleventh, had made Tommy very uneasy whenever there were planes on the news, as though any further tragedy might have been a personal attack against him.

Tommy motioned back toward the remote, but Rachel grabbed it before he could. They looked at each other for a moment, the televised fire reflecting off the right side of Rachel's face, and the left of Tommy's. "I think we need to talk," she finally said.

Breathe in.

Tommy turned back to the television. "What do you want to talk about, Rachel?" The images before him sent shivers up his spine.

She stumbled with her words. "Tommy, listen. It's nothing serious. Not really. Well, it is for me, I suppose. But I just wanted to make sure you know what I'm feeling." She placed the remote out of his reach on the other side of the bed, and then lifted Tommy's thick arm around her. "Baby, don't you think it's time I moved in here with you?"

"Are you serious?" Tommy reacted as though Rachel had asked him to split the atom right there on the bed.

"I just feel a little lonely sometimes. Do you know what I mean?" With her nose pressed into the itchy fabric of Tommy's sweater, Rachel could smell both last winter in Morningside Park and the past summer on the windy beach of Montauk. He wore that stupid sweater everywhere. "I have to come in from Queens every day just to go to school right around the corner from you."

Queens. Tommy shivered again upon hearing the word. Ugh. He didn't venture outside of Manhattan very often, and if he did, it was usually to go watch the Rangers play the Devils in Jersey. He would save the Long Island trips for when Rachel begged him to visit her family in Montauk, or if there should ever be a playoff series against the Islanders. Thankfully, neither occurred very often.

She continued to talk, not requiring any form of answer from the man. "And it just seems...sort of silly to me. That we're not, well—*you know*—living together."

Tommy stopped for a moment to consider whether the Blueshirts had a game that night, but he was never very good at remembering the team's schedule. "What do you mean you're lonely? There's got to be five million people in this city, Rachel."

"Yeah, and I push my way through ten thousand of them a day. But I just— I don't know, Tommy. I just feel this way when I'm not with you. And I've been feeling it more and more lately."

It didn't happen often, but Tommy had no idea how to respond. He turned down to look at her little face staring up at his. The glow from the television licked her ivory skin.

"How long have we been together now, Tommy?"

"You don't know?"

"Of course I know. This is *me* asking *you*."

"I'd say three years? Maybe four?" Tommy had a tendency to reconsider his answers after he'd already given them. "No, three."

"How long would you say is long enough to wait?"

"Wait for what, Rachel? Listen, are you mad at me?"

"I'm not mad at you, Tommy. I just—I'm just ready for *more*, is all."

He hated that word. *More*. Mostly because he never wanted more; his life and everything in it was just enough for him. Why hope for more than that?

Tommy couldn't turn away from her; Rachel's gaze was unrelenting. Her eyes had always been the most intoxicating part of her. The news report had switched to a story about a university shooting in Boston. Tommy held up his index finger for a moment but then curled it back inside his palm, stopping himself from saying whatever he'd intended.

"What do you say?" she asked, clearly unprepared for the smallest amount of disappointment.

Tommy looked at his hand as though the response he almost had a second ago was still held inside of it. "Do you know what almost happened there, Rachel? I almost forgot where I was."

"I don't understand."

"Having you move in would be great," he said.

Her eyes lit up. Just before walking up the five flights of stairs to have this talk with Tommy, Rachel had almost convinced herself it would be an entirely pointless endeavor. Tommy was the most stubborn person she'd ever known, and he was an impossible man to change.

Tommy continued his thought. "We could merge our book collections together. Or we could each take a shelf and do whatever we wanted with it. After a few months, I'd probably even think of a clever way to propose to you. Maybe serve the ring to you with breakfast in bed, or maybe for dinner. Squeezed around a chicken finger or drowned in a bowl of hasenpfeffer. We'd get married. We'd paint our walls every year. Solid colors. Maybe an accent wall with stripes or polka dots. We'd plant our own little garden somewhere in the city. Somewhere so heartbreakingly corny there'd be a story about us on the morning news. We'd circumcise our kids, and then pet them on their heads, and send them off to university. We could just sit there getting older and older as we watch the Atlantic Ocean roll in every morning from our house in the Hamptons. It all sounds pretty terrific, doesn't it?"

It did sound pretty terrific, she thought to herself. Even if she had no clue what hasenpfeffer was supposed to be. Was that Yiddish?

"That's what *almost* happened just then. But then I remembered where I was, Rachel. Everything here is just the way I want it to be. Everything is perfect in this city. That's why I came here in the first place. And I don't want any of that to change. I *don't* want more."

Rachel sank back into the sweater which now smelled like the night a year ago, when Tommy was drunk and embarrassed her and his friends by quoting lines from "Zardoz" before throwing up outside the Lafayette Station. She can't believe the things that come out of his mouth sometimes. "You can't be serious, can you?"

"I'm not prepared to give up what makes me happy for the things that I'm not so sure about, Rachel. That's just how things work. I came to New York to have everything I wanted, not to have any regrets."

"So, I've just wasted three years. Is that what you're saying?"

"See? I *knew* it had been three years!"

"I wish we had talked about this sooner, Tommy. Rather than have our expectations ruined."

"What expectations?"

"Is it so wrong to want a little more out of something? To expect *more* from someone?"

Ugh. There was that word again. Tommy lifted his arm from the girl who only wanted to be held. He shuffled across the bedroom and switched the television off manually, rather than having to reach across Rachel for the remote.

"How about a vacation at least?" she asked him while the room was opportunistically silent.

"I hate vacations."

"You've never been on a vacation, Tommy."

"That's because I know I'd hate it."

"So, does that mean marriage is out of the question too? And kids?" Clearly, Rachel had never learned about the quantity of potentially disappointing answers this man could generate from any number of her questions. "What about those hypothetical kids of ours you were sending off to university a minute ago, Tommy?"

"You know what hypothetical means, don't you?"

She had no immediate answer for him. She sat on the bed with her arms crossed, hoping it would be enough to make him give in.

"How many kids do you think you want anyway?" he asked her.

She flicked her tooth with a fingernail while she carefully pondered the most honest answer. It probably should have, but the fingernail thing never bothered Tommy. Finally, Rachel said, "I, um—I guess I always imagined us having, well—lots."

"Lots? In *this* city? I think Manhattan's crowded enough as it is, without us adding to its population problems. Don't you?"

"Who says we have to stay in Manhattan?"

Tommy couldn't bother dignifying her with an answer to her question. "How many is lots anyway?"

"I don't know. Four?"

Tommy shot her a look; a look which asked, *Are you out of your mind?*

"What's wrong with wanting four kids?"

Tommy heard the question, but he didn't answer right away. There had been many girlfriends in Tommy's life up to that point. There were many relationships, both serious and casual. And they had all ended in much the same way. Carla Barclay kicked Tommy out of her apartment when he suggested she might consider washing the dishes and cleaning the bathroom before he came by the next time. Sarah Rosenthal left Tommy standing alone in the Dunkin' Donuts lineup when he pointed out the restaurant now served salads. Isabella Keller simply hung up the phone when Tommy called her by the wrong name. Keekee Kaufman actually jumped off the Triboro Bridge when Tommy blatantly hinted she might in fact be mentally unstable (Keekee survived, but had no recollection of the event or of Tommy himself when she finally woke up four days later in the Bellevue psychiatric ward). That nameless girl he only danced one song with in the jazz club on Bleecker kicked him in the balls when he kissed her neck and proclaimed she tasted like the men's room. And Luisa Reyes excused herself from the lecture hall, never to be seen on campus again, after Tommy read a short story aloud to the class, explicitly detailing the two hours of sex they had three nights previously.

If Tommy had considered any of those relationships, if he'd used that moment to reflect upon his past, he might have had a different answer for Rachel Ponzini that night.

"What's wrong with wanting four kids, Tommy?" she repeated.

But he didn't consider any of the mistakes he'd made before Rachel. Instead, he just opened his mouth and joked, "It's a vagina, Rachel. Not a clown car."

And yet, Tommy knew the very second those words were released so haphazardly he had made yet another mistake. It would have been hard to tell where this one might have ranked amongst the others, but he didn't have much time to dwell on it. He thought he was cracking a joke, but Tommy Mueller was simply too impetuous sometimes. Yes, there were times when he said the most beautiful things, but the power of his words could also be incredibly devastating.

With tears welling in her eyes, Rachel stormed out of the apartment. Of course, he had said dumb things before, but Rachel had always come back. Tommy wasn't so sure this time. And neither was I.

CHAPTER SIX

Tom's Restaurant – Morningside Heights

"It's a vagina, not a clown car?" Kate asked. "What the hell were you thinking, Tommy?"

"Well, obviously he *wasn't* thinking," Jesse added. "It's no wonder she left him."

Tommy pleaded, "Hey, how about a little compassion here?" Just as Jesse and Kate had arranged earlier, they met at the coffee shop after work. The two of them sat across from Tommy, who had been there since Rachel left the apartment a couple of hours before. It had been one of those gloriously blue New York fall days, but black clouds had clouded the sky the moment Rachel left. Tommy ran through the pouring rain just to get to the restaurant. "And Rachel didn't *leave* me," he added. "She's just not here currently."

Kate couldn't leave it alone; she had to twist the dagger a little deeper. "You can really be an insufferable idiot sometimes. You know that, Tommy?"

"Of *course* I know that! You tell me every day, Kate. Whether I'm the Insufferable Idiot, the Narcissistic Prick, or the World Champion Ass-Hat. But, come on. Don't you guys think it was funny?" He was hoping for maybe just the smallest trace of a smile from his friends, but Tommy wouldn't receive any response at all. "Not even a little bit?"

"I think it's funny," said a fat, balding man who was seated at the counter and listening in on the group's conversation. "It's a fucking riot." He didn't turn around though; he simply continued to shove another fist-sized bite of a reuben sandwich into his mouth.

"Mind your own goddamned business, asshole!" Tommy retaliated.

The restaurant went silent, and some uneasy diners exchanged fearful glances. One couple immediately got up, paid the cashier for their unfinished meal, and exited into the preferred comfort of the rain. Tommy knew they were tourists; any true New Yorker could easily have put up with such a fine sampling of the city's time-honored belligerence.

"I don't think I've ever called you a World Champion Ass-Hat," Kate muttered.

"Besides," Tommy said, turning back to his own table. "Rachel's left before and she's always come back."

"God only knows why," Kate continued, mumbling deep into her coffee cup.

Jesse finished mixing his concoction of two-parts ketchup/one-part mayonnaise, and dipped a flimsy, tepid French fry in. "Has she called you yet?" he asked.

Tommy shook his head. It was hard to tell just how much Tommy cared for his girlfriend, since he almost never talked about her. And he was always happiest there at the restaurant, where more often than not it was just himself, Jesse, and Kate. What was apparent to both Kate and Jesse at that moment was the argument Tommy had with Rachel was not what had been weighing on his conscience. But neither of them was prepared to broach the subject. Tommy felt the balled-up letter in his pocket with the palm of his hand, knowing he had to plant it on the table again.

"You'll be just fine, Tommy," Kate reassured him, even if part of her wanted to believe otherwise.

"How about you, Kate?" Jesse inquired. "Have you thought about what you're going to do?"

"Not yet." Kate had been looking over the restaurant's menu for the last ten minutes, trying to decide whether she should get dessert. Milkshake? Cheesecake? The black and white cookie? "There are far too many choices in life sometimes. And I always seem to make the worst ones." Flagging the waitress down, Kate pointed to the cheesecake.

"You won't regret it," the waitress told her before scuttling off.

"I kind of wish there was an actual reason for me to divorce him, you know? Like if he was cheating on me, or if he wanted kids."

"Or some weird sex thing, right?" Tommy added.

"Everyone's got weird sex things, Tommy."

"Everyone? Even Gene?"

"Well, he likes to do this one thing—we call it the Fondue Pot. And—"

"Whoa! Whoa!" Tommy and Jesse both pulled a napkin from the dispenser, Jesse to shield his eyes and Tommy to wave a surrendering flag. "I think that's more than enough information for now, Kate."

"What's wrong with you guys? We always used to come here and talk about sex."

"Yeah," Tommy said. "But that was back when you were actually having sex, Kate."

"As far as I can tell, you two boys aren't doing much better."

"How about we just change the subject," Jesse suggested.

"I've got just the thing." Tommy straightened his legs under the table, and pushed himself up enough to reach deep into his pocket. He slumped back down in the booth and held out a closed fist for his friends.

"What's that?" Jesse asked, licking the pinkish sauce from his fingertips.

"Pick one," Tommy said, as though he had extended more than one hand to choose from. Jesse took the opportunity to poke Tommy's hand with his fork. Tommy opened it up to reveal the crumpled letter.

"Oh no," Kate sighed. "Again with the letter?"

Unfurling the paper orb in his hand, Tommy flattened the letter out along the edge of the table. He cleared his throat and read it aloud word for word, not allowing for any interruptions. They had their suspicions and hunches as to whom the letter might have been from — jogging their memories and considering crossed paths and chance encounters from the past — but neither Kate nor Jesse seemed totally convinced until Tommy had read the very last word.

"*Patrick?*" Jesse asked, almost spitting his drink onto the table. He knew now why Tommy was in such an anxious mood earlier, and he felt bad for not giving him a chance to share his own troubles, to throw them into the pot with Jesse's struggling post-Edie love life and Kate's failing marriage to Gene.

The cold rain did not let up, and it continued to machine-gun against the thin windows of the coffee shop.

~~~

It had been eleven years since Tommy Mueller, Katherine Prince, Jesse Classen, and Patrick Kohn sat together in the small Pike Place coffee shop. It was graduation day, and the four of them decided to meet for coffee to plan their futures rather than going to the upscale hotel in downtown Seattle with the rest of Franklin High. They were all wearing their graduation gowns, wet from the West Coast storm raging outside, but warm from the comfort of the small café. Jesse was the only one still wearing the hat. He had also spent the late afternoon constructing the table's current avant-garde centerpiece: a ramshackle, pyramidal apartment complex made up of napkins, straws, and honey and cane sugar packets. Every time the door opened, he had to shield the delicate ziggurat from the breeze.

Earlier that morning, Tommy had received notice he'd been accepted into the Hunter College literary program. And subsequently, he had a plan for them all.

"Congratulations, Tom!" Patrick declared, raising his latté.

"Listen," Tommy started. "I know you guys are still deciding or still waiting to hear back from other universities, but I wanted to take this moment to see
~~~

if I could maybe sway the lot of you. This acceptance isn't just for me. It's for *all* of us."

"What are you saying?" Jesse asked, dipping a torn ribbon of cinnamon bun into the mixture of honey, black pepper, and candy sprinkles on his plate.

"I'm merely suggesting you guys come with me."

Kate couldn't fully grasp Tommy's intentions sometimes. "What? You expect us to just follow you to New York? That seems incredibly presumptuous, doesn't it?"

"I don't think it's presumptuous. I just know you guys, is all."

Tommy and Patrick had been best friends since the tenth grade, ever since Tommy's brother had died. Patrick was happy to fill that void for Tommy and he did it well. In the eleventh grade, Patrick started dating Kate, who had been in all of Jesse's art classes. By the middle of their twelfth year, the four of them were inseparable, and they were perfectly content not to socialize with the rest of their graduating class. Of course, Tommy was right when he stated how well he knew his best friends. He was fully aware that if he suggested it, they would come along with him to Manhattan.

And that's exactly what they did.

Five weeks later, the quartet boarded a train in Seattle and stepped off into Grand Central Station. They didn't know where they were upon emerging from the station; they found themselves in the middle of a massive, breathing, concrete beast. With countless limbs and organs and arteries, it was sometimes impossible to tell day from night. But Tommy knew exactly where he was going; he'd had every street in Manhattan mapped out inside his head since he was eight years old. And the other three knew well enough to follow him.

By fall, Tommy was attending Hunter College, while Kate and Patrick were both studying at NYU. Jesse had taken a series of part-time art classes, photography courses, and architecture programs over the years until he realized he really had no idea what it was he wanted to do with his life. It didn't matter though; they were all happy in New York, just as Tommy had predicted they would be. Jesse sometimes thought he might have made a mistake by not accepting enrolment at the Columbus College of Art & Design, but his faith in Tommy had always been unwavering. The four of them lived together for what felt like only a sliver of time, on the first floor of that 113th Street apartment in Morningside Heights, but Kate, Patrick, and Jesse gradually bounced around the city every couple of months to wherever the rent was cheapest.

Kate and Patrick had lived together until the morning she awoke to find him gone. It was almost one year to the day since they'd left Seattle. It wasn't until later that evening, when the four of them were supposed to meet at the very same coffee shop they would meet in for the next ten years, when suspicion was aroused: Patrick didn't show. And he hadn't returned to their apartment that night either. Kate received his phone call from Seattle the following day. He told her he dropped out of university. He told her New York City wasn't the right place for him. He told her the subway trains freaked him out and the pigeons' stares made him uncomfortable. He told her he wasn't sure if he loved her as much as he should have, but he did love her enough to cover the next two months of rent. He went on to explain how the money he'd left behind was inside an envelope, tucked into the back pocket of a pair of Kate's pants hanging in the bathtub, still wrapped in the dry cleaner's plastic. His description of where he left the rent money was far more explanatory than his justification for why he'd ever left in the first place. And that was the last time the two of them spoke.

It was the first time any of them truly felt lost and misplaced.

It was the first time any of them thought moving so far away from home had maybe been a mistake.

It was the first time any of them were faced with disillusionment.

The first time Patrick reached for independence.

The first time Kate would have her heart broken.

The first time Jesse realized the complexities of adulthood.

And it was the very first time Tommy flirted with the idea that maybe his friends didn't love him as much as he loved them.

Of course, Jesse was the first to forgive Patrick for his selfish decision. Kate, always the tough nut, seemed bitter for a while but she eventually got over it. Patrick was the only guy she had ever dated, but Kate forgot all about him and welcomed the idea that she now had every reason in the world to sleep with as many men as she wanted.

Tommy, on the other hand, had lost a very significant piece of himself the day Patrick Kohn disappeared. Patrick was the peg filling the hole left open when his brother died. Tommy's imaginings of a perfect life had become reality, but he was suddenly faced with ideas he couldn't understand. Feelings he didn't want to feel. Questions he couldn't solve. And, most importantly, he didn't want to see or think about Patrick Kohn ever again.

~~~

If asked what the greatest moment of his life had been, Tommy's answer would only ever be: "*Right now.*" He loved his life that much. If Kate or Jesse had thought to ask him that question on that rainy night inside Tom's Restaurant, Tommy would have had a different answer for them. He would have answered: "*This morning.*" He would have told them: "*It was the moment right before I checked my mail and found that fucking letter.*"

None of the information within the letter, no matter how vague it might have been, had mattered at all to Tommy. What was of greater importance was why Patrick had decided to send it in the first place. "What would possess someone to write a letter like this?" he asked. "It's the kind of letter that should never be sent. Nobody's talked to the guy for how long? And who mails *letters* anymore anyway? Do we not all have email by now?"
~~~

"Don't you miss him, though?" Jesse asked. "Even just a little bit, Tommy?"

"Nope. I don't. Do *you*?"

"He was our friend. He was one of us."

Tommy crumpled up the letter, reverting it back into the spherical shape he was much more comfortable with. He spiked it across the table at Jesse. "Well, that's the difference between you and me, Jess. I don't carry around all of that sentimental bullshit."

"You don't have to be so cold, Tommy," Kate said.

"Oh, I'm sorry, Ice Queen. Did you want to say something?"

"Guys, guys," Jesse interrupted. "What happened in the past is in the past. I don't think we have any reason to be mad, do we?" Tommy and Kate looked at one another. "Forgive and forget, right?" Jesse's positive spin was almost heartbreaking in its nostalgic sympathy.

"Jess is right," Kate agreed.

Tommy wanted to say something constructive, but he could only flick his finger against the napkin dispenser in front of him. He flicked it a second time, hard enough to knock it over. "The guy's a class-A jerk. That's all I have to say."

"You know, it's really not like you to be this negative, Tommy. That's more of a Kate thing."

"Jess has a point," Kate hubristically acknowledged. "I can't believe you're still harboring these feelings against Patrick. I know you're not one for sentiment, Tommy, but isn't holding grudges basically the same thing as being sentimental? It's all about how you choose to deal with a memory, right?"

Tommy set up the napkin dispenser only to knock it over once more. He turned to see if the fat man with the sandwich was still at the counter, hoping to at least vent in a stranger's direction, but the man was already gone. A heaping pile of grease-stained napkins was the only evidence left behind.

Jesse took a moment to unfold the letter, and he looked it over for himself. He wasn't surprised at all to discover Patrick had typed it, rather than having written it by hand. However, he was more than a bit surprised it was typed entirely on one single page. Just as Tommy had always been the group's big talker, Patrick had always been their biggest thinker. He would never have restricted himself to a one-page letter in the past. It was almost as if he'd run out of ways to express himself. Or maybe he was afraid of saying too much? Jesse wasn't sure. "I guess the thing we should probably figure out here is: what do we do next? How much do we let this letter affect our lives?"

Tommy kept his mouth shut. He leaned back with his arms folded over his chest. To his left, he could see a stranger press her face to the rain-soaked window. Once again, he pounded his fist on the glass, sending the latest voyeur running away.

Kate finished her last spoonful of matzo ball soup and tarped the remainder of her cold fries with a napkin. She didn't want to be the first one to answer Jesse's question either.

Breathe in. Breathe out.

"Well," Jesse started, and carefully folded the paper back into its wrinkled, but original envelope-sized, rectangular shape. That letter had already been creased and crumpled so many times it was starting to resemble tissue paper. He left it in the middle of the table, between all three of them. "I for one, think this could all be happening for a reason."

"God hating us is *not* a reason, Jess," Tommy finally muttered.

Jesse ignored Tommy's comment. "Look at it *this* way, guys: if Kate and Gene are getting divorced, she can get back together with Patrick. It would be just like the old days!"

"I really hope you're joking," Kate said with a red fire in her brown eyes.

Jesse didn't mind the hostile response. "It's far-fetched maybe, but still a possibility. Don't you think?"

Tommy never missed an opportunity to razz Kate, and he smiled a little at Jesse's evocative proposal. "Yeah, Kate. Come on. It'd be just like old times. We could all move back in together too. Grocery shopping trips on the weekend. Sharing the chores. I call dibs on vacuuming!"

Now it was Kate's turn to sit back with her arms crossed. "Do you guys really think I'd be dumb enough to jump back into a relationship with Patrick Kohn? I haven't seen or talked to the guy for ten years! Do you know *anything* about how women work?"

Tommy raised his hand. "I'm pretty sure I don't. Why do you think all of the female characters I write are either prostitutes or murder victims?"

Jesse snuck a French fry out from under Kate's covered plate, and dipped it into the still-potent mound of sauce in front of him. "You know, Kate. I recall a time when a certain gal confessed to a certain fella that the only relationship she felt she'd ever totally valued was the relationship she had with a certain guy named Patrick."

Instantly, Kate regretted that one drunken night from years back, when she and Jesse passed out in the middle of the Washington Square fountain. In fact, she was so extraordinarily drunk that night, she might have also blatantly confessed to Jesse her jealousy towards Tommy's literary success. But she could barely remember the details of that evening, apart from her waking up in a downtown detox. "Forget it, Jess. I may just pull the trigger on this marriage, but I have absolutely *NO* intention of getting back together with Patrick." Even while saying the words, she couldn't help but glance at the letter between them and take a moment to consider how much Patrick might have changed over the years. The idea flashed in her head for perhaps only a second, but it was still enough to note. Was it more a question of unfinished business between the two of them that had Kate considering what was, what is, and what could have been? Kate asked, "Not to change the subject here, but what about *you*, Tommy? What are you going to do when Patrick shows up?

You can't ignore him forever. What are you planning on saying to him?"

"Well," Tommy started, "I might not have to worry about that."

After a brief explanation of the news he saw on the television that afternoon, Tommy presented to his friends the possibility of another scenario: one where Patrick may not have made it to New York.

Jesse and Kate could only sit with mouths hanging open. A chewed-up French fry fell from Jesse's mouth in much the same fashion as the bite of apple had fallen from Tommy's mouth that morning. "*What?*"

"Was he on that flight?" Kate asked, checking the facts on the discarded letter. "Was he coming back today?" But there was no indication on the letter.

"I don't know. But what do you guys suppose the chances are?"

"Hold on a minute, Tommy," Jesse said. "Are you actually *hoping* Patrick was killed a plane crash? That's awful!"

Tommy was quick to defend himself. "That's not *exactly* what I'm saying. But it's not like I was looking forward to seeing him either."

"It'd be nice if you at least tried to show some interest," Kate said.

"And even if he *did* show up here, even if he showed up right here in this coffee shop right now, do you guys think I would be itching to be all buddy-buddy with him again? Should I pretend everything's just like it used to be?" Tommy grabbed the letter from Kate's hand and waved it madly in the air. "Should I fool myself into thinking a fucking letter as inconsiderate as *this* one could possibly mend any metaphoric fences?"

"I don't see why not," was Jesse's more-than-optimistic reply.

"The answer you were looking for, Jess, is *NO*. A resounding and unabashedly profound *NO*."

Kate hated it when Tommy used words like that. *Unabashedly* should be restricted to novels, and never for real life.

Tommy slapped the letter back down on the table, and for the moment, the coffee shop was silent again. The only thing anyone wanted to hear was the thunderous rainstorm outside.

But Kate was always the first to break a good silence, and she spoke up again. "So, what do you guys suppose the chances are? What's the chance Patrick was on that plane?" She caught a tear as it snuck out of the corner of her eye.

"Jesus Christ, Kate!" Tommy yelped. "That's the second time in one day I've seen you cry! What the hell's going on with you today?"

"What's going on with *ME*? You're sitting there wishing a friend of ours was dead!"

"Wishing? I just don't want to see the guy again. You really think I'd wish for anyone to die in a plane crash?"

"You want *everyone* to die in a plane crash," Jesse answered. "Just like your brother did."

In the eleven years he'd been in New York, Tommy had yet to return to Seattle or travel anywhere else for that matter. Not that it was much of a surprise to anyone at this point. Even his book tours were restricted to the New York area and that one-time bus trip to Philadelphia. Tommy turned to Jesse. "I didn't want *you* to die when you went to the Star Trek convention years ago."

"That wasn't a Star Trek convention. That was the Comicon."

"Well, I'm not an expert on distinguishing one type of nerd from another, but I'll just assume there's a difference, okay?"

"Would you two please stop arguing like a couple of girls?" Kate interrupted.

"I say we just assume he's dead and leave it at that," Tommy suggested. It was a reasonable enough solution to him. But Jesse was quickly withdrawing himself from the discussion, like he often did when conversations become too intense.

"Come on, Jesse," Tommy relented. "I don't mean to be like this. I was just so angry when I opened that letter this morning. All I could think about today was how things like this are always just the start of even worse things. And then I saw the news and I thought maybe that was the best chance we had to avoid it all."

"Patrick was one of us, Tommy. I loved him as much as I love the both of you. I know you don't feel the same, but jeeze—" With his sleeve, Jesse had to wipe the emotion clean off his glasses. "You shouldn't ever wish for somebody's death. And why are you making Patrick out to be such a bad guy, anyway?"

"I'll bet you guys never knew that Kaspar Delancey was modeled after him, did you?"

"Who?"

"Patrick."

"No. Who's this Kaspar guy?" Kate asked.

"Kaspar Delancey. The character from 'Blanc.'" Tommy didn't get a reaction. "My first novel?" he added, hoping to clear up the matter.

Jesse thought about it for a moment. "I never noticed a resemblance. Did you Kate?"

"Was he the, ah—was he the owner of the pet store?"

"What? *Pet store?* Kaspar Delancey was the amnesiac serial killer."

"Amnesiac serial killer? How the hell did that book become a hit, again?"

"It's all about the characters, Kate. You write a good character and people will believe anything."

"To tell you the truth, Tommy, I never actually read the book."

"Excuse me?"

"I flipped through it once though. What was the deal with all those blank pages?"

"That's when Kaspar Delancey loses his memory entirely."

"Seems like an easy way for a hefty page count to me."

"Fuck. I'd like to think if one of *you* wrote a best-selling novel, I would be a decent enough friend to read the goddamned thing! Did you at least see the movie?"

"I saw it," Jesse noted. "Who was in that again?"

"Michael Vartan. And Shaquille O'Neal."

"Really?" Jesse asked. "Maybe I *didn't* see it—"

"What about *you*, Kate?"

"I never read the book and I didn't see the movie," Kate reiterated. "Shoot me."

"Unbelievable!"

"Can we move along here?" she asked. "I think the point we're at is this: what are we going to do next?" Kate motioned toward Jesse with her right hand, and said, "We have the one extreme—"

"I still think things can be how they used to be," Jesse said on cue.

And then she turned her left hand toward Tommy, saying, "And we have the other—"

"I'm just going to assume he's still burning somewhere in Kansas."

"I don't know which of you guys is the more delusional. But what if we're in for something else? Something that's maybe somewhere in the middle?"

"You know, Tommy," Jesse piqued. "Kal-El's rocket ship crashed in Kansas."

"What are you saying, Jesse? That Patrick Kohn could turn out to be Superman?"

"I'm just saying, is all. Sometimes there's good in what seems like a bad situation."

Tommy clenched his fist so hard the tips of his fingers could have burst through the back of his hand. He wanted to bang on the window beside him as hard as he could. He wanted to shatter the glass and feel the heavy rain blow in sideways and drench the three of them and wash the letter away. But right now, there was no one outside to shoo away. "Your gift for wisdom is astounding," Tommy responded. "Shouldn't you be reading palms somewhere in the East Village, Madame Jesse?"

"I'm just saying," Jesse repeated.

The three of them remained there for a long while. They stayed long enough for the night waitress to begin her shift, and she refilled their coffee and cleared the evening's mess off the table. Tommy and Jesse had assumed the balled-up letter from Patrick had been tossed in the garbage with their dirty napkins; they didn't notice Kate had slipped the letter into her purse before generously leaving a twenty on the table and exiting the coffee shop.

After Jesse said goodnight, Tommy sat until he was the only customer left. Unmoved, he dwelled on the past. I could feel him there in Tom's Restaurant. I felt his weight on the bench, his eyes on the wet, foggy glass beside him: the only thing separating him from the world looking in. He remained there long enough for the rain to die down, which was exactly the amount of time it had taken for him to eat the last four pieces of pie in the display case. While he ate the first piece, Tommy wondered where Rachel was. Was she back at his apartment waiting for him? He ignored the very realistic possibility that if she *did* want to talk to him by now, she probably would've tried to call. He fingered the phone in his pocket but it still refused to buzz. He considered the feelings of Kate and Jesse as he slowly consumed the second and third pieces. Was it a mistake to mention the letter to them? He had expected his friends to mirror his own thoughts on the matter but he couldn't have been more wrong. I could feel him slowing down. The waitress suggested he maybe not finish the entire strawberry-rhubarb pie, but Tommy dismissed her rudely. The uncertainties of Patrick Kohn had been saved for that last piece. However, many of the details had begun to blur from stomach pangs. The dessert might have seemed excessive, but it didn't really mean anything to Tommy. He had lost count after the first two pieces anyway.

Tommy stumbled back home along 112th Street. He made a concerted effort to step in as many puddles as he could because he loved the sound his heavy foot made as it stamped through a fresh New York rain puddle. He refused to admit to himself the possibility that any puddle splashing would sound the same no matter which city he was in. But if he had been anywhere else, the buildings would not have been the same. The architecture would not have been so perfectly exact, and Tommy could only love those specific echoes bouncing off New York's weathered structures.

He stopped for a moment and sat on the front steps of St. John's Cathedral. Again, I felt the weight of his newfound misery as he sunk into the stone. It didn't take him very long to throw up everything he'd consumed that evening. He cursed out loud, and hoped there would be more rain coming to wash his insides away. Maybe it could take all of his rancid discharge and drop it off in New Jersey.

He tried his best to recall the last time he'd felt so angry. Maybe it was when Patrick Kohn had disappeared in the first place? It was such a long time ago, but I'm certain that was it. Maybe not so long ago compared to some events, but it was long enough for Jesse — and apparently even Kate — to find a certain amount of forgiveness for their friend's impetuous and unexplained actions. Tommy couldn't grasp why his two best friends had found so much hope in that letter, and yet, the only hope he could glean from it was that Patrick might have died in a plane crash somewhere in Middle America. Was it a destination he deserved? All Tommy knew was Patrick did not deserve New York; he'd already blown that chance.

Along Amsterdam Avenue, a couple walked by. Tommy watched them intensely but they paid him no attention. They should have been holding hands, but they weren't. The man was talking on his cell phone, yelling at whoever had the wretched misfortune of having to listen to him. The woman was completely engrossed in the most important text message of her life.

Those stupid little keys beeped gleefully with every depression. Tommy hated the man for ignoring the woman, but she wasn't doing much better herself, now was she? Neither of them seemed happy with their situation, and yet each of them had more than Tommy did at that moment.

~ ~ ~

When Tommy returned home, he had hoped Rachel would be there. He hadn't missed a call from her all evening, so he was certain she'd be in his bed. Probably naked, although preferably waiting in that mesh bodysuit thing she would sometimes pull out for him. But she was not there. The envelope from Patrick's letter still sat on the couch; an empty coffin whose contents were alive once again, and were somewhere in the city haunting anyone who had tried in vain to forget them.

I felt it once more: Tommy's heavy frame as it slumped onto his bed. He contemplated Rachel, reconsidering his feelings for her and for all the others who had left him. Maybe Keekee Kaufman was right when she shouted out a methodical list of all of Tommy's faults just before jumping off the Triboro Bridge. Maybe Polly Robinson had a point when she left Tommy to find his own way home from New Jersey. Maybe Patrick Kohn's reasons for leaving his friends behind in Manhattan were not so far-fetched. Did he really just compare Rachel to Patrick Kohn, of all people? Tommy's blood boiled just thinking of the man. But the fact remained that all of them had left Tommy and none of them had ever seemed to regret it. Surely, he could do the same with Rachel Ponzini. Three years was not such a long time, was it? Her memory wouldn't stand a chance. Tommy fell asleep thinking about just how easy it would be. Not surprisingly, I was not entirely convinced.

SEVEN

Fulton Street – Lower East Side, 1937

With his grip still tight around the woman's neck, Kaspar Delancey knew instantly he had made a mistake. For just one night before, he was kissing the very same girl outside the gloomy bar. Warm vermouth still lingered on her lips. And the kiss was genuine, too. How could things have gone so quickly from one extreme to the other? He could feel the bone and cartilage caught between the gnarled fingers of his left hand. He recalled her neck as having the most pleasing aroma to it: something like fresh cut wildflowers and talcum powder. He eased his hand, and the broken, bloodied body tumbled and rolled over itself down the hotel's elaborate spiral staircase before coming to a stop like a heap of wet laundry. It was by far the worst act he'd ever perpetrated, but lately — and more and more often now — Kaspar Delancey was finding himself forgetting such frivolous details. Details as inconsequential as murder.

He cut through an alley. The wet steam smelled of fried pork and wonton soup. Chicken feet and steamed buns. He climbed all six stories of the rickety fire escape; the cat trap of rusted metal teased him as it seemed to bend with his every move. His window was left wide open, the threadbare curtains flapped sharply in the night air. Kaspar peered into the room with caution, making sure no one was waiting for him. The first image that came into his mind was that of his own father armed with a heavy cue ball wrapped in a woolen sock. But his drunk, abusive father had been dead for more than fifteen years, so why was the memory still haunting him? Cracked, dilapidated walls revealed ramshackle wooden boards and mouse holes. His apartment was just as empty as it should have been, but the floor was cold and wet. The building must have flooded again. He knew he should speak to the landlord, but Kaspar had been distancing himself more and more from him of late. The two of them used to consider one another friends, but now it was all Kaspar could do to avoid the fat little French man on a daily basis. Climbing the fire escape had been his latest in a line of furtive returns. In a city as dense, shady, and filth-ridden as New York, it was child's play to go unnoticed if one wanted to.

The floorboards breathed the water in and out of their cracks like blood surfacing from a fresh cut. Just like from the neck of—? Hmm. He couldn't believe it, but her name was already gone from his memory. His first instinct was to soak up the water with some bed sheets, but Kaspar had long been out of clean sheets, so the wet floors would go ignored. Perhaps, he thought, flooding the entire building would be the only way out of the mess he'd created for himself. But just as he contemplated the many ways he'd already discovered to get away with things as simple as disappearing and as complicated as murder, he spotted a note under the door. Kaspar hadn't been in his apartment for a couple of nights now, so he didn't know when the paper had been slipped through the splintered crack.

He captured it with his one good hand. Because of the water, some of the ink had bled to the paper's edges, but he could still make out the chicken-scratched message left for him. Though a creature of whim and chicanery, Kaspar Delancey still could not help himself from believing every fact ever presented to him. Most of what Kaspar knew was from what others had told him. The letter he held in his grip was no different. He understood all five words written on it:

GET OUT OF MY CITY

CHAPTER EIGHT
Ugly Ollie's Speakeasy – Greenwich Village

She was singing something about friends. Everyone could relate to the words, but they could never have written them as eloquently as she. Her voice was crisp, thunderous as the 1-Train emerging from the 122nd Street tunnel and out into Harlem. Scratchy like the first words after a heavy sleep. Exhilarating as a newborn's cry.

Of the seemingly endless supply of tattoos, the most interesting were written up and down her arms. They proclaimed words like UGLY, BROKEN, and ANGRY. MISPLACED. BUSTED. BRUISED. WANTING. STRUGGLING. FALLING. HUNGRY. HOMELESS. WORTHLESS. She said the tattoos came from a dark place in her life, one she was not proud of, and one she didn't think she'd ever escape from. But she did escape, and now the words which once defined her had become more than that: they were challenges to be met. And she had conquered them all. The most important one, the UNLOVED on the back of her right hand, was what she focused on every time she strummed her guitar, serving as fuel for her euphony.

She was so beautiful and so talented and so perfect in every way it was hard to look at her and not be excited for her. Her lyrics were both searing and dreamlike. Truthful and shattering. She had a lip stud, pierced a little off-center, just enough to make you want to question its placement. Her shaved head, tattoos, and electric blue cowboy boots were far beyond a mere statement anymore; they were all simply, amazingly her.

Jesse focused on every melodious reverberation she put forth. Every letter within every word within every lyric must have meant something so extraordinary to her when she first put them on paper. There was a salty tear behind every sweet thought. Jesse was a fool if he thought this girl was not worthy of being in his life; if he couldn't afford her even a shred of himself.

She was singing something about friends. And like most friendships, her song came to an end just as the crowd expected more. They applauded but didn't know why she had to leave them.

Breathe out.

Sharona walked off the stage and sat directly across from Jesse at his tiny table for two. She locked her guitar back inside its case and set it on the floor. Jesse had already downed one Bacontini and two Green-Eyed Monsters, and he'd long since finished mixing the remaining drops of both martinis in with the bowl of shrimp cocktail sauce and one piece of chewed licorice bubble gum. It had created such an unexpectedly harsh aroma, he wondered when the waitress would be by to clean up his mess. Where the hell was she anyway? Had she forgotten all about him? If only Sharona didn't have to show up first and be witness to the most peculiar of his many habits.

"I didn't think you'd come," Jesse noted, sliding the bowl away from her.

Sharona swallowed an entire glass of water, ice and all. The frozen cubes were visible as they slid down her throat. "I sort of *had* to be here," she answered. "There were posters all over the Village for this thing."

"No, I'm sorry. What I meant was, I didn't expect you to come and sit down with me."

"There's no reason to be sorry, Jesse." Throughout her set, everyone in the club had noticed each time the songstress stared at the solitary man seated at the table for two. It was plain to see where her lyrical attention had been focused. Of course she was going to step off that stage and sit down with him. "So, what have you come up with?"

"What's that?"

"It's obvious you've been sitting here thinking about what you want to say to me." She withdrew both a cigarette and a lighter in one motion from her pants pocket. Jesse wondered how that single cigarette could have remained so perfectly straight within Sharona's denim compartment all night. "So, what's it gonna be?"

"Listen, Sharona. I don't have anything to say except I'm sorry for cancelling on you the other night."

Sharona lifted the cigarette to her mouth before realizing the smoky club was actually smoke-free. She still couldn't get used to the fact every club in Manhattan now had the same asinine restrictions. Surely even the city's steamiest dives could still allow smoking inside, couldn't they? I must admit, a part of me missed it too. "That's it, then?" she asked. She tried to be cool, to say the words with the cigarette dangling from her lips, but it was too difficult to pull off. It fell into her empty glass the instant she uttered those TH-words.

Jesse couldn't help himself from being intimidated by Sharona. Truthfully, he was quite afraid of most women in general. He had almost bolted the moment Edith Galloway first opened her front door for him so many years ago. "That's really all I'd come up with."

"No. I mean, that's it for *us* then?"

"What, *us*? We only had *one* date."

"Plus, whatever you want to call this."

"Honestly, I don't know what I'd call this. But it couldn't possibly be considered a date, could it?"

"No. I guess not." Without the distraction of the cigarette, Sharona repeated herself. "So that's it, then?"

The best Jesse could utter with was, "Yes." But *Yes* was the honest truth, so it really was all he needed to say.

"That's cool."

"Really?"

"Yes, really. You figured me for a fighter?"

"A fighter? No. I thought you'd be a little more pissed, actually. I guess I just assumed there'd be more to this, is all."

"Whatever this is, right?" Sharona waved the cigarette at Jesse, in rubber-pencil style. "Do you mind coming outside with me so I can smoke this stupid thing then?"

"Sure."

She had been singing something about friends. The words were still echoing in Jesse's head, something about how friends will always be there for you when you need them. Even for the littlest of things in the smallest of moments. Even when they don't really want to be there. And then they'll leave you just as you're wanting more.

~~~

Jesse and Sharona had been sitting outside Ugly Ollie's Speakeasy for maybe ten minutes without a single word between them. The truth was Jesse didn't know what to say; he didn't know exactly why he was there at that moment. And Sharona? She just wanted to finish her cigarette. He'd only known her for a few days, but Jesse had already decided upon the oddest thing about her: she must have been the most talkative creature on the planet, but when she smoked, Sharona was as silent as a funeral procession. Of the passersby, no one paid any attention at all to them, and the only conclusion Jesse came to, was that the two of them must have appeared to belong together. That had to have been the only possibility. When two people are so right for each other they blend effortlessly into their surroundings. So why then was Jesse trying so hard to distance himself from her?

Sharona flicked the wet stub of her smoke high into the air, almost hitting the opposing sidewalk. Its wispy trail dissipated in a perfect arc over MacDougal Street. Her skills were fantastic, weren't they? "You know," she finally began, slicing the silence in two. "If you'd told me you were coming by
~~~

tonight, I could have gotten you in for free."

"Then I would've felt like I owed you a better explanation."

"You expect a lot from people, don't you?"

"Do I?"

"You do. Especially from yourself. You don't have to overthink everything, Jesse."

"I overthink?"

"If you need to ask, then you've already answered."

She's so powerful and clever, Jesse thought. Like The Thing and Mister Fantastic in one. The streetlight bounced off the mystifying shine of her plum-colored eyes. Sharona's sealed lips still seemed to hold the last of her cigarette's smoke. Like there was an invisible fire inside her. Fuck, she's just like Invisible Woman and the Human Torch as well.

"What are you smiling at?" she asked him, putting an end to his fantastical daydreams.

"Nothing." Jesse tried to come up with an answer that would be more something than nothing; the kind of something that would actually be believable. "You know, I work with these two guys who are always trying to get me to join their band."

"I didn't know you played an instrument."

"I don't."

"So, what, do they want you to be their lead singer?"

"I can't sing either."

"Manager?"

"I don't think so."

"The drummer then?"

"Like I said, I don't play an instrument."

"You don't have to have any actual talent to be a drummer. Drummers are the most overrated members in any band."

"Then why do people always say drummers are the coolest?"

"Well shit, Jesse. The other guys in the band just go along with it because they need a drummer."

"Maybe they *do* want me to be the drummer then—"

"What's the band name?"

"I think right now they're calling themselves 'Mayor Naisse'. But it seems to always be in flux."

"Seriously? Who are these guys?"

"Pond and Germ."

"Pond and Germ? Maybe you *are* the coolest of the bunch."

"Ah, they're okay. Do you want to know the dream I used to have when I was younger? I liked to imagine myself playing a wicked guitar solo in the pouring rain, wearing a leather vest with flowing tassels and standing on top of a moving train. Like in one of those rock videos from the Nineties."

"That's a pretty specific imagination you've got there, Jesse. Maybe you should join them then."

"Ha, ha. Very funny."

"No, really. If that's a dream of yours then you should grab onto it. There's nothing worse than losing sight of a dream."

Jesse took a moment to imagine himself once again; his long hair blowing in the wind from the moving train. He couldn't help smiling; he hadn't concocted that image for such a long time now.

"You're doing that smiling thing again, Jesse."

"I think I'm just wondering why you're not pissed at me."

"You want to know why I'm not pissed?"

Jesse nodded cautiously. He wasn't sure if he did want to know.

"It's because I'm from Canada, Jesse. Canadians have an innate ability to see the truth in everything."

"They do?" Mystified, Jesse stared at her, as though Sharona had just leaked government secrets. He also felt a tiny bit uncomfortable, like she could see right inside of him.

"Of course they do. And all Canadians have webbed feet and can spit out of their ears."

Now he wasn't sure what to believe. "So, what's the truth then?"

"The truth is this: you want to stop seeing me? That's cool. You're an interesting guy, Jesse. Maybe one of the most interesting guys I've met in this city. I actually like your stupid superhero t-shirts that are supposed to look retro and those dreadful sideburns of yours. But I'm okay with you feeling the way you're feeling right now because I know you're the type of guy who'll change his mind. And I'd like to save all of the awkward *'Can't-we-give-it-another-try?'* bullshit. I've done all of that before, you know?" Sharona pulled another cigarette out from somewhere. Maybe it was from her pants pocket again, but Jesse couldn't be sure. Just like her words, her movements were far too fluid to follow completely. Nonchalantly, she asked some guy walking by if he had a light, and he was only too happy to stop and oblige her, before telling her to have a great evening and moving along to wherever it was he was supposed to be going.

Jesse stared at her blankly. Who was this girl with the power to stop strangers in the street? He didn't know exactly what Sharona was talking about just then, but something told him she was right.

She didn't mind the empty stares though. She was the kind of girl who seemed used to it. "What I mean is, sort out whatever you feel like you need to sort out. Get over it, and then come find me again." Sharona slapped the palm of her one free hand against the streetlight beside her. "You'll find the poster for that future show right here. Come on by, and we'll start up right where we left off. Is that cool?"

Jesse didn't know what it was that brought him to the Village that night. He also wondered why he hadn't talked it over with Kate and Tommy. Why couldn't he tell his best friends about this girl, and any of the dates he did or didn't have with her? How the hell did Edith Galloway leave such an embarrassingly large hole in his soul? How long were the feelings supposed to last anyway? "Listen, Sharona," he finally started. "I've been through a lot of shit in the last year."

"So, get over it."

"It's not that simple."

"That's what *everyone* says, Jesse. But nobody's problems are so incredibly special. We all grow up and go through and get through the exact same horrible problems, don't we? Yeah. We do. We all have our hearts broken at some point, don't we? Fuck yeah, we do. So, all I can tell you is: whatever that shit is, get over it already."

Jesse hung onto her words for a moment. They were harsh, but they were also incredibly truthful. "You know, maybe what I'm going through isn't all that special. Maybe everyone is hurting as much as I am. But I still think I need to talk to somebody about it. Would that be okay with you?"

"I've got two ears, Jesse. And all they've ever been good for is listening."

Jesse told Sharona his story. As advertised, she listened closely to every word of it. It had been almost one full year since Jesse's art show in New Jersey. That was the warehouse space Edie had spent her own money on. That was the night she had left the note behind for John, who hadn't a clue about his wife's affair with the unassuming comic store clerk. The funny thing was, Jesse saw her leave the note behind, and he remembered thinking: *"What if John was to show up?"* Jesse had considered grabbing that stupid yellow note when Edie wasn't looking. But he didn't. It was sitting right there on the table, like an invitation to ruin all three of their lives, but Jesse didn't do a damn thing about it.

The art show was like a real-world stage for the spectacle of comic books. He created giant-sized comic book pages, life-sized Manhattan street scenes with battling heroes and villains, all constructed from drawings, explosions and word balloons cut out from actual comics. The comic books were all from a Lower East Side store's twenty-for-a-dollar bin. Jesse cleaned them out and ended up paying a couple of hundred bucks for it all. The finished pieces were a fantastic sight, like he'd created his own world, his own unique version of New York City.

Jesse was right in the middle of giving a very awkward, very impersonal thank-you speech to everyone in attendance when it happened. He wore the tuxedo Edith had bought for him, but articulated his look with bright red gloves and a domino mask. He was speaking from the sidewalk he'd crafted himself, standing on such words as "BRAAK!" and "PTOOM!" when John Galloway made his appearance. In fact, Jesse just happened to be thanking the lovely Edith Galloway for her constant and enduring support. Thank you, Edith for making the show's success possible. Thank you, Edith for allowing such dreams to become real. Thank you, Edith for making yourself available to me because your husband was never available to you. Something along those lines anyway. And it was exactly then when the two men spotted one another. John recognized Jesse immediately, even behind the mask. His ancient memory was uncanny: John Galloway could still recall the names of all eighteen kids in Mrs. Hartman's first grade class and he never forgot to reset his clocks for Daylight Savings Time. Jesse could only watch as the man put the pieces together inside his head. The connection was made. It was feasible that over the three-year period some suspicion of his wife's indiscretions had already been aroused within him. It was entirely possible that neither Jesse nor Edith had ever been as clever as they had liked to believe. But John was not a dumb man, and what he knew then was that some of his immense power had shifted to the insignificant employee of Midtown Comics. To that one, stupid kid whose eyes had lit up at the simple prospect of attaining nothing more than some smelly, yellowed comic books.

John grabbed his wife by the arm, and insisted they leave the show immediately. She fought back, slapping him across the face. She was certainly a feisty woman, and even more so when she was undeniably drunk. He grabbed her other arm. She swore at him. Her colorful collection of atrocious language was impressive beyond belief. Jesse was certain he'd heard words he never believed had existed. And when John Galloway threw his wife against the wall, the crowd rippled in nervous reaction.

Everything slowed down around Jesse. The crowd had frozen. The lights above them were no longer flickering, and they burned right through him. Surely, he thought, the snow outside had also stopped in mid-fall. Jesse didn't know what to do; he looked around to his best friends for answers. Kate was in the middle of flirting shamelessly with some guy at the open bar when the commotion started; of course, Gene had not accompanied her that night. Kate had mistakenly believed the man was from Australia, but it turned out he was from Nebraska, and just had an odd accent derived from some mild cerebral palsy. Tommy and Rachel hadn't even shown up yet. As good as Rachel was at improving on so many of Tommy's faults, she was notorious for making the two of them late any time they had promised to be someplace.

Jesse realized it was all up to him. He was the only one who could do anything that night. Save the city. Win the girl. Three years of incredibly poor decision-making had all led to that moment, hadn't they?

~~~

"So, what did you do?" Sharona asked.

In the process of baring his soul to Sharona on the wet sidewalk, Jesse intentionally skipped the best part of his story. First and foremost, his was a tale of great loss, and he didn't want to spoil it by telling her the one part that had always made him smile. That wouldn't have been right.

So, he saved it.
~~~

"I didn't do anything," is what he told her instead. "John threw Edie into his car with the intention of bringing her home and figuring out where they'd gone wrong in their marriage. But they didn't make it back to Gramercy. He lost control of his car in the Holland Tunnel. The police said it was the road conditions, the wet tires from all the snow. But I don't know if it was the snow that stopped them, or if Edie was still struggling inside the car. Or maybe John had never intended to make it home in the first place. And I'll never know if Edie was maybe just growing tired of me altogether. Maybe she'd left that note behind on purpose."

Sharona wanted to ask, but she couldn't. She wanted to know the outcome of Jesse's story, but she didn't want to hear it. She could only guess. She stared at him, into those big brown eyes which seemed unnaturally dry. Maybe he'd told his story too many times before? Told it so many times already that he had come to be unaffected by its details. And yet, she wanted him to go on. All the while, the songwriter part of her had hoped the words Jesse might murmur would make for some good, future lyrics.

In his mind, Jesse couldn't help but recollect the sight of the accident. He and Tommy drove through the tunnel the day after, on their way back from New Jersey where they'd been cleaning up some pieces from the art show. There was still the twinkle from the clusters of broken glass, reflectors, and metallic chips. A dark brown stain streaked across the STAY IN LANE painted on the road. Tommy said it looked like blood, and he carried on about how most people will assume blood is always red but because of the iron's oxidization, dried blood will turn brown. He'd learned details like that when he was doing research for his novels. Jesse didn't want to think about it. There were no longer any police on the scene, but Jesse imagined what it must have looked like the night before, the red and blue lights reflecting off the tunnel's wet, tiled walls. The underground echo of the body bag zipping tight. The sirens blaring forever beneath the Hudson River.

When Jesse's lips had finally parted, the only words to come forth were the very same ones Sharona had already heard him say. "Like I said, it's been a shitty year." There was a scrap of newspaper at Jesse's feet. He noticed it was an advertisement for Midtown Comics. "Sometimes I wonder if I've *always* made the wrong decisions."

Sharona sucked on another smoke. She held her cigarettes in such a way, it made everyone else want one too. It seemed that perfect. "Everyone is going to make the wrong decisions. I mean, what the hell are the chances that we're all going to make the exact right decisions every single time?"

"Not very good."

"Exactly." She finished the last cigarette, and flicked it across MacDougal Street, just like the one before it. And whether Sharona meant it to or not, the second cigarette landed perfectly flush with the first one. Of course, Jesse noticed these tiniest of details. "But it sounds to me like maybe you made one questionable decision, and you're simply applying it to everything bad in your life. So, what was it?"

"I'm sorry? What was *what*?"

"What brought you *here*, to this city, to this sidewalk, and to me right now, Jesse?"

The flickering streetlight above him suddenly became static. The wind temporarily vanished. The smell of impending rain seemed to become something else entirely, as though it was not signaling the near future, but rather, the scent of right now.

Breathe in.

Jesse was second-guessing his intentions for being there, beside the marvelous girl on that particular foot-stamped sidewalk. He wanted to tell Sharona it wasn't going to work between them. Because it really wasn't, was it? The truth, he contemplated, was that he was getting tired of it all. Jesse assumed he would fall in love with the city he'd read about for years, the city he'd grown up with but so far apart from. He was lingering on the fallout from his accidental relationship with Edith Galloway. He continued to hang on to the memories of Patrick Kohn. And he was still hoping that sticking with Tommy Mueller was the answer to it all.

Breathe out.

"I don't know if I can be in this city anymore," Jesse finally uttered as the winds once again pushed the rains ever closer. "It just feels like I'm sitting around waiting for something to happen. Something that never does."

"Something *is* happening, Jesse."

"I used to believe everything Tommy ever told me about New York. He told me the Flatiron Building was really a giant arrow that pointed toward the location of some long-ago buried treasure. He even said the United Nations Building was originally designed to be a giant skateboard ramp, and that there was a big magnet inside the Washington Square Arch that held Manhattan in place."

"You actually believed all that?"

"I'm not sure if I did. But I think I *wanted* to, because it all sounded so fantastic. Like this was the one place in the world where any of that could really be possible." Jesse looked back down to the torn newspaper ad between his feet. He scrunched the paper under the wet sole of his shoe. "But now I'm thinking I never should have seen any of it in the first place. Maybe I should have stayed in Seattle or gone to art school in Columbus. But I think I'm afraid to tell Tommy. I'm afraid of what he would think of me."

"All right then." Sharona was smart enough to know she had gotten as far as she was going to get. "Don't do it for me, do it for yourself. Get over this, Jesse. I don't know how you'll go about doing it, but you need to get over it." She stood up and slapped her palm firmly against the streetlight again. The rings on her fingers sent a hum which reverberated all the way up to Midtown. "Just look for my poster here when you're done."

Jesse paused for a long moment before finally opening his mouth again. "I still don't know why you're not pissed at me, Sharona."

She didn't answer him. Jesse assumed she was silent because she finally was pissed at him, but when he turned around he realized it was because Sharona simply wasn't there anymore. He stretched his neck to look down MacDougal Street, both to the north and to the south. But just like the Invisible Woman, she'd disappeared completely.

~~~

Jesse was lying face up in the mud in Morningside Park. He was right on top of second base, trying his best to ignore the instinct to recall any of baseball's sexual metaphors that Tommy might have told him over the years.

Jesse had decided to walk all the way home from Greenwich Village, and he'd made it nearly one hundred city blocks before the rain had begun to fall again. By the time he reached 110th Street, he chose to cut through Morningside Park, but he slipped in the mud of the baseball diamond. The rain passed quickly. He lay there in the mud for another hour counting the stars and considering his next move. His fingers clenched the mud and dirt so tightly, as though he was trying to hurt the city itself. Jesse was still a little woozy from the three martinis he'd downed earlier, making it harder and harder to keep track of the glimmering specks in the sky. Tommy and Kate could always hold their liquor much better than Jesse, as evidenced by the photograph on his refrigerator in which he's falling from the tip of the Alamo. Jesse was growing exceedingly frustrated, losing track of the stars after only counting ten or so. He tried again, but he'd now found himself stumped even sooner.

He was so tired of making mistakes. Throughout his entire adult life, Jesse had actually attempted to keep track of the number of mistakes he'd ever made, the small ones and the big ones. But just like the shimmering stars
~~~

above him, he was beginning to find it hard to admit he might've finally lost track. Still, he had to wonder if sending Sharona on her way was yet another in his latest series of regrets. But really, how could he possibly ever keep up with a girl like that, a girl with that much power? Nevertheless, the decision to let her go still hurt. Was it his intention to make Sharona as gone as Edith was?

Jesse stared into the black of night between the jagged claws of clouds which had begun to form, but then simply stopped moving. He had to wonder if the world had slowed to a stop again or if it was really that painfully quiet. He considered how, from his vantage point, the stars in the night sky all seemed so close together, almost to be viewed as a singular thing. The stars were just like all the people in New York: so close from afar, but really billions of miles away from one another. He asked himself: Was that so bad? Does one star worry about the actions of another?

Jesse's thoughts of Patrick were confusing him too. On the one hand, Patrick Kohn's return to Manhattan might just be the launching pad for a whole new chapter in the lives of himself and his friends. On the other hand, Jesse was finding himself taking Tommy's side in the whole situation. Maybe the return of Patrick heralded the beginning of something worse? Or perhaps it was simply the wet mud creeping under his shirt and into his shoes that was generating such unwarranted negativity?

He reached his hand into his coat pocket, hoping to find a dollar or two for a cab. After crossing nearly the entire city he was ready to give in with only four more blocks to go. His wet, muddy wallet was ruined, but it did not contain anything of value anyway and certainly nothing close to what he was searching for. An ancient subway token. Three incomplete Wing King's stamp cards. A CKY Grocery receipt for two liters of milk bought seven years ago. Yet the lack of money or anything else of importance at that moment yielded the appearance of something new: John Galloway's business card was stuck to the bottom of his pocket. That same card had sat in the same pocket of the very same coat he'd worn four years ago.

I waited as Jesse considered Sharona's last words. She didn't know how he was going to go about getting over his past, but she told him he'd have to find a way.

CHAPTER NINE
Kate & Gene's Brownstone – Upper West Side

It was two in the morning and Kate was sitting in the cold, yellow, plastic booth of the McDonald's at the 103rd Street Station. Holding the final bite of cheeseburger in her hand, she had not only noticed she was the last one in the restaurant, but also realized she inevitably seemed to return to the same place whenever she felt like she was doing something wrong. Stuffing her face with crap and wishing it would kill her. Kate's stomach was attempting to send out the appropriate warning signals, but she refused to acknowledge any of it. She was well aware she had so far not spoken a single word to her husband that day, and cramming cheeseburgers down her gullet seemed to be the best way to keep from doing so. She held up the final greasy bite, and considered the possibility it might end it all. Maybe it could find itself lodged in her throat? Surely there'd be worse places in this city to die than at the McDonald's. Defeated, she dropped the remains of the burger onto the plastic tray when she realized there undeniably was not. Kate sucked back the last of her vanilla milkshake. It tasted unremarkable, and a little bit like the wax lining of the cheap cup it was served in.

She held the letter in her hand. She could barely even remember the blip from her childhood that was Patrick Kohn. Their relationship seemed to be over just like that. Kate recalled Gene's mustachioed little face in bed that morning and wondered what she had to feel guilty for. So what if she didn't love Gene anymore? Was she the first person to ever fall out of love? Not even close.

Finally, Kate convinced herself she should listen to Tommy's advice. She would tell Gene that for the sake of everything good in their marriage, their marriage had to end.

~~~

With the letter between her teeth, Kate unlocked the door to the brownstone on West 107th Street. Her bag slumped to the hardwood floor just as she manifested a wet milkshake burp. Some of the coffee shop's matzo ball soup had found its way back up as well, and as she disgusted herself with the taste in her mouth, Kate also imagined Jesse being jealous of the unique flavor combination.

The place was as quiet as ever. Gene had never once said anything to Kate about her late nights out. It started innocently like anything, with some overtime at the office; it was that ridiculous cookbook which needed to get pushed out. Why her editor had decided to put a rush on that one was anyone's guess. Recipes written by 1980s Saturday morning cartoon characters? Who was ever going to buy that? No one, as it turned out. The Pendulum stockroom was full of them and office parties would still see such dishes served as Captain Caveman BBQ Ribs, Rubik the Amazing Cubed Fruit Salad, or California Raisin Pie with Jem and the Holo-Graham Cracker Crust.

The late nights at work ran seamlessly into late nights at the coffee shop with Tommy and Jesse. Kate had never considered telling Gene where she might be or when she might be home, but Gene had never asked either, and there had never been a single argument about the whole situation. Kate often wondered who would be more at fault should a dispute ever arise. She thought it was wonderful to be able to have that kind of confrontational foresight.

At the front door was a small round table and on it sat a picture of Gene and Kate, smiling like they'd just paid for expensive oral surgery. The only other thing on the table was a glass dish full of loose change, dead skin, and expired Metrocards.
~~~

Kate took her time walking up the stairs. All along the wall were more pictures; each of them embarrassingly outdated and all were of Gene's family and friends. Kate knew only a handful of the people in the photographs and she'd met even fewer of them. In one, Gene's mother sat in her favorite armchair, clutching a glass of scotch. In another, an aunt was flying a kite at Brighton Beach. Gene's brother Andrew held up his "We're Number One" foam finger at a Yankees game. Some other guy was playing an accordion on an outdoor stage.

Kate climbed higher. There was a picture of Sporty Gene just before he'd rappelled the Hearst Tower for a work charity function; Gentle Gene posing on a Central Park bench with three of his nephews; Teen Gene on the hood of his first car, sporting what could have been his very first mustache; and Little Gene about to board the school bus for his first day of grade school.

In the upstairs hallway, Kate touched the picture of a scruffy dog from Gene's youth. It was next to the dusty picture of a man standing proudly in front of a barber shop, which was underneath the faded picture of two kids in costume who could have been Gene and his brother, but one was in a Mickey Mouse costume while the other was dressed as Minnie. Kate had never asked who was who.

A feeling came over her. It was a feeling Kate had never experienced before. The farther into the house she went, the deeper she got, the less relevant she became. Most of the furniture in the house was Gene's too, sitting in the same spots they'd been in since Kate first moved in. If it weren't for that first picture by the front door, her clothes in the bedroom closet, or the trace of her perfume in the house, it might be very hard to tell whether or not Kate had ever existed.

The first thing she saw upon entering the bedroom was the last thing she had seen when she left that morning: through the hanging picture frame, Gene was fast asleep. She thought about how a picture frame was supposed to make things better, to highlight a memory that was never meant to be forgotten. That picture frame only made her husband far less than perfect. It revealed all of the man's flaws and imperfections. All of the times he would decline invitations to visit with her friends. Kate knew for certain now she'd wasted the last three years of her life. If it wasn't for those ridiculous hanging frames, she might not have ever come to the realization. Their interior decorator had the audacity to suggest them in the first place. Maybe she should call her right now and thank her? That picture frame had been the root of her troubles all day. The very spot on the carpet where she stood was exactly the same spot Kate had decided she didn't want to be in that relationship anymore. And after an entire day thinking about it, after talking so candidly with Tommy, Jesse — and yes, even Dwayne the Temp — she still had not changed her mind.

<div align="center">~~~</div>

Kate had first met Gene Schneider in the lunch lineup at Schwartz's in Midtown. He later confessed he'd seen her there one afternoon a couple of weeks before, and that he'd come back during lunch every day thereafter in the hopes of seeing her again. To Kate, the most flattering part of the whole story was the fact Gene didn't even like Schwartz's sandwiches, which was also so ridiculous at the same time since they were the best sandwiches in the city. But still, he fought through the heart-burning pain of sixteen liverwurst sandwiches for the chance he might talk to Kate.

They were married somewhere between five to nine weeks after that (it would all depend on who was telling the story), and Kate had soon learned how comfortable it was to live on the salary of a busy Manhattan dental surgeon. Tommy and Jesse were never envious of Kate's marriage, nor did they ever feel the need to tell her she may have made a big mistake. Neither of them ever knew what to make of Gene Schneider. His anomalous lumberjack mustache and preposterously parted hair aside, he seemed like a decent enough guy and he had a non-threatening, almost professorial look to him. Quiet, a little withdrawn, and not very adventurous with food, Gene always surprised folks when he told them his favorite films were classic 70s horrors, but then disappointed them when he revealed the existence of his Canadian stamp collection. He didn't voice his opinion often, but he was certain about basically everything, and he was a difficult man to convince otherwise. Kate sometimes speculated whether she had been doing Gene a favor by marrying him, or if it was the other way around. Tommy and Jesse were satisfied knowing she had simply chosen to settle, rather than date yet another What's-His-Name for yet another two-to-ten-day period of time.

And the truth was Kate had always known she'd made a big mistake. She knew from the very beginning. She knew while she spoke her wedding vows aloud while on a rooftop overlooking Central Park.

Kate wondered whether she should wake him. Should she just come out with it? How long would that whole conversation take? Five minutes? An hour or more? And then what? She certainly wouldn't be able to take her regular spot in the bed and just fall asleep beside him like it was any other night. No, things would only get that much more complicated, wouldn't they?

Breathe in.

Thoughts of Patrick Kohn came to mind. What was it about the boy from her youth that sparked a chain reaction resulting in Kate marrying Gene Schneider? Her memory flashed back to the day so many years ago when she awoke to discover Patrick was gone. Could she disappear now, just like Patrick once had? Maybe she could leave her ring behind in the back pocket of Gene's pants? He was just lying there, unmoving. His bushy mustache whistled with every breath, his breathing crackled like a dirty old record.

But she couldn't do it. She couldn't wake him and spill her heart. More specifically, Kate couldn't find the strength within herself to make her life everything it should have been.

Passing back through the stairwell of unfamiliar memories, Kate went down to the kitchen and poured herself a generous glass of white wine. The wine was left over from a dinner party they had last week: Gene had invited some other dentists from the office over and each was encouraged to bring his wife along, for surely the three wives would have just as much in common as their three boring husbands, wouldn't they? If Linda could marry the overweight and fashion-unconscious Marvin, if Janet could marry the ugly, smelly, and humorless Ken, and if Kate could marry the awkwardly haughty Gene, then surely the three women themselves would also share a connection of their own. Tragically, but not surprisingly for Kate, it was the exact opposite of a connection that night; nothing but uneasy stares, plenty of bathroom breaks, and jokes without punchlines.

Kate took the wine downstairs into her office. Leaving the lights off and sitting at the desk, she listened quietly for anything outside that might distract her thoughts. However, West 107th Street at three in the morning is never the ideal place to be if one is waiting for action. Kate sat patiently for nearly twenty minutes, but there was nothing that could possibly have taken her mind off Patrick Kohn. She was surprised when she discovered she was still holding his letter in her hand.

The day Kate met Patrick was the same day her dog Mitch died. She never really cared for the family dog though; she just wanted to feel as though Patrick could fill a void for her like he had done for Tommy. Back in high school, they all thought they knew everything and assumed no one was paying any attention. They were the smartest group of kids in Seattle. But aren't they all? Kate sees the same in the kids she passes on a daily basis. Along the sidewalks. On the subway. Eating cheeseburgers across from her at the McDonald's at two o'clock in the morning. It's the same everywhere. The same anywhere. They all act identical, oblivious to the fact they really don't know everything and they never will. Unaware they'll one day realize the truth about themselves, and it won't be anything close to what they expected.

It was well past midnight in Seattle, but Kate knew her father would still be awake. There was no fighting his insomnia anymore, it was entirely full-blown, but Gordon Prince still refused to speak with his doctor or even acknowledge his condition. The phone rang seven times without the answering machine ever kicking in.

"Hi, Dad."

"Katherine! How are you, Pumpkin-Pie? Boy, it must be late over there."

"Yeah, I'm not really sleeping tonight."

"Lately your mother's been trying to convince me she can't fall asleep without me beside her. But I just tell her to close her eyes and turn the other way. Who's going to know, right?"

"She can be difficult, can't she?" Kate couldn't possibly explain to her father that her problems were the exact opposite.

"Hold on. You're speaking so quiet. Let me turn the boob tube off—" Gordon Prince liked to watch the sports channel for the highlights. He'd watch it all night too, even if it was nothing but the same footage looped every thirty-to-sixty minutes. There was grunting and a stifling clatter on the other end of the phone, like her father was trying to turn off the television by throwing balled-up socks at it. Whatever he did, it seemed to work. "How's Gene doing?"

"He's fine, Dad."

"How's your book coming along?"

"Dad, it's great. It's all just great. Listen, did you hear about that plane crash today?"

"The one from Seattle?"

"Was there another?"

"Hmm—I don't think so."

"Then why would you need to ask?"

"I'm just used to clarifying I suppose. Your mother's so scatterbrained sometimes I need to ask a kajillion questions just to find out what's for dinner."

"Dad, did you hear Patrick Kohn was coming back to New York? Did you know that?"

"Yeah, I just talked to Jerry yesterday. He said Patrick was going to be running part of the family business over there on the East Coast." Jerry Kohn still lived a block away from the Princes, in the same house Kate had been in at least a hundred times in her youth.

"Did Jerry say when Patrick was leaving? Do you know which flight he was on?"

"No. I don't think so." Kate's father had never been good at putting two and two together. "But I think it'll be good for him after what happened with his wife and all."

Kate's mother had called maybe three months before to tell her Natasha Seward-Kohn had died from a very sudden case of brain cancer. It was horrible news, sure, but with the all-too-common positive spin: *"It happened so fast, at least she didn't suffer long."* Kate was never one to try and pull something good out of something negative. And for whatever reason, she didn't pass the news along to Tommy or Jesse. Kate wasn't sure why she chose to withhold the information, since all three of them had known Natasha from high school.

Once again, she looked over the letter in her hand:

"To be honest, things in Seattle are not so good right now," it said. *"I'm not certain how much news might have gotten around. I'm not sure if friends and family talk the way they used to,"* he wrote.

Kate knew exactly what the words had meant when Tommy read the letter aloud that morning, but she still chose to not say anything.

However, it was obvious her father didn't know or hear anything more. Kate wondered if that was good or bad news, but she knew it was meaningless to press her dad for any further information. She made him promise he'd get to bed soon, if for no other reason than to make sure her mom would fall asleep.

Kate got up to refill her glass, this time taking the bottle back to the office with her as well. She turned on her computer and glossed over the first three pages of her manuscript before deleting the entire thing altogether. She even emptied her computer's recycling bin just to make sure she didn't open it again that night. This was not as dramatic a move as she had convinced herself, for there was also a version backed up on her external hard drive, one on her computer at work, and even a printed version she kept hidden in a location undisclosed to anyone who pried. But it was out of sight and out of mind for the moment at least, which was enough. Kate took as much wine into her mouth as her mouth would allow and opened up a blank journal from the shelf beside her desk. She stared at it for a minute or two before finally swallowing the wine and scratching the first page with a crooked, tooth-riddled pencil. She began with:

CHAPTER ONE: THE LETTER

Tom,

I'm sorry to contact you in such a way, but you were the only one I was certain I could reach. I've got to say, I do sometimes miss your shameless predictability.

Suddenly, Kate was back to paper fences.

Breathe out.

PART II

~~~

THE RETURN
~~~

CHAPTER TEN

Tommy's Apartment – Morningside Heights

ONE WEEK LATER.

Tommy awoke to the sound of rain. With his palms, he rubbed his eyes then took a minute to piece together his surroundings as the white blotches slowly dissipated from sight. His room was empty; emptier than it typically was. Empty except for a bed, a dresser of drawers, a bookshelf, and a few lingering memories. The first three books on his shelf were Bukowski in the Bathtub, The Complete Calvin and Hobbes, and a cultural anthropology encyclopedia Rachel had left behind. The books were all so incredibly varied, while the memories were all painfully alike. The muffled pounding of the rain against his window seemed to be much farther away, far more distant than it should have been. Tommy stepped out of bed to investigate.

Moving to the window, he was actually not surprised at all to find the glass now set behind iron bars. His long fingers trickled through them to touch the windowpane. It seemed thicker than it should have been, perhaps the reason behind the deadened sound of the rainstorm. But Tommy was still not convinced anything around him was amiss. His sixth-floor view of the brick wall across the courtyard had now been replaced by a vast expanse of water; the building next to his was gone, but he did not consider the implausibility of it all for even a second.

Outside, the city was soaking. The streets were drowning under two stories of murky water. Tommy could see the shadowy outlines of rusted cars, mailboxes, and long-abandoned storefronts on the ocean's adopted floor. He watched as the water's surface crept another notch up a dead streetlight.

Gripping the bars now, he peered out across the makeshift river between skyscraper banks. The horizon was nothing but gray; sky and water melting indiscernibly into one another.

Tommy wondered when it must have started raining, but then he suddenly knew it really didn't make any difference, realizing finally that it was nothing but a dream. And who in a dream would ever care about such a matter?

And then he woke up with a startle.

Tommy had had a different dream for seven nights in a row, each of them worse than the one before it. He dreamed the city and everything around him was shrinking but he remained the same size; his hands becoming so big that it was getting harder and harder to touch or hold onto anything he loved without breaking them. He dreamed Central Park was gone, replaced by Hoboken, New Jersey. He dreamed the New York Islanders won the Stanley Cup and the victory parade went by outside his building, along 113th Street from Broadway to Amsterdam and back again. And again. And again. He dreamed he and Kate and Jesse had entered the Coney Island hot dog eating contest; he watched as his two best friends' stomachs burst open, spilling out into Lower Bay. He dreamed Rachel returned, but only because she had forgotten a six-pack of vanilla cream soda in his refrigerator. He dreamed of razor blades under his fingernails and toenails. And he dreamed of his twin brother Leyland, drowning in the Pacific Ocean and calling out to him relentlessly.

~~~

Tommy loved his brother for many reasons, but at the top of that list was the fact Leyland was born first. Before they were married, the Muellers had agreed to name their first son after the baby's great-grandfather, Leyland Mueller, who had come to America from Austria just before the Great Depression. As Tommy's luck would have it, he was the second born by only seventy-two
~~~

seconds and as such did not have to grow up with the name he knew his twin brother had always detested so much.

Growing up, the Mueller boys were constantly confused by relatives. This seemed incredibly strange to Tommy, since it was actually quite easy to tell them apart: Leyland was the one who received all of the attention. They were both tall for their age, both had dark skin, blonde hair, and hazel eyes, but Leyland was the boy who strangers would smile at first. Tommy made note of every time Leyland's hair was playfully ruffled by the girls at school (it was a lot), he counted the number of candies tossed into their sacks at Halloween (Leyland always ended up with more, though he would share with his brother anyway), and he kept track of the number of instances where Leyland was picked before him in gym class or for games of road hockey (it was every time). It didn't really bother Tommy, but he did find it peculiar. Maybe, he thought, it was simply a by-product of his brother's unfortunate name, possibly an unconscious act by others to help the boy find forgiveness for his parents' ignorance about any of the 101 Most Popular Baby Names.

Still, the boys were inseparable. Their mother enjoyed telling them stories from when they were babies. She told Leyland his first word was *Tommy*, and she told Tommy his first word was *Leyland*. She often indulged them with accounts of their bath times together, which naturally neither of the boys found any pleasure in listening to. When they were older, Leyland enjoyed playing mix-up, pretending each of them was the other; sitting in on the other's classes; kissing one another's girlfriends. These games had never seemed like fun to Tommy. Tommy was happy just being himself, and he was happy to have Leyland for a brother. It seemed silly to want to pretend it was the other way around. He only ever agreed for the sole purpose of wishing for the extra attention from others, but somehow things still continued to work in Leyland's favor.

The boys were in the ninth grade when they were finally separated. It was a school trip to Japan. Tommy didn't want to go because it wasn't a trip to New York. Seattle was already far enough away from where his heart truly wanted to be; he didn't want to be any farther. As his mother and father kissed Leyland goodbye at the airport, Tommy stood back and watched the arrivals and departures board. There was one plane leaving for New York at that moment, and another was just arriving from JFK. He wanted to see what the passengers looked like; he wanted to know if he would be able to tell which ones were the real New Yorkers and which were the tourists. He was too distracted to even say goodbye to his brother one last time. Leyland called out to him, but Tommy didn't hear.

The following spring, when Tommy had no one else, he met Patrick Kohn.

~~~

It was the sound of the door buzzer that woke Tommy from his nightmare, and he knew for sure Rachel had returned. Rachel possessed an ever-evolving buzzing style, and she would change it up constantly with no warning whatsoever. Tommy hated that. He liked to know that when Jesse came by it was always going to be a buzz-bu-bu-buzz-buzz, buzz-buuuuuuzzzzzzz, and when Kate showed up it would no doubt be one long buuuuuuuuuuuuuuuuuuuuuuuuzzzzzzzzzzzzzzzzzzzz, most likely with the full force of her fist, or perhaps an elbow or a knee if her hands were full. But when Rachel dropped by: who knew? It could be anything. Maybe one short buzz; maybe two. Or any possible combination of every sound capable of being produced through that sixty-year-old speaker.

The sound of the buzzer that morning was something akin to a dying puppy. Rachel must have forgotten her keys. Or maybe she'd thrown them onto the tracks; it certainly wouldn't have been the first time she'd flown from Tommy's apartment in a fit of frustration and tossed her keys somewhere. And yet, Tommy took an outlandish sort of pleasure in the idea that keys to
~~~

his apartment were scattered around areas of Manhattan. Tommy pulled his ass out of bed to hit the intercom, but of course it was on the fritz. All he heard was an alien static. Throwing on his ANGER sweater, Tommy marched down the five flights of stairs to let her inside.

Expecting to see the familiar slim shape of Rachel Ponzini through the murky translucency of the door's glass, Tommy stopped when he noticed the form of a man instead. Tommy didn't say a word. He carefully inched closer toward the blurry figure behind the glass. "Tom?" it said to him. "Is that you there?"

It was him. Tommy just knew it. Patrick Kohn was alive and standing on the other side of the door.

Breathe in.

Tommy remained silent, as though he could will himself invisible behind the glass, as if he had the power to take on a ghost-like form rather than his own. As though it was all still a horrible dream.

The dark shape pressed further. "Hello?" But wasn't it Patrick who was playing the part of the ghost at that moment? Was it not just one week before Tommy had proclaimed his former friend dead? Had the plane crash on the evening news not already wiped Patrick Kohn from existence? Had it not swallowed the man deep down into a place where Tommy could at last be done with him? The two of them were both at eye level now; the mottled glass was the only thing separating the fuzzy, gray blobs of their heads.

"Come on, Tom," he said. "Don't do this."

Tommy wondered if that glass was not between them, how he might react to his uninvited guest. The fire inside him wanted to bang the window, to send Patrick away. Could he hit the door with enough force to send him all the way back to Seattle? Or better yet, to put him in the fiery grave in which he belonged? Fuck, he thought, giving his head a shake. Both Kate and Jesse were right when they would tell him how preposterously dramatic he could be at times.

The blurry head outside the door pressed on. "Don't do this, Tom," it repeated.

Silence.

"Tom, it's me."

Just steps to the east, the giant, red door of the Engine Company 47 firehouse suddenly rolled open. Patrick had to raise his voice over the scrambled commotion of fire fighters and the growling of the truck's engine as it awoke.

"TOM, COME ON!"

The fire truck blasted out of the hall, heading west up the one-way street, its siren blaring past the two men. And yet, Patrick's faltering desperation could still be heard.

"TOM!"

If Tommy had felt the deafening racket could hide him from reality, he was suddenly aware of its blatant inefficiency. He no longer had the willpower to remain in the one-sided standoff. "What are you doing here?" he finally asked, hating himself a just little bit for opening his mouth. He would have hated himself even more had he known Patrick Kohn was just about ready to give up and turn away.

"Tom!"

"What are you doing here, Patrick?"

"Didn't you get my letter?"

"I read the letter. But I'm not asking a letter, I'm asking *you*. What the hell are you doing here?"

There was only silence outside now. There were no fire trucks or car horns. The shape of the man behind the glass did not move. Patrick was frozen. Was he regretting his decision to come back?

Inside, Mrs. Horowitz from 406 was shuffling her way into the lobby. The crinkling of her giant ball of plastic bags never failed to give her presence away, nor did the squeaky wheels of her walker. Tommy knew she was on her way to Mintz's Meats because she went to the pungent delicatessen every Tuesday morning. She'd been on the same schedule since Tommy moved in eleven years ago, and it was just as she'd been doing eleven years before Tommy moved in. Tommy threw up his arms, blocking the door to let Mrs. Horowitz know she would not be leaving out the front this morning. She gave Tommy a perplexed look, but knew well enough about younger people to not ask them questions.

"Tom, come on. I was only in Seattle. I wasn't dead. Don't treat me like I'm dead!"

Tommy pointed toward the glass with his thumb, and mouthed the word "Terrorist" to Mrs. Horowitz. He covered his mouth with one hand and held the other out like a gun, looking more like a Wild West train robber than a terrorist, but she got the idea. The old woman had an absolute fear of terrorism, so much so, she went out of her way to avoid Apartment 104's wooden-legged Middle Eastern man, just in case. Of course, she was never a big fan of Tommy either, and with a dismissive wave, some under-her-breath muttering, and an uninterested glare, she wheeled her cart around and headed for the back exit.

"Maybe you're *not* dead," Tommy finally replied. "But you are to *me*."

"What do you want me to say here, Tom? What can I possibly say that would make you open this door?"

Tommy thought it over for a moment. If it had been a girlfriend outside, there was no doubt he would have had the skill to say something to drive her away again. So why couldn't he find the words to make Patrick do the same?

The door between them was the very same door they stood at eleven years ago when Tommy and Patrick first came to look at the apartment. Tommy didn't want to tell Patrick at the time, but when he had pushed the buzzer, he was more nervous than he'd ever been in his life. Tommy recognized how big a change they were about to make, committing themselves to a brand-new life in the great big city.

"Is this how it's going to be then?"

Eleven years ago, Tommy knew he couldn't have made the choices he'd made without the backing from his friends. In Kate and Jesse and Patrick, he found the strength to make any decision.

"Tom?"

But Tommy had cut that cord between himself and Patrick, and he sometimes wondered if that severing had strengthened him, or if he had been running at three-quarters speed ever since.

Tommy placed a palm to the glass and said, "Go away, Patrick." Turning, he removed his hand and walked away from the door. "Just go away."

Patrick remained on the stoop long enough to see the sweaty hand print dissolve from behind the glass.

The dreams Tommy dreamed became worse and worse every night. But he would have wished any of them more real than the reality of Patrick Kohn returning to Manhattan and destroying absolutely everything.

CHAPTER ELEVEN
Tom's Restaurant – Morningside Heights

Tommy hid inside his apartment for another two hours intent on ignoring any incoming phone call or buzz at the door. When he was satisfied he'd waited long enough, he threw on his coat and scarf.

But before closing the front door, he spotted the copy of "Blanc" still sitting atop his desk. He stared at the thing adamantly like it was a wild animal that had found itself trapped in the apartment. Since the night he typed the book's final words, Tommy had been optimistic in thinking Kaspar Delancey might be kind enough to stay folded within its covers forever. Now he found himself cursing his own creation and his reasons for ever deciding to bring Kaspar into his world in the first place. He closed the door, locking up as many foolish thoughts as he could.

After his daily detour to the CKY Grocery, Tommy walked back up Amsterdam Avenue, Spartan in hand. He was surprised to find all of the grocery's apples had been uncharacteristically bruised that morning. The best apple he could find had a mealy consistency and lacked any crunch whatsoever.

Tommy approached the corner of 112th and Broadway with more trepidation than ever, for there was still something not sitting quite right. Patrick Kohn's appearance earlier that same morning not only meant the man was officially back in Tommy's life, but it also meant he was back in Tommy's city. Patrick knew the coffee shop was their eatery of choice because he'd been in its familiar booth himself only ten years earlier, and he'd eaten the very same rubbery scrambled eggs and cardboard pancakes that were still being served ten years later. What was to stop him from being there that morning, waiting for the gang to meet like they had always done? But what could Tommy do? He wasn't going to change his life to accommodate Patrick. Tommy had to be sure though, and he peeked through the coffee shop's window: Jesse was sitting alone at the table.

Tommy swung the restaurant door wide open. Ringing bells indicated his arrival but not a single head turned. Jesse was giggling quietly to himself as he read the morning paper. It was reassuring how Jesse would always find something in the funnies to laugh at, no matter how bad they were. Kate's coat was sprawled across the opposite seat, and Tommy plastered it against the wall as he made himself comfortable.

"Hey, Tommy," Jesse muttered, without lifting his head. Tommy had no reply, yet Jesse still knew something was amiss. "Are you in a mood today? I don't know if I can handle one of your moods this morning."

"I think it's going to be one of those days," Tommy said. "Do you realize how shitty it's been so far?"

Jesse answered with nothing more than shrugged shoulders.

"It's been *so* shitty I didn't even feel the need to point out the misspellings on the sign this morning."

"Hobolicious?" Jesse asked.

Tommy nodded. Hobolicious was the homeless man who occupied the corner of Amsterdam and 110th Street, and every morning he would have a new sign scribbled in crayon on the inside of a cardboard box lid. Tommy enjoyed correcting the man's spelling and sentence structure, justifying his actions by dropping a dollar or two into the plastic Double Bubble pail. Tommy, Kate, and Jesse gave Hobolicious his nickname so long ago they couldn't recall how or why they'd ever decided on it in the first place. Tommy's best-guess was that Kate had found the man to be exceptionally good-looking. This best-guess was typically followed by another punch to the arm.

"That *does* sound shitty."

"Yeah, well. You don't even know the half of it." Tommy squashed the coat into the bench a little more. "Has Kate been in the bathroom all morning? Was she cramming down cheeseburgers at the McDonald's again last night?"

"Very funny," Kate said, returning to the table and sitting next to Tommy.

"Shouldn't you kids be at work today?" Unintentionally, Tommy would sometimes speak down to the two of them. Kate believed his condescending nature to be an extension of his success and their lack of the same.

"I'm covering Germ's shift later. He's got some band meeting in a garage in Queens somewhere."

"And you, Kate?"

"I should be at work," she said. "But I'm thinking of quitting today."

"What?" Jesse dribbled some coffee onto his Aquaman t-shirt, but seeing as the cheap shirt was already brown it would probably conceal most of the day's stains anyway. "Why would you do that, Kate?"

"I just can't take the corporate bullshit anymore."

"What corporate bullshit?" Tommy asked. "You edit manuscripts."

"You wouldn't understand, Tommy."

"How does Gene feel about all of this?"

"I — I still haven't spoken to him. Not about my job. Not about our marriage. I think I'm just afraid he'll give me some reason not to leave him. If that makes any sense."

"I guess so," Jesse agreed half-heartedly.

What Kate really wanted to tell her friends was she'd started writing a new book. She was excited about it, so naturally, she wanted them to be as well. Still, Kate didn't want it to seem as though the other things in her life didn't matter right now.

"Hold on," Tommy said. "You said you were *thinking* of quitting? But that would mean you haven't quit *yet*. So, it would *also* mean you should be there right now sitting in your crummy corporate office chair, wouldn't it?" Tommy flagged the waitress for a cup of coffee. "So, what are you doing *here* then?"

Kate asked, "Isn't it too early, Tommy?"

"For what?"

"For being a jerk. What's gotten into you, lately? Is it Rachel?"

Tommy sighed. "No. I've just been having some bad dreams lately."

"God. Tell me about it," Kate sighed. "I had a dream the other night I gave birth to a two-dimensional baby. Like it was made out of paper. And then I accidentally dropped it through a sewer grate. And it was gone. Poof. Just like that. The strange thing was, I wasn't even all that worried about it."

Tommy didn't know what to say about that. "How about you, Jesse? Are you still having your Alan Alda dreams?"

"Unfortunately, yes," Jesse admitted.

In Jesse's recurring dream, he was grocery shopping with Alan Alda. For months, he couldn't put his finger on who this person in his dreams was; he could only remember a certain familiarity to the tone of his voice, and that they would be doing different activities together every night: five-pin bowling (always as teammates), chasing pigs through mud (always as competitors), driving across the prairies of Saskatchewan (usually in a dark blue Ford Prelude, but not always), and most disturbingly, masturbating to reruns of "Taxi" together (but at least they sat on different chairs, *"So it wasn't as if there had been anything gay about it, right guys? Right?"*). But it wasn't until he'd seen a late-night episode of "Scientific American Frontiers" hosted by Alan Alda, when Jesse finally made the disturbing connection. From that point on, the only thing Jesse Classen and Alan Alda would do together in his dreams was shop for groceries, and they would bicker with each other the entire time like an old married couple.

Kate needed some clarification on the matter. "Is it always the *same* shopping trip, or do you guys keep going back?"

"I think it's the same trip. Whenever I put something in the cart, he takes it out when I'm not looking. I don't think we've ever made it to the checkout."

Finally, Kate asked, "What about you, Tommy? What are these bad dreams of yours?"

Tommy had not even flirted with the idea of telling his two best friends about the surprise visit he had that morning. He wasn't ready to make Patrick Kohn's return any more certain than it already was. "I've just been having your basic, run-of-the-mill movie nightmares. You know, a Joe Pesci pen in the neck. An Edward Norton curb-stomping. The Polar Express. That kind of thing." The waitress delivered a fresh cup of coffee for Tommy, and he stirred some sugar into it. He clanked his spoon against the ceramic mug as loud as he could in the hopes he might divert any further questions away from himself.

Through the window, a young boy peered into the restaurant. He was wearing a bright costume, some sort of superhero get-up, even though Halloween was still more than a week away. Tommy didn't know what to think. He wanted to bang on the window but something stopped him. The boy stared at the three of them with a blank expression, almost like he couldn't actually see them. It was unnerving. "What the fuck, kid?" Tommy asked through the glass. Taking Kate's coat from the seat, Tommy pressed it up to the window to block the boy's vision.

Moments later, the restaurant door swung wide open. Tommy, Kate, and Jesse all ignored the ringing bells, just as they always did. Then a familiar voice shouted, "Ho! Manhattanites!" Like he was a Viking or something. Instantly, Tommy knew his morning was not about to get any better.

Kate and Jesse turned to the door, stunned. It was him. Certainly more bald and bloated than they'd remembered, but there was no mistaking him. After ten long years and one strange, short letter, Patrick Kohn had finally returned to Tom's Restaurant.

"Patrick!" They burst from their seats and ran over to him. Tommy stirred some more sugar into his coffee cup as the three friends hugged one another excitedly.

"Hey, Fart Tart," Patrick said to Kate. It was the same bizarre nickname he had always called her. "How you been?" As happy as he appeared, there was still a hint of something not quite right about him. Like something had broken him somewhere along the way. The boy in the costume was directly behind Patrick. He tugged on the sleeve of Patrick's blazer and quietly asked if he could go to the bathroom. Without stopping to think, Patrick pointed to the washrooms. Tommy watched the boy apprehensively until he disappeared from sight.

The group wrapped up their greeting, sharing brief stories of reported plane crashes and sleepless nights, before making their way back to the table where Tommy remained. Jesse and Kate sat back down, and Jesse wiped tears from his eyes. Patrick held out his hand to Tommy. "It's good to finally see you again, Tom."

Tommy inched his hand cautiously toward the middle of the table. If Patrick Kohn was planning on hurting him again, he wouldn't have committed himself so fully. It appeared he was generously welcoming back the past. But Tommy refused to shake the unwanted paw before him, and neither man made any mention of the morning's cheerless encounter.

Patrick asked the waitress for another chair and for two glasses of orange juice, as if he already owned the place. He then sat down next to Jesse, trying to position himself comfortably, wriggling his rear end into the cushion. "Lordy! These booths sure haven't changed much, have they?"

Against his better judgment, Tommy fixed his gaze upon his old friend. Rubbing his eyes and scratching his scalp, Tommy tried to find the best way to say whatever needed to be said. But he couldn't do it. He couldn't find the words. The din outside was deliberate in its attempts to spoil his concentration: the chirping; the barking; the honking; the yelling. Even Patrick ruined the moment for him too. "You haven't changed a bit, Tom," he said.

"Disappointed?"

"Not at all. Are you?"

Tommy did not have an answer for the man. For that matter, he realized he hadn't one for himself either.

Patrick had probably changed more than Tommy, Kate, and Jesse combined. This was really no surprise to Tommy, since he saw leaving New York City as being the easiest way in the world for a person to change, and never for the good. Trapped somewhere beneath the receding hairline, rounded face, wrinkled eyes, and graying chin, was the same young man with the same old dreams. He was never one to resist change and he was always positive about the uncertainties any change might bring.

But Patrick Kohn certainly was not the same man he used to be. When he was younger, he tried his best but he could never match a pair of pants to a shirt to save his life. Now he wore pressed suits and sparkling ties. His morning diet once consisted of nothing more than two cups of coffee, now he drank orange juice with a piece of toast. He used to bite his fingernails to no end, but his hands now appeared as smooth and clean as surgical gloves. His favorite color used to be blue, now it was green. His favorite movie used to be "Jaws" but now he didn't have one. His preferences for music, books, and humor had once been so incredibly specific, but they had all changed as well. And just as he could always be expected to articulate on any discussion topic, he would now only fall silent. If pressed, Patrick would rather agree with someone than force himself to voice a singular opinion. And still at other times, he found himself incapable of finding an opinion on anything at all.

He used to be able to sit completely motionless. Now, he could barely stay still for more than a few seconds. He used to enjoy watching magic tricks for their sheer mystery; sometimes not knowing what existed behind a closed door was enough to make him smile on a bad day. But now he couldn't be happy unless he knew all the answers to everything. Patrick once believed in the freedom of unanchored decisions, but now his world was one of stifled business acumen and legalese. Numbers coursed through his head constantly. Where once he had to think about reaching out for a handshake, it was now done instinctively.

His elbow skin was forever peeling, like a bird in a constant molt. He had a scar on his right leg from a childhood knee surgery which resembled a branch of winterberries. Both of his earlobes still had the noticeable pinholes of piercings from long ago. The one sound he hated more than any other was the sound tissue paper makes when squeezed between fingers. In fact, he really could not bear the rubbing sound of any paper, and yet, if given the choice at grocery stores, he would always opt for paper bags over plastic. He was slightly neurotic, and didn't like to sit anywhere but at the back of a bus or movie theatre, where he could view everyone at once. He had a laugh that could only be described as "maniacal." Jesse used to say Patrick's laugh was not unlike a super villain's upon discovering his arch-enemy's single weakness. Without meaning to, Patrick would often scare people away who happened to be anywhere in his vicinity when he found something funny.

When he was a boy, he would stare into the window from the backseat on family car rides; but his attention wouldn't be focused on what was on the other side of the glass, but rather on his reflection. He was fascinated by his own dark, brown eyes. Now he could barely stand shaving in front of the mirror, in the chance he might accidentally catch a glimpse of his eyes.

As far as Tommy could tell though, Patrick's brown eyes were still the same as they'd ever been. Perhaps they were the one part of him that had not changed at all.

Patrick boasted, "I knew if I came to this coffee shop, I'd find one of you guys here. I didn't count on all three! Nothing ever really changes, does it?"

Tommy did not wish to answer Patrick's question. Instead, he asked one of his own, spitting out the one question that had been on his mind for what seemed like forever: "Why'd you leave us, Patrick?" Patrick's sudden disappearance was hard on them all, but to Tommy, it was nothing more than an outright betrayal.

"Lordy, Tom. That was so long ago." Patrick was not really fazed by the question, since he'd expected it to come sooner or later. "We were just kids, weren't we? There were no limits to the number of stupid mistakes we made back then." The four of them all took turns glancing at one another. They had all made different mistakes over the years. Some of their mistakes affected the group while some had no impact whatsoever, or even went completely unnoticed. "You know when people tell you to roll with the punches? Well, that's a bullshit suggestion. The truth is, sometimes when we take a punch, it's really hard to recover."

"I want to say it never bothered me," Tommy said. What he really wanted to say was he had some amount of interest in throwing a punch of his own at that moment. "But it *did* bother me, Patrick. It bothered all of us."

The waitress came with the juice, and Patrick almost swallowed a full glass in one gulp. "All I can say is I'm sorry, Tom. That's it." He shrugged his shoulders, indicating that really was the best he could do.

With nothing more than a thumb's up for the waitress, Tommy indicated he would have his usual for breakfast. "But you still didn't answer my question," he reiterated. "Why did you leave all of us? We had something good back then, didn't we? We did everything together, but before I knew it, I was standing in that tennis court by myself, looking like a big loser."

"What tennis court?"

"You don't remember? We had plans to finish our tennis match in Riverside that morning. I waited for you, but you never showed."

"Tennis? Is that what's bothering you? The fact we never finished a tennis match?"

"It's just *one* of the things."

Patrick looked over at Kate. It was easy for him to recall every time she'd ever looked at him, but there was still something different beneath the surface now. Ten years was enough time to damage anybody. "Listen guys," he finally said. "The truth is I had to choose between Kate and Natasha. I left because I chose Natasha."

The truth hit her hard, but Kate remained silent.

"Natasha Seward? Your burnout ex-girlfriend?" Tommy had nearly forgotten all about her too. "I can't believe you would dump our Kate to go back for seconds with Natasha C-Word."

Patrick sat silent for a moment. He shifted in his seat a little. "It was the choice I made, Tom. It was killing me being in New York, realizing I'd left so many unanswered questions back home. And it hurt too much to have to explain myself. Especially to *you*. So, I just left. I hate to say it, but playing one last tennis match was not a priority of mine at the time."

"What about Kate, then?"

"What's that?"

"Shouldn't you have at least explained yourself to Kate? Instead of abandoning her, I mean."

"It's okay," Kate said in her own defense. "It's forgotten. Really. Just let it go."

Tommy took a sip of coffee and turned his attention back to Patrick. "So, what, did Natasha dump you before you could leave her too? Is that why you're back?"

Again, Jesse and Kate looked at one another. In one quick look, they both knew instantly that the other was aware of the same thing. And neither of them was sure if they should say something. Just as Kate's mother had called her with the news, Jesse found out when his own mother called to wish him a happy birthday last month. Obviously, no one had said anything of the matter to Tommy.

"Natasha's dead, Tom," Patrick said. He stated it quite matter-of-factly. "She died just a couple of months ago."

Tommy wanted to say he was sorry. He really did. But all he could do was stare across the table. Some tourists materialized outside the window, but he could not even summon the strength to shoo them away. He noticed Patrick's phone face-up on the table, softly buzzing with an incoming call. Patrick ignored it, but Tommy noticed the picture on the phone: it was a picture of Patrick, Natasha, and the same boy who was still in the coffee shop washroom. Natasha did not look anything like he remembered; she seemed taller, fuller, darker, and more beautiful. She seemed like a completely different person. Maybe she was. Their son looked like a nerd though. And Patrick was wearing exactly the same coat he was wearing at that moment.

"One morning she didn't feel so good," Patrick spoke sullenly. "So, she went to the hospital for some tests. When the doctor called a week later, I watched her from the other room. I don't know why, but I think I was more scared than she was. Too scared to even hold her as she listened to the worst news in the world. She sat at the kitchen table, and she put down the phone and smiled at me. That's when I knew." Patrick didn't flinch or squirm or shed a tear. "She came over to me and said she wasn't ever going to see another winter. No more Christmases. And that was all we said. She loved the winter so much. It was her favorite time of year."

Jesse put a hand on Patrick's shoulder. It was one thing to know what had happened, but it was another to hear it from the person who had been hurt the most by it. Patrick wasn't embarrassed by himself though. He didn't quiver. He didn't tremble. He didn't try to wipe his tears away discretely. All he did then was get up from the table. "I'm sorry," he said. "I should go see if

Sheldon's okay." He made his way to the back of the restaurant, toward the washroom.

"Sheldon?" Tommy asked. "Who or what is a Sheldon?"

"That must be Patrick's son," Kate figured.

"The kid in the costume?"

"Go easy on him, Tommy," Jesse encouraged. "Don't you think Patrick's been through enough already?"

"If today is going to be all about Patrick, then I'm not interested."

"The guy's gone through a lot of shit recently," Jesse continued.

"His shit is not *my* shit Jesse. Why should I be expected to deal with it too?"

"Because we're friends," Jesse said. But Tommy could only cross his arms and huff. "Because we *were* friends. Isn't that enough of a reason, Tommy?"

Hoping again for some passerby to come to the window, Tommy twisted his head to get a look up the street outside. But there was no one interested in Tom's Restaurant at that moment.

It wasn't too long before Patrick returned to the table with the costumed boy in tow. "Guys, I'd like you to meet my son, Sheldon." The boy managed his best wave, but he was really not keen on meeting a table full of new people. Especially these strange New York people.

Sheldon's costume was a baggy, bright yellow number with a blue cape, gloves, and a mask which was trying as best as it could to cover his bulbous forehead. He wore a pair of scuffed red rain boots which were obviously not part of the package. Everything about the boy seemed meek. He scrunched his fingers together awkwardly. He stood as though he didn't want to be where his feet were planted, but he seemed to lack the capacity to do anything about it. At eight years old, he shared an uncanny resemblance to a much younger Patrick, but to Tommy, Sheldon Kohn could have been any other kid from anywhere else in the world. "Come on, Patrick," Tommy said. "*Sheldon?*"

"What?" Patrick said. Sheldon sat down in the booth beside Jesse. Patrick sat at the end of the table and slid the untouched glass of juice over to his son.

"Why didn't you just name the kid Poindexter? That would have been just as traumatic for him. He'd probably get beaten up just as much."

"Sheldon Seward was Natasha's father's name. The name was *her* choice." Even if he had meant to be, Patrick remained unapologetic about the name.

Tommy turned his attention to the boy. "So, what's the deal with the costume, kid? Isn't Halloween still a week away?"

Sheldon didn't say anything. He tasted the orange juice cautiously, unsure whether he should trust it.

"He insisted on wearing it," Patrick replied.

"I can't blame you," Jesse said to the boy next to him. "Superheroes are pretty astounding. Which one are you supposed to be?"

"I don't know," Sheldon finally spoke.

"I think it's just a generic superhero costume," Patrick said. "Natasha bought it for him months ago."

Still, Jesse had to wonder. He couldn't fathom the idea of a superhero without a name. It wasn't right. There was some sort of universal imbalance to it. "So, what, are you Captain Common then?"

"I don't know," the boy repeated timidly.

"How about Non-Specific Man?"

Sheldon shrugged his shoulders.

"General Generic?"

Patrick leaned over to his son hoping to clear up any confusion. "Uncle Jesse works at a comic book store."

Sheldon spoke softly. Even for an eight-year-old, the boy didn't carry much of a presence. "I don't like comic books or superheroes. I just like wearing the costume."

"That's exactly how Kate feels about lesbians," Tommy joked.

"Shut up, Tommy," was her reply, although it wasn't what she wanted to say. Kate didn't know much about kids, but she did know swearing in front of them was generally frowned upon.

"I don't understand," Sheldon said.

"Hold on," Jesse said. "Uncle Jesse? Which one was that? And please do not say Dave Coulier."

"I'm pretty sure that was John Stamos," Tommy said. "Either way though, you realize you're still going to think Dave Coulier now every time the kid calls you Uncle Jesse, right?"

"Wonderful."

For a moment, the four adults sat without a word and watched Sheldon silently guzzle his juice. It almost felt like they were all eighteen again. The dark clouds parted, and the morning's first sunlight bounced off the table's scattered cutlery. Out of all the days that had ever been, there had never been a New York day like this one. It was imperceptible to the naked and unassuming eye, but the sky had never been this kind of blue, and it never would again. Should it have been painted exactly as it was that day, the artist surely would have been accused of smearing his sky with a falsified hue.

Patrick's phone buzzed again, but this time he gave in. "Sorry, guys," he said, rising from his seat. "I've got to take this." He answered the phone only when he was entirely out of earshot. The others watched him as he crossed the coffee shop floor, through the dust motes caught within golden sunlight beams. Jesse was ecstatic with the sudden return of their old friend. Kate couldn't help but compare the mistakes she made when she was nineteen to the ones she was currently making now. Sheldon finished his juice.

Tommy picked some apple skin out from his teeth, before turning back to Patrick's son. It was the perfect opportunity for another question or two.

"So, what's your deal?" Tommy asked him, as if the boy knew how to answer the question.

"I don't understand," he said.

"Well, I assume you go to school, yes?"

"Yes." Sheldon stared at Tommy as though the man was a masturbating monkey at the zoo. He didn't want to look, but he was still a little curious. "But I'm transferring to a new school here."

"Well, duh." Tommy didn't realize in the very few times he ever talked to kids, he would channel the dialogue devices he used himself when he was much younger. Kate and Jesse silently witnessed their friend's failing attempt at being folksy with the boy.

Sheldon reached into some hidden pocket in his costume and pulled out a small plastic object. "What have you got there?" Tommy asked. "Is that a toy?"

Putting the device to his mouth, Sheldon said, "It's my inhaler."

"Asthma?"

The boy nodded as he sucked back a couple of bursts of air. "I also have Attention Deficit Disorder."

"That's bullshit!"

"*Tommy!*" Kate refereed, tossing a red card onto the field. "You don't need to swear in front of him."

"Come on, just look at him! That's the most placid kid I've ever seen. There's no way he's got ADD. It's just one of those titles parents slap onto their kids so they never have to admit they don't know what to do with them."

"Excellent prognosis, Doctor Freud." Jesse was well aware Tommy had no idea what he was talking about, but there was definitely something off with Sheldon. Of course, losing his mother couldn't have been easy for the boy.

Patrick surprised them as he sat back down. "Sorry guys. It's been crazy trying to find somewhere to live while dealing with work and looking for schools. But it sounds like there's a place on India Street we can take a peek at this afternoon."

"India Street? Isn't that in Brooklyn?"

Now it was Jesse's turn to referee the conversation. "Don't judge, Tommy. There's nothing wrong with Brooklyn."

"Sure there isn't. Unless you live on India Street."

"Well it beats living out of suitcases at the Beacon Hotel. I'm hoping we won't be staying there any longer than we have to."

Kate recalled the conversation she had with her father about Patrick the week before. "What are you doing for work, Patrick? I heard you were helping your dad with the family business?" The three men all wondered about the source of Kate's quality Intel.

"Yeah. I took my father's advice and relocated to New York. He said a change would be good, and he needed somebody to run the new warehouse out here."

"That's super news," Tommy muttered. He didn't like the way Patrick said the word father. It was so cold and clinical. There was no reason for him to not say dad instead. "Just fantastic."

"What's the business?" Jesse asked.

"Titanic Utilities. We manufacture and distribute the latest in self-cleaning toilet seat technology."

"Titanic?" Tommy mused. "That sounds like you're producing toilet seats for giants. Or people with really big asses."

"Actually, we do make over-sized seats too."

"Who knew there could be a career in toilet seats?" Kate wondered.

"They're mostly for bulk orders. You know, for airports or restaurants or shopping malls. I'll be working out of an office in Midtown and running our warehouse in New Jersey."

"Good for you." Kate didn't want to sound like she was patting a child on the back for finishing third place in the science fair, but that was how her words came out. Patrick knew the life he was living was not the life he imagined when he first came to New York City a decade before, but he knew whatever he was doing now, he was doing for his son.

Sheldon excused himself to use the bathroom again. Tommy meanwhile, started to wonder if the boy suffered from Irritable Bowel Syndrome as well. Or maybe he had the world's youngest cocaine addiction. No kid should be disappearing into the bathroom so often.

The waitress came with Tommy's usual: two soft poached eggs, extra crispy bacon, and sourdough toast. He doused the eggs with pepper, and began slopping them up before realizing the yolks were hard. "This is bullshit," he said, pushing the plate away into his coffee cup, spilling some on the table. A week ago, his life was perfect. And now it was all he could do to stop himself from screaming. He wished his lungs were the size of Madison Square Garden so he could scream even louder.

"Listen, Tom," Patrick started. "I'll admit what I'm going through right now is not easy for me. I've seen my share of bad news. I'm sure Jesse and Kate have too. But awful things will happen to everyone eventually. Everybody falls at some point."

"Not me," Tommy said, hoping again for a shadow to appear outside.

"When Natasha was diagnosed, I was in such a horrible place. But she seemed to be at peace almost right away. I don't know how she did it. And when she died, her father told me about what he called *The Falling*. I think it was some Ukrainian wisdom. He told me everybody falls eventually, and the best thing we can do is be prepared to know how to get back up again."

Kate considered her marriage and her novel just as Jesse thought about Edith and the talk he'd had with Sharona the week before.

But Tommy did not think about the past. He did not stop to consider any of his own mistakes. "Don't worry about *me*," he tried to reassure them all. "I've got a great girlfriend and a new book coming out. I'll be just fine."

"But Rachel's gone, Tommy," Kate reminded him.

"She'll be back. I'm not worried about it."

With his coat still on, Patrick stood up and removed some money from his wallet. Jesse got up from his seat and slipped his own coat on. "Come on, Patrick. I've got some time before work to come with you and look at that apartment." Tommy remained motionless, arms crossed in front of him.

"You can come too if you want, Tom," Patrick offered. "It wouldn't bother me."

Tommy glared him. Patrick was not the same person Tommy used to know. Leaving New York had changed him completely. So maybe that was enough reason to give the man a chance, to let him back into his life again. The past had passed.

"It wouldn't bother me at all," Patrick reiterated. He dropped some bills onto the table for the two glasses of juice.

"Sorry," Tommy said begrudgingly. "I've got a meeting with my agent today. I might even play some tennis too if I feel like blowing off some steam."

Kate reached over for her coat too, and kissed Tommy on the cheek. "Things really aren't so bad, Tommy." She buttoned up just as Sheldon came back from the bathroom. The four of them were all lined up and ready to go. Kate added, "And it could always be worse, you know?"

They said their goodbyes. Jesse even threw his arm around Patrick as they exited the restaurant together. From the window, Tommy glared at them all as they walked down Broadway. His three oldest friends and the strange little superhero. The season's first snowflake fell from the sky and stuck to the window. It only took a moment for it to melt, but even as it did, Tommy was already on his way out the door himself.

CHAPTER TWELVE
Midtown Comics

Let me tell you a bit more about Jesse Classen. One day into the job at Midtown Comics, he had already felt as though he belonged there. One week into the job, Jesse had begun to worry about having made another mistake; it seemed to be how his brain was wired. Five years in now, and Jesse Classen was reconsidering every move he'd ever made up until that point in his life. Worst of all, he was now unsure about his reasons for ever having come to New York in the first place.

The only day of the week Jesse could ever feel like he still loved his job was Wednesday: the day new comics arrived. He was looking forward to reading through the latest issue of "Captain America"; the day had been circled on his calendar for a couple of months now, since it signaled the end of a gripping storyline which would see Steve Rogers' last-ditch attempt to escape from the Nazi-infested ruins of Castle Zemo. It also marked the end of a landmark run of issues from the same writer/artist creative team, so something big was sure to happen. The fan boards had mostly been clamoring for the demise of Cap's sidekick, Nomad, but Jesse had suspicions it was Sharon Carter whose ticket might be getting punched.

But certain events never happen as planned, especially when certain days are simply destined for misfortune.

As it turned out, due to a shipping error, there were no comics on that particular Wednesday. Jesse had been on the phone with his distributor for seventeen minutes, enough time for his neck to strain from holding the receiver with his shoulder. Seventeen minutes was also more than enough time that, if he chose to, he could have simply walked over to the Marvel Comics studios on Fifth Avenue and read the book there instead. The phone call was going nowhere. It was one of those conversations in which neither party had any interest in being the one to finalize the squabble, but fortunately neither had to.

Stampeding into the back office, Pond hammered his meaty fist on the door frame as though his unwieldy entrance had any chance in the world of going unnoticed. "Yo, Jess! There's somebody here to see you." Pond's headphones clasped his neck like a wall-mounted spring grip holding a mop. His music was only slightly louder than his shouting.

Waving Pond away, Jesse ended his phone conversation without either a solution or a compromise. He already knew how quickly he would tire today of telling every customer: "Sorry, but the books won't be in until tomorrow." It was hard not to sound irritated when giving the same disappointing answer to the same exact question to every person in the store; like repeating oneself to incessant children who were all suffering severe, short-term memory loss. What Jesse really needed to do, he thought, was craft a sign displaying the same information, one he could simply point to, rather than having to open his mouth at all.

But all the signs in the world would not have helped Jesse when he approached the gentleman who had been asking for him. It was John Galloway. He was flipping through a third edition trade paperback of "The Man Without Fear," still dressed impeccably; far too erudite for the Midtown Comics rabble. It had been four years since the man had been there. Four years since he'd personally handed Jesse the key to his own ruination in the form of a crisp business card.

Jesse moved cautiously like a Stanley Kubrick ape at the Dawn of Man; John Galloway seemed no less perplexing than the legendary black monolith. Through the glass display case — behind the Ultron-13 maquette — Jesse watched the man's old hands holding the book: his craggily, contorted fingers turned the pages slowly, gradually. Not at all like the voracious hands of the shop's regular mass of loiterers.

"Are you the manager?" John asked before Jesse could fully ready himself. He extended his right hand, looking for the same in return.

"I'm the assistant manager," Jesse answered straight away. "Still just the assistant manager."

"Still?" John withdrew his hand, returning it to again brace the spine of the book he held.

Jesse nodded his head guardedly. "Listen," he spoke quietly enough so as not to cause any commotion. "I don't want any trouble."

John's brow furrowed. He looked to his left, and he glanced behind himself as though the young man might have been speaking to someone else. "I'm sorry?"

"Would you like to speak in the back office? I'd prefer to not make a scene."

John chuckled, "You don't even know what I'm here for, my boy." He was about to return the book back to the shelf from where he'd taken it, but he couldn't help noticing the number of identical copies on display. "Tell me, how many of these reprinted editions are produced?"

"That one is the third edition."

"Wouldn't all of these newer ones lower the value of the originals?"

"Not really. Trade paperbacks are only produced so often because the originals are so hard to come by for the casual reader."

"But if I can read *this* book, why would I need to spend more for the same thing?"

"It's called *collecting*." Jesse couldn't help himself from being short with the man. "Sometimes you can't put a price on collecting what you love. Just ask any pannapictagraphist."

"Excuse me? I don't think I'm familiar with that term."

"Comic book collectors are also called pannapictagraphists."

"I see." John placed the book back. He removed his hat and said, "If you don't mind, I think I *would* prefer to speak in the back office."

~~~

Earlier that morning, Jesse had accompanied Patrick to Brooklyn. His footsteps felt lighter, his stance not quite as sunken as I'd known. He was ecstatic to see his friend again after so long, especially after a week of worrying whether he was alive or not. He had been too afraid to call home for the answer. Jesse, Patrick and Sheldon took a tour of the modest, two-bedroom apartment on India Street which was being sold for a not-so-modest price. Still, it was supposed to be one of the up-and-coming neighborhoods, and there was also a school nearby. Jesse's wish was for Patrick to return to Morningside Heights so all of them could be closer. But Patrick was ready to make an offer on the apartment just when Jesse had to leave for work. He took the subway back to Manhattan before disembarking from the 7-Train at the 42nd Street Station.

As Jesse ascended the station's steps from underground to street level, his hands once again found John Galloway's business card buried deep within his pocket. Instantly, he considered Sharona's words from the week before, and how he'd later found himself lying in the mud of Morningside Park, promising to find a way to forgive John. It was the only way he was going to move on, he told himself. In fact, Patrick Kohn's reappearance that very morning served as a wakeup call to remind him the past was only a fleeting, incorporeal concept at times, and that anything was possible. So, he called Midtown Comics, and told Pond he would be coming in late.

Like déjà vu, Jesse found his way back to the Galloway home in Gramercy, only this time it was with the full intention of confronting John, rather than hoping to avoid the man while fooling around with his wife. With his old
~~~

familiar heavy feet, Jesse climbed the front steps before finally planting himself upon the doormat. "The Galloways," it still read, like a cruel joke. He tried to peer in through the window. The curtains were shut tight, probably as they had been since the first day John returned home alone, but Jesse could not see anything worth noting. Like a wolf at the door, Jesse was hungry. He found the courage to ring the doorbell. *RING DING DONG.* The chime from inside was a sound he did not recognize, and Jesse silently acknowledged he may not have ever heard the doorbell before. The Galloway home was not a popular destination for casual guests, socialite parties, or even trick-or-treaters. Perhaps their mail had been sent directly to John's office as well, for no postman had ever found his way up those steps either.

Jesse waited for another two minutes, but there was no answer. The stone steps cringed once more under his weight. He felt the fear well up inside his throat, but he choked it back like a snake swallowing a rat. Jesse Classen knew himself well enough to know it would be some time before he might find himself back at that door, before he could possibly ever find the strength to attempt forgiveness. I know it was within that moment when Jesse also understood Tommy's feelings toward Patrick, and of his refusal to move on. Maybe the past is not so fleeting at times; the damage the past can inflict might not be so momentary. Perhaps, Jesse considered, forgiveness is something meant only for the future.

<center>~~~</center>

The back office at Midtown Comics was not so much an office as an extra room to store the piles of merchandise the staff had not yet dealt with. The rest of it was something of a comic book museum, with full-size replicas of Iron Man's invincible armor, Cap's mighty shield, Batman's utility belt and cowl, and the hammer of Thor; all proudly on display in glass cases occupying the four corners. The stacks of comics and dog-eared trade paperbacks were there for "quality control," as Jesse liked to put it. Beneath the mass of toys, posters, statues, boxed collectibles, and a chugging computer, sat one desk with two chairs, either of which could probably be considered medieval torture devices for their significant lack of lumbar support. Jesse rarely sat in them though, choosing the ratty couch as his preferred spot for doing business. The corduroy sofa was long enough for three people, though one spot was reserved for the life-sized stuffed Spider-Man doll.

Jesse seated himself at the desk in a lackluster effort to pretend he held some sort of power. John produced a business card from his breast pocket and laid it in front of him. He immediately sat on the dusty couch, not intimidated at all by the wall-crawler next to him.

Flipping the business card from front to back to front again, Jesse inspected it for some kind of clue. "What's *this* for?"

"It's a business card," John mocked. "It's for doing business."

"What kind of business are you suggesting here, John?"

"I've got a rather sizable collection of comic books I'm looking to sell."

So many questions surged through Jesse's head, but he kept his mouth shut, allowing the man to continue.

"My father bought most of them for me when I was little. Too little to understand the value of keeping them in decent shape, mind you. But I'm certain they must still be worth something to a collector."

It would have been safe to say Jesse had no idea what was transpiring at that moment. Was John Galloway's folksy manner his way of attempting to bury the proverbial hatchet, or had he forgotten all about the exact same conversation now four years removed? The business card was the same as the one from before, the one Jesse had found in his pocket only one week prior. It was still two inches by three-and-a-half in size. It still had the same phone number. It still smelled of Lucky Strike cigarettes and also of that extraordinary home in Gramercy Park.

John continued. "I realize that, technically speaking, it may not be a *collection*, since it's mostly just a random assortment of books in varying condition. But you're free to come and have a look at them."

One week ago, Jesse Classen had been lying in the mud of Morningside Park when he rediscovered John Galloway's business card. It was the same night he had decided he would find forgiveness from the man whose life he destroyed. That wasn't even an exaggeration, Jesse remembered thinking. He had swooped into John's life and tarnished everything the man loved. But when he had finally gathered the courage it took to approach the Galloway home that morning, John did not answer the door. Jesse felt he had reason to be suspicious.

The man's old gray eyes scanned a few of the items on the desk. The sculptures collecting dust. These were not the same as the heroic paraphernalia which occupied the corners of the room within glass cases; these were objects of enormous power, tools of villainous desire from the scattered dimensions of comic book netherworlds. The Cosmic Cube. The Infinity Gauntlet. The Serpent Crown. The Satan Claw. The Evil Eye of Avalon. John Galloway must have been drawn to them instantly.

"You can come by any time," the man offered.

Jesse knew the first sign of a good super villain is no sign at all. A truly prolific arch-villain is one who will bide his time, one who carefully plans his next move. His greatest move ever. The diabolical plot that will finally rid the world of the hero he's come to loathe above all else. For that is his only purpose; the only reason for having to share the same dirt of the world. Jesse knew all of this of course, so there was no possible way he could have the wool pulled over his eyes.

"I think I know someone who might be able to help you," Jesse finally answered, rising from his seat. "I'll be sure to pass your information along."

"Wonderful," John spoke smoothly. He too rose from his seat, and Spider-

Man's head flopped backwards as the weight was released from the couch.

Breathe out.

The two men still did not manage a proper handshake, and John continued out of the office without one. He turned to Jesse before parting and said, "I'm sorry, but I just realized you haven't yet introduced yourself."

The only answer Jesse had for him was: "I know."

John Galloway scratched his head, and exited Midtown Comics for the second time in four years. Jesse watched him from the window, wondering what to do next. The tip of the Chrysler Building seemed to be swaying more than it should have been. Jesse did not think it should have been swaying at all, but perhaps he'd simply never noticed before.

CHAPTER THIRTEEN
Pendulum Publishing – Midtown

"Kate? Kate, are you alright?"

The *WE ARE HAPPY TO SERVE YOU* slogan on the paper coffee cup stole Kate's attention away from where it should have been. She was sitting in the middle of a one-on-one meeting she had initiated with Troy "The Shark" Dunlop, but she couldn't shake the irony of the message her coffee cup was delivering.

"Kate?" Troy asked again. "Are you listening to me?"

She thought to herself: "*No. I am most certainly NOT happy to serve you.*"

"Sorry, Troy," she responded, snapping back into her cruel reality. "I zoned out there for a moment."

"Holy shit. You fucking freaked me out!" In high school, Troy Dunlop was nothing more than a pot-smoking meathead, and at times, his linguistic skills still reflected his previous life. "Remember what happened to Jackson Horvath last year? When he spaced out in that meeting and then he tried to run through the window? Fuck. I thought the same thing was going to happen."

"I'm not planning on throwing myself out a window, Troy. This is in no way a suicide meeting." Anyone else in the office would definitely not have believed her today, based on Kate's choice of skeleton leggings and a dark, flannel pajama top. She'd wrapped a strand of pearls around her neck but had not made an effort to do anything with her hair before coming in to work with plans on quitting. "Besides, even if I *was* going to kill myself, there's probably a *gazillion* other places I'd rather do it than *here*."

"Shit. That's good." Troy rubbed the back of his neck with his hand, but it was only as a means to flexing his bicep. His barbed wire tattoo was clearly visible, and he knocked back yet another half-liter of energy drink in one gulp.

Kate straightened herself out on the cold plastic chair. "I just think I need to do this for myself. I've accepted failure for too long now."

Troy explained, "The thing is, I can't let you just quit without some notice. Two weeks is the norm." The Randy Couture bobble head on his desk bounced a little in complete agreement.

"What about a leave of absence?"

"Do you know how much paperwork a leave of absence requires?"

"This is my *life*, Troy. You don't want me sitting over there being miserable, do you? Doesn't that ridiculous sign on your door say some crap about motivating your employees?"

"That's right. *Consumer/Media Relations and Employee Motivations.*"

Kate rolled her eyes. "Nobody here even knows what that means."

"Well, it's a complicated job. The thing is though, we really need to follow proper procedures and protocol here, Kate."

"Protocol? Talking to *you* is protocol, isn't it? Believe me, I'd much rather speak directly to some other jackass who can actually make a difference around here, but protocol tells me I have to go through The Shark first, no matter how futile an idea that is."

Troy finished the last drop before crushing the can in his hand. His attention had diverted to other matters, matters of far, far less importance. "Hey, have you ever taken something from somebody's desk and hid it somewhere in the office?"

"I'm sorry?" For a moment, Kate worried Troy Dunlop might know something about Dwayne Reamer's missing yogurts. "Are you accusing me of stealing?"

"No, I just mean hyperthetically."

The abuse of language did not go unnoticed by Kate. Did this guy just say hyperthetically? Seriously, how did he ever get a job in publishing? "Why would I want to hide anything?" she asked.

"Just to fuck with them. How many floors do we have here at Pendulum?"

"Five."

"Think about it. There must be what, at least two hundred cubicles here. Dozens of offices." Troy began counting on his right hand, starting with his thumb first. "Lunchrooms. Supply rooms. Meeting rooms. Bathrooms. Closets. You name it. There's so many places they'd have to look." He returned his fingers back into the palm of his hand, but left a thumb's up just for the hell of it. "I think it'd be fun."

"Are you drunk? I'm not here to have fun, Troy. This is an office building, and it's full of a bunch of no-personality deadbeats."

"Hey, I'm just trying to lighten up the 'sitch here, Kate." Like a Starfleet Commander, Troy whirled his over-sized leather power chair around to face the window and the view of West 39th Street it offered. On a late night, he could look straight into the building across from him and see the Korean cleaning ladies. Troy Dunlop had been urging Pendulum to hire the "Clean & Happy" cleaning service instead of the one with all of the old Portuguese guys they currently used. But at nine-thirty in the morning, all Troy could see from his office was the glare from the rising sun, a window washer, and some pigeons. "It's important to keep things light around here." Then he wondered if window washers ever got a free show from horny businesswomen. *Man, that would be awesome!*

With Troy's back turned, Kate took his advice and swiped the Randy Couture bobble head from his desk, tucking it into her bag. "I'm leaving Pendulum Publishing, Troy," she said. "It's important to me."

The Shark swung back around to face her. He seemed to notice something was amiss or out of place, but he'd had the bobble head on his desk for so long, he couldn't tell for sure what it might have been. The longer we see something, the less we notice it. "What could I do to stop you, Kate?"

"At this point, there's really no way you could convince me to stay, Troy. I just need to separate myself from all of this."

"No, I meant physically. Like, could I jump over this desk and put a submission hold on you? Or maybe something like a Python Kick."

"Python's don't kick, you idiot."

"No. I know. That's just the name of my move."

Kate crinkled her face. "Seriously. Are you drunk?"

"I'm mostly just shitting you here. The thing is, if you really *did* quit your job right now, it would just be an ass-load of paperwork for me. And a shit-load of interviews I'd have to set up in order to replace you."

Kate didn't know whether an ass-load was more than a shit-load or if they were even comparable at all. "Honestly, I don't know who put you in charge of anything, but I don't really give a crap either. Like it or not, this is your job, Troy. Deal with it." She rose from her seat, but realized she had one last favor to ask The Shark: "And could you please not stare at my ass on my way out?"

<div style="text-align:center">~~~</div>

Kate was cleaning up every trace of her existence at Pendulum, collecting everything that was a part of her into one single, legal-sized cardboard box. She took her last box of Frankenberry cereal from the top shelf in the Nineteenth-Floor kitchen. She pulled packets of Nicorette from her desk drawers. She crammed in as many sticky notes and red correction pens as she could, all stolen from the supply closet. She was pulling some comic books from her desk just as the squeaky wheels of the Temp's mail cart made Dwayne Reamer's presence known.

"What have you got there?" Dwayne inquired, pinching one of the books from her hand.

"It's nothing, Dwayne." Kate tried grabbing it back, but Dwayne deftly moved out of the way.

He flipped through a few pages and began reading some of the dialogue. "*'I don't know why you and your computerized comrades invaded my city. I can't imagine your reasons for causing such wholesale destruction! But I've had enough! ENOUGH!'*" Dwayne yelled the words across the office. "Wow. Spider-Man just ripped that robot's head in half! That's impressive."

"Give it back, prick!" She finally snatched it back.

"I didn't know you collected comic books, Kate. Is that a rare one?"

"You could say that." Kate turned the book over to an advertisement on the back cover. It was an ad for the GAP, and even through the baggy flannel shirt and denim overalls, the model was suspiciously familiar.

"Holy shit! Is that *YOU*?"

"It is."

"But—how? Why?"

"When I first came to New York, to help make ends meet, I did some modeling. And this GAP ad was the height of my career, if you want to call it that. It appeared for three straight months, pretty much exclusively on the backs of comic books."

"You were probably every thirteen-year-old nerd's wet dream in 1996."

"Yeah. Just me and Heather Locklear. I also starred on the packaging for a medical eye patch manufacturer."

"That is *unparalleled*. I don't think Heather Locklear ever did eye patches."

Kate continued to pile the remnants of her past into the box. From two cubicles away, they could hear Teresa on the phone with her veterinarian. From the sounds of it, Andrew the cat had taken a turn for the worse. Yes. Andrew. The cat.

"Why are you packing up all your stuff anyway, Kate? Are you tossing it?"

Dwayne couldn't help but notice Kate's abysmal wardrobe selection. "And why are you dressed like you live in downtown Beirut?"

"I'm leaving, Dwayne. I've quit Pendulum."

"*What*? You can't be serious?"

"I am."

"Did you find another job?"

"No. I quit so I can work on my novel."

"Paper Fences? Nice!"

"Actually, I've quit that too. I started a new book. Nothing but changes for this girl! I wrote another two chapters just last night."

"What's it called?"

"I've decided this time around it would be good for me to not get so wrapped up in titles."

For the record, this was quite possibly the first time in his life Dwayne Reamer was ever, truly, utterly speechless. He was already beginning to imagine how boring his job would be without Kate around.

"You'll be fine, Dwayne," Kate reassured him. "Really. This place will be much better without me dragging it down."

In the three minutes Dwayne had spent with Kate that morning, he could already tell she was different from the person she was the day before. "So, if it's nothing but changes, I take it you had that talk with your husband?"

And just like she assumed avoiding Gene was the smartest solution to her problems, Kate decided ignoring Dwayne's question was also the best move she could make. Without a word, she continued to pack her personal items into the box.

"I'm guessing that's a NO." Dwayne reached back into the box and began flipping through the Spider-Man book again.

"Listen, Dwayne. I've already gotten into *four* arguments this morning and it's only ten o'clock." Dwayne didn't ask, or even lift his head up from the comic book, but Kate continued with the details anyway. "I told Clint Baxter — the guy who's always playing online Scrabble with his wife? — that she's probably using a word generator since she always seems to beat him. I actually told Teresa she might be better off letting Andrew the cat die. Somebody had to! I told Dieter I'm sick and tired of repeating myself, even to a deaf guy, and that he should think about investing in a better hearing aid. I actually emailed him a Google search of quality hearing aid products. And I just came out of an agonizingly inane meeting with The Shark, so I really don't want to have to argue with you too."

"I just think you should talk to your husband. That's all I'm saying, Kate."

Kate wanted to say something to Dwayne about the return of Patrick Kohn. Of course, she had never mentioned Patrick to him before; she'd never talked about him with anyone at all. But ever since she exited the coffee shop with Patrick that morning, Kate was uncertain what she should be feeling. Most importantly, Kate was afraid of rediscovering feelings for him. She wondered why it was that she could be so ready to accept failure in one part of her life but not in another.

"All I'm going to do is work on my novel, Dwayne. That's my *only* plan right now. I'll deal with Gene when the time is right."

"That's really not being fair to him though, right?"

"I don't want to talk about it, Dwayne."

"If not now, when? Come on, Kate. There's so much about the guy that drives you crazy. Like, what about the picture frames and the mustache?"

"Yeah, yeah. And the toenails and the nurse fetish."

"Toenails and nurses? Tell me more!"

"I mean, is it weird that he likes me to dress up as a nurse?"

"I believe *all* men have the nurse fantasy, Katherine."

"No, I mean a *real* nurse. Like in hospital scrubs."

"Err, that's not normal."

"I didn't think so."

"See? You need to talk about this with somebody. What will you do without *me* around?"

"I've got friends, Dwayne. Real ones. Not just temporary ones."

"Ouch. Is that all I am to you?"

"That's all it ever has been, Dwayne. What made you think otherwise?"

"I guess I don't have a reasonable answer for that." He dropped his head back down into the pages of the comic book. "You know, you never did respond to my email from last week."

"Yeah, about that. You and me? That's not a good idea. I'm not entirely sure what it is I need right now, but I know that much is true."

Dwayne stared at one of the pages for a moment before reading another line out loud, albeit, a little quieter this time: "*I know the very idea of a guardian angel seems pretty ridiculous in today's jaded world, but there's great comfort in knowing that someone is watching over you, someone who really cares!*"

Teresa's sobbing became noticeably louder, enough to shake Dwayne out of the book. "Seriously," he whispered. "Who names their cat Andrew?"

Digging into her bag, Kate pulled out the bobble head and held it out for Dwayne. "What's that you've got there?" he asked, even though he recognized it immediately. He dropped mail off for Troy every morning.

"The Shark's doll. I want you to hide it somewhere."

"Hide it? Why?"

"It'll be good for a laugh. Trust me."

"You're on, Huron!" Dwayne tossed the comic book back into the box, and he took the bobble head into his hand. "You just might be my guardian angel, you know that?" Kate didn't flinch as he kissed her gently on the cheek. "Keep in touch, my temporary friend."

CHAPTER FOURTEEN
The Mercury Agency – Midtown

Juliana Florentine could have been a model; she was gorgeous. Men became tongue-tied and couldn't walk straight around her, and she knew it. Her corn-colored hair was as straight as the Nebraska wheat fields where she grew up. Her flawless skin lacked even a freckle and her lips could have doubled the sales of any cosmetic product. But Juliana didn't want to sell lipstick; she loved books more than anything else she'd ever known. She left the family farm to come to New York City, where she would eventually find work as a literary agent. From a midtown tower that stood straighter than even the wheat from her youth, Juliana had a 33rd-floor view of the fields of Manhattan. She would watch the sunrise every morning from her window, creeping up from behind Brooklyn and over the East River; the sun turning the Queensboro Bridge into nothing more than a thin jumble of matchsticks.

When Tommy finished his final draft for "Blanc," he queried every agent in the city. His literary professor at Hunter College suggested the Mercury Agency, and Juliana Florentine specifically. She was an up-and-coming agent, not yet jaded by the industry, and she'd be eager to find the right fit for Thomas Mueller's debut novel. After reading the manuscript, Juliana was excited about the book's potential and she asked Tommy to come see her. Tommy couldn't concentrate in that first meeting, and it wasn't because of the extraordinary opportunity he had within his grasp. No, it was because a button on Juliana's shirt was undone, and he had to continually stop himself from glancing toward the lacy pink bra underneath. It was wholly distracting, and Tommy was happy when the meeting went about as quickly as a meeting of its nature could possibly go.

Tommy still had high hopes he might see the pink bra again, but it had been almost ten years now without a second sighting.

Tommy's latest work was supposed to go to the printers in a couple of days, but Juliana asked him to come in for another meeting first. As soon as he sat down across from her, Tommy knew it was there. Then he saw it peeking through her shirt: the pink bra had returned. And its reappearance was sure to herald the greatest of things.

The manuscript for "The Manhattanite" was sitting on her desktop. Juliana chose her words carefully, tapping her pen up and down between her teeth. "I don't know what to tell you, Tommy."

"That is a pretty terrible way to begin a meeting you scheduled yourself."

"Okay. The situation is this: our publisher is suddenly having second thoughts about the book."

"Are you shitting me?"

"Certainly not. I've convinced them to go ahead with it, but I wanted you to be aware of the position we're in here."

"Come on, Juliana. You know I'm trying to do something important with this book. You liked it, right?"

Juliana thought about it. Her pen found its way between her teeth once again. "I *read* it."

"That doesn't answer my question," Tommy muttered. "Actually, I guess it does." He slumped back in the chair as far as he could without falling out.

"I know we have a book deal with you, Tommy. That's why I was hesitant to say anything after I read it, but now our publisher is seriously afraid they're going to lose money on it."

"So what? Haven't they made enough off of me so far?"

"It's never enough, Tommy. You know how it works."

"What didn't you like about it?"

She flipped through the dog-eared manuscript, thinking carefully about the scope of the story. "You've got a guy who meets a girl. That's about it. Nothing really *happens* in the book. Nothing at all." There were red circles and underlines and giant X's all over it. Tommy noticed one page was even torn in half; whatever the reason was, he had no idea.

"What do you mean, *nothing happens*? They're in *love*. Love happens!"

"What about *change* though? Adversity? Misfortune? What about loss and heartache? Isn't that what we've come to expect from great novels?"

"But I don't want anything more to happen to them. They're happy the way they are. It more a love letter from me to this great city."

"That's part of the problem too. Your main character? You tell the reader repeatedly that he loves New York as much as he loves his girlfriend. How is that possible, really? They're two completely different things."

"I don't see why they can't be mutually exclusive."

"It just seems a little preposterous to me. And more than a little pretentious."

"Pretentious?" Tommy couldn't help the feelings he had, and he was certainly not going to apologize for them. All he ever did was love his city. He loved how Manhattan could make him feel so small. It was a strange feeling, to appreciate being so small, maybe bordering on insignificant. But the city ruled Tommy, it owned him, and he didn't want it to be the other way around.

Tommy forgot all about the bra. "I like it the way it is." He stared out the window toward the stream of headlights on the Queensboro. Manhattan always seemed to be letting more bodies in than the number it was sending back out. How many of them were coming into the city with fresh novels of their own?

"Tommy?" Juliana was used to losing Tommy to her window. She knew how much power the view had over him. But there was more to writing about Manhattan than simply writing of it.

Tommy took the printed manuscript into his hands. He flipped through the pages, absorbing every word he'd written, taking it all in as though he was the world's fastest speed-reader. He recalled writing the original version. "The Manhattanite" was the first book Tommy had written by hand on paper. The scratching of lead and the scent of sharpened pencil helped him create a distinctive new voice. He began writing it within a tiny Harlem café. He remembered how it really didn't start coming together until the day he met Rachel Ponzini. As soon as the final draft was done, as soon as THE END was written, Tommy plugged all of the words into his computer and printed out the manuscript for Juliana. His soul had never felt so good; like it was exactly in the place it was meant to be.

"I was trying to write a real novel here. This was meant to be where my career really started, you know? It's obvious they just don't get it."

"And me?" Juliana asked.

"I guess you don't get it either. I put my *heart* into this book." The funny thing was Tommy didn't realize until after Rachel left him that he'd written so deeply about love. Like he never had before. He tossed the manuscript back over to Juliana. What he really wanted to do was to toss it in the garbage. He stood up, indicating the meeting would be coming to an end under his terms.

"I just think you'd better start working on your next book. And I think your *next* book should be more like your *first* book." She clenched the manuscript in her hand to help emphasize her words. "To ensure *this* book is not your *last* book. You've got an audience to think about here, Tommy."

"What am I supposed to do? Spend my life writing about murders and conspiracy theories and mistaken identities? When can I stop appeasing the masses and start pleasing myself?"

"It's *all about* the masses, Tommy." Juliana gestured at the window, out toward nowhere in particular. "They control all of this. Not you. If they want vampires, we give them vampires. If they want harlequin romance, we've got a million authors just waiting to churn another one out. If they want Kaspar Delancey to come back from the dead, then he'll have to eventually." She held the manuscript back out for Tommy. "Do you want to take this with you?"

~~~

As soon as Tommy walked out onto the East 53rd Street sidewalk he dumped the manuscript into the nearest garbage can. Maybe some lucky bum could find a tiny bit of enjoyment from it. Maybe use it for toilet paper.

He walked only a few steps more before stopping suddenly. Through the fluid wall of yellow cab traffic, Tommy spotted Patrick. He was outside the Duane Reade, talking to someone Tommy didn't recognize. Tommy froze, unsure what to make of such a surreptitious meeting on this crowded corner of Manhattan. Tommy hid behind an oversized, concrete planter in an attempt to go unnoticed. He looked closer. It was definitely Patrick Kohn. But this other man; who was he? Tommy assumed the only possible role the man could play would be as a real estate agent, but he certainly did not appear so. He was overweight and had long, greasy hair. He was eating a hoagie, the kind of sandwich one might find in the back of a 7-11. Sauce dribbled down the side of his face and he wiped it off with his hand only to relocate it to his dirty sweatpants.

Before any further evidence could be gathered, a delivery truck stopped for a red light, obstructing Tommy's view. He scuttled down the sidewalk far enough to see past the vehicle, but Patrick and the other man had already begun walking away, heading west along 53rd Street. Tommy had no desire to wait for the next pedestrian light, so he slipped through the oncoming traffic instead. Three or four horns bleeped at him, but he didn't care. He followed the two men at a safe distance for another block, before they turned again onto Lexington.

Tommy ran into the blitzkrieg of late afternoon foot traffic. Men and
~~~

women in power suits saturated the sidewalks; six-dollar coffees in one hand and electronic gadgets in the other, all of them working their meetings around tee times and pedicures. Tommy tried to see above them all, but was only met with Midtown's furious lunchtime cacophony. The clinking of café dishes over soft jazz. The futile honking of gridlocked traffic. The constant growl of engines. Rolling suitcases trailing behind fresh-faced tourists. Pigeons cooing. A child laughing. Another screaming. Every kind of heel click-clacking across concrete sidewalks, iron basement hatches, wooden planks, and crumpled newsprint. A truck backing up. Squeaky messenger bikes and motorcycles whizzing, making up their own traffic pattern rules. Even in the distance, the seagulls could be heard, yelping like wild dogs.

Tommy lost sight of the two men.

There was a subway station on the corner, and after a moment's consideration, he decided his best chance would be to take a closer look. He loved that smell every time he went underground. As diverse and ever-changing as the city's scents were, its subway system somehow maintained the same aroma at every station. He swiped his Metrocard and darted from one end of the station to the other. His heartbeat reverberated off the wet tunnel walls. Astoundingly, there were not many people waiting for the train, so it was easy enough for Tommy to scan each and every body. But there was no sign of either Patrick or the oddly mysterious man anywhere.

He'd definitely lost them.

He sunk a little further down into the island. Tommy was dumbfounded how anyone, especially Patrick Kohn, could lose him in his own city. It simply was not possible. He had to be somewhere, amidst the city's steam and sewage and cables and wires and concrete and glass and parks and puddles. Once again, Manhattan had forced Tommy to recognize just how small and powerless he really was. Only this time, he realized he did not relish it quite so much.

And the city breathes in.

PART III

~~~

THE REVENGE
~~~

CHAPTER FIFTEEN

Tom's Restaurant – Morningside Heights

ONE WEEK LATER.

When winter hits Manhattan, its attack is unrelenting. What begins as a cleansing snowfall blanketing even the ugliest streets with a white serenity, soon turns into a chaotic slop of wet, gray grunge and grit. The snow continues its pursuit of tranquility however, but it will never stand a chance, disintegrating into the grubby traps of tire treads and footprints. Like a new pet, winter is loved for its first few precious moments, but is quickly tired of by anyone but the most devoted, becoming an unwanted beast, requiring a constant audience to manage its disorder. Yet, even as the clouds pull themselves apart like torn denim, and as the glass and concrete towers take advantage of a moment's bleak respite by scraping the open sky once again, the city still braces itself for the next imminent wave.

Tommy no longer ventured down to the CKY Grocery. He popped in one day when the store had no Spartan apples at all. Believing the Persian man had a personal vendetta against him, Tommy brusquely discontinued his patronage. Now, he habitually grabbed a thirty-five-cent banana with the morning paper from a nameless Broadway newsstand. The bananas were always arranged upright, and Tommy could not help but make-believe they were tiny, yellow skyscrapers. And even though he carefully selected the firmest of the bunch, Tommy's chosen banana was still guaranteed to be brown by the time he reached the coffee shop.

Kicking the slush off his sneakers as he entered the coffee shop, Tommy realized his regular booth was currently three-quarters full with brash university students. He spotted a girl sitting alone at the counter, an aura about her. She had a guitar case and a backpack at her feet. Her hair was just long enough for the beginnings of a bleach-blonde mohawk. She had tattoos up and down her arms, words which seemed to act as warning signs for the unsure. One in particular, on her left forearm, stood out to Tommy: FALLING. Sharona had played at a Morningside Heights hotel club the night before, and she paid the manager fifty bucks to let her sleep on the stage for a couple of hours. Had she known that Jesse Classen lived only a few blocks away, she might have called him instead.

Tommy tossed his banana peel and its cocooned, mushy brown stump into the trash. He sat next to her. She was just planting the last syrupy bite of waffle in her mouth.

Tommy was justifiably mystified. "Waffles? When did they start serving waffles here?"

"I asked for them," she said simply, not even turning her head. Sharona had never been bothered by strangers making small talk. She was actually flattered by how often it happened.

"I can't remember the last time I got something I asked for," he said. Tommy shook the newspaper, loosening it up in the same manner his father would do. Intuitively, he always opened the New York Times to unveil the literary section, but today it opened to the obituaries instead. He flipped back and forth until he found the review for "The Manhattanite." He didn't know why, but Tommy wanted to read it out loud to this girl beside him. "The key to reading any review, whether it's for a movie, restaurant, or book, is to read nothing but the first and last sentences." He cleared his throat in preparation for the self-assured, ostentatious event. "*Imagine for a moment, that you are looking forward to reading Thomas Mueller's much-anticipated sixth novel, 'The Manhattanite'*"—"

Before he could finish, Sharona snatched the paper from his hands. As counseled, she read the second of the two most important sentences: "'*Now try to imagine yourself wishing Mueller had chosen instead to stop at five.*'" She dropped the paper and looked at Tommy, his mouth hanging open with incredulity. "You're right. That's one succinct review."

Without a fight, she released the paper back into Tommy's hand. He began to read the entirety of the review, finally spurting out, "I don't believe this horseshit! Who wrote this review anyway?" He double-checked the reviewer's name, but failed to recognize it.

"Why so concerned?"

"That's *my* book. I'm Tommy Mueller. And this asshole writes about me like I killed his parents or something."

"Do you know the difference between a critique and a criticism?"

Tommy ignored the girl's pondering completely. "The kid who wrote this review is probably some uneducated intern who thought 'On the Road' was brilliant."

"Who are you, Truman Capote? What's not to like about 'On the Road?'"

"I guess I never could appreciate the fact Sal ever left New York."

Sharona thought for a moment. She recalled the conversation she had with Jesse two weeks before: when he told her he was thinking of leaving New York but he was afraid of what his friend Tommy would think. "So the book tanked, Thomas. So what? It happens to all of us."

"People don't want different. They can't handle change. They want everything to stay exactly how it's always been. The same old comfortable crap packaged in the same familiar font as the last book."

"Are you saying your other books were crap?"

"Of course they were. But they were purely *intentional* crap. 'The Manhattanite' was supposed to showcase my real talents."

"You might have wanted to think about the title then."

Tommy said the name to himself. He didn't think there was anything wrong with the title.

"Well," she began again. "I don't know the first thing about agents or editors, but what did *yours* tell you?"

"She told me my readers wouldn't like it."

"Well, there you have it, my man." Sharona gulped down the last cold drop of her coffee. "You can't let it slow you down, though. I've had terrible reviews too, but I didn't let them get to me. I still had something worth saying. Don't you?"

"I thought I did. That's why I wrote this book." Talking to this girl made Tommy think about Rachel. He missed having conversations like this with girls like Rachel.

"So, write another one then. You've done it before."

The two of them enjoyed one another's silence for a few minutes more. Tommy reached for a menu for probably the first time in ten years, and was a little surprised to see waffles right there at the top of the breakfast list. He asked the waitress for exactly that, but was told the kitchen stopped serving them at eleven. He was never in the habit of paying much attention to coffee shop waitresses, but Tommy was certain he did not recognize this one. He ended up ordering his usual, having to carefully explain exactly what his usual was. How could she understand? This middle-aged mom working this part-time job to save some money to put toward her kids' college funds.

"Everything's so different up here at the counter," he said to Sharona, and noticed the crowd that had been gathered at his favored booth was now dispersing. He gathered his still-wet coat and scarf into his big hands. "Do you want to move over there with me?"

"I don't think so," she said. From somewhere, Sharona pulled out a few bills and plopped them on the counter. "This girl has got to get moving. If I stay in one place too long, it's inevitable I'll start loving it too much."

"Is that a bad thing?"

"You tell me." Sharona slipped her coat on, covering up the tattoos. Disguising the details which defined her the most. Tommy could only stand and watch as she slung her bag over her shoulder. "Listen, Thomas," she began. Instantly, Tommy knew the following words would be the last ones she would say to him. The women he knew always used that same tone just before they left a room. "Manhattan is not for everyone, you know? And it is certainly *not* the center of the universe." She picked up the rest of her belongings. "Just make sure you treat your friends right, okay?"

Tommy was right: Sharona walked right out the door without another word.

~~~

Tommy read the review in the newspaper at least fifteen times over, trying to find something to make the negative parts more redeeming. It wasn't long before Kate and Jesse entered. Kate threw her bag on the seat next to Tommy, but sat across from him with Jesse.

"Why don't you ask Tommy?" Kate said to Jesse, continuing whatever conversation the two of them had been having before they entered the coffee shop.

"All right," Jesse started. "We just saw this dog eating some dog food out of a bowl, and I said to Kate that I always thought dog food looked pretty tasty."

Tommy was stumped. "Was that my question?"

"The question is: do you think dog food looks delicious?"

"Well, believe it or not, Jess, I've never eaten dog food before, so—"

"That's not what he's asking," Kate interjected. "It's not about whether you would *eat* it. Just, do you think it *looks* good?"

"Dry or wet?"

"Either."
~~~

"I'd have to say—sure. The dry stuff looks like cereal, and the wet stuff kind of looks like beef bourguignon."

"See?" Jesse said to Kate. "I told you."

"You're both crazy," she said, throwing her arms up in defeat.

Jesse's eyes lit up when he saw the newspaper spread out before him. "Hey, wasn't your review in there, Tommy?" He reached for it, but Tommy was quick to pull the paper back toward himself.

"No. I think the guy who was supposed to write it died before he could."

"What? Really? That's horrible!"

"Yeah. It's a fucking tragedy."

"Tragedy," Kate mimicked. Tommy could tell from her tone and from her one, single word she had already read the review. "Now that *definitely* sounds like a good word to use."

Tommy turned to the window, but Broadway was extraordinarily quiet that afternoon. He would curse at the falling snow outside but he didn't want his friends to think he'd completely lost it.

"You alright, Tommy?" Jesse asked. "You seem bothered."

Tommy should have known better than to assume his two best friends would not read him so easily. "I don't know how to say this, guys. But I think I'm falling."

"What?"

"Remember what Patrick told me? He said everybody falls at some point. And he said I was next."

"I don't think he said you were *next*, specifically," Jesse analyzed.

"Come on," Kate said. "You don't actually believe Patrick, do you?"

"The point I'm making is not whether I believe him or not. The point is that Rachel's gone, and, according to the New York Times, my novel clearly sucks."

Jesse needed clarification. "Wait, I thought the review guy died?"

Tommy ignored the question entirely. "Don't you see? All of this shit started happening as soon as Patrick came back."

"What shit?" Kate asked. "That's two little things, Tommy."

"Oh sure! Little to *you* maybe, but what about the guy it's happening to? How do you think *I* feel?"

"So, are you saying that Patrick Kohn came back to New York just to ruin your life?"

"Maybe. Or maybe he's just starting with me." Tommy leaned closer toward the two of them and lowered his voice as though the coffee shop was wired. "Maybe you guys are next. And perhaps Natasha's death was not quite as cancerous as we were led to believe?"

Kate and Jesse turned to one another. Tommy's ominous suggestion seemed a little too peculiar, and much too malevolent, even for him.

"I'm sure Patrick was only joking," Kate said. "Nobody's fortunes or misfortunes can be predicted as simply as that. Why don't you just ask him when he gets back?"

"Where has he been, anyway? I haven't seen the guy since the day he showed up." Tommy never did tell his friends about how he'd spotted Patrick with that strange man on the street the week before.

Jesse was already mixing some salt and pepper together on a napkin. "He said he had to go back to Seattle. Something about business."

Tommy questioned the story. "Doesn't that sound suspicious to you?"

"He operates a *business*, Tommy," Kate noted. "That sounds like a pretty reasonable excuse for not being here."

Tommy didn't like to think about the day ten years before when Patrick Kohn had seemingly vanished forever, but a part of him hoped the same thing might have happened again. It was strange how Patrick had resurfaced so suddenly; odd how he could stomp back into their world tossing around hints of things to come, only to disappear all over again. To Tommy, it felt as though things were back to normal with just the three of them in their coffee shop. He wanted everything to be the way it was, but everything good seemed to have a sour note to it now.

"And what about you, Kate?" he asked. "Where have you been lately?"

"Writing. Quitting that job was the best thing I could have done. I've gotten so wrapped up in it, and accomplished so much already."

Tommy was proud of Kate and the creative surge she was experiencing, but he knew her well enough to know she had not yet said a word to her husband about the subject of their marriage. Of course, he couldn't stop himself from asking anyway. "What about Gene? Have you spoken with him yet?"

"Just the mundane husband/wife stuff. He tells me the garbage stinks and I tell him to take it outside."

"Ah. Marital bliss!" Tommy exclaimed. "It's what we're all striving for, isn't it?"

The waitress finally came to refill Tommy's coffee. But she neglected to take his dirty plate away. He doubted whether the crusted remains of egg yolk could ever be washed off that plate. And before Kate or Jesse could order anything for themselves, she had already disappeared again.

"I think you need to say something to him," Jesse said to Kate. "It's eating *me* up inside and I'm not even *in* the relationship."

"Guys, listen. What I have with Gene—it's *comfortable*. I've decided to stick it out for now only because it's what's easiest for me."

Jesse couldn't believe it. "That's the *worst* reason, Kate. You've got to come up with something better than that." Jesse knew better than to suggest anything along the lines of divorcing her husband and getting back together with Patrick. Mentioning things once to Kate was one thing, but mentioning things repeatedly was a surefire way to make the woman do exactly the opposite.

Besides, Kate was already changing the subject. "How are things going with you and Mr. Magoo, Jess? Has he made any more appearances?"

"Not yet, no." From the corner of his eye, Jesse swore he saw Sharona out the window, hailing a cab from a snow bank on the other side of Broadway. Whoever the girl was, she was definitely carrying a guitar case, but she had jumped into the taxi before he could get a better look. Jesse had been so preoccupied the past week wondering what John Galloway must have been planning, he had yet to consider his own next move with the enigmatic Sharona. He certainly wasn't ready to go looking for her promised poster on the streetlight quite yet. "I stopped by his place again, but there was still no answer."

"For an old dude, he sure gets out a lot," Kate mused.

"Either that or he's dead," Tommy suggested.

"I think he's just biding his time. He's planning something." Jesse couldn't help it: he enjoyed believing his relationship with John Galloway was one based entirely on fictional heroes and villains. "If only I could find out what he's up to. Maybe I should set up a sting operation or a stake out."

"*Now* who sounds like a conspiracy theorist?" Tommy blurted out. "I don't get it, Jess. A week ago, you would have been happy if the guy had decided to forget you altogether. Now you want to stalk the old bastard because you're wondering why he's forgotten all about you? That's fucked up."

"I wish I could disagree with you." Jesse cracked his knuckles under the table, just like he always did when he knew he wasn't being rational. The three of them used to be able to solve any of their problems at this coffee shop table, but for some reason, things were slowly becoming different now.

Tommy knew what the reason was, and it was suddenly staring at them from outside the window. Patrick Kohn had finally come back. Even the falling snow seemed to want to avoid him as it spattered around his feet. Tommy resisted the urge to bang on the glass, to scare Patrick away for just a little bit longer.

It took Patrick no time at all to remove his wet coat and scarf and join the three of them at the table. He sat down in the empty seat, right beside Tommy.

It was incredibly surreal how normal it was to have him back. It made Tommy wonder what the point was. Why did they have to spend so much time trying to forget? What was the point of questioning any of his actions if Patrick was simply going to slide right back into their lives?

"Hey, guys," Patrick said. "Miss me?"

Tommy wanted to tell him they'd already done their missing the first time he left them. Nothing remained for a second time. But instead, he kept his mouth shut.

"Where's Sheldon?" Jesse asked.

"He's at the hotel. I've got some errands to run today, so I didn't want to drag him around against his will."

"Are you kidding?" Kate's jaw dropped. "You left your eight-year-old son alone in a hotel room? Is that a good idea?"

"I'll only be gone for a couple of hours. Should I not have—?"

"It's *Parenting-101*, Patrick. Not that any of us here would know any better." Kate was only trying to make a joke, but Patrick wasn't laughing. In fact, Patrick hadn't much of a reaction at all: he sat motionless, staring out onto the bustling, blustery Broadway. The other three just looked at him.

"I don't know what I'm doing, do I?"

"None of us do, really."

"With my son," Patrick said, ignoring Kate's comment altogether. "I never did. Natasha was always so good with him. I didn't even know how to hold him when he was a baby; always thinking I'd break his neck or something. Now he's sitting by himself in a big New York hotel."

"The Beacon's not *that* big," Tommy muttered, for no real reason at all.

"Listen, guys. I bought the apartment in Brooklyn. And I've got to deal with the paperwork today. Would one of you be willing to watch Sheldon for a bit?"

"I've got a chiropractor appointment in an hour," Kate admitted, massaging her lower back. "Too many years in that cheap Pendulum office chair. And I've already waited four months to see this guy. I can't cancel now. He's the best in the city."

"Jesse?"

"Patrick, I'm sorry. They need me at work today. The new books are in and there's no way Pond or Germ can manage without me." He looked across the table to Tommy. "But *you're* free, aren't you?"

Tommy ground a layer of enamel off his teeth.

Patrick turned to his left. "What about it, Tom?"

But all Tommy could say was: "Who was that man I saw you with on the street last week?"

Patrick's brow furrowed, but no words accompanied his reaction.

"Over on 3rd Avenue," Tommy clarified. "He was particularly fat, and eating a hoagie the size of a small child."

Patrick squirmed away from Tommy a little bit, but eventually answered the question. "Oh, you mean Jules? He works at the warehouse. I just bumped into him on the street." Patrick waved down the waitress and he asked her for a piece of toast and an orange juice. Kate and Jesse took the opportunity to order something as well, but the waitress still did nothing about Tommy's plate. "What were you doing over there, Tom?"

"Meeting with my agent."

"Oh, yes. I saw your review in the paper this morning."

"I bet you did."

"Sounds like the people just want more Kaspar Delancey."

"Well, you can't believe everything you read," Tommy muttered. He removed the plate himself, placing it on the empty table behind him. "Trust me, 'The Manhattanite' will catch on eventually. These things just need time."

"I'm sure."

"Me too."

Kate and Jesse could do nothing but stare at the two men as they passive-aggressively one-upped each other. But the banter stopped when Patrick's phone buzzed. Tommy noted the family picture on the phone had already been replaced with nothing but a blank white screen. Patrick looked at the caller ID but did not answer it.

"Is that Jules now?" Tommy asked.

"Why does it seem like you never believe a word anyone tells you, Tommy?"

"Because that way I never feel bad when someone's lying to me."

Patrick reached into his back pocket for his wallet and removed a business card. The strong smell of the leather wallet indicated it must have been brand new. Once again, Tommy failed to suppress any suspicion. Patrick slid the business card in front of Tommy; on it was the address and phone number for somewhere in New Jersey. "You can call Jules right now if you don't believe me, Tommy."

"I'm good, thanks."

Kate couldn't stand it any longer. "What's wrong with the two of you? You're like a couple of idiot school girls arguing over whose tits are bigger! Just stop it already."

"I don't even know what it is we're arguing about," Patrick stated.

But Tommy didn't want to hear anymore. He snatched his coat and scarf, he stood up on the bench, and he stepped across into the booth behind him. It seemed easier than having to ask Patrick to get out of his way.

Jesse meanwhile was looking over the information on Patrick's business card. "Fairmount? Wasn't that the street my exhibition was on?"

Tommy stopped. Even though he didn't know the first thing about Jersey

City's streets, his suspicion was officially piqued.

Kate took the card from Jesse's hand and read the address herself. "You know what? That might be the exact same place."

Jesse took one more look, as though the answers were somehow woven deep into the card stock. "I think it *is* the same place! What are the chances of that?"

"I didn't even know you had an exhibition, Jesse," Patrick noted. "That's an unusual coincidence, isn't it?"

Breathe in.

At once, all three of them turned to Tommy, each with their own reasons for doing so.

Tommy didn't know what to think of the coincidence though; he was not a big believer in twists of fate, flukes, or chance. Characteristically, he was not a suspicious person, but he'd never felt warier than he had for the past week, ever since Patrick returned. One time in his life, for just a few minutes, he was certain destiny had to be real. It was the night he snapped open the Chinese fortune cookie and found a tooth. He thought it was maybe a clue to some ancient, lost fortune, but his mother just grabbed the tooth from his hand and phoned the Better Business Bureau. Wing Fung's shut down one week later. So much for destiny.

Tommy's friends were the most important people in his world, but his world seemed to be spinning the wrong way lately. He considered what the girl at the counter had said to him before leaving. She said: "*Just treat your friends right.*"

Patrick broke him out of his reverie. "So, will you help me out, Tom? Can you take Sheldon for a few hours?"

"Wait, did you just say *hours*? Because I almost said yes there."

"Tom, would you just—"

"Yeah, yeah. Of course I'll come pick up the little shit."

"Please don't call him the little shit when you see him. Can you meet us at the hotel in an hour?"

It was preposterous to think Patrick Kohn was back in Manhattan for ulterior reasons, wasn't it? The man was not a problem maker, but he was not a problem solver either. If anything at all, he was a problem avoider; leaving them all ten years before without a word was evidence enough. Tommy loosened his scarf and smiled at the absurdity of his thoughts. He knew all about giving the benefit of the doubt. He knew well enough he should treat his friends right. He also knew he really didn't have anywhere better to be that morning, so he sat back down at the table.

"I'll be there, Patrick."

"It's good to be back here with you guys," Patrick noted, holding his glass of orange juice in the air as if to toast them all.

"Here, fucking *here*," Tommy muttered cagily.

CHAPTER SIXTEEN
Manhattan

An hour later, Patrick and Sheldon were waiting under the blue awning of the Beacon Hotel. The morning's snow had already been swept off the awning by the hotel maintenance crew. Sheldon was wearing an **I♥NY** t-shirt under his winter coat; the white cotton shirt was still so new it hurt his eyes too much to stare directly at it. From the opposite side of Broadway, Tommy poked through the Fairway Market fruit stand, watching the two of them out of the corner of his eye. He was sickened by the market's sub-par selection of apples. Worms were practically squiggling around under the dusty, brown skins.

"Tom!" Patrick spotted him and called out, yelling over the busy traffic. Tommy tried his best to ignore him for just another few seconds, but he finally gave up on the fruit and hopped across Broadway, jumping through the median and over its knee-high chain fence.

"Ah, finally! Thanks, Tom. We really appreciate this."

"Both of you?" Tommy asked in jest, but still somewhat hoping for the boy's partial agreement on the matter. He wouldn't receive any eye contact, much less a verbal response.

Patrick was already hailing a cab, eager to get a start on the morning's business. Tommy noted how much he looked like a tourist, for only tourists hailed cabs in New York as though they were mimicking what they'd seen on a movie screen. "So, you'll show him around the city, then? I can't think of anyone better for the job than you, Tom."

"Sure, Patrick," Tommy began unenthusiastically. "By the end of the day, this kid will be an honest to god New Yorker." He ruffled Sheldon's much-too-neatly-parted hair with his fingers. Sheldon tried in vain to move out of arm's reach, and still without a word, he shoveled his hair back into place with his big blue mittens. "He'll be swearing like a pro by the time I'm done with him!"

"I hope not," Patrick challenged him. "Just make sure he takes his medicine."

"Medicine?" Tommy shuffled away from Sheldon as though he was carrying the bubonic plague.

"For his asthma. He's got his bronchodilator inhaler in his bag."

"His *whoozzit whatzzit*?"

Sheldon unzipped his coat, lifted his t-shirt, and pulled the inhaler out of his fanny pack. Tommy recalled when the boy pulled his inhaler out in the coffee shop a week ago. He didn't, however, spot the fanny pack before. Tommy rolled his eyes and pulled the boy's shirt back down. "Kid, you're going to make me look like a tourist by association with the shirt and the pouch thing you've got going on there."

The taxicab screeched to a stop. Some slush from the curb sprayed out onto Patrick's shoes. "Be good," he instructed his son, not believing for a moment the boy could possibly find trouble on his own. Tommy knew the words had been meant for him.

Patrick shot into the back seat of the cab, sticking to it like a fly. The cab drove north along Broadway, and within seconds it was indistinguishable from the rest of the city's yellow traffic.

Tommy and Sheldon looked at one another, each waiting for the other to make a move. Tommy broke first. "So, Shelly. Where are we off to?"

Sheldon ignored his newly acquired nickname. "I've never been to New York before," he said quite simply. "I don't know what there is to do here."

"You can do *anything* you want in this city. Anything at all. That's what makes it so great!"

Sheldon looked at him, waiting for a list of possible options from which to select. Tommy gripped the pole of the hotel awning to test its strength. "We could start by climbing this pole. Kids like to climb, don't they?"

"I don't know."

"You *are* a kid, aren't you?"

"Yes."

"Do you like climbing?"

"Not really."

Tommy looked north to West 75th Street and south to Verdi Square. He imagined he could very easily kill an entire day within the three-block span, but he was pretty certain Sheldon would be bored within minutes.

"You hungry?"

"We ate breakfast already."

"What did you eat?"

"Fruit."

"Fruit? From where?"

Sheldon pointed across Broadway back to the fruit stand.

"Come on! Kids aren't actually eating froufrou fruit salads for breakfast these days, are they? How about a hot dog?"

"For breakfast?"

"Sure! Hot dogs are a crossover food. You can eat 'em any time of the day." Tommy directed Sheldon's attention down the street. "Gray's Papaya is only two blocks that way."

"Isn't papaya a fruit?"

"That's just the name. They've got the best hot dogs in the city."

"But I don't want a hot dog. I already ate."

"So, we'll think of something else to do then. What did you do for fun in Seattle?"

"I liked it when my dad took me to see the trains."

"Trains?" Tommy asked, confused by the boy's answer.

"And I have a train set in our garage at home."

"You mean you *had* a train set. Watch your tense." Tommy never had a problem correcting anybody, even if it was a motherless child who'd just had his entire life ripped out from under him. "So, what are you, some kind of enthusiast?"

"I don't understand."

"Do you like trains?"

"Yes."

"Fine. Let's start there then. I think I know just the place we can go. Follow me!"

Tommy immediately took off, oblivious to the amount of attention that was required when escorting a boy through New York City. Sheldon had to run along behind Tommy just to keep up. Through no fault of his own, Sheldon assumed these promised trains would be waiting for him mere footsteps ahead, or, at most, just around the corner. But two-and-a-half blocks later, it was obvious that would not be the case. It wasn't until 77th Street when Sheldon finally spoke up. "How much farther is it?"

"What do you mean, *how much farther*?" Tommy couldn't understand how New York might have seemed no bigger than the tiniest of Seattle suburbs in Sheldon's unassuming eyes. "We're going up to 97th Street and then we just have to cut through the park. The trains are only another couple of blocks after that."

"Where's 97th Street?"

"Well jeez, Shelly. We're at 77th now. Do the math."

"I don't understand."

"The whole city's numbered! You can count from Houston to two-hundred-and-twenty, can't you?"

Sheldon looked at Tommy, as though he was speaking in some crazy, outer-space moon language. Like he was asking the kid to walk to the sun and back, or to Mars at the very least. Truthfully, the solar system was a much easier concept to most eight-year-olds than metropolitan grid systems.

"Is it okay if we sit down?" Sheldon asked. "My feet are tired."

Tommy huffed in much the same way he'd expected to hear from the boy. They crossed the east side of Broadway and sat on a bench beneath the morning shadow of one of the median's tall London plane trees. "Do you want to take a cab from here?"

"My feet are tired."

"Yeah, yeah. I heard you."

They sat there for a few minutes longer. There were no further words exchanged between them. Of course, Sheldon was not used to being thrown into the care of a complete stranger, and Tommy had never had to act as tour guide for the under-eighteen crowd, so they were simply doing their best to feel out the situation they had both been forced into that morning.

"What was your name again?" Sheldon asked.

"That's a good idea," Tommy said ambiguously.

"I don't understand."

"I mean, maybe we should start from the beginning," he said. Tommy held out his hand. "The name's Thomas Mueller. I'm a washed-up novelist."

Sheldon reached out and they shook hands. It seemed silly to him, meeting a man he'd already met, but he hoped the handshake would only bring him to the trains that much faster. "Sheldon Kohn. I'm in the third grade. Pleased to meet you."

"It's nice to meet you too, Sheldon."

A man came up to them and immediately asked Tommy for a cigarette.

"Do I *look* like I'm smoking?" Tommy asked him, insulted.

"What's the harm in asking?" the man wondered.

"If I was a smoker, I'd have a cigarette. And if I had a cigarette, I'd be smoking it. But I'm not and I don't. And I don't and I'm not, so fuck off already."

"Fuck you, too!" The man walked about ten feet away before asking another non-smoker the exact same question.

Sheldon looked up at Tommy, his eyes wide with caution. "My dad warned me you'd be using a lot of swears today."

"The way I see it, Shelly, is that kids have to pick 'em up sooner or later. And the sooner the better. Less questions, right?"

"I guess so."

A silence grew between them once again, sneaking up from unknown recesses. "Do you want to give me a swear word?" Tommy suggested. "It doesn't have to be one of the big three."

Sheldon didn't have any idea what the three worst swear words might have been. They all seemed equally bad to him. "I don't curse," was all the boy could say. "And neither should you."

A blonde twenty-something woman jogged up onto the median, and came to a stop right in front of them, resting herself against a waist-high railing. She pulled out her phone, although where it might have been pocketed was a mystery to Tommy since her clothing left virtually nothing to the imagination. She was wearing brown yoga pants and a tight shirt which exposed her belly button. The steam from her sweaty body was thick in the crisp morning air.

Sheldon noticed the amount of attention Tommy was paying to her and he asked him, "Do you know her?"

"No. But I wish I did." Tommy turned to Sheldon and cracked a smile he hoped the kid would understand. He failed miserably. "Have you ever had a girlfriend, Shelly?"

"No. I'm just a kid."

"Kids can have girlfriends. I had a girlfriend when I was a kid."

"Do you have a girlfriend now?"

"I did until a few days ago." Tommy had thought about calling Rachel, but he was too afraid he would have to leave a message. The pressure of leaving the perfect phone message was too much. Tommy didn't know where he and Rachel stood, but the wrong message could decide it for him, and he wasn't ready for chance to play any part in it. "But I'm not sure what you'd call it now."

"I don't understand."

"Neither do I, Shelly. Neither do I." Tommy considered his statement for another moment. "And I'll tell you, I don't think I ever will."

Sheldon could only stare at him blankly.

"What I mean, is that women are complicated, and mine is no exception. She's got the shifty eyes of a card shark and a face as unyielding as one of those British royal guards. You know those guys with the big fuzzy hats? Rachel's just like that. She can infuriate me like the mosquito you can't seem to swat but she's also my best-kept secret. I hate her, and I also feel like I should love her. But I'm not entirely sure if she loves me. So maybe I *did* love her. Maybe I *used* to. Maybe I still do, or maybe I'm just waiting to."

"I don't understand."

"Kid, if you had your own catchphrase, *that* would definitely be it."

"What's a catchphrase?"

"You know when your dad always says, 'I'm the world's biggest jerk for abandoning my friends?' Well, that's *his* catchphrase."

"I've never heard him say that before."

Tommy had to stop himself from opening his mouth again. He knew if they sat there any longer, he'd only continue to spout negative and partially untrue feelings about the boy's father. Probably with a few more carefully selected swear words tossed in for effect.

He thought the answer would be obvious, but Sheldon carefully asked anyway: "Have you ever kissed a girl before?"

"Well, duh! Of course I have!"

"What's it feel like?"

Tommy had to think about it. "Where do I start?" Of all the words he'd ever written, he never once had to describe what kissing a girl really felt like. "The first time I ever kissed a girl I went in too quick and we both broke our noses."

"How did you do *that*?"

"I honestly have no idea. But it turned out she already had a boyfriend. He threw a punch at me when I wasn't ready, and broke my nose again."

Sheldon squirmed. Who knew kissing would be so much trouble? Tommy angled his head just right to show the boy his crooked nose. "My only advice is: when you're finally ready, just make sure you're not kissing the wrong girl."

The woman in front of them had tucked her phone away, and was stretching at the railing. The cropped shirt clung to her breasts like the tight skin on a ripe nectarine. Beads of sweat streaked from her chest to her belly. She turned around to lean over the railing again, lifting her right foot up high to stretch her leg as far as possible. As she bent forward, she looked back to see Tommy and Sheldon sitting across from her; she smiled at the two of them before standing up straight and picking up her run where she'd left off.

"Are you sure you don't know her?" Sheldon asked again, but he would get no further response. Tommy continued to watch the girl as she hopped across Broadway with a deer-like prance.

He shook his head back to reality. "Come on, Shelly. Let's get moving." He didn't hail cabs often, but Tommy was good at it; maybe the best in the city. The two of them climbed into the back of the first taxi that appeared. "Ninety-seventh and Madison," he barked at the driver.

The thick, gruff cabbie was born and raised in Brooklyn, but Tommy Mueller made him feel as though this was his first day in the city. "You got it, pal," he said gregariously, stepping hard on the gas and swerving out into the traffic.

They had only moved a couple more blocks north before the taxi found its way wedged into the morning's muddle of cars. Sheldon stared at the First Baptist Church, its pointed red towers reminding him of a toy castle. The draft of air coming toward them from the old Zabar's building pleasantly filled the cab with the aroma of smoked fish and cheese.

Tommy sneered at Sheldon's **I♥NY** t-shirt as they idled. He hated those shirts. He thought the city should establish some sort of screening process for people who bought them. Or a questionnaire, at the very least. He disliked it when tourists bought them, but he disliked it even more when he had to see tourists wearing the shirts on the sidewalks of his city. Drinking his coffee. Walking through his Central Park. Sitting on his subways. They didn't love New York as much as he did. They never would. When he was a little kid, he wore his **I♥NY** shirt every day, because all he ever knew was that it was completely true. "Is this right?" he asked, tugging at the boy's shirt. But Sheldon was just as confused as he'd been all morning and had no response for him. Tommy pinched the collar of the shirt between his fingers. "How much do you really love New York?"

The boy took off his mittens and unzipped his coat all the way. He looked closely at the big letters on his chest. He didn't care much for the shirt; in fact, he didn't even really know what it had meant. "My dad bought it for me."

"Listen, I don't think for a moment that you're buying all your own clothes, but you must have an opinion on the matter, don't you? How do you *really* feel about New York?"

Sheldon wanted to look inside Tommy, to try and figure the man out. Just last week, Sheldon had built a model train and he finished writing a school report on sugarcane. He had good grades in school, so he knew he wasn't stupid, but Sheldon really had no idea what Tommy was talking about most of the time. He turned back to the window. He didn't know Tommy very well yet, but he already knew he didn't want to disappoint the man. He didn't want to tell Tommy he was already feeling sick from the cabbie's erratic driving; he was too embarrassed to show weakness around him. It wasn't all that different from being on the playground; he only wanted to be liked. Tommy just happened to be a good twenty years older than all of those other kids. Sheldon considered the question again. How *did* he really feel about the city?

Out the window, Sheldon noticed two old men with sunken eyes sitting at a bus stop, completely unmoving. They could have been sitting there for the last forty years for all he knew. He spotted a bookstore with its shelves of dirty paperbacks out on the sidewalk. What was stopping people from simply taking them all for nothing? Was that the idea? Were the sidewalks a free-for-all in this city? There was a diner with a handwritten sign on the window that read, "NO MILKSHAKES!" It seemed like a mean thing to be bragging about. He saw a woman wearing a long, black vampire cape carrying the biggest paper bag he'd ever seen. The vampire walked past a peculiar man who was looking for something on the ground, as though he'd dropped a coin. He was on his hands and knees with a look on his face like he just might die if he didn't find whatever it was he was searching for. And there was an older man and a younger woman arguing. She was flailing her arms around a lot, mad at the man for something. He was smoking a cigarette as though he didn't care a whit about his upset companion. He flicked the cigarette at her feet before yelling something Sheldon couldn't make out; although he was certain he didn't want to know what the words were.

Sheldon turned back to Tommy. "I don't like it here," he said. "Everything and everybody seems so strange and mean."

"Including *you*, kid." Tommy thought it was impossible for anyone to not love his city just a little bit, and it was an insult if they should ever criticize it.

The taxi began moving again, lurching ahead slowly before suddenly taking off at a torrid pace. The weathered tires humped the sidewalk's edge. Slices of Manhattan zipped by the window, before they once again came to an impulsive stop at 87th Street. Tommy pointed out the doorman in front of the Montana Apartments. He explained to Sheldon how the two of them once got into a fistfight, right under that very awning.

"Why would you do that?" Sheldon asked bewilderedly.

"Well, I was stumbling up this sidewalk one fine evening when I overheard that ass-clown complaining about his job. He said some crap about how the Upper West Side could suck his—I mean, how this neighborhood wasn't exactly to his liking. I stopped and asked him to please apologize to me and all other New Yorkers for his obscene thoughts."

"Did he?"

"No. He sure didn't. He took one look at my sweater, and he said the Rangers sucked. Right to my face he said that! He said he was an Islanders fan through and through. Well, as you might have already assumed, I was a little drunk that night."

"I wasn't assuming anything."

"Well anyway, let's just say I couldn't let it go. And let's just say he took a swing at me. And it goes without saying that I hit him right back. I cold-cocked him. I knocked his stupid little hat off. He fell into a puddle and got his stupid striped coat all dirty."

"Really?" Sheldon looked at the doorman as the taxi idled in traffic. He shrunk in his seat a little, hoping the man in the hat and striped coat wouldn't see them.

"That's what Jesse told me anyway. I don't really remember much of what happened that night, but I still sneer at this guy when I walk by here." Tommy rolled down the window, stuck his head out and shouted, *"Hey! Islanders suck!"* The man recognized Tommy instantly, and yelled something horrible back their way.

Sheldon worried that Tommy would be yelling at people all day. He wasn't sure if he could take much more yelling.

The taxi continued toward its destination, but the conversation in the backseat had come to an end. North of 87th they passed the Wing King's. As the cab turned east on 96th Street, they snickered at a guy selling sparkling, pink purses. Piles of black garbage bags were lined along the sidewalk, like a solid plastic barricade. A little person was begging for change outside of a hotel, using a plastic blue sand bucket rather than a hat. They passed a few more churches and Sheldon wondered why there seemed to be so many in Manhattan. Upon crossing Columbus Avenue, the green and white swath of a snow-covered Central Park had come into view, always a welcome relief from the city's tapestry of concrete, steel, and glass.

As the cab crossed Central Park West and drove into the park, the city had all but disappeared. The stone walls along the side of the road barely kept the monstrous foliage at bay. Soon, the walls also gave way to sheer cliff faces, the greenery kept out by a mere chain link fence. The concrete peak of Mt. Sinai loomed beyond the treetops. Emerging from the tunnel below the East Drive, the gridlock of traffic was the most obvious sign that they would soon be re-entering the civilized world. A hint of a playground could be seen to the south: the glistening handles of a ladder at the top of a slide; the chains of swings hanging from the top bar; the ears of a colorful giraffe. The crowds parted like a curtain, as though the intermission was over and the next act was about to begin.

The driver stopped at 97th and Madison, exactly where Tommy had requested. Sheldon still wasn't sure how far they'd traveled, but the preciseness of it all astounded him. Tommy dropped a handful of bills into the driver's hand before reaching across Sheldon to open the door. "Let's go," he said, nudging the boy out onto the sidewalk. So far, there had not been any sign of any trains. Tommy led Sheldon into the Dunkin' Donuts, as though completely forgetting why they had come all this way in the first place.

"What about the trains?" the boy asked.

"Just grabbing a coffee first," Tommy responded. "Should I get one for you?"

"A coffee?"

"You gotta grow up fast in this city, kid."

It seemed every customer in the dusty donut shop was wearing hospital scrubs. It was strange to Sheldon, as strange as anything else he'd already seen that morning. He wondered if there was some sort of dress code he and Tommy were not adhering to, but the two of them were served nonetheless.

Tommy brought the coffee cup to Sheldon's mouth. "You want a sip?" The steaming, shimmering, brown liquid smelled something like a strange sort of hot chocolate, but it was hard to tell what it was that made it any different. Still, he tasted a sip and tried his best to pretend he didn't hate it. He was trying his hardest to grow up fast.

"Yea or nay?" Tommy asked, twisting his wrist from a thumb's up to a thumb's down. "Needs some sugar, doesn't it?" Tommy grabbed some sugar packs and tore them open with his teeth, dumping the white crumbs into the cup. He didn't stir them in, but Sheldon wouldn't have known any different. "You know, my feeling is that you can tell the most about someone by the way they prepare their coffee." He put the plastic lid on, covered the small opening with his thumb, and carefully shook the contents until the sugar dissolved. "Do they add cream? Milk? Sugar? Vanilla? Cinnamon? What order do they add their ingredients? Do they stir the coffee or do they shake it? I've never met anyone else who shakes their coffee, but that's just *my* thing, I suppose."

Sheldon had learned a lot about Tommy so far, but none of it seemed to have anything to do with coffee.

Tommy offered another sip, but Sheldon decided to refuse from there on out. "All right then. Next stop, trains!" Tommy proclaimed boisterously, and the two of them ran back out to the sidewalk.

~~~
~~~

Even before they arrived at Park Avenue and East 97th Street, Tommy noticed how much Sheldon had perked up. The kid's big blue eyes grew even bigger as soon as he heard the clacking of the trains up ahead. But when Sheldon stopped at the railing overlooking the tracks, the train had already disappeared, swallowed up into the cave below his feet. The exposed tracks stretched out north along the island, cradled crudely within Harlem's dilapidated tenement buildings, and over crumbling parking lots. There was not another train in sight.

"How long until the next one?" Sheldon asked.

"I don't know," Tommy replied. He bragged to most everyone about the wealth of information he knew regarding his city, but it didn't take all that long for the kid to stump him. "I guess we'll just wait for it."

"I don't like waiting."

"Come on, Shelly. You're six years old! What do you know about having to wait for anything?"

"I'm eight."

"Is there a difference?"

"There's a big difference!" he exclaimed. "When I was six all I ever did was watch cartoons and play army men. Now I like trains."

"Seems like one rung down on the cool ladder to me, Shelly."

"Why do you keep calling me that?" he finally asked.

"It's just a nickname. Haven't you ever had a nickname?"

"Nope."

"Hasn't your dad ever called you *Slugger* or *Chief* or *Squire*?" Tommy always wondered why his own dad had chosen to call him Squire when he was younger. He didn't really care though; it was still better than Leyland.

"No. Do *you* have a nickname?"

Tommy considered all of the names that all of his ex-girlfriends had ever called him, but they probably weren't the most appropriate names to be throwing into the conversation as examples. Instead, he gave Sheldon a little piece from his past. "When me and your dad and our friends were younger, we had a limit to the number of E-names we could use at one time."

"I don't understand."

"What I mean, is that it was always *Jesse*-this and *Katie*-that and *Tommy*-this and *Patty*-that. All the E-names in our group were getting out of hand."

"Who's Patty?"

"That was what we called your dad. But it was me who decided that I would be Tommy and Jess would be Jesse. From that point on, Katie and Patty were only to be called Kate and Pat. Or Patrick, if we felt like being more formal. I'd been Tom or Thomas for most of my life, and I was ready for a change. I wanted to ride with Tommy for a while."

"Seems like you make a lot of the rules around here."

"Rules are what keep everyone in line, Shelly."

"But I don't want an E-name either. I don't want to be called Shelly."

Tommy considered the alternatives for a moment. "Well, how do you feel about Poindexter then?"

Sheldon only had a couple of seconds to think about the name change before he was distracted by the rumbling below him. His little hands grabbed onto the railing and he strained his neck as far out as possible to get a better view. Tommy lifted the boy up by his armpits and held him on the top bar. A chain-link fence behind the railing separated the sidewalk from the tracks, and Sheldon's fingers clawed the dirty, rusted metal so intensely he almost bent them in his exuberance. Suddenly, the MTA train burst into the outside world. Sheldon's head nodded up and down as he counted every car that zipped past, thundering along the tracks and out into the distance.

Tommy recalled the first and only time he sat on that train. It was the first time he ever saw New York with his own eyes; the familiar skyline he'd always seen in movies and dreamed about was suddenly right there in front of him. Patrick, Kate, and Jesse had never told him, but they all sat back and watched Tommy that day. They were so impressed by the complete idolization of the city he was beholding. Sometimes the memory of seeing the great city for the first time would come back to him. It would return in fragments at the oddest of moments. When he caught himself staring at a stranger on the subway or when he wrote a sentence that left him breathless. That would be when he saw the Empire State Building again. Perhaps he would be selecting an apple from the grocery or watching a butterfly dance outside his window. He could be slicing into a thick steak or rinsing his toothbrush under the tap and suddenly the Chrysler Building would appear again. The moment he first lost himself in Rachel's eyes was when he remembered seeing the twin towers for the first time.

Sheldon felt the same in that moment; he was fixated on the train below him.

When the train finally disappeared, the boy turned to look at Tommy and thanked him for the greatest gift ever. With their eyes locked, Tommy was trapped in a sort of father/son moment he couldn't explain. If he could have explained it, he would probably have described it as a big brother moment at the most, or a friendly uncle moment at the very least. Either way, he wasn't sure if he liked the feeling.

Tommy said, "When I was a kid, all I ever wanted was to be here. I've explored every dirty corner of this city, and every day I still feel like there's more I need to see." He turned to Sheldon expecting a specific look in return, a look that would lead to the boy telling him about the kinds of things he wanted from his own life. He hoped Sheldon might formulate the answers for wherever it was he wanted to discover, the type of girl he hoped to fall in love with, or which mementos he would save in a cardboard box so he might experience them again when he was older. But there was no look. "It's all right," Tommy said to him. "You'll figure everything out when the time comes."

Soon enough, another city-bound train appeared in the distance, through the Bronx's gray haze. And just like the first, this one also disappeared under their feet. 97th Street vibrated a little more, welcoming the newest visitors into the city.

"Where do they all go?" Sheldon asked, pressing his face as far into the grimy chain-link fence as possible, trying to see into the tunnel below them.

"They all converge in a magical place known as Grand Central Station."

"Can we go there next?"

"Why would you want to do that?"

"To see the trains."

"You just saw them."

"I want to see *all* of them."

"If we stand here long enough, you will eventually. Now don't get whiny. Your dad told me you have a tendency to get whiny."

"No he didn't. You just made that up."

Tommy looked at his watch. "Isn't it about time we gave you your medicine?"

Removing the inhaler from his fanny pack, Sheldon sucked back a couple of short bursts of air.

"Thatta boy," Tommy encouraged, in his best friendly-uncle demeanor. "It's no fun being sick, is it?"

Sheldon shook his head.

The first thought that came to Tommy was of Natasha Seward. He didn't want to say anything, but for some reason he did anyway. "Listen. I'm sorry your mom was so sick. I knew her too. A long time ago."

"My mom was never sick."

"What's that?"

Sheldon inhaled once more, not responding to the question.

"You don't believe your mom was sick?"

"No."

Tommy persisted. "Do you know what cancer is?"

"I don't think she ever had cancer."

Tommy wanted to laugh, but knew it would have been inappropriate. He moved in closer, like a detective digging for information from his key witness. "So, what do you think happened to your mother?"

Sheldon took one last inhale with his device before putting it back into his pouch. "You have to promise to not tell my dad," he spoke solemnly.

Of course Tommy wouldn't tell Patrick any secret. The best secret was one he didn't have to share with people he didn't trust. Tommy even surveyed the sidewalk to ensure no one else was within earshot. "I won't," he agreed enthusiastically.

"I think my mom got killed."

"Your mom *was* killed." Tommy corrected. "Why would you think something like that?"

"It's my dad."

"What about him?"

"I think he did it."

"*Excuse me*?" It wasn't so much that Tommy didn't hear the words, as it was he simply wanted to hear them again.

"I think dad killed her."

Breathe in.

Kaspar Delancey, you glorious bastard, Tommy thought. *You've struck again, haven't you?*

"But you can't tell him I said that," Sheldon quickly reiterated. "You *promised.*"

Tommy watched the boy for another moment as Sheldon looked out to the horizon, waiting for the next train to roll into view. Tommy carefully considered his moves. Sheldon was so unruffled by his own confession, it was obvious he hadn't just made it up; he must have been thinking about this for a while, just waiting for the right person to talk to.

Tommy knew there wouldn't have been anyone better than himself.

He put his arm around Sheldon and led him down the sidewalk toward Park Avenue. "Poindexter, my boy, you just might be my good luck charm. Follow me!"

CHAPTER SEVENTEEN
Midtown Comics

The taxi pulled up right outside the entrance to Midtown Comics. Sheldon immediately recognized the images of Superman, Spider-Man, and the Hulk on the store's second floor windows, but he was unsure about most of the other colorful characters. He'd never read a single comic book in his life, and he was a little confused as to why Tommy would take him to a place such as this.

But Tommy needed to speak with Jesse, to pass on the vital information the boy had leaked. He didn't want to take the subway, even if the 96th Street Station had only been a block away. He knew Sheldon would want to take his time down there, with all of the trains clacking and the wind blowing through the tunnels. A cab ride down Park Avenue – with block after block of innocuous offices of dermatologists, dentists, chiropractors, and plastic surgeons – would sufficiently quell any wide-eyed enthusiasm. Tommy sat in the back of the taxi nervously, replaying in his head the conversation he'd just had with Sheldon. He wasn't sure what to make of it, and the feeling was not entirely unlike eager anticipation, as though he'd just won the New York Lottery and was about to have the giant novelty-sized check passed to him.

They entered the front door, and walked up the single flight of stairs which led into the store. Tommy directed Sheldon to the rows of new comics and pulled an issue of "The Incredible Hulk" off the shelf, handing it to the boy. "Here," he said. "Read this over. There'll be a quiz on the material later."

"Okay," Sheldon said timidly. He wasn't sure what Tommy had meant by a quiz, whether he was joking or if he'd actually planned it out in advance, but he graciously flipped through the book anyway.

Tommy knew Jesse would be in the back office, and he bypassed any security measures Pond or Germ would surely have let slide anyway. "Jesse!" he yelled and banged on the office door. "We need to talk."

Jesse opened the door. "Tommy? What are you doing here?"

"I'll tell you what I'm doing here. I'm letting you in on a prime little nugget of information I garnered this afternoon."

"*Prime nugget?* Is that a saying now?"

Tommy didn't answer; instead, he let himself in and closed the door. He sat on the couch and wasted no time in parlaying to Jesse exactly what Sheldon had said earlier. "I think Patrick killed Natasha."

Jesse dropped his empty, over-sized, plastic Thor mug onto the floor, and leaned back in his seat, as though winded from a punch to the stomach. He didn't know what to say; he was speechless up until the Mighty Thor had finally stopped spinning. "What the hell are you talking about? Where'd this come from?"

"The kid told me so himself!" Tommy exclaimed. "Remember what I was saying this morning? About how all this bad stuff started happening as soon as I found that letter?"

"Yeah," Jesse said. "But I thought you were only joking." He got up from his seat, grabbed the mug and placed it back on the desk. He came around to the front of the desk and leaned against it, wiping his brow with his sleeve.

"At the time I was joking. Mostly. But maybe the truth of it all leaked into my subconscious?"

"You mean like a sixth sense?"

"I thought sixth sense meant seeing dead people?"

"You never even saw that movie, did you?"

"No. But only because that asshole on the subway ruined the ending for me."

"A sixth sense is really just a general clairvoyance."

"Not the *dead people* thing?"

"Trust me. I read forty comic books a week." Jesse shook his head so he was thinking straight again. "Seriously though. You're saying Patrick Kohn has come back to New York to rub us all out? That's *crazy talk*, Tommy!"

"Is it? Think about it, Jess. What were the chances that Patrick's toilet seat business just happened to be set up in the same warehouse as your art show? I'll bet he had it all planned out years ago. Is it really so far-fetched?"

Jesse considered the facts. Patrick's sudden disappearance ten years before. The heartbreaking death of Natasha Seward. And Edith Galloway. That letter. The plane crash. The warehouse in Jersey. "Yeah, it is. It's just a big coincidence, Tommy."

Tommy turned to the stuffed Spider-Man seated beside him on the couch, but the web-slinger was being no more cooperative than Jesse. "So why would the kid say something like that to me? He must've had some reason to believe or he wouldn't have said anything at all."

"Maybe he was just screwing with your head?"

"Why would an eight-year-old want to screw with my head?"

Jesse shrugged his shoulders. He didn't really understand how and why kids did anything. He watched them come into the store and had to wonder sometimes how they ever managed to dress themselves.

"I'm telling you, Jess. He had a look in his eyes. Like he was scared of something."

"Really?"

Tommy thought about it. He recalled the exact moment that transpired less than an hour before, and he tried to find anything in his memory he might have missed at the time. "Actually," he began. "He wasn't scared. He just told me very matter-of-factly. Like it was information that couldn't be disputed. Like it was something he'd known for a long time." Tommy got up from the sofa and cracked the office door open. He looked out across the store to where Sheldon was standing, right where Tommy had left him. The boy was still flipping through the same comic book, studying it intensely. "There's something wrong with that kid, though. I think Patrick really messed him up. But maybe it's just because he's an only child?"

Jesse stayed right where he was. "Tommy, we're *all* only children. Me. Kate. Patrick. You too, ever since your brother died."

"Yeah. My brother." Tommy closed the door again and lowered his voice. "How far back do you think this thing goes?"

"What thing?"

"With Patrick. Do you think he had something to do with my brother as well?"

"Like I said. I think you're crazy, Tommy. But that's just my personal opinion."

"Maybe I *am* crazy. But I'll tell you what I'm not: I'm not naïve, Jess. It's naïve to assume everything's a coincidence. What's the *real* reason Patrick came back here? Where is he right now? What's he doing today that he can't even watch his own kid?"

"I don't know what he's doing. But I'm pretty sure he's not sitting around planning out our great demise. You need to stop trying to connect Patrick to Kaspar Delancey. They're not the same person."

"Sure they are. Why would I have come up with the idea in the first place? It must be that sixth sense thing again."

"So, you've got murder theories *and* super powers now? Why can't you just let things be as they'll be, Tommy?" On the desk sat the many comic book sculptures, the ones that were considered evil. They were the objects John Galloway couldn't seem to take his eyes off of a week before. Jesse removed one of them from its display holder; it was a semi-transparent cube, and it fit perfectly in the palm of his hand.

"What is that?" Tommy asked.

The sunlight came in through the window behind Jesse, making the cube glow in his hand. "This is the Cosmic Cube."

Tommy had to shield his eyes from the reflection.

Jesse slowly twisted the object around with his fingers. It sparkled like a square disco ball. "Whoever wields the Cosmic Cube can use its power to reshape reality. The impossible can be made possible." He liked the feeling of it in his hand. It was hard to tell whether or not Jesse actually believed the words he uttered. There was conviction in his voice. But then again, he did read forty comic books a week.

It didn't happen often, but Tommy had no idea what to say.

Jesse blew the dust off the top of the cube before placing it back down on the desk, back into its reserved resting spot. "It's really no more conceivable than what you're proclaiming, Tommy. I think Patrick's words just got you all freaked out. You know, what he said about The Falling."

"Maybe I *am* freaked out. But you still can't explain the warehouse."

"And you still can't accept the coincidence, can you?"

Tommy slumped back into the sofa and considered his options. He knew Jesse wasn't going to voluntarily believe him. He would have to come up with an idea that could maybe do the convincing for him.

Jesse was already making a move for the door. "Are we done, Tommy?"

"How about you come to the warehouse with me then?"

"In New Jersey?"

"Yeah."

"Right now?"

"No. Tonight."

Jesse paused. He opened the door and took a look at Sheldon himself. He tried his very best to see Patrick in him. He challenged himself to recognize any of the same qualities he'd always known in his friend. But Patrick had never seemed so lonely. So quiet. So unhappy. Jesse thought about high school, and how those days can seem like the unhappiest days in the whole span of every human's existence. But Patrick Kohn had never once seemed so gloomy. Jesse certainly had, but not Patrick.

For the moment though, Tommy still believed he had Jesse's full attention. "We'll go there tonight and find the answers we need," he said. "And if we don't, I'll drop it."

Jesse continued to stare out beyond the threshold. As if feeling the eyes on him, Sheldon Kohn looked up at Jesse. He recognized him, and smiled the world's thinnest smile.

"He seems so sad out there," Jesse said.

"Sad? That kid is sadder than Christmas lights in June." Tommy got up and stood beside Jesse, getting a look himself. "He does seem to like the trains though. I'm lucky I found *something* today to perk him up."

Jesse knew he wasn't prepared to go back to New Jersey. But maybe it wouldn't be so bad. Maybe it wasn't the same warehouse that held his art show one year before. Maybe it wasn't the same place he'd seen Edith Galloway for the very last time.

"Well?" Tommy said. "Why don't you think about it, Jess? Maybe you'll come around to the idea."

"Maybe," Jesse answered slowly and turned to Tommy. "And maybe *you* will too."

"I always do, eventually," Tommy said. But Jesse wasn't really sure what he'd meant by those words. Tommy's phone buzzed in his pocket, and he removed it to check the caller ID. It was Patrick. "Well, look who it is," he said, holding the phone up for Jesse to see. The two of them had exchanged numbers earlier in the coffee shop so Patrick could call when he was ready to pick up Sheldon. Tommy had no other reason to exchange numbers. He answered his phone, and spoke with only a few muffled grunts and confirming mumbles. "We're at the comic store," Tommy said.

Pause.

"Yes. With Jesse."

Pause.

"Fine then." Tommy put his phone away and turned back to Jesse. "Patrick's coming. Is it alright if I leave Sheldon here with you?"

Jesse said it wouldn't be a problem, and Tommy disappeared as quickly as he could and without another word.

~~~

When Patrick did arrive, Jesse didn't want to seem overly cautious. But he was. He didn't want to let any nervousness slip. But he did. Jesse knew himself well enough to know he was the worst liar in Manhattan — and the city certainly had a generous helping of bad liars — so he made sure to keep the conversation as brief as possible.

If Tommy's crazed account was somehow even partially true, Jesse simply wanted to get the boy out the door as quickly as possible. Patrick thanked him. Jesse said it was no problem. "Actually," he said. "It's Tommy who should get the majority of the gratitude." He knew he had already said too much.

Patrick wondered where the boy's blue mittens were; he had them when he left that morning. Sheldon suggested maybe he forgot them in the back of the taxi. Jesse took note of the look in Patrick's eyes, but he wasn't sure if he was reading the reaction properly. Quickly, Jesse reached for the comic shelf, handed Sheldon a stack of Invincible Iron Mans, and perked his ear toward the office, pretending the phone was ringing his name. Forget New York; Jesse Classen just might have been the worst liar on the entire eastern seaboard.

Jesse glided over to the window, his favorite viewing spot, and peeked out from behind the cardboard Incredible Hulk. He watched Patrick lead Sheldon by the hand out along Lexington Avenue, toward Grand Central. He thought
~~~

he caught Patrick sneaking a look back to the comic shop window. He replayed the conversation, as concise as it was, in his mind. And he was certain Patrick must have dropped some hint somewhere within his minimal amount of words.

And then Jesse realized, that by his suspicion alone, he was simply following Tommy again. He'd done so his whole adult life, why wouldn't he now? Like the Cosmic Cube, it was unfathomable the amount of power that man had.

~~~

Jesse was about to lock the door when the phone rang. He had already set the alarm, flicked the last light off, and had the key braced in his hand.

"Midtown Comics," he said with his usual greeting.

"Jesse! It's me."

"Tommy? What's up?"

"Do you remember that scene in 'Blanc' when the detective returns to his apartment and finds that Kaspar Delancey has burnt it to the ground?"

"I guess so. Why?"

"I think you already know why."
~~~

EIGHTEEN
Hell's Kitchen – Midtown, 1941

Detective Broome sifted through the smoky rubble. Already, whatever evidence might have been recovered would probably be nothing more than ash anyway. Still, he kept digging. Buster Broome had lived in the same apartment for five years now, ever since he got his badge. He felt like he'd been after Kaspar Delancey since day one, which was not so far from the truth. The two men shared a symbiotic relationship by that point: one would predict the other's move and vice versa, but neither could ever finish it. The closest Broome had come was that night at the Flatiron Building. But he didn't have the guts then.

Every time he passed the Flatiron at the corner of 23rd Street and Fifth Avenue, he couldn't help but recall moments from his youth. With his friends, chewing bubble gum and waiting for girls' skirts to blow up from the draft of the underground trains. That was the windiest corner in the entire city. Usually, the boys were chased away by the officers and their clubs, but every once in awhile they'd be lucky enough to see what they had waited so patiently for. Every little detail seemed so simple back then. At times, this case had been no less fun; the prospect of catching Kaspar Delancey with his skirt over his head was thrilling. Broome knew it would be unavoidable, even if some of the other guys in the precinct had begun to doubt it months ago.

"Well?" Oster dropped his hand onto Broome's shoulder. "What have we got here?"

"It's as done as it's going to get," Broome mumbled with hidden delight. He made sure to keep his foot exactly where it was so as not to draw attention to where he stood.

"But is this our man?"

"Ours? Oster, you know this one's *mine*."

"Don't be such a romantic. This is the worst serial killer New York has ever seen. There's no way you're doing this alone, Broome."

Detective Broome had yet to point out the fact the scorched building was actually his own. And he didn't plan on mentioning this was far more complicated than a simple cat-and-mouse relationship. It had never been that simple. Even when the inevitable day would come when he would catch Kaspar Delancey, he knew the two of them would still never be free of one another. It went much further than the cop-and-robber mentality. It was vengeance, pure and simple.

"Right, Oster. You got it."

Sergeant Oster covered his face; the smoke was becoming too much to bear. He made his way back out toward 11th Avenue where the sporadic red and blue lights lapped the wet brick walls. He stepped carefully over whatever charred evidence might have still been left to investigate.

As soon as he was gone, Broome kicked the blackened mirror away from under his foot. He bent down and picked up the small, metallic egg which he hoped Oster wouldn't see.

He examined it closely; the unmistakable key design on the side of the egg was definitely the piece of evidence Broome had been hoping for, and the inscription only made it that much more palpable. Kaspar Delancey was a fool if he thought this was over.

CHAPTER NINETEEN
Titanic Utilities Warehouse – Jersey City

Tommy, Kate and Jesse emerged from the cab, and were hit instantly by the smell of New Jersey. The scent was like something caught between the Fulton Fish Market on a hot summer day and mildewed newspaper. Their thick-bearded driver had followed Jesse's explicit directions without fault, but he was still a little tentative behind the wheel. After four other cabbies on Broadway said, "I no go Jersey," (and after Tommy subsequently responded with, "I don't blame you, pal"), they finally found a driver who reluctantly agreed to take them to the once-familiar warehouse. The three of them were so calm and stiff along the way; the only signs of life in the taxi seemed to be the empty coffee cups and candy wrappers sliding back and forth across the dashboard.

Without trepidation, Jesse was the first to approach the dark building. The address was exactly the same as the one on Patrick's business card.

Tommy paid their fare and the taxi sped off back to Manhattan. He shivered as he studied his surroundings, and slung a backpack over his shoulder. His Rangers sweater and heavy hoody would keep him warm, but he still felt a chill under his skin. The large, dark shapes slowly moving around in their vicinity did not go unnoticed by Tommy. They were probably just the homeless and harmless, but he still did not feel entirely at ease standing on the broken sidewalk, directly under a flickering, yellow streetlight.

"Where are we, anyway?" Kate asked.

"Feels like the corner of Berkowitz Lane and Date Rape Avenue to me," Tommy suggested.

Kate looked around, trying to recall the night of Jesse's art show. "Honestly, Tommy. I don't remember ever being here. This place doesn't ring a bell to me. Maybe it's not the same warehouse after all?"

"Well, you *were* pretty drunk that night, Kate. But this is *definitely* the place. Trust me."

"You know I hate it when you say *trust me*."

Suspicious they may have been walking right into some elaborate trap, Tommy called for Jesse to wait up.

Kate groaned, "I still don't know how you convinced me to come here with you guys."

"I'm telling you, Kate. I had a bad feeling about Patrick from the start. And after his kid tells me he thinks his dad is responsible for his mother's death, I come home to find my building in flames. Doesn't that smell the least bit fishy to you?"

Tommy was dumbfounded by the poor response time from the firehouse. Even though Engine Company 47 was right next door to his apartment, it may as well have been ten blocks away, since the firefighters had to suit up and the great red truck still required those precious seconds to roar to life. Evidently, living right next door to a firehouse does not make things any safer. Neighbors' reports claim the fire started in 104, and the Middle Eastern man was rushed to the hospital, although apparently just for smoke inhalation. There was no word on whether or not his wooden leg survived the flames. Mrs. Horowitz claimed she heard a bomb go off in the apartment, hoping to substantiate her terrorist claims, but there had not been any evidence of an explosive device.

Tommy couldn't ignore the fact that apartment 104 was where he once lived with Patrick, and it was the address on the letter which had been mailed to him from Seattle, so it was not hard to figure Patrick Kohn may have believed Tommy still resided there. Still, there was enough smoke damage to temporarily force the occupants of the building's west side out. Tommy ended up crashing on Jesse's couch for an hour or so before deciding to gather the gang and head to New Jersey.

"Still," was all Kate had to say in return.

Tommy continued to present the facts. "And then we've got Patrick's business being run right out of here? The very same warehouse as Jesse's art show? I'm telling you, Kate. It's got suspicious written *all* over it."

"Or coincidence."

Jesse was already at the front door. The tiniest of signs above the door read: TITANIC UTILITIES. The sign was already peeling and there was a screw missing from one of the corners. Just like the garage door beside it, a burglarproof metal shield was rolled down to prevent any after-hour break-ins.

Kate asked, "If this *was* a trap, don't you think the front door would have been left open for us?"

"That would be way too obvious, Kate. I've seen my share of slasher movies to know you can't plan for everything." Tommy tried the door himself, hoping to roll the metal covering up with the palms of his hands. He tried to physically out-muscle the best warehouse security money could buy, as though he was superhuman. Not surprisingly, he was not met with any success. Kate and Jesse turned to one another and both knew for sure they would be leaving here momentarily and empty-handed. They probably should have asked the cabbie to wait for them. There was a pipe on the front of the building which only went about halfway to the roof. A rickety, wooden telephone pole seemed like the best option, but Tommy questioned the safety of its tangled spider web of wires and nails. Across the street, there was nothing but a large, bare fence and a cold brick building with some undecipherable Chinese characters. "Come on," Tommy suggested. "Let's take a look around back."

~~~
~~~

The small parking lot to the side of the warehouse was easy enough to get into. There was another door, but it too was secured with a metal screen. A large, green dumpster was pressed against one of the walls. Tommy assessed the situation, and figured if they could push the dumpster far enough, the three of them could scale the building's three tiers to the rooftop.

"And then what?" Kate asked. "Crawl in through an air duct maybe?"

"Maybe." Tommy tried his best to cover up his exuberance. The possibility of crawling through an air duct actually sounded pretty cool. If nothing else, the night's adventure might serve as some excellent first-hand research for another novel.

Jesse remained as quiet as he could. The parking lot was the very last place he had seen Edie, where her husband dragged her away through the snow and tossed her into the car that would later lie crumpled and burning within the Holland Tunnel. The smallest of flakes began to drift down from ominous clouds.

"I didn't really bring my best climbing gear, Tommy," Kate noted. She was wearing her famous purple cow-patterned leggings under a long, woolen sweater and a bright blue ski jacket. She looked like a homeless vagrant, but she claimed it to be her "New Jersey Drifter" outfit, which, at the time, was enough to get a smile out of Tommy. For now though, he was only frustrated at her attempts to back out of the plan.

"Why don't you stand out there then," Tommy suggested, pointing back out to Fairmount Avenue. "We should probably have someone on patrol duty anyway."

"Patrol duty. Right." Whatever Tommy wanted to call it, Kate assumed it would be better than climbing to the top of a warehouse on a freezing October night. "Should I walkie-talkie you or fire the flare gun if there's any trouble afoot?"

Tommy did not appreciate the humor. "Don't make fun, Kate. This is serious shit. I'm not about to do any jail time for this."

"Jail time?" Jesse asked, snapping out of his melancholy. "We couldn't actually go to jail for this, could we?"

"It's a *B-and-E*, Jess. You're in the big leagues now."

Kate meandered back to the sidewalk, and Tommy directed Jesse toward the dumpster. Their fingers nearly froze to the metal, but the two men managed to heave the steel receptacle close enough to the wall so they could climb up and grab onto the rooftop's edge. Tommy scrambled up first and then gave Jesse a hand. From there, the second tier was easy to grab onto individually, and they both ascended to the next level. "All right, Jess," Tommy said, not nearly as out of breath as Jesse already was. He held his hands on his hips boastfully, as though he was about to reach the peak of Mount Kilimanjaro. "Now you've just got to give me a boost to the top."

"I don't know, Tommy. I think I'm starting to reconsider this whole thing."

Tommy's arms fell limply back to his side. "Are you kidding me? Don't wuss out on me now, Jesse Classen!"

Jesse looked up into the night sky as an airplane soared into sight; he noticed how it seemed to be slowing down. The plane vanished behind a thick cloud but it refused to reappear, as if it had come to a complete stop midair. Impossibly, even the distant roar of its engines had silenced. It was happening again: Jesse was second-guessing himself. He had to crouch down and brace himself on the rooftop. He looked back to the parking lot below him and out to the sidewalk. Kate was looking right at him with her arms spread wide, wondering what was going on.

"Hey!" she yelled, not caring a whit about their mission of stealth. "Don't wuss out on us, Jesse Classen!"

Jesse was once again being led by Tommy. When would the inevitable separation occur, he wondered? When would he find the strength and the courage to follow his own conscience?

Tommy placed a hand on Jesse's shoulder, just as the plane re-emerged from the clouds. "I know it's hard for you, but I *need* to do this, Jesse. And I *need* your help."

Jesse stood back up. Without saying a word, he gave Tommy a lift to the rooftop. Perhaps there were still demons within the warehouse Jesse needed to exorcise? If Tommy was going to be so selfish, maybe, just for once, Jesse should take the opportunity as well?

Standing atop Jesse's shoulders, Tommy stretched his long arms far enough to reach the top of the warehouse. His fingers clasped the ledge, and as he dangled, Tommy couldn't get Patrick's ominous warning out of his head: "*Everybody falls.*" Still, he laughed the words off, confident he would not fall now, nor would he ever. Rachel may have left him, his novel might have been an astounding failure, and he may have even been smoked out of his apartment, but Tommy was certainly not on the verge of falling. If for no other reason than to prove Patrick Kohn wrong.

Jesse pushed up on the bottoms of Tommy's feet until Tommy had enough leverage to pull himself the rest of the way. From the very top of the warehouse, Tommy turned to see the glow of Manhattan in the distance. The brilliant blanket of light could scarcely conceal all of the dreams, desires, feats, and triumphs that lay within. And yet, Tommy now felt as though the radiance was reaching out for him, begging him to relieve the city from the darkness Patrick Kohn had brought with him. And he wasn't simply being dramatic. He wasn't being selfish or idealistic. His friends could think what they wanted to, but Tommy knew they would thank him later. New York City was not meant for everyone. It did not welcome anyone but a handful of the world's chosen few. Tommy knew Patrick had already been chosen once. But he was now deemed unfit to tread the pathways of the world's greatest metropolis.

"Tommy?"

"Huh?"

Jesse was not even aware Tommy's attention had drifted away for the moment. "I said, how am I supposed to get up now?"

"Don't worry so much. I already thought of everything." Since Tommy couldn't enter his apartment, he had the prudence to pick up a backpack and some other supplies before coming out tonight. Kate and Jesse wondered what was in that SpongeBob SquarePants backpack, but not enough to actually ask him. From the bag, Tommy pulled out a length of rope. He tossed one frayed end down to Jesse. "Grab on, Jess. It'll be just like Batman and Robin."

"Am I right to assume I'm supposed to be Robin in this scenario?"

"Correct again, old chum! You've always been my Boy Wonder."

"Which version? Dick Grayson? Jason Todd? Burt Ward? Chris O'Donnell? Which one am I?"

"What? Whatever, Jesse. I'm not about to pretend I know the difference."

It didn't really matter all that much to Jesse which role he was going to be playing; he just wanted to get up to the roof. As unmovable as Lady Liberty, Tommy held the rope tight while Jesse rappelled up the side of the building. Once on the roof, Jesse brushed himself off. "One of these days I'm going to teach you everything you need to know about superheroes."

Tommy only grunted an answer under his breath before noticing the stairwell door to his left. It definitely lacked any of the security measures of the building's ground-level entrances. Tommy had written enough warehouse scenes in his Detective Broome novels to know his best back-up plan would be the rooftop access. Without a second thought, Tommy pulled a crowbar from the backpack and wedged it into the door frame.

"Where did you get a crowbar?" Jesse asked, stupefied.

"Hardware store on Columbus. Haven't I always said you never know when you might need a crowbar?"

"I don't recall you ever saying that."

Using the crowbar to bend the handle off, Tommy forced the door open. Jesse shook his head, letting Tommy know he had little desire to enter first. The stairs led straight down onto a small catwalk, overlooking the warehouse floor. Through the darkness, they could make out a few rows of shelves below them, less than half-full of stock. Without hesitation, Tommy continued down the stairs, switched on the overhead lights and began to peruse the shelves.

When the lights came on, the memories instantly flooded Jesse's mind.

He gripped the railing of the catwalk.

Even though a year had passed since he'd been inside the building, Jesse could still visualize everything. Every last miserable detail. He recalled the exact way everything had been the moment John Galloway entered the warehouse. Kate drunkenly flirted with some guy at the open bar. The DJ reached for another disk. A cute photographer from the Village Voice slithered her way through the crowd. Comic books had been strewn across the floor as decoration, eventually trampled into a colorful, crumpled carpet. Edith Galloway watched Jesse with a sparkle in her eyes he'd never noticed until that night.

From the catwalk, Jesse could see himself on the stage. He was wearing those flashy red gloves and domino mask. Jesse spent a full year working on the pieces for the exhibit, all with the financial compliments of Edie Galloway, and he wanted to be sure he looked as super as the show itself. Along one wall stood three unique twenty-foot pieces: from a distance, they appeared to be an exact duplication of three authentic and carefully selected comic book pages, but each was a finely constructed collage made up of much tinier images. Like a photomosaic image for posters and puzzle games.

Another wall of the warehouse held a life-sized corner of a city block, constructed out of wood and covered with layer upon layer of comic book pages. Black and white windows fashioned exclusively with word balloons.

Gaudy sidewalks of brightly colored, jagged explosions of onomatopoeia. Billboards and newsstands of intricately layered cover pages. A darkened alley was composed of the most nefarious of images. Store mannequins dotted the street scene, each one posed as — and plastered with — specific character images. Some were engaged in battle with one another; some seemed to cackle menacingly; some simply patrolled the rooftops searching for signs of trouble. And yet, none of them seemed to take notice when trouble eventually manifested itself.

Jesse was standing on the colorful sidewalk, stumbling through his ill-prepared speech, when John Galloway entered, creating such an uproar and eventually throwing his wife into the wall of giant comic pages. The party came to a sudden stop. The crowd separated itself from the commotion. Even Jesse's friends were of no help. Kate was too drunk to do anything about it, and thanks to Rachel, Tommy had yet to show up. Even the heroic mannequins remained motionless. It was the moment in which Jesse forced himself to make the decision he had.

"I punched him," Jesse said. His words quietly echoed inside the near-empty warehouse. He finally released his sweaty hands from the railing.

"What's that?" Tommy asked, still picking his way through some boxes on the shelves below.

"I punched John that night. I'd never hit anyone in my entire life, and then I go and punch an old man."

Tommy came out into the light and looked up at Jesse. "I know. Kate told me all about it. You wouldn't believe how pissed I was that I missed that. Stupid Rachel and her stupid being late all the stupid time—" With two hands, he picked up one of the boxes and shook it hard. Something heavy rattled around within.

Jesse sat down now, on the edge of the catwalk. "When Sharona asked me what had happened, I told her I didn't do a thing. I told her I just stood there and watched. But I actually socked him in his old, wrinkled face.”

Tommy moved to the foot of the stairs. He didn’t know why Jesse was still up there, why he wouldn’t come down to where it was safer. Perhaps Jesse thought it was safer? Just a little bit further away from his past. “Sharona? Who the hell is Sharona?” he asked, with his hands on his hips.

“Sharona was the girl I went out with a couple of weeks ago.”

“Ah. Wing King’s and Wicked.”

“That’s the one.”

“And her name is really Sharona? Like the song?”

“I think that’s her real name. To be honest, I never asked her.”

“Why didn’t you tell her about the fight?”

“Well first of all, I obviously don’t want to be bragging about punching an old man in the teeth.”

“Obviously. If he *had* any teeth, that is.”

“Right. But I think the real reason was because I actually enjoyed the moment. That fight with John—it was the most *incredible* feeling I’d ever felt, Tommy! When we were throwing punches on that stage, in the fantasy city I’d built with my own hands. It was awful, but also amazing. I mean, he was my arch-enemy. My evil nemesis. I was even wearing a superhero costume, for Christ’s sake! And we trashed it all. Everything I’d created was ruined, but I didn’t care. I threw a fake garbage can at him. He knocked me through a papier-mâché wall, and I hit him back with a cardboard lamppost. It was so surreal, like everything I’d ever dreamed about and read about as a kid was actually coming to life.”

At first, Tommy didn’t suspect coming to the warehouse would have much of an effect on Jesse, but he realized then, he probably should have seen it coming. Jesse had bottled up so much of the past year, it had to come to surface eventually; as easily as bubbles in a water cooler. But Tommy also understood no matter how fantastic that moment might have been for Jesse, it could not possibly cover up how he still felt about Edith Galloway. "I'm sorry I missed it, Jess," he spoke solemnly.

"Am I a bad person for feeling like this, Tommy?"

Tommy didn't have an answer for his friend. He wondered if there was anything wrong with finding a little bit of pleasure in something awful.

"And yet, the more I think about it now, the harder it is to believe any of it ever happened in the first place. The harder it is to remember what my life was like with her in it. Does that make sense?"

Tommy didn't want to, but he couldn't help thinking of Rachel again. "You were happy," he discerned. "Even if she's gone now, that's the important thing."

For a long moment, Jesse took another look around him. "But I didn't move a muscle when John threw Edie into the car and killed her." He gulped back a bad taste in his mouth. "Did you know tomorrow is the one-year anniversary of her death?"

"I don't know what to tell you, Jess. Kate would probably say some crap like: *'You've got to remember the good stuff from any relationship.'* I'm not sure if I believe that myself, but I guess it beats focusing entirely on the bad stuff."

Jesse couldn't comment on Tommy's words, but it did sound like something Kate might say. Finally, he walked down the steps to the warehouse floor, planting his feet firmly. Maybe that was enough for now.

Tommy went back to the shelves, although he was obviously frustrated by whatever it was that he found. Or what it was he wasn't finding. A few hundred toilet seats in various models and colors filled the shelves. All of them were innocuous though, and did not seem to be hiding anything suspicious. Disappointed, Tommy kicked the steel frame of the shelf unit. "Maybe there's an office in here," he suggested. "You know, where we might find some paperwork or something."

"How about a business license?" Jesse suggested.

"Nice thinking, Boy Wonder! If there's no business license, that would mean there's no business. And if there's no business, this warehouse is just a front for something else."

The two of them froze suddenly when they heard banging at the front door, but they loosened up a little when they remembered Kate was still outside.

Tommy pointed to the front door. "Do you think we should let her in?"

"I think she'd kill us if we didn't," Jesse responded.

Strangely, there didn't appear to be any sort of alarm system on the door. If there was one, it hadn't been armed in the first place. Jesse rolled up the metal guard on the outside and unlocked the door. Kate was shivering on the other side; the hood of her ski jacket was pulled tight around her face. "About time," was all she said as she pushed Jesse out of her way and crossed the threshold. "I think I saw Gene outside."

"What?"

"I'm not sure, but I'm certain I saw his car drive by."

Tommy was quick to close and lock the door behind her. "You're not sure or you're certain? That's two completely different perspectives, Kate."

"Oh, shut up, Tommy. Did you know there are hookers out there too? I had to hide behind a fence when I saw the JCPD coming down the street."

"I don't think prostitution is illegal in New Jersey," Tommy said. "It's pretty much a lawless state. Besides, I doubt you could pass for a hooker in that outfit. New Jersey or not."

Kate ignored Tommy's comment. "What are the chances Gene's driving around Jersey City picking up whores?" she asked. "What if he's been doing it for years?"

"I think you're probably just imagining things, Kate," Jesse said, acting as the voice of reason. "Didn't you say Gene was working late tonight?"

"That's *exactly* what she said," Tommy intimated, emphasizing all the wrong words. "Can we just focus on why we're here without creating new problems? I don't know if you two have forgotten, but we're supposed to be looking for clues."

Kate tried to warm up by rubbing her hands together. "Just for the record, Tommy, I think you're totally nuts. You might have convinced Jess that Patrick's intentions are reprehensible, but I just don't see it."

"Hey," Jesse started. "I never said I was convinced. I'm just examining the particulars of the situation."

"Right," she said. "Like there's a difference. You're the easiest guy in the world to convince of anything, Jess."

"I am?"

"Point proven," Kate smiled.

Tommy ignored her and found a small office around the corner. The door was slightly ajar, making it easy to reach in and flick the light on. The office was nearly bare: a computer, a coffee mug, and an empty file folder were all that sat atop the desk; there was a shelf unit with nothing but a ream of blank paper and a moose stuffy; the only additions to the white wall were a small "I Hate Mondays" poster, and a free calendar from a New Jersey real estate agent which featured a monthly selection of classic cars. October was the cherry red 1963 Corvette.

"Look at this place," Tommy said. "I couldn't stage a fake office worse than this if I tried. It's obvious he's hiding something in here."

Jesse picked up the coffee mug, inspecting it closely. There was some cartoon printed on it, with a golf joke he didn't understand. The inside of the mug had the familiar brown stains of dried coffee. "I thought Patrick didn't drink coffee anymore?"

There was an unlocked drawer on the desk and Tommy slid it open. He ruffled through the newspapers and fliers he found inside, but again there was nothing of interest anywhere. He looked up, exasperated.

Jesse wondered, "Maybe you don't need a business license for a warehouse?"

Tommy didn't know much about running businesses, but he knew enough about the situation to know he didn't like it. He walked outside of the office and surveyed everything at once. "I think this is a bust," he finally admitted.

Kate said, "I don't know what you were hoping to find in the first place, Tommy. You shouldn't let Patrick intimidate you so much."

"He doesn't intimidate me," Tommy said, clenching his teeth.

"Is it really so bad that he's back in New York?" she asked. "Why does it bother you so much?"

"It's that letter," Tommy reacted. "That letter scared the shit out of me. We were all so pissed when Patrick disappeared, but I thought we'd gotten over it."

"I got over it," Kate said, wasting no time with her response.

"Me too," added Jesse.

"Well, I didn't. Maybe I took it more personally than you two did. So, when I got that letter in the mail, I knew I didn't want to have to go through all those feelings again. And then there was the plane crash. The possibility of avoiding those feelings was almost too thrilling to ignore. But when he showed up at my door—well, obviously things have been getting worse ever since. Maybe you guys can get over it — maybe you can look beyond the warning signs — but I'm not prepared to. I don't know why I hate Patrick so much, and maybe I wish I didn't. But I do. And I don't want to have to make apologies for that."

Jesse and Kate tried to comprehend Tommy's feelings, but they couldn't. "Let's just get out of here," Kate finally suggested, and she made her way back to the front door.

Tommy pulled a toilet seat from one of the shelves. It was labeled the "HyGenieSeat-3000, Complete with Perineal Spray Attachment." He proudly slid it under one arm. "Might as well take a parting gift, huh?"

Kate was already outside. She looked back at Tommy, confused by his temerity. "You're not seriously stealing a *toilet seat*, are you?"

"I am. You guys should grab one too while we're here."

"This isn't a shopping spree, Tommy," Jesse pointed out. "I don't think any of us deserves a prize for what we've done."

"Suit yourself, Jess," was Tommy's only response.

The two men were slow to exit the warehouse, knowing that any haste was certain to not make a difference anyway.

However, Jesse slowed a bit more when he reflected upon Tommy's counsel from a few minutes earlier. "You know, Tommy. You were happy once too. Isn't that the important thing?" He continued to walk past Tommy, abandoning his waning memories in favor of the cold outside. But Jesse had no idea that Tommy was close to answering the offered supposition. He was so incredibly close to admitting Jesse was right.

~~~

The three of them sat on the curb until their taxi came. It didn't matter how cold the wind was, since it had started to feel even colder inside the warehouse. None of them had uttered a single word for a few minutes. There was a prostitute sitting alone on the curb across the street, but she did not seem nearly as lonely as they.

Tommy was still clutching the stolen toilet seat. "You know," he finally said. "Picking up hookers may not actually count as having an affair."

"Thanks, Tommy. That sure helps a lot."

A police car coasted by listlessly, but its occupants didn't appear to want to get involved in whatever it was Tommy, Kate, and Jesse were doing outside the dark warehouse at that time of night. Tommy waved at the car, but it turned the corner and disappeared.

Tommy continued, "I'm just saying. If you're looking for something to
~~~

blame Gene for, I maybe wouldn't try the affair card. It's just a hooker."

Kate did not thank him for his constructive insight a second time.

Jesse, meanwhile, simply wanted to change the subject. "So, what did we learn from this, Tommy? Do you still think Patrick's up to something? Is there an ulterior motive here?"

But Tommy wasn't sure anymore if he did have cause for suspicion. He felt like they were so close to putting all the loose ends together, and now all of the parts weren't adding up like he hoped they would. He had every piece of the puzzle, but the only thing they seemed to form when put together was nothing more than a coincidence.

Thankfully though, the cab pulled up before Tommy had any further opportunity to admit to anything.

Each of them sat quietly during the drive back to Manhattan. They tried to put the evening's adventure behind them, and considered their own personal circumstances. Kate would have to talk to Gene eventually, wouldn't she? Jesse knew he needed to visit Edie in an attempt to find some closure and finally move on. And Tommy decided, maybe the first time in his life, that he would start to take a look at his own mistakes and failures, rather than pick apart everyone else's.

Breathe out.

PART IV

~~~

THE FALLING
~~~

CHAPTER TWENTY
Tom's Restaurant – Morningside Heights

THE NEXT MORNING.

I was watching Tommy at the table, scribbling something on the top piece of a stack of wrinkled papers. Beside him was a closed telephone book. Kate watched him too, through the window from a safe distance across the street. Tommy was becoming increasingly harder to differentiate from the rest of the city's crazies; Hobolicious, Gwyneth Paltrow, and the like. On the tabletop sat a brown banana peel and a coffee cup that was currently being used as a receptacle for his writing instruments. Whether or not there was still any coffee in the cup was unknown, but nothing would have surprised Kate at that point.

Tommy had no idea she was observing him.

She decided the best thing to do would be to enter the restaurant, rather than spy on her best friend from afar any longer. Tommy paid no attention to the ringing bells of the front door. Kate sat down across from him, yet still kept as much distance as she could. When Kate got out of the cab the night before, she caught Tommy crying in the back seat. He wasn't bawling like a baby; he was wiping wet eyes with his sleeve while trying his best to shield himself with the pilfered toilet seat. Jesse didn't seem to notice, but it had bothered Kate all night.

"What are you working on, Tommy?" she asked carefully.

"Check this out," he said, sliding the papers across the table, not concerned at all when some of them flew away from the pile. The top sheet had nothing but a list of women's names on it, some of which Kate recognized, but most of them she didn't. "I've spent the morning compiling a chronological list of every girlfriend I've had since moving to New York." He drew an invisible line with his finger, from the top of the page to the bottom. "It starts here at Mince Wilson, and goes all the way down to Rachel Ponzini."

Kate pushed the papers back to Tommy. It was astounding to think how Tommy could actually recall all of the information he was presenting; Kate didn't realize he'd had such a copious number of girlfriends over the years. "I'm sorry I asked. Because now I have to ask: why the hell are you doing this, Tommy?"

"I'm not really sure yet," he said. He leaned back in the booth and scratched his head, as though only just realizing the mess he was making. "I thought this might be useful. Like it might help me try and remember the person I used to be. The person I really am. I actually thought it might be cathartic."

"Sounds like the emergence of a spectacular mid-life crisis to me," Kate said. She signaled the waitress, making the universal hand sign for coffee: a hand in a claw shape, and slightly twisting it at the wrist. "Honestly though, I figured I'd have beaten you to it."

"Me too." Tommy opened the phone book beside him. The coffee shop's dusty tome was quite a few years old, and it sat at the front on the cashier's table, barely used by anyone anymore. Flipping through a hundred pages, Tommy stopped and jotted a number and address down beside one of the names on his list. "You ever wonder why there's no email book? You know, like a phone book, but with email addresses instead."

"It's probably because that's a terrible idea," Kate responded bluntly.

In record time, the waitress arrived with a fresh cup of coffee. She almost topped up Tommy's cup before noticing it was full of broken pencils and blunt crayons. She joked, "Should I bring you another cup or just some more crayons?"

"Just the coffee, thanks." Tommy replied, wondering when the coffee shop waitresses started getting so snarky. He glared at her as she approached another booth with her coffee pot. "What would be so terrible about an email book?" he finally asked Kate.

"Oh, I don't know. Would *you* be happy if anyone in this city could just email you at any time?"

"I already get emails from people I don't know. And you know what I do? I delete them. I'd much rather get email spam I can delete than have to answer phone calls from people I don't want to talk to." Tommy flipped through another handful of pages in the directory until he found the next name on his list. "I tell you," he said, jotting the number down. "People take their emails far too seriously."

"You might have a point there, Tommy." Kate recalled one of the last conversations she had with Dwayne Reamer. The *Did-You-Get-My-Email* conversation. Having gone from working in an office for eight years, to a week of sitting home alone with nothing but her computer, some wine, and the occasional cheeseburger, was a fairly drastic change. When Kate left Pendulum a week before, she hadn't said another word to Dwayne. But there was something about the mail room temp that Kate found herself really missing at the oddest of times. She couldn't recall ever missing Gene no matter how long she went without seeing her husband. "Gene wasn't home when I got in last night. I was already asleep when he finally showed up. He didn't tell me where he was, and I never asked him."

"Did he smell like a Jersey City hooker?"

"No. I think *I* did though."

Tommy sniffed in her direction. "I think you *still* do."

She managed a smile. "It would be so much easier if I could just bust him though, don't you think? Then we could just end the whole damn thing."

Tommy mused. "Relationships seem to be so much harder to end than they are to start. Why is that?"

Kate thought the answer was obvious. "It's probably got something to do with having actual human emotions, Tommy."

"Yeah, probably." Tommy sat back and thought for a moment. He flicked his tooth with a fingernail while he deliberated, just like Rachel used to do. "Do you know I can remember absolutely every place I've had a relationship end, and yet I can't remember where any of those relationships *began*?"

Kate shook her head, in an effort to try and find some common ground. "Nobody really knows where relationships begin, Tommy. It's all about that first kiss. That's what we remember."

"Well, that's just what I mean, Kate."

"You don't remember the kiss?"

Tommy sat back, arms crossed. His answer was obvious.

"Come on. Where did you and Rachel have your first kiss?"

"I don't remember."

"Tommy! It was just a couple of years ago!"

"Three, actually."

"Three can be a couple, can't it?"

"Three's not a couple, Kate. *Two's* a couple. That's the *definition* of a couple."

"No, no. I've always been told a couple is two or three."

"Well, you've been horribly misinformed."

"I really think you're wrong."

"Right. Well, the next time I ask you for a couple hundred bucks, I'll be sure to expect a little extra for my trouble." Tommy suggested.

"Since when do you ever need money from me?"

"It was just a hypothetical example, Kate. How the hell did this discussion get off *me*? The point I was trying to make was: how come I can recall *where* my relationships ended, but for the life of me, I can't tell you *why* they ended?"

"Maybe you should consider asking some of your ex-girlfriends?" Mockingly, Kate pointed at the list of phone numbers right in front of Tommy. "I'm sure *they* would be more than happy to jog your memory."

"Right. I know Keekee Kaufman would be extremely anxious to answer *that* phone call," he snickered. But Tommy thought about the possibility for a few seconds longer. "That'd be a real 'High Fidelity' moment though, wouldn't it?"

"Book? Movie?"

"Pffft. The movie, of course. I love a good book, but when a movie gets something right, it's gold." Tommy mulled over many of the High Fidelity-inspired Top-Five lists he and his friends had come up with over the years. There had been some really good ones. "Maybe I should talk to them?" He looked down at the names in front of him. "Yeah, you know what? I *should* give these girls a call!"

"No, Tommy. You definitely shouldn't."

"What? But you just said—"

"If you knew *anything* at all about women, you'd know I was kidding."

"Well, I'd like to think I'm capable of doing anything John Cusack can do."

"Trust me, you're not." It was obvious Kate wasn't going to change her stance on the matter. Sure, maybe the idea had just come to him, but Tommy thought it was still much better than any other one he'd had in the last couple of weeks. It wasn't spiteful, or based on revenge, or born out of fear; it was simply along the lines of self-discovery. If alcoholics and over-eaters and sex addicts can have their own laid out steps to recovery, why couldn't Tommy? Still, Kate could see the wheels turning inside his head and she wished they would just come to a screeching stop. "Please don't do it, Tommy. You'll only end up hurting yourself more."

"That's the idea, isn't it?" Heartache is always followed by a little additional pain, like it comes free of charge. It's all part of the human condition. Tommy was never one to dwell on failed relationships, but he didn't mind the supplemental aching that came with them.

Tommy's Top-Five songs to listen to after a breakup (in no particular order) were:

Sunday Night *by Buffalo Tom*

A Long December *by The Counting Crows*

Say Hello, Wave Goodbye *by Jools Holland*

After Laughter (Comes Tears) *by Wendy Rene*

Come Pick Me Up *by Ryan Adams*

"So how come you're not writing today?" he asked Kate.

"It's the whole Gene mess."

"What happened to that 'easy comfort' you had, or whatever it was you called it?"

"Obviously I was lying," she admitted.

"For the record, I didn't believe you for a second. I doubt Jesse did either, and we all know he's the worst liar in New York."

"I was thinking of following Gene on his lunch break."

"What? When? Today?"

"Yeah. I figured I just need to hang around outside his office when he leaves, and then I'll see where he goes. It might help make my decision easier."

Tommy snorted. He couldn't believe the audacity Kate had sometimes. He joked, "What are you going to do, wear some big, dark glasses and a trench coat, and hide behind a newspaper?" She didn't answer with words, but Tommy could tell his facetious summation was exactly what Kate had planned. "God, that is so cliché!" he blurted. "Do you want to borrow *my* trench coat, or did you already stop by the Spy Store?"

"I've been hiding a trench coat in the back of my closet for years," Kate confessed. "Just in case."

Tommy shook his head in disbelief. "I know you're probably going to tell me I don't know anything about women, but I'm going to ask anyway: Why would you hide a trench coat for the off-chance that you'd need it to spy on your husband? That is so fucked up."

"Well, I can't wear a coat Gene would recognize."

"You don't know *anything* about men, do you? Trust me, Gene's not keeping track of those kinds of things. He's got no idea what your coat collection looks like. Now, your underwear on the other hand—"

"What about my underwear?"

"Men always know their women's undergarment options. Heck, they even know the options *other* women have. But trench coats? Forget about it."

"Okay, fine. But if I can just catch Gene in the middle of something incriminating, then I'd finally have a solid reason for leaving him."

"You already *have* a reason: the guy's a weird loser with a crazy-ass mustache! And you don't love him! Isn't that enough?"

"I know but—" Kate looked out the window and saw Patrick on the other side of 112th Street. He was on his phone and seemed particularly distressed about something. Patrick noticed both Tommy and Kate in the window, and held up a single finger, letting them know he'd be inside in another minute.

The two of them turned to one another. Kate was worried they were about to get busted for breaking into Titanic Utilities the night before. Did she touch anything? Did she drop something accidentally? Were there video cameras? Oh god, they never even looked for cameras, did they?

"I feel kind of stupid now for breaking into the warehouse," Tommy uttered. "Partly because we never did find anything of importance, but mostly because I can't believe I let myself get so carried away."

"You should probably tell Patrick that."

"Are you kidding? I'm not saying *anything* to him! If I did, I'd probably have to give back the HyGenieSeat-3000. We installed it in Jesse's bathroom last night. It's fucking awesome." Because of the fire, Tommy had spent the rest of the night at Jesse's apartment. Earlier that morning, the fire department had given the okay to the tenants of Tommy's building, and they would all be moving back in that afternoon.

"As awesome as a toilet seat can be, you mean?" Kate pontificated.

Patrick did not seem to be getting anywhere with whomever he was talking to. He leaned up against a tree and a clump of snow fell from its branch onto his shoulder. He didn't even bother to brush it off.

Kate asked, "Where *is* Jesse, anyway?"

"I think he was going into Brooklyn today to visit Edie. He didn't really want to talk about it, so we didn't. He was still on his bed psyching himself up when I left."

"Poor Jess."

Finally, Patrick entered. He had his choice of seat, and decided upon sitting next to Kate. She feared it was so he wouldn't have to look at her, angry because of what she'd done. Tommy was just happy he didn't have to move his coat and bag from the empty seat beside him. Before Patrick returned to New York, Tommy never had to move his things for anyone.

"Hey, Patrick." Kate squeezed the words out almost against her will. "Where's Sheldon?"

"You guys are not going to believe this. My warehouse was broken into last night. That was Jules on the phone just now. He said he gave a report to the police."

Both Tommy and Kate just sat, waiting for the other shoe to fall.

"I've got to go over there today and assess any damages." He slammed his fist down on the table hard enough for everything to jump: the napkin dispenser, the salt, the pepper, the sugar, and even Tommy's mug of pencils. "Seriously, though. We only set that place up a couple of weeks ago. That's some shitty luck."

"Who would even want to steal a toilet seat?" Kate asked Patrick but stared directly at Tommy. Tommy gathered his pencils and paper, stuffed them all into his SpongeBob bag, and threw on his coat and scarf. "Where are you going, Tommy?"

"I can't just sit here all morning. I've got to go check on my apartment, and then I'm off to High-Fidelity my life."

"You're going to do *what*?" Patrick had never read the book, seen the movie, or even heard of such a reference before. It was embarrassingly astounding how many things Patrick had never experienced in his life, how much he had absolutely no clue about. He didn't know who Dustin Hoffman was. He thought India was somewhere in Africa. He couldn't name one Major League Baseball team. And, purely by chance, he had never actually seen a picture of the Mona Lisa. Not even once in his entire life.

"Don't listen to Tommy," Kate advised. "He had a rough night."

Tommy dropped some money on the table for his meal, and said goodbye to the two of them.

"Hold on, Tommy," Patrick started. "Before you go, I wanted to ask the both of you something."

Tommy muttered under his breath, "Uh oh—"

"*Uh oh*? What's that supposed to mean?"

"What did you want to ask, Patrick?" Kate was quick to add.

"I just thought we should all go out tomorrow night. Jesse too. Aside from sitting in this coffee shop, we haven't spent any meaningful time together since I came back. I thought it would be nice."

Tommy didn't want to make a flimsy excuse, but what was really so wrong with his coffee shop anyway? It was where he felt safest. "Tomorrow's Halloween though," he said. "All the crazies are going to be out there."

"Didn't *we* used to be those crazy ones? Weren't *we* once running around drunk in New York and screaming at all of the uptight people? Come on guys, it'll be fun. How about the Temple Bar at eight o'clock?"

Their first evening in New York was spent at the Temple Bar in NoHo. The four of them showed their fake Seattle ID's and they all got in. It was a fantastic night, celebrating their newfound independence, until getting kicked out at three in the morning. Jesse assumed the reason they were standing on the sidewalk was because somebody had finally found out about the ID's. Not realizing it was simply closing time, Jesse yelled drunkenly at the bar staff. He had assumed Manhattan bars never closed.

"I don't know—" Tommy wavered.

"Come on. We should all wear costumes too," Patrick suggested. "What do you say, guys?"

Tommy looked over to the woman at the front cash, as if she could possibly help him out with the decision. She just shrugged and continued to count the money in the register. The framed picture of Cosmo Kramer seemed to nod, as if saying everything would be okay. "Fine," Tommy finally said. "I'll see you guys tomorrow night." Tommy exited out onto Broadway with his pile of paperwork, scratching his head and trying to decide which direction to head first.

Patrick turned to Kate, now that it was just the two of them. "Why does Tommy keep acting like that? He's been so indifferent and obstinate ever since I came back."

"I think he just misses you," Kate said without really even thinking about it.

"Yeah. I guess so." Uninterested, Patrick flipped through the menu a few times before realizing he didn't want anything to eat. He sat as far back in his seat as he could, and huffed. "Now, where the hell am I going to find a costume for tomorrow?"

Kate stirred her coffee slowly, not really for any reason. "This is New York," she said. "You can have whatever you want, whenever you want it."

"Do you really believe that?" Patrick asked.

"I do," she said. "And if you stick around long enough this time, you'll see it's true."

Patrick tried his best to not think about why he had ever left so many years ago.

CHAPTER TWENTY-ONE
Greenwood – Brooklyn

Jesse took the R-Train from Times Square to the 25th Street station in Brooklyn. There were some unsavory characters loitering on the corner outside the Dunkin' Donuts, so Jesse picked up his pace. He'd never been as confident as Tommy; Tommy could walk anywhere he wanted in any of New York's most disagreeable neighborhoods. There was a gravestone and monument manufacturer only a half-block from the cemetery; its grim entranceway a sort of Halloween display of graves and tablets, marking the final resting place for nothing more than discarded cigarette butts and fast food wrappers.

Jesse had never been to a cemetery. Before Edie, he'd never lost anyone so close to him. He remembered his high-school art teacher, Mr. Freyberg, who had died suddenly while walking to work one morning. A crowd of kids had formed around his unmoving body on the sidewalk, not one of them knowing what to do. Up until a year ago, Mr. Freyberg's was the only death that had any consequence on Jesse's life. After Edie died, Tommy, Kate, and Jesse had snuck into the funeral home on 2nd Avenue for her funeral service. Tommy claimed he had the best egg salad sandwich in his life at that funeral service. They all agreed going to Brooklyn for the subsequent burial was definitely out of the question.

Green-Wood Cemetery was an expanse of nearly five-hundred acres, and Jesse wandered under portentous clouds for nearly an hour before heading to the office for proper directions. Trudging through Lot 106 with a visitors' map in his trembling hands, Jesse wondered whether things might have been easier if graveyards had been organized in a similar way to comic book collections. He imagined that if the dead could be slid into coffins of polypropylene storage bags with acid free backing boards, and then filed — alphabetically first, and numerically second — into corrugated cardboard or plastic boxes, finding the appropriate marker would be a much easier task.

But as promised, the marked pathway eventually led all the way to the grave of Edith Lenora Galloway.

Jesse didn't take his feet off the path, as though stepping off would transport him somewhere he didn't wish to be; sending him to the same place of darkness that Edie would always know for the rest of eternity. He could still read the tombstone from where he stood however, so there was really no need to get any further away from the living than he already was.

The marker lacked any description, aside from Edith's name and the dates which indicated her time on the earth. It was one year ago to the day since she died. Of course he'd thought of her often over the past year, but Jesse found it much more difficult to actually see her name etched in the stone. Jesse scanned around him. It seemed as though he was the only person in the cemetery, the only sign of life, like he was in a dream of his own creation. But in his dreams, Edie was still alive. In Jesse's dreams, it was John who had died beneath the Hudson River on that cold, snowy night. But the callousness of reality bore on.

A drop of rain the size of Jesse's fist exploded on the rim of the tomb. Another, as full as Jesse's heart, punched into the earth, no doubt trickling its way through the dirt until finding the coffin.

In comic books, a hero seemed to die only to be brought back to life. It was inevitable, and to the vast majority of readers, almost expected.

In 1993, Superman had been beaten to death by the alien monstrosity known as Doomsday. He returned mere months later, revived by the Eradicator's Regeneration Matrix.

The X-Men's Marvel Girl sacrificed herself in 1980 to save the universe from the Dark Phoenix — a cosmic entity of unimaginable psionic power — but her body was later discovered within a healing cocoon at the bottom of Jamaica Bay, created by the Phoenix Force itself.

After the destruction of Coast City in 1994, Hal Jordan went on an insane rampage, becoming the villain Parallax, and using his Green Lantern powers to kill all of the Guardians of the Universe on the planet Oa. Only two years later, Jordan had a change of heart and sacrificed his life when he re-ignited the sun. Implausibly, his soul was later selected to embody the unearthly being known as The Spectre, and Jordan became the Spirit of Redemption.

And on and on it goes. It's unfair the real world doesn't work as simply as comic book logic. Yes, Patrick had returned to Manhattan, but even if that had once seemed impossible, it was still a completely different situation.

Jesse raised his foot, and prodded the ground with the tip of his scuffed sneaker. His frayed shoelaces tickled the blades of grass. The earth wheezed as he planted his foot firmly. The grave yielded no response. He inched closer, putting his other foot down now. A wind blew around him; it twisted through his legs and arms. Jesse wanted to feel as though it was welcoming him, but he sensed the exact opposite. The wounds inflicted by the past had not yet mended; the cuts were still waiting to scab over. Either forgiving or forgetting would be the only path to recovery. He knew it at that moment, and he knew it when he watched John Galloway from the window of Midtown Comics. He planned on waiting for John to make the next move, but Jesse had yet to hear back from him about that persisting comic collection.

Jesse crouched, and ran his fingertips along the dewy grass. A brown, crusty leaf fell from the sky, seemingly out of nowhere, and it had somehow disregarded the intensifying winds. The leaf landed directly on top of the grave. Jesse had less than a moment to consider what it must have meant.

There was a woman's voice behind him.

"Hello? Can I help you?"

Still crouching, Jesse turned to see a woman standing on the path, probably no older than Jesse himself. Beside her stood John Galloway. She held John's arm tightly.

"I'm sorry," Jesse stammered. He stood so he wouldn't have to look up at John. "I was just leaving."

John seemed more focused on keeping his hat atop his head than considering the reasons for why Jesse Classen was standing in front of him at his wife's grave. It was almost as though John was trying his best to not recognize him.

"Did you know Miss Galloway?" the woman asked. She had a rich Southern accent, the kind that seemed to transport listeners to another time.

Jesse glanced back and forth between the two of them. The woman clutched John's arm a little tighter. "Edith, was a friend. Of my mother's." Jesse didn't care if John believed him or not; he was going to call the old man's bluff. Still, his words garnered no reaction. "But I was just on my way. Excuse me."

"You can stay longer if you'd like to. It's fine with me. I'm sure it'd be fine with John, too." She looked to John for confirmation.

"Yes," the man said quietly, slowly shaking his head in agreement. "It's fine."

Jesse couldn't put it together. John seemed like a completely different person. He appeared so frail, as if the wind might blow him over at any moment. He held the woman's arm tightly, lacking the stubborn show of independence he had exhibited in the comic store's office the week before.

"John is Miss Galloway's husband," the woman said. Jesse did his best impression of a stranger, trying to pretend he didn't know any better. "My name is Esther. I'm John's nurse." Waving her hand graciously, Esther let go of John, and she sat down on a nearby bench.

The two men stood side by side. Jesse strained his eyes trying to look at John without having to turn his head. Without a word or any care at all for Jesse, John stared straight ahead at the grave. His gaze was simultaneously intense and nebulous, and both were making Jesse uncomfortable. Jesse knew he had to say something to his enemy.

The brown leaf remained static on the grave. Another gust of wind blew toward them, and Jesse told himself he'd say something to John if the leaf did not blow away. That would decide it easily.

But it didn't budge.

Jesse closed his eyes, and counted down from ten in his head. If the leaf was still in front of him by the time he reached zero, he would finally speak his mind.

...Three...Two...One...Zero. The leaf had not even shifted an inch. But Jesse still could not do it.

Defeated, Jesse sat down beside Esther, collapsing onto the cold bench. She was running something back and forth under her nose, sniffing it. It was a cinnamon stick. Forgetting all about John for a moment, he stared at her with a fresh curiosity. "What are you doing?"

"My mother loved the smell of cinnamon so much she'd rub it on her clothes." She inhaled deeply. "Sometimes on her neck too. It's my favorite memory. I always keep a stick of cinnamon in my purse so I can remember her anytime I want."

Jesse responded sincerely. "That's nice." He wished he could carry every scent with him that he would need to remember everyone and everything he ever loved. The beach. Bubble gum. Dandelion weeds. Cigarettes. Ratty old comic books.

Opening her handbag, Esther carefully placed the stick of cinnamon back inside and sealed it tight again. She inhaled deeply through her nose, bringing herself back to reality. She asked softly, "You're the young man who was sleeping with Miss Galloway, aren't you?"

Jesse glanced quickly over to John, hoping he didn't hear her words. It was obvious he hadn't. "How did you know that?" Jesse asked her quietly.

"Your smell was all over that house," Esther said, tapping her nose.

"Does *he* know?" Jesse asked, directing his attention back to John. The man's back was still turned toward the two of them, his head lowered. "He doesn't seem to remember me."

Esther steeled herself, as though preparing to say something she did not wish to speak of. "The poor man's mind has been slipping lately. Sometimes he remembers the littlest details about the littlest of things. Just yesterday he recounted all nine innings of a Dodgers game he saw when he was just a boy. And then he went on about some tie his father made him wear to the World Fair. This morning, it was all about stock prices on Wall Street in the Sixties."

"Really?"

"Mm hmm. But then at other times, he doesn't remember a thing. Not his name, not where he's going, or where he's been. It's all just blank. The way he describes it, it's something like a white emptiness."

John Galloway scratched the back of his head. He looked around him, as though temporarily forgetting where he was. Turning to the bench, he recognized his nurse sitting with the stranger. With the back of her hand, Esther pointed toward the grave behind him, and he turned again, suddenly remembering his reason for being in the cemetery.

"His doctor said the first time it ever happened was the night Miss Galloway died. He told me about an accident in the tunnel. Said it happened while he was driving."

Jesse's thoughts jumped back to the brown stain of dried blood in the tunnel. He remembered the patch of blood was shaped like a checkmark; like some sort of soulless higher power had approved the accident. "I've tried my best to forget everything that happened that night," he said. "I've been trying for a year now, but I still can't erase the memories."

Esther directed Jesse's attention toward John. He was completely oblivious to the rain which was starting to come down around him. "Do you suppose you'd be happier if you were in that man's shoes?"

Jesse didn't have a reasonable answer for her. He had never once wished to be John Galloway. Esther opened her umbrella and walked over to the grave. She led John to the bench and handed the umbrella to Jesse. "Will you wait here with him?" she asked Jesse. "I think I should bring the car over. No sense getting him more wet than he already is."

Jesse didn't want her to go, and his unsteady eyes couldn't disguise it.

"Relax," she said to him. "You'll be just fine." Nurse Esther left, leaving the two men together with their collective misery.

Jesse didn't know what to say. He felt guilty for having been so suspicious of John the last time they'd met, how he had him playing the villain to the hero in his mind. But now, there was a space between the two men that did not exist before.

Jesse considered the white spaces — the gutters, they're called — between panels in a comic book, and how they are used to represent time. But it could be just a moment they signify, a sliver in time, or it could be a million years later, or even no time at all. Sometimes they will take the reader through space and time, going into the past, or perhaps to an alternate reality. Maybe a flashback? Maybe the same moment, but at a different angle? Sometimes those spaces are used to hold important details; sometimes nothing at all. What they represent is never predetermined: it is determined only by what happens in the next panel.

He turned his head slowly to look at John, at first from the corner of his eye, but eventually turning his head all the way toward the man on his left. John did not move however, and kept his gaze fixed upon the grave marker. Jesse wondered about the white spaces that must be dividing John Galloway's memories, separating one random moment from another.

But then John mumbled something he couldn't quite make out. "What was that?" Jesse asked, reticently.

"It was Preston Mayne's office."

"I don't understand?"

"That was when I met her. Preston Mayne had a tiny office in the Empire State Building. It seemed larger than it was though, because there was practically nothing in it. Edith Lenora Harrington was his secretary, but I knew from the moment I saw her, she deserved so much more than that menial office job."

Jesse didn't know what to say, but he expected John would continue his story. He waited for the white space to pass; for the page to turn.

"That girl who gave me my bagel, she dropped the tongs on the floor. She didn't think anyone saw her, but I saw her. I didn't say a word though. I just threw it right in the garbage."

It was not clear just how much time the blank space had represented, if indeed either of John's memories were real. Jesse was spooked a little by the disconnectedness of the man's recollections. He thought he should share a random memory of his own but he wasn't sure where to start. Eventually he said, "When we first came to New York, Tommy, Kate, and Patrick were all attending universities, but I never knew what it was I wanted to do. I spent so much time, so many years, just trying to discover what it was I *really* wanted." It was unclear if John was listening, but Jesse carried on anyway. "I was so lonely back then. I was so *lost*. But I never wanted to tell them how I really felt."

Finally, John turned to Jesse. He did not say a word, but with his eyes, he still managed to indicate he knew exactly what Jesse must have gone through.

Jesse smiled. "Did you know I even tried stand-up comedy once during an improv night?" John shook his head. "No, of course you wouldn't know that.

I didn't tell anyone about that. God, it was such a massive failure. I don't think anybody laughed at all, except out of pity. It was *horrible*. The vulnerability of naked nerves on that stage."

"There was a stage—" John said. His mouth seemed exceptionally dry, even with the rain blowing up from under the umbrella. "I came home late to find the note she left for me. I wanted nothing else but to be with Edith." Jesse gulped, not because he knew what night John was talking about, but because he was afraid of how far the memory would go before the white space in John's mind ended it. "I was on stage with this strange masked man, in the middle of his strange city. He laughed at me, and then he punched me, and then I woke up in the Holland Tunnel. I couldn't remember where I was going to, or where I was coming from. And then I saw Edith being carried into an ambulance where she died."

Jesse felt dizzy. He felt a cold sweat pour over him. The rain came to a stop when everything else around him froze. He was trapped in his own white space; in the gutter between the panels of his own world. He felt awful. But Jesse didn't know if he felt that way because John was remembering what happened to Edie, or if it was because John had been completely unaware of Jesse's role in the whole story.

But before Jesse could decide, John continued. He seemed so much more lucid than before, as though talking about his memories made them that much more real. "After the accident, I wanted to get rid of everything that ever meant anything at all to me. The next day, I took my paintings to Sotheby's. It didn't take me long to sell the house. I smashed all of my vintage wine from the rooftop. I tore up my Hemingways."

Jesse hesitated for a moment. He wanted to know, but was afraid to ask. He was sure John did not recognize him, so what was the harm in asking? So, he asked: "What about your comic books?"

John faltered, but eventually had an answer. "I talked to a man about saving them for me." There seemed to be an awareness of sorts in his old grey-blue eyes. It was apparent John thought his visit to Midtown Comics had happened after Edie's death, and not actually three years before. His memory either jumped around or created complete inaccuracies. Obviously, the man had never sold the Gramercy home as he claimed. And still, he failed to recognize Jesse at all.

"I lost someone important too," was what Jesse said. But it didn't seem to faze the man at all, as John turned back to the grave where his wife was laid. After a long pause, Jesse asked, "Did you ever sell those comics?"

John shook his head, but not to say no. He shook his head to say he couldn't remember.

"Well," Jesse said, recollecting the words that had been shared between the two men just a week before. "I know someone who might be able to help you with that."

Without flinching, John reached into his breast pocket and took out a familiar business card, handing it to Jesse. It was the third time Jesse Classen had been handed that same card. "Wonderful," John said. "Why don't you come by?"

Breathe out.

Just as Esther brought the car to a stop, the rain halted and the clouds parted. She stepped toward the two men, surprised to see them talking to one another. "Well, isn't that just the way it goes sometimes?" she spoke in wonderment, and to no one at all. She helped John into the passenger's seat. Jesse watched as the man wriggled under the seat belt and clenched his jaw. Before driving off, Esther asked Jesse if he got the chance to say the things he needed to.

Jesse thought about it. "If I could go back in time and fix it all, I would."

"Honey, that's what everybody says after they've messed it all up. Just don't blame yourself."

The one thought that came to Jesse's head was: Things always happen for a reason. He hated it when people used that line as a way to justify when things don't work out the way they wanted them to. He hoped the nurse would be good enough to not utter such an irrational axiom. Jesse expected more from her.

But then she said: "Life has a way of going exactly the way it's meant to go."

It was essentially the same thing, but Jesse told himself it wasn't such a bad thing to hear.

~~~

From the sidewalk, the Brooklyn Superhero Supply Company looks no different than a hardware store or a keysmith's shop. Jesse expected bright colors, posters, and signage, not unlike the displays at Midtown Comics, and he almost walked right by before spotting an advertisement for Telepathy Gel at the last second. He had known about the place for a while now, yet it seemed like one of those establishments spawned out of an urban legend, created solely for mystifying comic book nerds like himself.

The real secret behind the business was that the store was merely a front for a one-on-one after school learning center. A place where neighborhood children could be helped to improve their writing skills. Inside the store, behind a shelf full of grappling hooks and secret identity kits, was a hidden door which led to the learning center.

But Jesse was not there to bump up his high school level of education. He had heard the best costumes money could buy were for sale at the Superhero Supply store, so he intended on stopping by the next time he was in Brooklyn. Jesse was not asked if he needed help, and truthfully, he would not have known how to answer; he was simply too perplexed by all of the products on display.
~~~

He studied the shelves full of Power Supplements (in large plastic vitamin tubs, but these were for increasing the users' own powers of weather control, optic blasts, and teleportation), containers of Unstable Mutation Catalysts, and spray cans for the application of invisibility, regeneration, and steel skin. Jesse didn't know what any of them actually contained — there was no indication on the packaging — but it was all for sale. Even the Bionic Implants (a display skeleton helped illustrate where/how the robotic attachments might be affixed) and the Villain Containment Unit: a human-sized cage with an intricate locking mechanism.

Upon finding himself in the costume department, Jesse was finally approached by a forty-something hipster who claimed to be an employee. He certainly did not seem to possess any super abilities of his own, but Jesse answered him with caution nonetheless. "I'm looking for a costume," Jesse spoke bluntly.

"Are you replacing an old uniform, or will you be looking for an all-new identity?" The man had a badge on, but it was nothing more than a comic explosion that read "POW!" Whether this was a nametag or not seemed irrelevant.

"Uh—"

"Do you already have a superhero moniker?"

"Um, no."

"Then a new identity it is! Don't worry. We'll fill out all of the necessary paperwork later. What kind of costume are you thinking? Single color? Two-tone? Stripes? Nationalistic? Maybe something dark for night patrols?"

Jesse looked around, far beyond the man who was bombarding him with stupid questions. On any other day, he would have savored the eccentricity of such a place, but he was having a hard time believing that any of what was happening was for real. Still, the man continued to stare at Jesse, waiting for an answer. "Well, I don't really want anything more than just a plain costume.

Maybe with a mask."

"Plain, huh? How about some upgrades at least? A utility belt?"

"I don't think so."

"Goggles? Deflector bracelets?"

"I'm not really into jewelry."

"Cape? You've got to have a cape!"

"Aren't capes sort of dangerous?" Jesse loved superheroes, but his fear of capes went back to his childhood when he was dressed as Batman and tripped on his cape at the top of the stairs. He tumbled all the way to the bottom, and cut his head open on the corner of a wall. He spent that Halloween night in the hospital, getting stitches instead of candy.

"Dangerous? Nah!"

"I think I'll just stick with the plainest costume you've got."

The sales associate riffled through some suits on hangers and pulled out a white bodysuit with black gloves and boots. His eyes bulged, never imagining someone would pick such a boring outfit over all of the other options. "Sheesh. Who are you gonna be, *Boring Boy*?"

It was just as plain as the costume Sheldon Kohn had worn to the coffee shop the week before. "I think I might go with *General Generic*."

"Who?"

"Never mind."

The man held the costume up in front of Jesse, proclaiming it to be a perfect fit, assuring him it would stretch everywhere it needed to. "Alrighty. All we've got to do now is register your superhero name and powers." He led Jesse toward the front counter and handed him some blank forms.

"There sure seems to be a lot of paperwork involved just to buy a Halloween costume."

"Hey man, this is more than just Halloween. This is a lifestyle choice. Besides, we can't have two guys running around the city with the same name, can we?"

"No. I suppose not." Jesse filled out the paperwork begrudgingly, settling on *The Midtown Minder* for his own heroic nickname. Under Superpowers he wrote: None. Under Special Abilities he wrote: None. Under Arch-Enemy he stopped to consider his answer, but eventually decided on: None. He passed the forms back to the man and waited a moment for everything to be put in order.

In that moment, Jesse noticed a small, waist-height table to his right. On the table were a dozen or so cans of Time Travel Juice. A sign indicated that drinking the juice would allow the user to move forwards or backwards through the time stream, letting him alter events of his choosing. The product just happened to be on sale, too. Jesse couldn't help but think about everything that had gone wrong in the last few years: Edith's death; John's memory loss; Kate's marriage; Natasha Kohn's cancer; Tommy's failed novel. What if Patrick had never left them? What if Jesse had never come to New York with his friends in the first place? What if he could fix it all? The solutions to all of his problems might have been right there on that table in front of him, canned and waiting to be opened.

He thought about the last thing Sharona said to him, before she left him sitting alone on that sidewalk in the Village: she told him to get over whatever he needed to get over. She said, *"I don't know how you'll go about doing it, but you need to get over it."*

It seemed to Jesse there were so many different ways to get lost; so many ways to break apart a life. And sometimes there's no way at all to ever fix it.

Jesse took one can of Time Travel Juice and placed it next to his costume on the counter. "And one of these too," he said.

"Alrighty," the man responded. "I'll just need you to recite the *Vow of Heroism* and then I can ring these up."

"Excuse me?"

The man behind the counter reached over and pointed to a sign in front of Jesse. At the top it read: "The Vow of Heroism," and there was a passage beneath it. Jesse looked around again, but he was still the only customer in the store. He cleared his throat and began to read: "I, Jesse Classen, also known as The Midtown Minder, promise always to use my superpowers for good. I promise that I will use the items I've purchased here today safely and in the name of justice. I promise to remain ever vigilant, ever true."

Satisfied with Jesse's speech, the man announced the total cost of the purchase, wrapped up the costume and the can of Time Travel Juice, and handed them to Jesse. "Always honor the vow," he said as Jesse walked back out into Brooklyn.

CHAPTER TWENTY-TWO
Mince Wilson's Apartment – Alphabet City

Mince Wilson still lived in the same old apartment building on the corner of Avenue A and 11th. Tommy wasn't surprised at all to see the familiar "M.WILSON" on the door buzzer, because Mince had always said she would never move from that spot. And she was without a doubt the least hyperbolic person Tommy had ever met; Mince never exaggerated.

She never lied, never stretched the truth, and never assumed something to be something it wasn't. And because of this, she was also always right. In fact, she was absolutely correct when she declared "The Garbage Pail Kids" to be the worst film ever made. It was true. And when she said "The Brothers Karamazov" was undoubtedly the *only* book anyone would ever need to read, she could not have been more accurate. She knew the best places in the city for milkshakes, borsht, sunsets, and public washrooms. It was uncanny just how right one person could be.

The singular untruth about her was her moniker: "Mince" was only a nickname, and yet, Tommy never once discovered what her real name was. And he'd never once asked.

Mince consistently amazed Tommy. To her, the best thing about this was that she never even had to try. She was the first girlfriend Tommy had in New York, and very nearly the first girl he'd ever spoken to in Manhattan. That alone was enough to satisfy him. To Tommy, having dreamed his whole life of coming to the greatest city in the world and making love to one of its native residents was surreal. There really wasn't much Mince Wilson could have possibly done to screw up their relationship. She always had Tommy wrapped around her finger.

Tommy pressed the buzzer. Nothing. He tried it again.

"Yeah?" said the voice on the other end, loud enough to speak over crying kids. The wonderful noise of the street traffic returned once her finger was released from the intercom.

"Mince? It's Tommy."

The screaming picked up right where it left off. "What?"

Tommy cringed a little from what sounded like some daycare of torture. "It's Tommy Mueller."

Pause.

"The guy from Seattle?"

"Seattle? Come on! I'm a New Yorker, babe!" Tommy didn't mean to confuse her, but he also didn't want to pretend he was anything he wasn't. Nevertheless, the door clicked open, and Tommy made his way back up the once-familiar stairs.

But the higher Tommy stepped, the more unsure he had become. The details of his relationship with Mince Wilson were now nothing but watered-down memories: he couldn't recall how long they had dated or where they had broken up, and it was no surprise the memory of where they had kissed for the first time was now misplaced too. It wasn't until he approached her door — behind which emanated the miserable squeals of malcontent children — that Tommy found one of the missing pieces: there was a fist-sized dent in the wall beside the door. The only physical evidence that the two of them had ever broken up was still waiting to be repaired. He placed his hand in the cavity just to make sure it still fit, but the door opened before Tommy could decide if it made him feel any better.

"Tommy? My goodness, it *is* you." The evidence that ten years had passed had never been more obvious than it was on Mince Wilson. But maybe that was still her being truthful about everything. She was noticeably heavier, and grayer at the temples, with her frazzled hair tied back in what was possibly the world's most unflattering ponytail. Her smooth, dark skin had somehow worn lighter, and was now covered with unappealing bumps. She was trying her best to hold on to a two-year old, who, much like Tommy, did not want to be there, and she failed miserably. The kid ran off somewhere inside the dark apartment, the exact opposite direction Tommy wanted to be at that moment.

"Hey, Mince."

"What are you *doing* here?" The television volume suddenly went up roughly eight notches. Some incessant cartoon was trying its best to out-yell the kids.

"Honestly, I'm not really sure now."

"Do you want to come inside?" Mince stepped back a little in order to give Tommy access to her cave of hell.

"God, no!" Tommy jumped back a little. "I mean, this will only take a minute. Could we talk out here in the hall?"

She stepped out and closed the door, muffling the noise only somewhat. Tommy noticed her t-shirt had ridden up a little above her bulbous waist, revealing the dark void of what was once the cutest bellybutton he'd ever stuck his tongue into. "What is it, Tommy?"

Tommy decided the best thing to do would be to simply cut to the chase. "Here's the thing. I just came back here to ask you why we broke up."

"What?"

"I don't want you to get the wrong idea—" The television went up again, followed by the sound of something hard hitting something even harder. Mince just ignored the clamor while Tommy continued. "I'm definitely not trying to spark an old flame or anything. I just—"

"Wait, you're not going all John Cusack on me right now, are you?"

"Uh—um. Yeah. I guess it sounds pretty stupid, but that's *exactly* what I'm doing."

Mince almost answered immediately, but then she took a little extra time to think about it. She glanced at the dent in the wall; Tommy imagined she ran her fingers along it every day, as though it was a precious memento left behind. A trophy for surviving the world's worst relationship.

Finally, she said, "The last time we ever ate pancakes at the Veselka. Do you remember that?"

"We ate a lot of pancakes at the Veselka," Tommy admitted. "You might want to narrow it down for me."

"You kept going on and on about some friend of yours. About how you were doing *this* with him, and then doing *that*. I couldn't get a word in. I just kept eating my rhubarb pancakes."

"I don't understand."

"I was fed up with competing, Tommy. I just felt like you wanted to be with *him* more than you wanted to be with *me*."

"Jesse?"

"Huh?"

"Was that his name?"

"No," she thought back. "No, it wasn't Jesse."

Tommy didn't want to say it. But he did anyway. "Patrick?" After all, Patrick was the reason why he came to Mince Wilson's apartment in the first place.

"Yeah, Patrick. That was it." She looked down the hall, past Tommy. As though that pancake breakfast was happening again right behind him. "Patrick always came first with you, and I just had enough of coming in second."

"Huh." As eloquent as Tommy considered himself, he had a knack for failing to recognize the times he wasn't. Times just like this. "Huh," he said again, with even less panache.

"We came back here. I told you what was what, and that was that. You punched a hole in my hallway and then you left."

Tommy took another look behind him. "In the wall's defense, that's really more of a dent than a hole," he noted. "But I see your point." Something ran into the other side of the door and started crying. Tommy jumped back a little more, while Mince didn't even flinch. "You gonna tend to that?" he asked.

"I'll get to it when we're done here," she said coldly. "I'll tell you though, Tommy from Seattle. I actually thought we were done ten years ago."

"I guess this was all just a waste of time then?"

Mince clutched the doorknob. Not because she was making a move toward the relative safety of her home, but simply because she felt she needed something to hold on to. "Goes to show you how little can change in such a long time."

The city breathes out. And Tommy exhaled. Mince Wilson was as perceptive and as frank as ever. Kate may have been right about the High Fidelity plan being a bad one. "Maybe Cusack was wrong," he pondered.

"Cusack's an idiot. And I don't care what anyone says, that book was much better than the movie."

"Are you sure about that?"

"Of course I am." She was never less than one hundred percent sure about anything. Mince opened her door and stepped back inside, just as the crying came to an end. "You know, Tommy. The truth is, you always were a chowderhead. And you still are a chowderhead." Then she closed the door.

Mince Wilson was right. She was always right. And there was nothing Tommy could do but agree with her.

CHAPTER TWENTY-THREE
Kate & Gene's Brownstone – Upper West Side

In the two weeks since she scratched "Chapter One" onto the first page of her blank journal, Kate had almost filled the entire book. Sure, some pages were crumpled at the foot of her desk, torn out of futility, and some fat, black X's were marked across them, but she had tenaciously scribbled nearly one hundred and seventy-five pages of quality fiction. Unlike "Paper Fences" before it, this still-unnamed new novel had direction, structure, and raw, involved emotion. She was actually proud of what she'd created and was genuinely looking forward to writing more. Her characters excited her, and her scenes made her want to experience them first hand. A few times now, her eyes watered up and her vision blurred, but she loved the feeling of tearing open her own soul and transplanting the meat of herself into the page. And the best part was that she could not even feel her cramped hand or lower back anymore.

Since walking away from Pendulum Publishing, Kate had only left her desk for sleep (sometimes in bed with Gene, but just as often on the couch), meals at the coffee shop (perhaps with another trip or two to the McDonald's for cheeseburgers. Who was counting?), and for the one disappointing adventure to New Jersey with Tommy and Jesse.

She opted against donning her trench coat and following Gene on his lunch break that afternoon. Tommy was right; it really was a horrible idea. On the other hand, she knew Tommy would still have gone through with his own asinine plan of self-discovery; as good as he was at dispensing helpful, friendly advice, he was never one to listen to any of it himself. The man was simply too bull-headed.

The box of personal items from work was still sitting on the floor below her desk. She hadn't yet decided what she would keep and what she would throw away, but Kate was leaning toward the latter for all of it. The longer you hang on to something, the harder it is to remove it from your life, no matter how important the item in question actually is.

The cereal bowl on her desktop was beginning to smell. There was a cupboard full of clean bowls in the kitchen, but Kate continued to refill the same one. Now it was sticky with dried milk and sugary crumbs. She reached for the bottle of wine in front of her, but realized it had been emptied hours ago. There was something about the combination of Frankenberry cereal and elderberry wine that not only sounded great together, but also created an incomparable flavor magic.

There were the muffled sounds of footsteps outside. A child's curious voice. Kate tried to peer out her basement window, but all she could see was the darkened street and her own clouded mannequin eyes looking back at her. Her head was heavy. Perhaps she'd been awake for too long now, or needed something other than sugar and wine in her stomach.

The footsteps came closer, crunching through the snow and up the front steps of the brownstone. The doorbell chimed, but Kate did not move. Gene was upstairs somewhere, so surely, he would answer it. After a moment's pause, Gene yelled for her to please get the door. The man was such an introvert he would never bark orders at anyone, so it could only mean he had not been sleeping much himself lately. He understood Kate's writing was important to her, but the truth was he also missed the warmth of her body in their bed.

The doorbell rang again, and this time Kate called up to her husband. She knew he would always cave in first, which was part of the reason why she was still refusing to admit defeat in their marriage; he was sure to break soon. And hopefully any time now.

From her office below the front stoop, Kate heard Gene's ratty slippers shuffling toward the door. There was some stifled chatter, but she could not make out a word of it. "Katherine!" he called. "You've got visitors."

Without too much hesitation, she trudged upstairs, and was surprised to see Patrick and Sheldon. Halloween was still a day away, but Sheldon was wearing his costume again, and he was munching on a miniature Three Musketeers bar. Gene Schneider loved Halloween so much, he'd had a bowl of candy bars at the front door for well over a week now. He loved candy. He never had a single cavity in his life, and he would mention it at the office any chance he got. When he was a boy, he was not allowed to go out trick-or-treating; instead, he and his brother got to stay home in their Mickey and Minnie costumes watching Charlie Brown and eating boxes of raisins.

"Hey, Fart Tart," Patrick said. It had not occurred to him that it may have been inappropriate to call Kate by her old nickname in front of her husband.

"What are you guys doing here?" she asked, her eyes adjusting to the light.

"We were just at the coffee shop for dinner. I hoped I'd see one of you there. I called Tommy, but he told me he was busy and that I should come here."

"Of course he did." Kate wasn't sure if introductions had already been made, so she familiarized the three of them with one another.

"Kate's never mentioned you before," Gene stated sullenly. He turned to his wife. "I thought it was only the three of you who came here from Seattle?"

But she no longer knew what information had been shared about whatever moment in her past, so she had nothing to say in response.

There was an awkward silence for a moment, and whether Sheldon had noticed it or not, he was generous enough to break it. "Thank you for the chocolate," he said to Gene, holding the empty wrapper out in his hand.

Gene was appreciative of the gratitude. "You know, the day after

Halloween last year, I had two separate patients who both needed oral surgery from razor blade injuries."

Sheldon dropped the wrapper onto the hardwood floor. It seemed to hit harder than it should have.

"Gene!" Kate snapped. "Why would you say something like that? You're going to scare the poor kid."

"I was only being precautionary. You need to watch what people in this city are handing out to kids."

"That's good to know," Patrick interjected. "Thanks for the heads up, Gene."

Gene was content knowing at least *somebody* found his cautions helpful. "Do you know I've never had a cavity?"

Kate picked the wrapper up from the floor. "Would you two like to come downstairs? I was just finishing up for the night." Patrick and Sheldon followed Kate to her office while Gene returned to wherever he had been, to do whatever it was he'd been doing.

As casually as she could, Kate asked Patrick what had come from his trip to New Jersey earlier that afternoon. Scratching his scalp, he said he wasn't sure. So far, it didn't seem as though anything was stolen, and the Jersey City police weren't going to pursue it any further, only suggesting Titanic Utilities might want to invest in better security.

The office was dark, since Kate didn't like working with more light than what her tiny lamp provided. She knew she would probably pay for it with some corrective eyewear before too long.

Patrick and Sheldon both scrunched their noses as they entered. "It smells in here," they noted simultaneously.

Kate was not easily embarrassed, and she only displayed minimal signs toward their reactions. "I suppose I've been holed up in here for a bit too long. Sorry. I could crack the window, but it's hard to do any constructive writing in my parka," she joked.

Sheldon reached for one of the Spider-Man comics from the box under the desk.

"What's with the comic books?" Patrick asked. "Are they for when Jesse comes over?"

Kate slid the book out of the boy's hands and turned it over to present the GAP ad on the back cover. Patrick recognized the model immediately, because it was exactly what Kate had looked like when he had left New York so long ago. It was the same way she looked in his memory for the next decade, until he returned. Still, his jaw dropped. "Holy—" he started. "What are you doing on the back of a comic book?"

Kate handed it back Sheldon, who could care less about an advertisement for denim overalls. The kid sat down on the big reading chair in the corner of the room, and immediately began analyzing the story inside. "It's not easy being a starving student in this city. I took whatever work I could get, and now I'm immortalized on the back of these funny books. You know, they wouldn't even let us *keep* the clothes?"

"That's a shame," Patrick noted. He sat down in Kate's writing chair and let out a long breath. "Sometimes I wondered about the things I might've missed when I left you guys. Things like that GAP ad. Or even your wedding, or Jesse's art show. And all of Tommy's success." He ran the palm of his hand over the rough surface of the desk. His wedding ring scratched roughly along the wood but it didn't leave a mark. "It must have all been really great."

Kate didn't need long to think about it. "It was. There were so many remarkable things I've experienced." She rubbed the nape of her neck as if trying to coax the memories out. "But you missed a lot of really crappy times too. I mean, New York is where I *really* grew up, not Seattle. Tommy and Jess and I were there for each other when we went through everything. But I still caught myself thinking it would've been nice if you'd been there for me, too.

It was hard for me to believe you were gone. You were here for too short a time to actually be gone." Kate turned to the window. She noticed the snow had begun to fall again on 107th Street. The tiniest of flakes, like the first few stars beyond the sunset, danced beneath the street light. "I'm sorry," she apologized. "I think I've been drinking too much wine."

"It's okay," Patrick told her.

"No. No, it's not. I don't want you to get the wrong idea about everything."

"What do you mean?"

"I mean, well—it's true that I missed you sometimes, Patrick. But mostly, I never thought about you at all. God, there were so many other relationships though. Terrible ones. You wouldn't believe."

"My heart was really only ever with *one* person," Patrick said. "I mean, I left because I finally realized I loved Natasha. And then we got married. And then—" His thoughts drifted away a little, but Kate knew exactly where they had gone. "Well, I wouldn't know *how* to start over with someone new now."

"While *I* only know too well," Kate said.

"That's not what I meant."

"No. I know. But it's true." She looked out the window again, but the snow had already stopped. Like it wanted to happen but decided against it.

On the chair, Sheldon continued to flip the pages. He was careful with the book, knowing how to properly treat objects belonging to other people. He was wondering why the pages of the comic book in his hands were glossy, while the ones at Midtown Comics were rough, like paper was supposed to be. He didn't care at all about whatever it was the adults were discussing.

Kate said, "I've dated more weirdos than I care to remember. The strangest always seemed to be from Staten Island. The coolest guy I ever dated was a bus driver, of all things. I dated a baseball player and a hockey player, but both in the off-season when there weren't as many of the perks to dating baseball and hockey players. So, no road trips with the team or tickets for box seats.

Did you know, in the off-season these guys just like to sit around and do nothing all day? Like, they play video games and eat Cheetos. And that's it. And then there was the museum guy."

"Museum guy?"

Kate explained how, on a whim, she went to the Metropolitan Museum of Art one day, and met a man while looking at the pre-historic cave paintings. They talked for a while, and when they realized they were both visiting the museum alone, they decided to continue on together. They breezed through the Chinese earthenware and Minoan Terracotta together before he kissed her in front of the headless Aphrodite statue. There was some extremely covert oral sex inside the Dendur Temple before having an argument whilst surrounded by the armada of armored knights on horses. From there, they split up, only to meet again in front of Leutze's "Washington Crossing the Delaware." They shared another half hour or so together, before calling it quits amidst a collection of Salvador Dali's.

"That's really horrific," Patrick said, keeping an eye on his son to make sure the boy did not hear too much detail. But Sheldon was still immersed in the comic book.

"It was. That relationship only lasted one day yet it was spread across the entire history of mankind. But no matter how good or how bad a relationship is, it feels like the letting go is always the hardest part." Or, as Tommy had told her that morning in the coffee shop, ending a relationship is always tougher than starting a new one. It was almost the same thing.

"I think you might be right, Fart Tart."

"I can't believe you're still calling me that," Kate said. "I don't think I ever knew where it came from or what it meant."

Patrick thought about it for a moment. He never really considered where the nickname came from. He called her that back in high school, but couldn't remember why. "There's not really a reason I can think of. I don't recall how it started."

"I liked it, though."

Sheldon broke the incoming awkward pause by getting up from his seat. He returned the book to the box and asked if he could use the bathroom. Kate led him around the corner. When she returned to the office, Patrick was digging around in the box himself. He held up a package of Nicorette, wondering why she had it. "You smoke?"

"No. I just like the gum. Actually, I don't even enjoy it anymore, but now I'm addicted to the stuff."

"That's ironic," Patrick noted. And then he admitted, "I only smoke when I'm stressed out. Natasha always used to tell me not to worry so much, because the more I worried the more likely it was I'd develop lung cancer."

"That's funny. She sounds like she was full of helpful advice."

"She was. She picked me up whenever I was feeling lost. And she always knew the right things to say to Sheldon when I had no idea. I still don't know what I should be saying to him sometimes. But I don't feel like I changed as much in the last ten years as I did when I was with you, Kate. So much of who I am today is because of the time I spent with you."

"That's because we're so much easier to change when we're young. The littlest of things affected us so much more back then."

"I guess so." Patrick dropped the Nicorette back into the box. "I guess that's why I left when I did. Maybe I was just being overly-dramatic. Maybe I should have stayed in New York. But I *do* know I could not have loved Natasha as much as I did if you and I hadn't first made the mistakes we had."

"*Love is what happens after you've had your heart broken,*" Kate said. She sounded like she was quoting a famous line.

"What's that from?" Patrick asked.

"It's something I wrote in my book." Kate reached for the journal on the desktop; she knew exactly what page to flip to, and held the open book up for him. Her left-handed printing was easy to read. The line stood out like it was the only one on the page. "What it means is, you can never know what love really feels like until you've been hurt by someone."

"I guess that makes sense."

Kate snapped the book shut and sat on the edge of her desk. "You and I didn't know anything about love back then. I'm still not entirely sure if I do or not."

Patrick took the journal and turned a few pages as he listened. He wasn't certain if he agreed with what Kate was saying; he thought he did love her years ago, but he could have been wrong. All he knew at the time he left New York was he loved Natasha Seward more than he loved Kate Prince. Of course, it wasn't fair to Kate, but an impartial love is inconceivable. "I can't believe you wrote all of this," he said. "It's really good, you know?"

"It's about friends who lose their way," she told him, even though Patrick had not asked about the premise of the novel. "It's about a letter that sparks a chain reaction amongst them all. And how they deal with the ever-changing feelings they have for one another."

Patrick didn't want to acknowledge the all-too-obvious similarities, so he didn't. He carefully turned the pages, reading sentences at random. "It's beautiful, Kate. I can't wait to read it when you're finished."

Kate wanted to finish the book; she wanted it more than anything. But as soon as Patrick said the words, she found herself afraid she never would. She was afraid it would never end, just like "Paper Fences." The incomplete sequel to the unfinished debut. All her life, Kate continuously built toward the future, but she found herself uncomfortable and unmotivated whenever that future inevitably became the present. She hoped her procrastination would put itself off for just a while longer. Long enough for her to simply be happy.

"Thanks, Patrick," was what Kate said, instead of showing any weakness. The snow had decided to come down again, and it was falling fast. The wind blowing from the tips of Midtown's skyscrapers was directing all of the snow toward that one, innocuous, lonely window. It was piling up, trying its best to keep Kate and Patrick trapped inside with one another.

"Shit," Patrick said when he heard the heavy flakes patter on the glass, like tiny hands clapping. "I think we'd better be going. Sheldon and I have to get back to Brooklyn before it gets even uglier out there."

When Sheldon emerged from the bathroom, the trio went back upstairs. Patrick thanked Kate for letting him read her work and Sheldon said thank you again for the chocolate bar. As they said their goodbyes, Gene called for Kate from another room, claiming to have a question for her which required an immediate answer. Kate knew the tone, and excused herself from the entranceway, promising to be right back.

Patrick and Sheldon waited, but soon could not help but overhear Kate and Gene arguing about something to do with inviting people over for dinner on the weekend. Patrick did not know if Kate was being selfish for wanting the time to write, or if Gene's friends were really as horrible as she had made them out to be. Either way though, he knew Kate did not love her husband like she used to, if she ever had at all. Patrick Kohn was never very good at putting pieces together; he'd always been much more proficient at taking them apart. But he managed to pluck as much from his earlier conversation with Kate. She said she had too much to drink, but there was still something obvious in her words. They stepped outside, and Patrick closed the door behind them quickly so as not to let the flurry of snow inside.

"What are they fighting about?" Sheldon asked his father.

Patrick knew Natasha would have had just the right answer for the boy, but he didn't know what to say. So, he didn't say anything. The snow was quiet enough he could still hear the stifled shouting from the other side of the door. Patrick thought about the phone call he made to Kate after he'd said goodbye to New York so long ago. He knew it would be much easier to make that call from twenty-five hundred miles away than have to explain his actions in person. Kate's fiery temper was intimidating, and was only further exacerbated by alcohol. Tommy had no problem matching her intensity, and if needed, Jesse probably could too, but Patrick had never learned how to handle a confrontation. He said nothing except, "Come on, Sheldon. Maybe we should just leave them alone."

They had made it only as far as the bottom step before the door behind them opened again. Patrick's first thought was he had not closed it all the way, but Kate was at the top of the stairs. "Hold on, guys." She already had her coat on. "I'm sorry about that," she said, joining them out on the sidewalk.

Patrick wasn't sure who was coming and who was going. And Kate wasn't giving any indication of where she was headed. "Are you okay?" he asked her.

"I'm fine," she said. "Do you guys want to go grab some cheeseburgers?"

"Cheeseburgers? At this time of night?"

"The McDonald's is just around the corner," she said, obliviously pointing in the exact opposite direction. It wasn't as if they could follow her shivering finger anyway.

"I've never been to McDonald's," Sheldon said, looking up to his father with big eyes.

"His mother never let him eat fast food," Patrick confessed to Kate, as though he needed to apologize.

"It's just fast food," Kate said. "It's not plutonium. Come on, let's go."

Patrick and Sheldon were in no position to argue the matter any further, and the three of them hurried down Broadway through the evening's sudden snowstorm.

~~~

She knew as soon as she awoke that it had been a mistake. Kate thought about leaving a note behind, maybe calling him when she got back to the Upper West
~~~

Side, but was sickened by the idea of having to come full-circle with Patrick Kohn.

She sat up, immediately feeling light-headed. Sliding her legs out from the sheets, she was surprised to find the floor was closer than she expected. There was no bed frame, only a mattress. And there were only a few boxes in the bedroom, or whatever room it was supposed to be. There was a sink on the wall, but it certainly wasn't a kitchen.

Kate peered out the window. There was no snow on India Street, not even a slushy puddle. It was as though Brooklyn existed in an entirely different realm than Manhattan. Maybe a whole other time period. She put her clothes back on as quickly and as silently as she could.

Kate was fully aware she shouldn't, but she still knew she'd tell Tommy and Jesse that she slept with Patrick. Tommy's reaction would be a self-righteous one, while Jesse would only be connecting the dots toward the inevitability of their reunion. *"You guys are just like Ross and Rachel,"* he would no doubt say. Ugh.

Trying to piece the previous night together, Kate could not reach any sort of reasonable conclusion for why what happened had happened. However, she did not overlook the irony in the fact she usually found herself at the McDonald's *after* making mistakes, not *before*. Still, it was not much consolation.

Behind her, Patrick began to stir. Kate did not turn around, hoping he would be man enough to say something first instead. When he started snoring again, she knew her stance was a futile one. She wanted to imagine being with Patrick felt just like it used to feel, but it didn't feel that way at all.

She sat on the hardwood floor and dug through her handbag. Aside from money, the only paper she found was the letter. The very same letter Patrick had mailed to Tommy. She knew she'd held on to it for a reason. On the back of the letter, in her muddled, right-handed printing, Kate wrote:

I'm sorry I'm still the same person I used to be.

-K

CHAPTER TWENTY-FOUR
The Temple Bar – NoHo

Every Halloween, the Empire State Building is lit orange in celebration. On that night, the night of the falling, the skyscraper's lights blended almost seamlessly into the red-brown glow of the evening sky. The cloud cover was so low, the lights of Times Square could be seen from just about anywhere in the city; all of Manhattan was captured within its glow. It was as if a higher power had been watching New York that evening. Waiting. Preparing for something important to happen.

The Temple Bar was one of those special places in the city that was all about wistful memories and nostalgic visits. With its plain green awning and thick-curtained windows, the nondescript bar had a way of luring accidental, first time patrons through its doors. And those who returned always did so for no other reason than to reminisce about the first time. Perhaps then, it was only fitting the four of them agreed to meet there that evening.

Eleven years before, they had slept on the train all the way from Seattle to New York, arriving in Manhattan in the very early morning. Tommy whizzed them around the city all day before finally coming to a stop outside the Temple Bar on Lafayette. Tommy, Kate, and Jesse had each returned at some point since then, all three with a first date on three separate occasions. The bar had not changed much over the years, still offering plush seats at mahogany tables next to red velvet curtains and dim lighting. It boasted a magnificent oak bar which served up an impressive array of international vodkas and romantic cocktails to a bevy of haute-couture consumers. But for all of its sophistication, the Temple Bar still had the slight odor of sordid debauchery.

Surprisingly, there were no other costumed patrons that night, as though Halloween had not yet stumbled upon the Temple Bar. Aside from some suggestively-clad waitstaff, Jesse and Kate were the only ones dressed for the occasion: Jesse in his newly-purchased Midtown Minder getup (with the addition of a pair of tennis shorts over his suit, as he was self-conscious about its tight-fitting crotch), and Kate in her puke-green hospital scrubs. The two of them had just ordered more drinks when Tommy entered.

"Ho! Manhattanites!" he yelled, not the least bit aware he was merely mimicking Patrick's entrance from two weeks before. Tommy was wearing a giant, foam Empire State Building costume, so stupidly bulky he had to duck through the doorway and maneuver judiciously around the tables. He tried to sit down, but failed to do so. Tommy chose to lean against the wall instead. The tip of the costume's spire tangled with the hanging light fixtures, but Tommy still refused to remove the hat, and he called to the waitress for a Whiskey Sour, even though he'd already spent the majority of his afternoon drinking.

Kate and Jesse were astounded by his preposterous choice of attire, and yet, nothing else could possibly have ever suited Tommy any better. "Where do you even find something like that?" Kate asked, trying not to laugh.

"We found it in a costume shop Downtown," Tommy said. His breath reeked of alcohol, but there was also a smoky smell that clung to him. "Rachel was going to dress as King Kong, and I was going to be the Empire State Building."

Jesse had to ask, "Shouldn't *you* have been King Kong?"

"Are you kidding me? I'm not putting on a monkey suit. There's a stigma attached to men in monkey suits."

"Right," Kate agreed half-heartedly. "It's much less reprehensible for a woman to wear a monkey suit, isn't it?"

But Tommy had no answer for her; he was already wondering what was taking the waitress so long.

Tommy's costume had been sitting in his closet since he bought it a month before, and the foam absorbed much of the smoke that had come in through the vents during the apartment fire. Kate twisted her nose when she finally figured out the source of the smell. "You stink," was all she said to him.

Tommy looked over Kate's uniform, recollecting the story of Gene's one peculiar sex fetish. "I do *not* want to know where that costume's been."

"I didn't have time to find anything else," she admitted, smelling her own collar for uncertain, precautionary purposes.

The waitress delivered their drinks: a Mint Julep for Kate, Tommy's Whiskey Sour, and another water for Jesse. She also handed them a complimentary bowl of popcorn with what appeared to be dried beets and carrots mixed in. Tommy shook the contents around to get a better look. "Jesus," he winced. Dissatisfied, he slid the bowl across the table toward Jesse, but Jesse also refused. "What's the matter, Jess? You're always the first to eat crap like this."

Jesse gulped down his glass of water. "I think I ate something bad earlier," he told them. He'd felt terrible all afternoon, ever since he decided to open the can of Time Travel Juice. He didn't know what was really in that can, but he chugged it on the subway, like some vagrant wino who'd run out of better options in his life. He finished every last drop. The liquid had a disconcerting taste, like pickled ginger or an unripe banana or licking a rusty pipe.

Worst of all, there had not yet been a single hint of any temporal variation; a dark grey cloud remained hanging just above them all.

"I've told you before, Jess. That Wing King shit is gonna kill you."

"I know, Kate." Jesse flagged the waitress for one more water. It was like he was completely dried out inside now. "But the worst habits are the hardest ones to break, aren't they?"

Whether Jesse meant to imply something about Kate's marriage was unknown, but Tommy certainly didn't want to miss an opportunity to follow up with her about the proposed events from the day before. "How'd the stalking go yesterday, detective? You get any hard evidence?"

"I decided against it," she said. "You were right. It was an incredibly stupid idea. How about *you*, Tommy? How far down the list of girlfriends did you get?"

Defensively, Tommy dug his hand into the popcorn and swallowed a mouthful. "You were right, too," he said. "I couldn't have come up with a *worse* idea." He wasn't lying; he just wasn't revealing the whole truth. And fortunately, neither of his friends cared enough to ask any more questions anyway.

Jesse excused himself to use the washroom while Tommy rooted through the bowl. He began picking out the vegetables, and just shoveling those into his mouth. Kate tried to stare as far away as possible, and slowly tore a napkin apart into ever-smaller pieces. She didn't recognize the music playing, but it certainly seemed like the saddest tune ever. Her shoulders went weak. She closed her eyes for only a moment before Tommy interrupted. "What the hell?" he asked.

"Hmm?"

"I can tell when something's up with you, Kate. And something is most *definitely* up."

Kate's lips parted, but no words came out.

"What's going on?" Tommy asked.

She looked around her cautiously, as though anyone else might have cared enough to be listening in. Every mistake she'd ever made in her life came flooding back into her memory, but Kate knew, even before she uttered the words, this was by far the worst one of all: "I slept with Patrick last night."

Tommy wanted to feel overwhelmed; he wanted to have a reaction that would go down as history's all-time greatest reaction. He wasn't sure what that response would have been, but it certainly wasn't what he gave up instead: staring blankly at Kate as she revealed the most awful of things. He didn't even spit the dried carrot out of his mouth; it just hung limply from his lips. The reappearance of Patrick Kohn had infected so much already, crept so far into Manhattan's veins, Tommy had simply reached the point where he was no longer affected by the man's presence.

Tommy's reaction was not what Kate had expected either, and it certainly wasn't helped by the absurd costume he was wearing. "Tommy? Did you hear what I just said?"

Mince Wilson's earlier admission that Patrick Kohn was essentially responsible for the end of her relationship with Tommy had left a bad taste lingering in his mouth. He hadn't left his apartment all day, hadn't spoken with anyone at all until coming to the Temple Bar. He thought about what he should do next, but failed to come to any reasonable conclusion.

Quite simply, Thomas Mueller was not the same man he had been two weeks before. Before Patrick's return to New York. Prior to that letter showing up in his mailbox.

The tip of Tommy's costume intertwined with the light fixture again. Finally, he gave in and moved out of the way. "Why would you do *that*?" he responded at last.

And Kate almost answered him too, but noticed the Midtown Minder was on his way back to the table. "I can't get into it right now. Just don't tell Jess, okay? I think it would only confuse him."

"Sure."

"I mean it, Tommy."

"You betch'ya."

"What are you guys talking about?" Jesse asked.

"Kate slept with Patrick!" Tommy blurted out.

"WHAT?"

Kate punched Tommy in the chest, but the foam skyscraper absorbed the impact. "I hope an infected pigeon shits on your fucking costume," she grumbled.

Jesse tried to process the information. "That's awesome," he said. "So, does this mean you guys are getting back together?"

"No, it does not," Kate responded with her mouth pressed into the glass of bourbon.

"And what about Gene?" Jesse persisted. "Where *is* Patrick, anyway? Does Sheldon know?"

Kate turned directly to Tommy. "See? *This* is what I was worried about."

"Come on, Kate," Tommy insisted. "Jess is a grown man, not a dog. He can handle it."

"Just please do not say anything to Patrick when he gets here, okay?"

Tommy asked, "But what are *you* going to say to him?"

"I don't know yet."

"Well, you'd better decide fast," Jesse said. Patrick was at the entrance, scanning the bar for his friends. He was wearing a green rubber frog costume, complete with flippers and bulging eyes on the top of his head. Jesse waved an arm to get his attention and soon they were all reunited: the Frog, the Nurse, the Superhero, and the Skyscraper.

Tommy was perplexed by the costume selection. "What the fuck is *that*?"

"I'm a frog. I wear this *every* Halloween."

"It looks like a gecko."

"Trust me. It's a frog." Patrick took a good look around him. He could barely remember ever being in the Temple Bar, but he knew for certain it was still the same. There was a scent — maybe it was the velvet curtains — that brought him right back to when they were just kids. When the four of them were so young, and so full of dreams, and felt as though greatness was nothing more than a simple matter of destiny. But then they had to grow up and figure everything out on their own. Each of them had picked up on that smell when they first arrived that night, but Patrick was the only one of them who could properly place the feeling.

"Where's Sheldon?" Jesse asked.

"He's at home." Patrick ordered a beer from the closest waitress. "The woman next door to me is watching him."

Tommy, Kate, and Jesse all looked at one another. Did Patrick really just leave his son with a stranger? Had he always been so gullible?

"Relax, guys. She's got two kids of her own. Her husband helped me move in too. They're great people. We took all the kids out trick-or-treating tonight. Hey, is it just me, or do people not give out as much candy as they used to?"

"It's a New York thing," Jesse said. "The health-conscious parents were worried about all the candy and artificial ingredients so they started handing out rice crackers and sunflower seeds. Then the kids stopped trick-or-treating because they didn't want any of that healthy crap. Now half the city doesn't bother to hand out anything at all."

"It's cyclical," Tommy added. "But I just go to Kate's place for candy since Gene's always got the best stuff."

Kate had been noticeably quiet since Patrick arrived. She had an aloof look about her, and all three men knew what it meant. Even the waitress noticed as she placed Patrick's beer on the table. Patrick asked, "Guys, do you mind if Kate and I talk in private?"

Tommy was quick to remove himself from the table. The truth was he needed some fresh air anyway; his own space away from Patrick. Jesse pecked Kate on the cheek before following Tommy outside onto Lafayette Street.

Patrick sat across from Kate, his rubber suit made a farting noise as it rubbed on the plush seat, but neither of them laughed. Reaching into the neck opening with his gloved fingers, Patrick pulled the famous letter out from somewhere deep inside. He laid it flat on the table, presenting Kate's miserable printing to her. "Listen, I know we probably made a mistake last night. But please don't say you're sorry, Kate."

"Why can't I apologize?"

"Because there's nothing to be sorry for. Especially not for something so silly."

"Silly?"

"Saying you're still the same person you used to be."

"Oh. I thought you were talking about the sex," she said. "But I *am* the same person I was. It's why things didn't work out for us years ago, and it's the same reason it wouldn't work now."

"You've got it all backwards, Kate," he said. "It's impossible for somebody to go through life unchanged. Especially here in Manhattan. I was only here for a short time, but it sure as hell transformed me. I just don't want either of us to get the wrong idea."

Kate only wanted to tell him she agreed, but she was finding the words impossibly hard to say. She opened her mouth, but nothing came out. And Patrick had already run out of words too. He knew there was more that needed to be said, but he was stumped as to how he might say it. He had convinced himself in the morning that he was so quick to return to Kate because it was the easiest way to numb the pain of losing Natasha. So why couldn't he say that?

The same, sad song was still playing in the background and Patrick's beer was already empty.

Taking the wrinkled paper back into his hands, Patrick turned it over to see the dutifully typed letter he had sent to Tommy just a few weeks before. He remembered how nervous he was as he sat down to type it. And he'd torn up eight previous drafts before settling on just the right words. Even if they had moved on or even forgotten him entirely, time had not eroded Patrick's feelings toward his friends. For every moment he experienced, good or bad, he wished they had been there with him. For every dream he had, he hoped they could have been a part of it.

But every dream lost is only replaced by something unexpected along the way. Inevitably, every letter not sent is still somehow answered. Every moment which passes by comes back eventually. Patrick understood all of this when he woke that morning to find Kate's message scribbled on the back of his own.

Kate hadn't noticed until then that there was a floor-length mirror beside her. She considered her own reflection for a moment before finally asking, "Were you ever afraid of anything when you were younger?"

Patrick thought about the question. "I don't think so." He spun the empty beer glass in slow circles on the table top. "When we were kids, we never wanted to be afraid of anything, did we? That's why we did whatever we wanted. But now that I'm older, I realize there's a limitless supply of things to be scared of. There's so much more to worry about, isn't there?"

"Yeah," Kate agreed. "I guess that makes sense. But there was one thing that always scared me."

"What's that?"

"Falling in love."

"I don't understand. How is falling in love with someone a bad thing?"

Kate thought about her next words carefully. It was not easy for her to be so vulnerable. "People always talk about not wanting to die alone. Like it would be the worst thing in the world. But what about the people who love them? What could be worse than loving someone for years and years, and then suddenly they're not there anymore? And what if they're so old there's no time left over to move on? I can't imagine anything worse than that."

Patrick was confused. "You're saying it would be better to die alone, rather than hurt someone so badly? What about Gene? Why did you marry him?"

"I think maybe I always knew it would never work out with Gene."

"Kate, why are you telling me all this?"

"Don't you see, Patrick? When we came to New York, I knew I was falling in love with you. I knew it more and more every day. That's when I started getting scared about being with you forever. But then you left. You just disappeared that morning, leaving nothing but that letter behind. And I felt so relieved. I was *happy* that I wouldn't have to go through all of that with you."

"You were happy?"

"Sometimes I'm happiest when I'm at my saddest, if that makes any sense at all."

"Yeah." Patrick sat back his seat. His frog suit squeaked on the chair again. "Yeah, I think it does make sense." He handed Kate a clean cocktail napkin and she wiped her eyes.

"Thanks for coming back, Patrick," she said with a smile.

~~~

There was a hazy fog over Manhattan. Where only minutes ago it was licking the tips of skyscrapers, the fog was now creeping ever closer to the streets below, engulfing anything and everything it could. The orange glow from the Empire State Building was gone, already consumed by the night's malignant cloud. To Tommy, it felt like the island was becoming ever smaller. Buildings which stood only blocks away had vanished from sight. But taxis still patrolled the streets as though nothing was the matter. Businesses continued to pile their garbage along the sidewalk, assuming it would be collected the next day as always. People remained lined up at the hot dog cart; the only need they had to fulfill was that of hunger. So why was the miasmic haze making Tommy feel so uneasy?

Stumbling along Lafayette Street, some drunken college kids mocked the costumes Tommy and Jesse wore. One of them commented on the Empire
~~~

State Building suit, and failed in his attempt at some sort of erection pun. It confused Tommy more than anything, and he felt ashamed of the city's education system, how it was wasted on such witlessness. The best costumes the kids could muster were fright wigs and eye patches.

Tommy had tried to sit down on the curb beside Jesse, but he found that simply lying on his back was much easier. At least the foam helped make the cold, hard sidewalk that much more comfortable. He persisted to fixate on one thing only: Patrick Kohn. Sure, he thought, maybe his apartment was not intentionally set on fire after all, and maybe the warehouse was not a front for some elaborate revenge plot, and maybe Natasha Seward really did have a tumor on her brain, but Patrick's presence still continued to prove Manhattan was far better off without him.

"Don't let Patrick bother you so much, Tommy," Jesse said to him. He had his head between his knees, nursing his sore stomach, but he still knew what thoughts Tommy was preoccupied with. "Don't let it consume you."

Tommy unremittingly stared up into the dark clouds. He knew Jesse was right, but he was too impossibly stubborn to change even his own mind.

"Patrick was right," Jesse continued. "We all fall, don't we? I tried to be strong enough to get past it, but I'm not." He dipped his boot into a mound of dead grey snow, one of the last remnants from the storm. It broke apart easily, quickly disappearing altogether beneath his foot. The Time Travel Juice bubbled and churned inside his stomach. "In a moment of weakness, I thought I'd found the solution to all of it yesterday. I was going to make all of us better again. I was going to fix John and Edie. Natasha. Even your brother. I thought I could maybe bring Rachel back too." He sighed deeply, but mostly for effect. "Why do we have to grow up and go through all of this shit? I mean, what's really the point?"

Tommy wanted to admit he didn't know what the point was. He wanted to acknowledge his own mistakes and all the negativity he harbored. But then he realized he had never once done so before, and he finally grasped just how hard it is to actually admit it to someone.

And just as Tommy recalled what the tattooed girl had said to him in the coffee shop, Jesse simultaneously recalled what Sharona had told him on that Greenwich Village sidewalk, only a few blocks from where he sat now.

She told Jesse nobody's problems are so incredibly special. She said everyone's heart breaks at some point; everyone will make the wrong decision eventually. And she told Tommy if he only ever did *one* thing, he needed to make sure he treated his friends right.

"I wish I could change everything back to the way it was," Jesse said. "But that wouldn't be fair to the way things are *now*." He looked over at Tommy who was still stuck on his back, a fallen Empire State Building. "You know, that costume really is ridiculous," he laughed.

"I think I've had way too much to drink today."

Jesse helped Tommy up, and they went back inside the Temple Bar together, just before the fog touched the sidewalk.

Breathe out.

~~~

Tommy stopped by the bar for another drink before heading to the bathroom, and then once more on his way back to the table. He must have knocked into every person along the way. When he got back to the table, Kate and Jesse and Patrick were all laughing. It was good to see smiles on their faces, especially after everything that had gone down over the past week. Patrick was telling them about earlier that morning and his poor attempts to explain to Sheldon why Kate had stayed the night. "I can't believe how many times Natasha and I had to lie to the poor kid," he said. "Sheldon's just got a knack for walking in at all the wrong times."

"Maybe that's why he's so suspicious of you," Tommy slurred. He was
~~~

sober enough to know it was the wrong time and place to go into detail about the boy's farfetched murder theories, but he was just drunk enough that he couldn't help himself.

"Tommy, why don't you sit down?" Kate suggested.

"I'll tell you why. Because my ass is literally the size of a city block!" he said. "I could barely even fit in the stall to relieve myself." Tommy leaned in closer to Patrick, a little too close for both their likings. "Do you know what the bathrooms in this place could use?"

"What's that?" Patrick asked, trying to push himself away.

"A nice, sparkly, HyGenieSeat-3000! I gotta hand to you, Patrick, those things work like a dream!"

Patrick glared at Tommy, unsure of what he should suspect.

"We just installed one at Jesse's place. I never thought I'd be a bidet man, but that shit's pretty great."

Patrick turned to Jesse, then back at Tommy. "Do you know the most peculiar thing about the break-in at my warehouse? There had only been one item stolen. We did an inventory check and the only thing missing was one, single HyGenieSeat-3000. They haven't even hit the public market yet. How on earth do you explain *that*, Tom?"

"Well, it's kind of a funny story actually," Tommy began. Kate and Jesse fell uncomfortably silent, since they had assumed their humiliating adventure into Jersey City two nights before would remain a secret between the three of them. But Tommy was far too inebriated to keep the lid on anything that night. "It was *me*, Patrick. You caught me! I broke into the warehouse. Well, *all* of us did, actually. Though it was all *my* idea, so don't start giving these jokers any credit or anything. But it came from a good place."

Patrick asked, "Which was—?"

Kate and Jesse could only try to bury their faces in their drinks, but the Temple Bar had notoriously small glasses.

Tommy didn't notice any of the awkward signals on the familiar faces around him. "I thought you killed your wife," he said. "And I figured you'd be coming after the three of us next."

"You thought I *WHAT?*"

"Well, I admit it was Sheldon who put the idea in my head to begin with."

"Sheldon?"

"Yeah. And then there was the fire in my apartment. And the fat man on the street with the sandwich."

"I told you already! That man's name is Jules and he works at the warehouse."

"And then there was the negative review of my novel, which doesn't necessarily have anything to with you, but there's still a chance, isn't there?" Tommy was now starting to look for some agreement. "Isn't there, guys?" But the more Tommy came clean, the more he found himself questioning everything all over again.

Patrick couldn't believe what he was hearing. "What the hell is wrong with you, Tom?" He raised his normally tepid voice louder. "Is *this* how you treat your friends? It's no wonder your girlfriend left you."

Heads in the bar began to turn their way. Kate thought the music had become noticeably sadder. Everything slowed down around Jesse. They both sat, staring blankly at the two men. They knew nothing could be said anymore that would make any difference.

At some point, everybody falls.

"You're one to talk," Tommy responded. "How do *you* treat *your* friends? By abandoning them? I was just waiting there with my tennis racket. I didn't even have any balls because you said you'd bring them."

"What is with you and that tennis match? Let it go, Tom."

"You and I bought Rangers season tickets too. They were in Section Fifty! *Section Fifty!!* I had to sell my stereo so I could afford them. But then you were gone and I had to trade them in for some crap-ass nose bleeders.”

“That’s so petty, Tom. What, are you going to accuse me of stealing toilet paper from you as well?”

“Ah ha! I knew that was you!”

“Have you been harboring all of this since the day I left? I can’t believe you would actually accuse me of hurting somebody. Especially Natasha.”

Tommy was almost running out of things to say. Almost. “And goddammit. Frogs are lame, dude.”

“Yeah, it’s much more awesome to be walking around in a giant foam skyscraper, isn’t it? Get over it, Tom. Just get over this city already. It’s not so fucking great.”

The last head in the Temple Bar turned, as though sensing what would come next. “What did you say?” Tommy asked, pointing a shaky finger in his friend’s face.

But Patrick had enough. He swatted Tommy’s hand away and got up from the table. “This obsession you have with New York, and who’s worthy enough to set foot on its sidewalks and who *isn’t*. Get the hell over it.” He turned away from Tommy and only took one step before he was pushed from behind. He only brushed against a nearby table, but it was still enough force to knock over a few glasses.

“Tommy!” Kate yelped. She tried to free herself from the table, but Jesse was in her way, still zoning out. Patrick tried to hold Tommy back, but it was no use. Tommy pushed him into the table again. Something smashed onto the floor.

Jesse watched the half-assed attempt at a fight. Patrick had always avoided confrontation; he didn’t know the first thing to do in a fight. Truthfully, he still hadn’t realized he was even in a fight. Tommy, on the other hand, was simply too drunk to register what he was doing anymore. Amid the chaotic scuffle, Jesse was recollecting the night of his art show, when he and

John Galloway had fought with one another. He couldn't help himself from pretending Patrick's frog costume was more like Godzilla, trying to destroy the city. Battling with a human skyscraper. He had to admit, it was a pretty cool visual. When Kate spotted the smile on Jesse's face, she slapped the Midtown Minder on the back of the head, snapping him out of it.

Somehow, Patrick succeeded in wrestling Tommy onto the floor. Caught like a turtle on his back, Tommy flailed his arms and legs without much result. The top of his costume, the tip of the skyscraper, had flown free.

He managed to sit up for only a moment before Patrick established the opportunity to land a solid punch. He accidentally hit Tommy square in the jaw, and Tommy's head hit the wall hard.

And that's when everything began to   fade to   blank......

The INEVITABLE FALL of TOMMY MUELLER

CHAPTER TWENTY-FIVE
NYPD 5th Precinct – Chinatown

On the day Keekee Kaufman was admitted to Bellevue, after throwing herself off the Triboro Bridge, she had an email waiting for her in her inbox. It was from an old boyfriend, the one who got away. Ralphie Muzatti was just as crazy as she was, but Keekee had always loved him more than anything. She knew one day Ralphie would realize they were meant for one another, and Keekee told herself that, as soon as Ralphie decided he loved her too, she would drop everything to be with him again. And even though Ralphie *did* make that decision to love her, Keekee Kaufman did not check her email that day. Instead, she got into one last argument with Thomas Mueller, and then proceeded to make her way to the East River.

The day John Galloway crashed his car in the middle of the Holland Tunnel, accidentally killing his wife Edith, was the same day he also saved a life. From his office window he witnessed a man collapse on Pearl Street. The man had a sudden heart failure; not only did he fall onto the sidewalk, but he also tumbled down a stairwell. John called for an ambulance before running outside, and he waited until help arrived. He only spent an hour in the hospital that afternoon, just long enough to make sure the man was okay, but during that time, Edith Galloway had dropped by John's office unannounced. She came by to not only confess to her husband her affair with the comic store clerk, but that she planned on ending it with Jesse Classen as soon as the art exhibition was over that evening. But John was not at his office, so Edith did not get the chance to tell him everything about the mistakes she had made. And by the time John finally saw her that night, Edith was already too drunk to admit anything to her husband.

The day Thomas Mueller fell, there were no warning signs at all. There was nothing that would have prevented him from hitting the bottom. He would have had to look back over his entire lifespan in order to find the signs he needed to save himself. Quite literally, he had to look as far back as the day he and his brother were born.

~~~

There was a voice. It echoed off empty walls; a bare room. It was only saying one word, turning the word itself into a question:

"Leyland?"

Was it questioning the word's authenticity? Questioning its very existence?

"Leyland?"

Tommy opened his eyes. He was right: it was an empty room. There was a table. Two chairs. Two people. That was it. Tommy was seated in one of the hard, wooden chairs, still dressed as the Empire State Building. Across the table in the other chair, was a police officer. His nametag read: Constable B.R. AVERY. Tommy couldn't believe it; it was almost too stupid to be true.

"Good to see you finally coming around," the officer said. "You took quite a hit there." Avery was an older man, with the kind of police mustache that's to be expected after years on the force.

Tommy was still a little out of it though. "What? Where am I?" He realized he was missing the top of his costume. The tip of the skyscraper.

"I'm sorry for putting you here in the interrogation room. You'll notice you're not handcuffed. This building fills up pretty fast on Halloween night, so we sometimes have to put the non-felons wherever we can."

"Non-felons?" Slowly, the memory of throwing a punch at Patrick started to come back to him. As did the memory of hitting the wall with his own face.
~~~

He rubbed his jaw. With his tongue, he could feel where his tooth should have been.

"Yeah, you lost your front tooth there. And your nose is broken. But no major damage inflicted." Tommy felt the bandages on his nose, crusted from dry blood. Avery sorted through some papers which were laid out in front of him, and he clicked the pen in his hand excitedly, as if trying to break a world record. "I've just got a couple of questions for you, Leyland. Well, one major one, really."

"Why do you keep calling me that?"

"Hmm?"

"Leyland. You keep calling me Leyland." Tommy didn't notice before that the inside of his mouth was cut. He licked the blood from his teeth. The warm, metallic taste reminded him of the time he got into a fistfight back in high school. He remembered Patrick Kohn sticking up for him that day.

"Would you prefer Mr. Mueller? I'm sorry, but I don't enjoy being so formal. Never have."

Tommy looked around for some kind of clue. If it was a practical joke, there would have to be a hidden camera somewhere in the room. If he was caught in the middle of a dream, then there would have to be something like a leprechaun, or maybe the floor would be made entirely out of marbles. But it was nothing more than a simple police interrogation room, almost exactly like any he'd seen in the movies. And there was only himself, Constable B.R. Avery, two chairs, and a table. As a last resort, he looked at his own hands, and was baffled by the dark ink on his thumb and index finger. "Am I in trouble here? Am I being arrested?"

"Your friend in the dragon costume isn't pressing any charges." Avery jotted something down on one of the papers.

"It's a frog. He was wearing a frog costume."

"Well, the file says *dragon*. But that's not really important."

"If you want to know why I beat the shit out of a good friend of mine, I'll tell you."

"Sounds like you got knocked in the head harder than we thought. Your friend is fine. And he's already been released. It's *you* who received the worst of it."

"What? You let him go? But he tried to *kill* me! He almost burned my apartment building to the ground!"

"If you'd like to file a case for a separate incident, be my guest. But Patrick Kohn is not pressing any charges himself."

"Charges? For what?"

"Well, for tonight's altercation and for the break-in at his warehouse."

Tommy didn't have anything to say. He knew any squirming in his seat was certain to be interpreted as a sign of guilt, but he couldn't help himself. He couldn't believe Patrick would rat him out like that.

"But I *do* have something to ask you."

"Well if it's an autograph you want, I only sign books."

"Uh huh. No, the reason I've got you here with me, is because we ran your prints, and they belong to one Leyland Mueller."

Tommy swished some more fresh blood between his teeth.

"But according to all the files we could pull, Leyland Mueller died fifteen years ago." Constable Avery rose from his seat and leaned in closer to Tommy. "Now, can you tell me why your fingerprints would match those of a dead man?"

"Leyland Mueller was my twin brother. My name is Tommy."

Avery huffed. "Right. But twins wouldn't share the same prints, would they?"

"I don't know how that works. You tell me."

"Trust me. That's how it works."

~~~

It was another hour before Tommy was released from the station. As he was led through the halls toward Elizabeth Street, Tommy noted all of the other ghosts, spirits, and specters that had been detained and were waiting for their names to be called. He didn't feel much different from any of them at that moment: haunting a world they were only temporarily a part of.

Kate, Jesse, and Patrick were all waiting for Tommy outside; the Nurse, the Hero, and the Frog. Jesse handed him the lid for his costume. Tommy took it, and continued walking toward the Canal Street Station without another word.

~~~

There was no serious damage to Tommy's apartment, and all those who had been temporarily homeless were allowed back inside the building that morning. He had only a vague recollection of spending the afternoon drinking on his couch before heading out to meet his friends at the Temple Bar. The smell of smoke hit him as soon as he opened his door. Tommy ignored the stench, picking up the phone. It was hard to dial the numbers in his bulky costume, but he was determined.

It was still just eleven o'clock in Seattle when his mother answered. "Hello?"

"Hi, Mom."

"Thomas! It's been awhile since we heard from you. How is everything? Have you seen Patrick yet? Has he called you?" Doris Mueller could never ask one question without asking three or four.

And Tommy could never answer any of his mother's questions without putting her on the spot first. Both of them were annoyed by the routine, but neither avoided it. "Mom, did you ever mix me and Leyland up when we were kids?"

"Leyland and *I*. I can't believe I'm still correcting your grammar. *You're* the writer, not me."

Tommy breathed heavily through his nostrils. He didn't say a word, since he knew his mother would just answer the question anyway.

She said, "You were identical twins, Thomas. Everybody confused the two of you at some point. I don't know why you both insisted on having the same haircut. But a mother can always tell."

"No, Mom. I mean, did you ever completely lose track of who was who? Maybe you put us down somewhere and forgot?"

Doris Mueller went silent for a long moment. Tommy heard something heavy on the other end of the phone, like a book falling. Or a heart dropping.

Tommy looked out his window, but all he saw was the plain brick wall glowing faintly from the street light. It was all he ever saw, but he still felt disappointed; as though he expected something more at that moment. "Mom?"

"When the two of you were just babies, you wore different colored wristbands so we could tell you apart. But they were getting so tight, you were both crying. So I took them off. It was while I was giving you both a bath. I turned away for just a moment — I think your father was calling to me from the other end of the house — but it was only for a moment. When I turned back, I'd forgotten. I didn't know who was who. But Thomas, I didn't think it would be a big deal."

"*You didn't think*? Jesus, Mom. It's a pretty fucking big deal!"

"What's happened, Thomas?"

"Put the pieces together, Mom. *I'm* Leyland. I always have been. That's Tommy lying somewhere at the bottom of the Pacific! Why wouldn't you have gotten our fingerprints taken?"

"I—I didn't think that would make a difference. Because you were twins."

"Well, apparently it makes a whole shitload of difference. There's a grave in Seattle with *my* name on it! I dedicated my first book to him. I dedicated a book to *myself!* Can you understand the difference it makes now?"

"Thomas, please do not yell at me."

"I'm sorry, Mom. But I've run out of people in New York to yell at."

Doris went silent again. She seemed to be thinking about all of the signposts along the way, but one life can simply have far too many to keep track of. "When you boys were first born, when Leyland was just a baby, he had always fixated on that plate in the kitchen. We had one plate for every state, but he never took his eyes off the one that said New York. I think he loved the big red apple on it."

"But that was *me*, Mom," Tommy said. "*I'm* the one who loved that stupid plate."

"Thomas, I'm sorry. If it means anything right now. I'm sorry."

Tommy hung up the phone. He knew he should've said something more, but whatever it might have been certainly would not have helped any. He sunk onto his bed, and considered the repercussions of it all. The weight of his soul had never been so heavy. So straining. Although it was his brother who had died in that plane crash, Tommy could not help but think it was himself lying there at the bottom of the Pacific Ocean.

Everything he had accomplished as Thomas Mueller was a lie of sorts. Tommy had never actually graduated from high school. Tommy had never written a single book. It wasn't Tommy who had made out with Jenny Duncan in the seventh grade: it was Leyland Mueller.

God, he thought. He hated that name so very much. And now it was his own.

He forced himself off the bed, cursing his decision for a Halloween costume. Maybe it was that unusual moment of clarity that led Tommy across the room to his dresser. Perhaps it was the lucid truth of it all that made him reach to the very back of his sock drawer, his fingers hunting for something long forgotten.

From a weathered cardboard mailing box, he removed a tiny stack of photographs taken the day he and his best friends arrived in New York. These were pictures of Manhattan's most recognizable structures: the Chrysler Building, the Flatiron, Madison Square Garden, and the World Trade Center. Upon Tommy's insistence, the four of them zigzagged everywhere that day. The Guggenheim; the Chelsea Hotel; the old wooden escalator at Macy's; Times Square; Katz's Delicatessen; the Apollo Theater; the Empire Diner; Morningside Park; and the Alamo cube. The colors were still so vivid in the photos. His friends thought it strange at the time that Tommy would be capturing so many of the city's landmarks. After all, the four of them had *moved* to Manhattan; they weren't tourists. The buildings would be there every day for the rest of their lives. But Tommy continued to snap away until there was only one shot left on the camera. He tossed it to a man passing by, and asked him to take a photo of the four of them. This was the object Tommy intended to find in his sock drawer. He knew exactly where it was. The picture of Tommy Mueller, Patrick Kohn, Kate Prince, and Jesse Classen standing outside a store on the Bowery that sold cash registers. They all had their arms around one another and their mouths hung open awkwardly, caught in a moment of extraordinary celebration. All of their dreams were concrete, obvious, and entirely possible. Jesse's eyes were closed. Tommy could still recall the feeling of Patrick's corduroy blazer rubbing against the palm of his hand.

And when a heavy tear rolled down his cheek, Tommy knew exactly what the photo had meant to him. Sometimes he missed the things from his childhood that he would never get back. Playing on the street with his brother. Running around with tree-branch guns. Learning to ride his bike with no hands. Their father teaching them how to spit off the overpass. When he awkwardly called a girl for the first time. His friends had always said they'd never known Leyland Mueller, but it was Tommy who they had never really known.

The truth was, Tommy sometimes caught himself yearning for a return to Seattle, just to be around everything he felt from his childhood. He was always too afraid to admit it though, even to himself. As big as he dreamed, Tommy Mueller never truly thought the life he'd made for himself was possible.

Tommy placed that one photo on his desk, and shoved the rest of the glossy pictures of buildings deep into the sock drawer from whence they came. Turning back to the brick wall through the window, Tommy decided if he was not actually the man he believed he was, he had a second chance now to fix his mistakes.

Some of the mistakes really didn't matter all that much anymore.

Some mistakes would be easy to fix, some not so.

Some could be entirely rewritten in his mind.

And so, he wrote.

CHAPTER TWENTY-SIX
The One Man Show – Harlem

THREE YEARS EARLIER.

It was probably the nicest fall morning Leyland could recall since he arrived in New York. Truthfully though, he felt each day was unavoidably better than the last. But this was different. Seventy-two degrees. No humidity. There was a special feeling in the air, a smell on the breeze. It was perfect. He was preparing himself for a book signing that morning, even though he told his agent on numerous occasions how he hated Tuesday signings. For some reason or another, all the perverts and stalkers and nutcases seemed to come out on Tuesdays.

Leyland was right there when it happened. He was at the Downtown Dunkin' Donuts at Church and Murray, shaking some sugar into his coffee when he heard it. The coffee rippled menacingly. The low rumbling was the kind of noise that instantly indicated something was wrong. Outside, people screamed. A few cars banged into one another, their drivers justly distracted. There was a stream of conversation unlike any Manhattan had ever heard. Word got around fast. The North Tower had been hit.

Fifty minutes later, he was unrecognizable amongst the masses crowding the streets and sidewalks for a good look. But five minutes after that, Leyland stood out like Cleopatra's Needle — the 68-foot-tall Egyptian obelisk in Central Park — as hordes of people ran as fast and as far away from the falling South Tower as they could. Yet, he remained standing. He anchored himself to the blacktop, watching the second building come down, swallowing itself up into its own dust and dirt. He didn't run. He didn't panic. As the mess of everything that once was blew toward him, he contemplated what it all meant, even considering the possibility he may have made a mistake when he decided to come to New York eight years before.

Amidst everything, he reached out and caught a paper in his hand. The paper was just one of millions — maybe billions — that were within the World Trade Center's walls. Most were probably incinerated. But this one piece of paper flew from somewhere within the South Tower, right toward him. As the chaos enveloped him, Leyland read what was on it. It was an email, sent the night before, and printed out at 8:43 that morning:

From: Yolanda Higgins [yoliggins@hotmail.com]
Sent: September-10-01 11:56 PM
To: Rondell Greene
Subject: Sorry

Ronnie,
I'm so sorry for everything that happened this afternoon. You must know I never meant what I said to you. If you still want me to, I'll wait for you at the One Man Show after work tomorrow. I'll be there at 7:00.
-Y-

Leyland didn't know why the email had been printed, but he could only assume that Rondell Greene would not have lived to make his seven o'clock date with Yolanda Higgins. Although Leyland was not the intended recipient of the message, he was quite possibly the only living person who was aware of its existence.

Obviously, the book signing had been cancelled, though there were no notices sent. It was one of the things about that morning: there had been far less communication on purpose, for much of the information New Yorkers would normally have emailed, instant-messaged, telephoned, or printed posters for had no need to be sent or received. It was all understood in a unique way on that Tuesday.

Like most, Leyland returned home much later than usual. It was impossible to catch a cab or ride a bus. Most people did not want to go into the subway stations. He ran like a crazy person out of Downtown, across Midtown, through Central Park, and into Morningside Heights. He looked back every minute or so, but the smoke was consuming everything behind him. It was as though he was running to avoid being wiped from existence too. He'd lost his cell phone somewhere along the way.

Television and electronics stores were crowded with people, both inside and on the sidewalks, somberly watching the flickering screens through the dusty front windows. He'd never seen so many people crying. And yet, the sky remained startlingly blue that day.

Once at home, he called Kate and Jesse and his family in Seattle to let them all know he was safe. But after that, even before showering the thick grime away, he pulled out his phone book and looked up the One Man Show. It was in Harlem, maybe a half-hour's walk from his apartment.

Tom's Restaurant was open, its television sets were crowded with patrons. Kate and Jesse were at their usual table, waiting for Leyland to arrive. He pressed his hand against the window when he saw them. The glass seemed to bend more than it should have. Leyland went inside, but he only sat with them for a few minutes. He was shaken, but there was a strength about him that needed to keep moving.

"Where are you going?" Kate asked when he got up from the table. She didn't want to tell him how much she needed him at that moment.

"Harlem."

"What the hell for?"

Leyland pulled the folded email out of his pocket and showed it to them.

"I don't understand," Jesse said. "You're going to meet this girl? Why?"

"I don't know, really. I just think I need to. To make sure she's okay."

None of them were big believers in fate, and on any other day this would have seemed like extremely bizarre behavior, even for Leyland. But on September Eleventh, the air was thick with inexplicable decisions and unquestioned actions.

"I saw the towers fall. They were falling right in front of me! I'm not going to let this madness be the only reason for getting out of bed this morning. Today has to have been for something."

With that, he headed to the mysterious One Man Show café. He didn't know Harlem even had cafés, but there it was, right between a laundromat and a fried chicken restaurant. It was an odd little place. Like many other businesses in Manhattan, it had an innocuous façade; a feeling of anonymity poured out onto the strangely tidy sidewalk. The One Man Show was a wholly different world inserted deep within the ghetto's intricate latticework of gangsters and prostitutes and garbage and drugs and fake storefronts and stolen taxicabs and ignorant travelers. Inside, there was not a soul in view, but he could hear the din of a television from one of the back rooms. He followed it. There must have been twenty people crammed into that tiny manager's office, each one smelled worse than the last. All of them watched the television without a word, but they still did not hear Leyland enter. He knocked on the door frame and waved the email he'd never once let go of.

"Does anyone here know a Yolanda?"

Every head in the room turned to him. They didn't seem to comprehend what the stranger was saying.

"I'm looking for Yolanda Higgins. Is she here? Does *anybody* know her?" He would have believed he was talking a different language if the big man who looked like a hound dog hadn't expunged himself from the crowd and approached Leyland.

The man explained to Leyland that Yolanda Higgins was a regular patron at the One Man Show café. No one had seen her, but it wasn't really a surprise considering how many plans would be changing without notice on that day. So many patterns shifting. The man's big eyes were extremely wet, and Leyland could tell, even underneath a day's worth of tears, his eyes were always that wet. Without warning, the man threw his arms around him. It was unexpected, but Leyland didn't fight it.

When he finally relaxed his grip, the man said, "I don't know if Yolanda will show up tonight, but you're welcome to stay if you want to." He returned to the back room, rejoining his associates. "There's coffee and beer behind the counter too if you'd like," he added. "Help yourself."

Leyland stood in the same spot for another few minutes, trying to make sense of everything that had happened. He had been preparing for his book signing only a few hours ago, and now, suddenly, he was standing in a Harlem café while the city teetered on the brink of ruin. He knew he should have run back to the coffee shop to be with Kate and Jesse, but he stayed there instead. He poured himself a glass of water, realizing then just how thirsty he was. He sat down at a small table for two, and he made the decision that he was not going to wait for whoever Yolanda Higgins might have been. Instead, he chose to write. Starting on the back of the filth-ridden email, he soon moved on to some napkins and scrap paper he found behind the counter.

The remains of the towers still smoldered as Leyland wrote about everything he never thought he knew.

~ ~ ~

Leyland had written the entire first draft of "The Manhattanite" inside the One Man Show. After a couple of months, he had really started to abhor that café, but he knew he would never get any real work done at the coffee shop, since everyone in his life knew they could find him there. Besides, the One Man Show had surprisingly better coffee than anywhere in Morningside Heights.

He hadn't seen the big man with the sad, wet eyes since the first time he entered the café. Leyland supposed he never actually worked there. That day felt like such an incredibly long time ago. It was almost as though Leyland had imagined everything that happened on the day of the attacks, but the One Man Show had an ability to generate its own strange illusions at times. There was no other place in Manhattan quite like it.

The nondescript Harlem café seemed to lure the city's most blatantly volatile visionaries. Bohemian bull-shitters who had been talking about change since the Sixties, but had yet to act on any of their complex — albeit, completely delirious — talk of revolution. Leyland knew if any of them had actually intended to change their worlds, they would have been down in the Village fifty years ago, rather than hiding in a dusty coffee shop in Harlem. Still, Leyland sat among them. He drank their coffee and used their toilet. But he was not really one of them. They paid him no attention either. They were far too busy trying to transform the world with their wasted ideas.

The second time Leyland came to the One Man Show, he brought his writing pad with him, continuing right where he'd left off on the flimsy napkins. Kate and Jesse didn't understand the sudden fury with which he had decided to write, but they did not question it. They knew better than to question anything he wished to embark upon. The scratching of pencil on paper was the only sound that would carry him through the story he wanted to tell. He wasn't at the café to amuse anyone but himself. This new book was not meant for anyone else. It was not for recognition's sake, not to make a name for himself. That had already been accomplished. And he was not writing for the purpose of saying something profound and prolific to entertain the masses. It was just for him. It might have all seemed very righteous and noble, but that was exactly where Leyland's biggest flaw lay. He thought only of himself any more.

The truth was, for the first time since coming to New York, Leyland

Mueller was beginning to lose direction. The falling towers had shaken something loose deep inside of him. His girlfriends no longer served any purpose, and he gave them nothing more in return that was of any greater consequence than a night or two of guilt-free sex. And most of the time, it was nearly impossible to find someone who desired anything more than that.

But on one mild December day, just as Leyland's writing was hitting a wall, he felt a pair of eyes watching him. There was a girl seated across the room. She sat just like everyone else around her, but while the crowd remained unnoticed in an unremarkable flurry of being, this particular girl was so still, he was convinced she must have been there just for him. Amidst a room full of idiots oblivious to the two of them, they had been exposed to one another.

Her eyes were extraordinary. Her eyes were not the same as any of the other girls Leyland had known. Her eyes were not forgettable. To him, this was the most important staring contest he had ever been a part of. If a blink could result in losing her, even for just a microsecond, he did not want to risk it.

And then he blinked. And she was gone.

~~~

Leyland didn't know why, but he expected the girl to show up again the following day. He awoke the next morning with the feeling he must have imagined it all, but he was clever enough to know he hadn't. He sat at the small, round table for two, exactly where he had always sat. Just like at the coffee shop with Kate and Jesse and even Patrick; he was particular in that kind of way.

He watched the door, waiting for her. Daring her to enter.

But it was his current girlfriend, Daisy, who had shown up first that morning. She had fire in her eyes. She hated that café more than he did. Daisy came to the table, but she did not sit down. It was obvious she was not
~~~

planning on sticking around long. It didn't really matter to Leyland just what it was she was angry about, but the safest guess would have been he'd said something insensitive to her the night before. Barely listening, he bit his upper lip in response to whatever accusations were being thrown his way. He had heard it said somewhere that to bite one's upper lip was a sign that one was hiding something. Whatever the case may have been, Daisy eventually slammed her hands down on the table, and charged back out of the café. She bumped into someone on her way out the door.

That someone came and sat down across from Leyland. It was the girl from the day before, but he did not notice, already having gotten back to his writing pad.

"I don't even want to know what *that* was all about," she said to him comically.

Leyland looked up into those glorious eyes of hers. They exchanged momentary and awkward greetings before proper introductions were made. "My name's Leyland," he said. "Leyland Mueller."

And she followed with, "Rachel Ponzini. It's nice to finally meet you."

Leyland bit his lower lip a little. He had heard it said somewhere that to bite one's lower lip was an indication of nervousness, which was an emotion that never came to him too often. So, suffice it to say, biting his upper lip was a far more natural reaction for him.

"Leyland," she mused. "That's an interesting name."

"It was my great-grandfather's."

Many of the One Man Show's patrons stopped and took notice of Leyland and Rachel sitting with each other at the small, round table for two. They looked on, noticing them both for the first time. Individually they could have vanished into their own little worlds, but together they were simply unavoidable.

"Don't do that," Rachel told him.

"Don't do what?"

"Don't put your pencil down." She pushed the pencil and paper toward Leyland, who reactively gathered them back up. "I've seen you in here many times before, always writing whatever it is you're writing. And you keep to yourself so perfectly. You don't care at all about these squabbling fools around you."

He took in the shape of her head. Round like the ripple from a raindrop, with a flawlessly pointed chin. Her complexion was almost golden under the soft lights of the café. Her brown hair curled around elfish ears, shaped like tiny crescent moons. Perfectly pouty pink lips which shone like wet paint. The scratching of lead on paper was a strangely complementary sound to the sincerity in Rachel's voice. But it was her eyes that really captured his attention. They were like tiny wet mirrored balls of energy. They were brown. They were olive. They were black. And they were brown again. The color of Rachel's eyes changed so rapidly, it was impossible to distinguish the dominant one. Her pupils were at once dilated and infinitesimal. Leyland could see himself in there too. And there was a thin, squiggly blood vessel on the bottom of her right eyeball, just above the lip of her eyelid. Rachel had just enough imperfections to make her seem as though she was someone Leyland had known his whole life.

"Do you know what a group of playwrights is called, Leyland?"

He didn't know what the right answer was because he really had no idea what she was asking.

"It's called a plot. A plot of playwrights."

"How do you know that?" he asked.

"I know all the inane group nouns used for identifying gatherings of the like."

How peculiar, he thought. This brilliant girl seemed as though she might be rife with trivial information. Rachel pointed to the opposite corner from where they sat, toward a congregation of egocentric dramatists. They were obnoxiously reading screenplays out loud to one another. "A condescension of actors," she called them. Without so much as twitching her eyes, she motioned toward the front of the café where a group of turtlenecked intellectuals sipped water as though it were red wine, and used words like henceforth and dichotomy. She pronounced, "A wrangle of philosophers." And she worked her way around the rest of the room, "A brow of scholars. An illusion of painters," all the while keeping her attention focused on Leyland.

"That information seems rather unnecessary. Where in the world would you have learned all of this?" he inquired, not really caring if she was telling him the truth or not. He didn't believe for a second someone like Rachel could have been from Manhattan.

"I live and breathe. I take in everything around me, and I can separate the weak from the strong. I see powerful minds being used recklessly, and I see the weak ones that will rise above. I see *you*. You are an undiscovered star in an exhaustively explored solar system. And I see something in those eyes of yours; something I've never imagined before."

Leyland stopped. "I have no idea what you just said."

"Yes, you do."

He looked back down at his writing pad. The last sentence he'd scribbled on the page was: *"Everything was possible. There was nothing in this city I hadn't already imagined."*

"I love your accent," he told her. "Where are you from?"

"Montauk."

"Where is that? Europe? I'm getting a Switzerland vibe."

"Montauk's on Long Island, actually."

"Ah. Close enough."

"You say that like it's a bad thing. What's wrong with Long Island?"

"If I have to explain it to you—" he started, but then decided to finish with:

"At least it's better than Jersey."

He'd never before felt what he was feeling now. It was intoxicating. He was relatively certain she liked him, but he still did not really know anything about her. He knew she hated these transparently erroneous revolutionists around him. He knew she liked to use big words like that too. And he knew her eyes were the key to discovering everything else about her he didn't know.

"Would you like me to buy you a coffee?" Rachel asked him. "Because it's obvious you weren't planning on offering."

Leyland apologized. He didn't want to admit her very presence seemed to make all common sense disappear. It sounded too corny, even just in his head. Instead, he requested: "A regular coffee, please. With sugar."

"All right, then." Rachel got up from her seat, and walked over to the counter. At the same time, those around them returned to life, as though the show they had been so focused on was now taking an intermission.

But when Rachel returned to the table, the patrons of the café once again began to take notice of the couple. She brushed her curls away from her mouth as she sipped her coffee. Leyland could tell exactly how much sugar she used by the expression on her face after every sip. He thanked her for the coffee. "But don't think I'm going to start expecting special treatment," he added.

"I hope you don't think me strange," she said. "And I'm not being presumptuous. I don't believe myself to be anything other than what I am. I know all about the importance of benevolence." She took another bitter sip of coffee.

Leyland leaned toward Rachel, and fixed his eyes on hers. "You don't need to justify yourself. I was just a little stunned, is all."

Rachel watched him as he reached into his bag and pulled out the most unremarkable pencil he could find. He sharpened it with a small pocketknife, and the shavings drifted onto the tabletop. Being with Rachel was as comfortable a feeling as he'd never known before. He didn't suffer from an obligation to entertain her. He didn't expect anything from her. He was simply *with* her, and that was enough. Still, he wasn't quite sure what he was going to tell Kate and Jesse, since it was obvious this was going to be more than a one-night stand.

"You must like writing a lot," she asked him, although it really was more of an observation than a question.

"It's pretty much my only talent."

"What do you write?"

"Have you ever heard of a book called 'Blanc?'"

"I saw a movie called 'Blanc.' Wasn't that Scottie Pippen?"

"Shaquille O'Neal."

Rachel gave him a look, as though Leyland was personally responsible for all of Hollywood's poor casting decisions.

"Obviously," he said, "it was *not* my choice."

"Let me ask you *this* though: have you ever written anything important?"

"Important? I've had five novels published!"

"But what else? Is there anything you're proud of?"

He thought about what Rachel might have wanted to hear. "Mostly just love letters to girlfriends." He glanced up at her with a transparent spark in his eyes.

She smiled, knowing she had just the right answer for him in return. "Don't you need to know something about love in order to write a love letter?"

The scratching of pencil on paper intensified as Leyland continued talking. "I've come here every day for three months now. I thought I had something important to say the day the towers fell. But I know now I never really had a reason to come here until yesterday, when I saw you across the room. And I just realized all of the shit I thought was worth writing about is really not very important at all. I've never really had anything to say until this moment." He blew the bits of lead off his paper, and shaved his blunted pencil some more.

The afternoon sun was breaking through the window behind him, and from inside his shadowy silhouette, Rachel could still see the glimmer in his eyes. The anticipation on his lips.

"Did you know you have a freckle on your right eyelid?" he asked her. "I notice it every time you blink."

"I didn't know that," she whispered truthfully.

Leyland excused himself, and he took his coffee cup to the counter for a refill.

When he returned, Rachel was drawing on his writing pad. He glanced over as he sat back down. It was a sketch of a cat, but one of its eyes appeared circular, while the other was drawn as an 'X':

He had to ask, "What is this?"

"This is a cat that is both *alive* and *dead*. You see, one of his eyes is marked with an X: the universal cartoon symbol for death."

"But, I don't under—"

"It's a paradox, Leyland. An experiment conducted in the Thirties proved that something — in this case a *cat* — could simultaneously be both alive *and* dead. The scientist, Schrödinger, placed his kitty cat in a box with a canister of cyanide connected to a radioactive device. If an atom in this device decayed, a detector would trigger a tiny hammer to smash the glass canister open, and the cat would die."

Leyland took a closer look at the picture. "I don't think I get it."

"Suppose there is a fifty-fifty chance of this happening. Clearly, when the box is opened, the cat would be either alive or dead. But is the cat alive or dead prior to the opening of the box?" Rachel took another long sip of coffee, giving him a moment to contemplate the conundrum. "Because radioactive decay occurs at the quantum level, where events are purely random and foreseeable only in a statistical sense, there is no way to know for sure what had happened to the cat unless the box was opened. The cat's entire existence is reduced to a statistic. A decimal point is all that keeps Schrödinger's cat alive."

He sat back in awe. Leyland could barely begin to comprehend everything that must have been in her mind, and he realized beyond a shadow of a doubt he would never know all the answers. Just sitting across from this girl was almost more than he could bear. His coffee was already cold. And it was exhilarating. "You're not really from Long Island, are you?"

Rachel didn't waste time answering the question. "I'd read about all of this years ago," she told him instead. "I find it stimulating how there can be so much going on we have absolutely no control over. It's all circumstantial consequence."

A lock of curly brown hair fell across her face. She smelled of jasmine. She blinked. As perfect as that freckle was, Leyland would have been satisfied if he never had to see it again in his life. It would mean he'd be looking into her eyes that much longer.

"Can I make a suggestion?" Rachel asked.

"Of course."

"I think it's time we got out of here."

And they did.

~~~

When they emerged from the 110th Street Station, they were only a few blocks away from Leyland's apartment. Rachel led the way there, as if she had already learned everything there was to know about the man from somewhere deep within his eyes. But it was probably just the alcohol.

They had stopped for some red wine after leaving the café, but ended up
~~~

downing the bottle in Marcus Garvey Park. It was freezing, but the unusually mild New York winter meant they would not have to lie in snow, and the wine kept their bodies warm. On the crisp grass, and beneath the setting sun, they held each other. They talked, but not about their dreams, because they were both living their dreams. And not about their desires, since nothing else mattered to them in that moment. Rachel didn't speak of her past, and she didn't ask Leyland about his.

They spoke of their lives. What they were doing today, not yesterday or tomorrow. Rachel liked slow music and fast movies. Leyland enjoyed just the opposite. White wine was Rachel's favorite, while he had no preference either way. And it really didn't matter why they'd opted for red.

In the distance, between two old tenement buildings, they could see the tallest of skyscrapers peeking out from midtown. They agreed to go to the top of the Empire State Building together one day, since neither of them had ever done so before. Leyland hadn't because to him there was nothing worse than feeling like a tourist, and Rachel hadn't due to her demophobia. She said she hated being in the middle of large crowds because she disliked the feeling of going unnoticed.

The setting sun directly behind the bare trees made their branches appear smaller, thinner than they actually were. Leyland wondered aloud why they had never met before they did, and he knew Rachel would have the right answer for him. She intimated that the two of them were along the same lines as the cat in the box: their lives were nothing more than random percentages of possibility. Of course, it was just as he thought she would put it.

And Leyland worried where he could hope to find a love like hers again, when she inevitably left him. He had never once considered a lasting love could ever be, so how could he possibly expect to ever find it?

Rachel didn't pretend to want a tour of the apartment. His other women played those kinds of games, where they acted as if they were there for an actual visit, and not just the sex. Rachel wasn't one for games, or concealing her intentions. There wasn't anything ambiguous about her. You knew if Rachel liked you or if she did not. You knew when Rachel wanted sex, and also when she'd had enough.

Leyland woke up and felt the still-lingering heat of her body next to his. He tried to pretend for an instant he didn't know where he was, that he was somehow misplaced in space and time. But he was quick to shake those silly thoughts from his head when he realized he didn't want to miss out on a single second of Rachel. And he decided that when he saw her next, he would tell her he loved her.

The note was waiting for him on the refrigerator, pinned beneath a "Calvin and Hobbes" magnet. Rachel knew he would find it there, as he had already explained to her the first thing he did every morning was go to the fridge for a swig of chocolate milk. He had no idea what time Rachel left that morning, he simply woke and she was gone.

The note was written with one of his pencils, torn from a page of his writing pad, and folded in half. He noticed it immediately. Drawn on the front was another picture of Rachel's famous cat. He couldn't tell if the cat was alive or dead.

Inside, she had written the following for him:

Leyland,
In my experiences, I've found you only ever hurt the ones you love.
The only roses you watch die are the most beautiful ones. But even
if everyone everywhere left everyone else forever, I'd still never
leave you.

Leyland planned on going to the coffee shop to meet Kate and Jesse for breakfast. He would boast about Rachel, and hoped the two of them would be just as excited about his new relationship as he was. But Jesse wasn't there that morning, and Kate was too busy complaining about her upcoming wedding to whoever this Gene Schneider person was. Leyland considered telling her marrying Gene could end up being a mistake, but he was still too distracted by thoughts of Rachel Ponzini.

Later, he passed the park where he and Rachel had shared the bottle of red wine the night before. Where they had dreamed of going to the top of the city together one day. The cork was still there, resting upon a wilted dandelion. Leyland knew that if the World Trade Center had not fallen that morning, months before, he would not have ever found himself in Harlem meeting the last girl he would ever love.

PART V

~~~

EPILOGUE
~~~

CHAPTER TWENTY-SEVEN
Riverside Park – Upper West Side

ONE WEEK LATER.

Undoubtedly, it had been the longest tennis match in the history of man. Between the time the match begun and the time it ended, Patrick Kohn had seen the sun rise and set in a dozen different countries. He had married, honeymooned in Venice, and watched as his wife suffered through two miscarriages before they finally had a son to call their own. He worked as a shoe salesman, a limousine driver, and an investments advisor. He bought a house in Seattle. He was involved in three car accidents, two of which were his own fault. He set up a model train set in his garage. He read forty-three books, most of which had been adapted into movies he'd already seen. He put on thirty-eight pounds. He'd been the victim of both mail fraud and a bomb threat. He found fifty bucks on the bus, but it had blown out the window when he opened his wallet, along with another fifty he was saving for a haircut. He watched his wife die from a brain tumor. He sold his house in Seattle and bought an apartment in Brooklyn. He made friends and lost friends and found friends again.

In the time between his first serve and his last, Thomas Mueller had written six novels and had articles published in every major American literary magazine. He dated and/or slept with thirty-one different women and saw his favorite hockey team win exactly one championship. He actually grew two inches. He walked every single street in Manhattan and he had been to Staten Island one time on a dare. He played the New York lottery once and won sixteen dollars, spending all of it on chocolate milk at the CKY Grocery. He discovered he wasn't the man he thought he was. He loved friends and hurt friends and found friends all over again.

It took Patrick ten years, four months, seven days, one hour, and thirty-three minutes to defeat Tommy, but he had finally done it. The two men sat together on a courtside bench, guzzling water and catching their breath.

"I didn't think I would *ever* beat you," Patrick said. "I thought you had me there."

"I had you ten years ago, but I guess you've learned a few tricks since then. That's quite the backhand you've got now." Tommy wiped the sweat from his brow with the sleeve of his Rangers sweater. Even though it was a crisp November morning, he still should have known better than to wear a hockey jersey for a game of tennis. But Tommy didn't care about a sweat-stained sweater, and he didn't care about losing the match to Patrick. He had only suggested they meet that morning at the once-familiar Riverside Park tennis courts for one reason: to apologize. "Listen, Patrick," he said slowly, with a lump in his throat. Tommy knew the only way he was going to say it, was to just let the words thump against his teeth and stumble out of his mouth. "I'm really sorry for everything that happened."

The only reason Patrick had agreed to play tennis that morning was so he could accept Tommy's apology. Still, he let his friend carry on a little longer first.

Tommy continued. "I know I can be a big, mulish idiot sometimes, but I had no reason to treat you the way I did. The truth is, I realize now all the shit that happened in the past few weeks was only inevitable. You were wrong when you told me about The Falling. Because the reality is that I had already fallen. It was ten years ago when you left us all."

"That's not true, Tom," Patrick finally said.

"Sure it is. For me, it was worse than when my brother died because I replaced him with you, but when you left there was only a void."

Patrick still couldn't shake from his memory the image of the boy with his head buried in the school locker. That was the first time he'd met him. Thomas Mueller did not cry often, but he had never been very good at hiding his tears. "But that was such a long time ago, Tom."

"Don't we all hold onto things a little longer than we should sometimes?"

Patrick knew it was true but he still did not have an answer.

"Why'd you come to New York with us if you couldn't stay forever? Sometimes I felt like it would've been easier if I had left first. Not that that would ever happen."

Finally, Patrick considered the mistakes he made years ago, the same ones which had obviously hurt Tommy so much. "When we're young, I guess we don't think things will matter as much as they do. All the small, selfish crimes we commit. The microscopic damages are never quite so insignificant."

Mince Wilson had said the same thing to Tommy, only using very different words. It's entirely possible Keekee Kaufman and all the rest would've agreed upon the inevitability of Tommy's needs surpassing their own. Certainly, Rachel would too.

After a long moment, Tommy said, "I've been thinking a lot about what I should say to Rachel."

"What have you come up with so far?"

"I thought I'd tell her that even if everyone everywhere left everyone else forever, I'd still never leave her."

Patrick turned his nose up, as if there was an unpleasant smell in the air.

"No good?"

"Tom, that's *awful*. That's like a line from a movie."

"I've got more. You've just got to let me get warmed up first. Here we go, how about this: You'll always be the same old someone that I knew. Won't you believe in me, like I believe in you?"

"What's *that* from?"

"It's Billy Joel."

"Come on, Tom. You're a writer! Have you told her you love her?"

"Not in so many words."

"It's only *three* words, Tom. And if you really mean them, they're pretty darn good ones. I'd suggest starting with that and seeing where it takes you."

Tommy realized if he had the same talk with Kate or Jesse they probably would have given him similar advice. Either that, or just told him to shut up and be a man. But Patrick Kohn always had a way of making everything seem possible. It was the same as when he pulled Thomas Mueller's head out of that locker in the ninth grade, and it was the same as when he said he'd go anywhere with Tommy, even when he knew Tommy's version of anywhere would only ever be New York.

"I'm glad you're home, Patrick," Tommy said. He held his hand out and the two men finally shook.

Patrick took a moment to admire the Upper West Side apartments peeking out from just behind the trees. It was quiet enough to hear the Hudson River to the west. "Me too," he said.

Breathe out.

TWENTY-EIGHT
Seventh Street – East Village, 1947

How peculiar it was that as Kaspar Delancey lay face-up on East Seventh Street, he could recall only the good that had ever touched his life: his first piece of Coney Island saltwater taffy melting on his tongue; his father opening the front door the day he returned home from the war; the apple tree in his backyard; tickertape parades; sitting on 23rd Street with his best friends, watching the girls' skirts blow with the wind; riding the cable cars to Battery Place.

The falling snow cleansed his soul, even as his mind was preparing to set his one last sin free. The heavy flakes danced upon his one good eye, but he did not blink them loose. The snow graced his cracked lips with a moment of wet respite; it tickled, but he could not bring himself to lick it away. That one last memory was slipping from his grasp, like singlehandedly trying to keep an ocean liner from leaving port, almost out of his grip entirely.

It was the other cop, Sergeant Oster, whom Kaspar had just wrung the life out of, as though the bullet wound would not have been sufficient. Kaspar left the bloodied man on the station platform before hustling back up to the street. Buster Broome, tenacious as ever, was still on his trail, and Kaspar knew as soon as he spotted it, the parked car with its engine running would be the fastest way back to the South Street Seaport. It was a United Nations limousine of all things, but there was no driver inside. Maybe he had run across 33rd for a pack of Lucky Strikes? Or maybe he'd stopped for an impromptu photo of the Empire State Building? Whatever the reason for such fortuitous charity, Kaspar did not consider it for long. He settled into the driver's seat and closed the door without anyone suspecting anything.

But before laying his weathered sole on the pedal, Kaspar stopped himself. It wasn't out of fear, because he knew for certain he would never be caught. Especially if Broome was the only one who insisted on doing the chasing. That detective was the only person to come close, but Broome would surely have to admit defeat sooner or later, wouldn't he?

Kaspar turned and released the key, and the engine slowly sputtered into silence. Maybe South Street was exactly where Broome would look for him? Maybe Kaspar should head uptown instead? Or leave the city entirely? No. He'd rather die than give in first. Opening the door, he stepped back out onto 33rd Street. There was a buzz in the air, but there was also an eerie silence. It was the kind of feeling one gets the moment before something horrible hits, before there's a chance to do anything about it. And that's when Kaspar Delancey saw him: Buster Broome was standing on Fifth Avenue, his pistol drawn, no more than two hundred feet away. The two men stared at one another, both knowing what they wanted to say, but neither willing to utter the first word. Kaspar stepped back an inch, just as Broome inched forward a step.

But no one around them paid any attention to either man. One woman turned her head up, noticing something in the sky. Another man pointed. The buzz in the air grew louder, the unnerving silence ever quieter. There was a scarf floating gently on a breeze, like a bird with no particular destination. Something else followed behind it, something much heavier than a bird. One man muttered something to Jesus. Another said something incomprehensible to God. Kaspar knew neither would be able to help. A woman shrieked. Another fainted, hitting the sidewalk hard. But not nearly as hard as Evelyn McHale hit when she fell from the sky.

Falling eighty-six floors from the Empire State Building's observation deck, Evelyn McHale crashed into the roof of the parked limousine with a heavy thud. If Kaspar Delancey had not second-guessed himself, he would have been just as dead as she. As Manhattan crowds often do, they gathered quickly. People shouted, and Kaspar only had a moment to see her body, smashed into the husk of the automobile, posed elegantly like she had meant to land just so. Her lips still wet with life; her eyebrows smiled, as if having a pleasant dream; her suicide already a work of art. Kaspar reached out for her just as Broome finally reached for him.

So many times, he had cheated death, and for what? Just to lie helplessly on East Seventh staring up at the snow and waiting for everything to simply stop? That didn't seem fair at all. The flickering light outside McSorley's Old Ale House seemed to be the one indication that life still persisted.

Drunken men hollered wildly inside.

Men hollering.

Inside.

With his mind now a clean, blank slate, Kaspar brushed the snow from his face and sat up. He couldn't recall when or why he ever decided to lie down in the middle of that street. Kaspar had no idea if the detective had ever managed to catch him; in fact, the name Buster Broome no longer had any meaning to him. Nor could he recollect the reasons for why he had forgotten all of the atrocities he'd ever committed. But for some reason — as his thoughts and his world slowly faded away — Kaspar Delancey was finally thinking of himself as a better man.

CHAPTER TWENTY-NINE
From Montauk to Morningside Heights

ONE YEAR LATER.

The wind bit into Tommy as he waited for the E-Train out of Jamaica. It didn't bother him though. If Rachel had told Tommy he would one day enjoy the two-and-a-half-hour train ride from Montauk, he would never have believed her.

The train station was full of sketchy and unsavory characters, but Tommy didn't mind them either. A pair of homeless men huddled in the corner, ignored even by the security guard who wandered listlessly on patrol. The two men could have been twins for all Tommy knew; with their scruffy beards, drab monochrome clothing, and matching New York Islanders hats. He had bought a wholly unspectacular Spartan apple at the station, paying for it with a crisp twenty, and Tommy tossed the men all of the change that had been rattling in his pocket ever since. They probably weren't *really* Islanders fans, he thought, in an attempt to justify his own charity.

Tommy had surprised the Ponzinis that morning when he showed up on their doorstep asking Dick Ponzini for his daughter's hand. Patrick told him the whole scenario sounded a little old-fashioned, but he didn't want to dissuade his friend from making any life-changing decisions. Tommy's father had done it the same way, as did his grandfather before him. No one in the family was quite sure how Leyland Mueller had proposed, but Tommy imagined it must have gone down in the exact same fashion. Just a day before, Tommy visited Ellis Island to find his great-grandfather's name; he felt it would serve as some sort of familial approval of his proposal to Rachel. It took him well over an hour to find the tiny name etched into the Wall of Honor. It was both comfortable and unsettling to read his own moniker nestled in amongst thousands upon thousands of faceless, long-dead immigrants. A year ago, Tommy considered going by his proper birth name, but the truth was he still hated it. He decided to stick with *Tommy*, rather than pretend things were any different than they had always been.

Heeding Patrick's advice from the day of the tennis match, Tommy agreed to simply tell Rachel he loved her. He paid her Columbia professor fifty dollars to give him ten minutes at the start of the lecture; Rachel's Socio-Cultural Anthropology class. Tommy put on a smelly tweed jacket and a fake mustache and proceeded to bore the entire lecture hall by bull-shitting about the societal merits of Super Mario Land for a full seven minutes. He hadn't practiced any of it, but the majority of students weren't really listening anyway. Rachel knew it was him right from the start, but she was simply too dumbfounded to do anything but smile at the man's lunacy. Eventually, Tommy just wrote "I love you, Rachel Ponzini" on the whiteboard. He asked her to see him after class, and then he left. Rachel moved into Tommy's 113th Street apartment exactly four days later.

The E-Train finally pulled in and it was even colder inside because somebody thought it would be a good idea to leave the air conditioning on. Still, Tommy refused to let anything bother him. The cars clack-a-lacked beneath Forest Hills and Queens Boulevard and Hunters Point, before thundering through the East River. Tommy loved the ease of the subway system, but if there was one thing he missed when riding into Manhattan from Long Island, it was seeing the glorious skyline of the world's greatest city coming into view. New York City never ceased to stand guard, ever vigilant as its people perpetually changed. They continued to face new ordeals every day, but the wisest of them knew it would always be so. Their ebbs and flows were not predetermined, but they were also not entirely unexpected. The city would always breathe in and out.

John Galloway died suddenly in his sleep on Christmas morning. By then, he'd entirely forgotten who he was, but he never forgot how much he loved his wife. Keekee Kaufman awoke one evening to discover she was perfectly fine; her schizophrenia was simply no more. She walked out of Bellevue and made her way across the Triboro Bridge. As she looked down into the East River, she found no desire within herself to jump off. Troy "The Shark" Dunlop was found dead and shirtless on the floor in the men's room after suffering a severe heart attack from massive energy drink consumption. Apparently, he had been practicing some ultimate fighting moves in front of the bathroom mirror when it happened. He never did find his missing Randy Couture bobble head doll. Dwayne Reamer eventually found himself in an editing position at Pendulum Publishing. He even garnered his own small office overlooking West 39th Street. His office was big enough for a mini-fridge, so nobody could steal his yogurts anymore. He had also been putting the finishing touches on his own book: "Catchphrase Me If You Can: The Next Generation of Great American Sayings."

Tommy transferred subways at the 50th Street Station, taking the 1-Train north. The station smelled particularly grimy that afternoon, but the grimier the better. To Tommy, that only meant the city was running as it should. It was comforting. He sat as far back as he could in the train's very last car. A beggar with no legs slowly patrolled the subway, pushing himself on a skateboard with his calloused hands. Tommy had no change left in his pocket, but he did find a pen which he dropped into the coffee tin hanging from the man's neck, claiming everyone could always use a good pen.

An unfunny lawyer named Hugh Morris contacted Jesse Classen one day in late January, letting him know something had been left for him in John Galloway's will. It was a comic book collection, still mostly unsorted and piled up in the basement of the Gramercy Park home. When Jesse went to collect it, he was astounded by the sheer volume of valuable rarities. At first, he refused to take them, but once his friends managed to convince him it would represent the final stage of the healing process, Jesse finally succumbed. There was a copy of The Amazing Spider-Man #1, an assortment of rare Buck Rogers and Lone Ranger comics, a three-hundred issue run of the newspaper edition Spirit comics from the 1940s, and, most incredibly of all, a near-mint copy of Detective Comics #27. Jesse quit his job as assistant manager at Midtown Comics and used the value of the collection to open his own comic book shop in the Lower East Side. He called it "Edie's Bunker," and he was the store's sole employee. When Jesse was ready to see Sharona again, he did just as he was instructed, and went to the streetlight on MacDougal Street to find the necessary information regarding her next show. But there were no posters to be found. There was only an ad for free computer lessons, and two of the nine phone numbers had already been torn off the bottom. And there was another girl there, taping up her own poster for a lost cat. It wasn't her cat, Jesse learned, but her friend's. Betty Bentley hated musicals and chicken wings and black licorice and comic books, but the two of them decided to give each other a shot anyway. Jesse soon found compromising was actually far better than living alone with regret.

The 1-Train came to a slow stop somewhere between Columbus Circle and Lincoln Center. The lights went out and most everyone onboard panicked. Tommy could easily tell which of the passengers were tourists and which were not by the levels of alarm they displayed. It was funny to him just how obvious people could sometimes be. He took the moment to appreciate the artwork spray-painted onto the tunnel walls on the other side of the window. There were areas of New York Tommy knew he would never get the chance to see, which bothered him more than most anything else. It was moments like these he really savored, considering himself even luckier than he was just the moment before.

Kate Prince and Gene Schneider divorced in March. It turned out Gene had never had an affair, nor did he want one, but Kate was done either way. She took enough time for herself to finish her first novel, "The Falling." She self-published the book, but failed miserably in promoting herself. She wasn't looking for fame or notoriety; she was just happy to have finally finished it, and she was proud of herself. When "The Manhattanite" eventually did end up being a success, just as Tommy predicted, Kate still did not let it get to her. Tommy deserved all the accolades he got. Eventually, she found an editing job at another publishing company, and the very first book she pulled from the slush pile turned out to be an award winner. Kate finally returned to the gym, but balanced her new lifestyle out by taking up smoking. She claimed to have curbed her Nicorette addiction through cigarettes. For her birthday, Jesse made Kate a collage. It was a collection of GAP ads taped together with the addition of comic book word balloons glued above Kate's head. The many denim-clad Kates were saying such things as *"Bow before the might of Doom!"*, *"Walloping web-snappers!"* and *"By Odin's Beard!"* It was very Warhol-esque. Kate kept the collage above her desk at home, proudly showing it off to anyone lucky enough to spend time with her.

From the Cathedral Parkway Station, it was only two more blocks to the coffee shop, but Tommy leisurely took his time. He was looking forward to meeting with his friends and telling them the big news, but he'd been in much less of a hurry lately than he usually was. Besides, he knew his friends weren't going anywhere. New York was no longer just his; it was *all of theirs.*

They still continued their attempts at convincing Patrick to get out of Brooklyn and move back to Manhattan, but they didn't push him too hard, since they all knew it was bound to happen eventually. Sheldon was already starting to show the signs of a budding Thomas Mueller. The boy loved being in the city, he loved hearing the trains underground when he passed a station stairwell or a grate on the sidewalk, and he quivered a little bit before heading back home to their apartment on India Street. Sheldon was quick to make friends with hotel doormen. He helped Uncle Jesse out every Saturday at Edith's Bunker. And once a month, he would bug Tommy enough to take him on the three-hour sightseeing boat tour around Manhattan. He loved listening to Tommy tell the stories of every building and every street and every bridge they passed, and never ceased in suggesting Tommy give tours for a living, since it sometimes seemed Uncle Tommy had nothing else to do with his time. Tommy's only response would be to challenge the boy to do the same.

As he approached the corner of Broadway and 112th, Tommy stopped for a moment to process everything that had gone through his mind that morning. He thought about his brother, and how much he would have loved to have had the chance to share the city with him. Everything was perfect there; it no longer mattered how much things changed or whether or not they remained the same. Tommy would continue to love New York City forever.

Patrick, Kate, and Jesse watched him from the window of Tom's Restaurant. I couldn't help but watch him too. His passion would never cease to astonish and baffle us all. Patrick almost gave Tommy another second to collect himself, but he chose to bang on the glass instead, snapping him out of his fervor.

END

From the Author

When I set out to write my second novel, I had only one thing in mind that I'd
write about. The important things (you know, the real meat. Like, *What's the plot?*
Who are the characters? And what are their motivations?), didn't matter at the
time; I only knew where this story would be set: New York City. As it turned out,
this actually was the most important thing about the book.

You can ask anyone: I've always loved New York, just like the eponymous Tommy
Mueller. And just like Jesse Classen too, my own vision of Manhattan was formed
from reading too many Spider-Man comics as a kid: those canyons between
skyscrapers, the visually striking water towers (we didn't have water towers on
Vancouver rooftops), and the stink fumes from back alley dumpsters (we *did* have
smelly alleys in Vancouver, but for some reason, I assumed NY's were far more
magical). These were enough to sell me on the wonder of the city.

So, it started with the setting, and from there I simply got selfish, writing the kind
of literary novel that *I* would want to read. I tried to explore all the corners of the
city which fascinated me the most. But it wasn't until I decided to turn the city
itself into the story's narrator when I knew the setting would actually be the
book's everything. It's not obvious, and I tried to not hit the reader over the head
with it, but it works, while also giving the novel its own uniqueness.

From there, The Inevitable Fall of Tommy Mueller became a fun story about not
much more than friends. It is a balancing act of characters who all have their
pasts, presents, and futures woven throughout every coffee shop discussion.
These are friends who first discovered the city in much the same way I once did,
and even though they all go through moments in the novel of considering
something else, Tommy, Kate, Jesse, and Patrick each receive their own scenes
which tell the story of why they love the city so much.

When asked which of my novels is my favorite one, I always answer *this one*. It's
not perfect; at times it can be a bit directionless, and yes, it's perhaps got
moments of pretentiousness, but it is definitely the type of novel I would fall in
love with, so I'm proud to call it my own.